The duke may have returned, but she has no intention of falling back into his arms...

W9-BWH-974

"I want to know the real reason you've come home. Is it because of my wedding?"

Will grinned at Beatrix and raised his glass. "I thought you said I wasn't invited."

"You're not. But if you were determined to make a scene in front of over five hundred people, I hardly think lack of an invitation would stop you."

"True enough," he said. "But now that I'm home, excluding me from the guest list will raise more eyebrows than inviting me would, don't you think? The Dukes of Sunderland are invited to every social event in Devonshire as a matter of course. Besides, wouldn't having me there be the best way of proving to everyone that you don't care tuppence for me anymore?"

"I don't need to prove that. Everyone already knows—"

"That you're still holding a torch for me?"

She smiled sweetly. "Only if I can use it to burn you alive."

"As I recall," he murmured, lifting his gaze to her face, "you and I never needed any torches to burn for each other."

By Laura Lee Guhrke

WEDDING OF THE SEASON
WITH SEDUCTION IN MIND
SECRET DESIRES OF A GENTLEMAN
THE WICKED WAYS OF A DUKE
AND THEN HE KISSED HER
SHE'S NO PRINCESS
THE MARRIAGE BED
HIS EVERY KISS
GUILTY PLEASURES

Coming February 2011

SCANDAL OF THE YEAR

Laura Lee Guhrke

Wedding of the Season

ABANDONED AT THE ALTAR

AVON

An Imprint of HarperCollinsPublishers

AVON BOOKS
An Imprint of HarperCollins*Publishers*
10 East 53rd Street
New York, New York 10022–5299

Copyright © 2011 by Laura Lee Guhrke
Excerpt from *Scandal of the Year* copyright © 2011 by Laura Lee Guhrke
ISBN 978-0-06-196315-5
www.avonromance.com

First Avon Books paperback printing: January 2011

Avon Trademark Reg. U.S. Pat. Off. and in Other Countries, Marca Registrada, Hecho en U.S.A.
HarperCollins® is a registered trademark of HarperCollins Publishers.

Printed in the U.S.A.

10 9 8 7 6 5 4 3 2 1

In loving memory of
Dixilyn Helen Noh
May 1, 1957—December 11, 2009
The truest friend anyone could ask for.
I miss you, Dixi.

And for her sister,
Kristen Helen Noh
December 13, 1963—December 11, 2009

And for their father,
Richard Noh
October 9, 1930—December 11, 2009

May God be with all of you. Rest in peace.

Prologue

The Earl of Danbury
Requests the honor of your presence
At the marriage of his daughter,
Lady Beatrix Elizabeth Anne,
To
William James Mallory,
The Marquess of Richfield,
Son of the Duke of Sunderland
On Tuesday,
The fifteenth day of September, 1896
At half past twelve o'clock
St. Mary's Church
Stafford St. Mary, Devonshire

From Mrs. Delilah Dawlish, journalist, in her weekly column for the society newspaper *Talk of the Town*, Monday, 7 September 1896:

My dears, a little bird has confirmed that the wedding of the season has been called off! Great tact and delicacy are being employed on both sides, needless to say, but this intrepid columnist is undaunted by such trifles. The call to truth and the people's right to know demand that I pass along the exclusive details to you.

Lord Richfield has been invited to accompany that great and learned archaeologist Sir Edmund Tavistock, to Egypt, and Lady Beatrix has freed him from their engagement. This columnist can only conclude that Lord Richfield finds searching for Egyptian mummies a more fascinating occupation than matrimony.

Poor, poor Lady Beatrix. One can only imagine what she must be suffering. We weep for our sister woman in her devastating humiliation. And if this reporter learns any more of the delicious details, I promise that you, my dear readers, will be the first to know.

—D.D.

Letter from Mr. Anthony Hale, Esquire, of the law firm Hale, Spencer and Teague, to William James Mallory, Ninth Duke of Sunderland, dated Wednesday, 21 November, 1900:

My Lord Duke,

My deepest sympathies on the passing of your father. I am sorry to hear that you are unable to

attend the investiture ceremony in the House of
Lords conferring ducal title, but our firm shall
be happy to undertake the filing of the official
documents and handle all matters pertaining
to the estates in your absence. Good luck with
your excavations in Egypt. What an adventure!
I confess, I envy you.

I remain, my Lord Duke, Your Grace's most
obedient servant.

～

From the *Weekly Telegraph*, Stafford St. Mary,
Devonshire, Friday, 26 April 1901:

*Despite the serious illness of her father, Lord
Danbury, Lady Beatrix has graciously offered
her presence again this year to open the May
Day Charity Auction for the Benefit of Widows
and Orphans. As is customary, this worthy event
will be held on the village green, next to the vicarage. The new vicar, Mr. Venables, has told the
Telegraph he is delighted by Lady Beatrix's gen-
erosity and her tireless devotion to the less fortunate and hopes all within the parish will pray
with fervor for the quick recovery of her father.*

～

Telegram from Baroness Yardley to her cousin,
Lady Beatrix Danbury, Tuesday, 11 June 1901:

DARLING EXCLAMATION CANNOT IMAGINE YOUR
GRIEF STOP YOUR PAPA VERY DEAR TO YOU I

KNOW STOP CATCHING ORIENT EXPRESS FROM
BUCHAREST TODAY STOP WILL BE IN DEVONSHIRE
FRIDAY WITH DAIMLER STOP TAKING YOU FOR
SUMMER HOLIDAY STOP NO ARGUMENTS EXCLA-
MATION YOUR LOVING COUSIN JULIA STOP STOP

From Mrs. Delilah Dawlish, journalist, in her
weekly column for the society newspaper *Talk of the
Town*, Monday, 9 September 1901:

*My dear readers, I have the most deliciously
appalling news. Lady Beatrix Danbury has
been seen cavorting in Cornwall! Since it is
her usual custom to spend August at Torquay,
we had first thought the worthy Lady Beatrix
to be hiding away in Cornwall for the proper
year of mourning and seclusion required by
the death of her father, the Earl of Danbury,
earlier this year. But no, I regret to say such
is not the case at all, and her purpose seems to
be neither mourning nor seclusion, but enjoyment! She is staying at the seaside cottage of
her scandal-ridden cousin, Baroness Yardley,
and has been seen riding in the baroness's motorcar at reckless speeds, drinking champagne
on the baroness's balcony, and walking (without either shoes or stockings!) on the beaches.
She even appeared in public, attending the St.
Ives Summer Ball last Tuesday evening.*

After the humiliating rejection she suffered at the hands of the Duke of Sunderland (Lord Richfield) five years ago, we had concluded in these pages that Lady Beatrix was destined to no greater glory than good works and spinsterhood. That conclusion seems to have been premature, however, for she was said to have enjoyed a full dance card Thursday evening, including two waltzes with the handsome, oh-so-eligible Duke of Trathen! His Grace, who has a reputation for impeccable manners and a commendable regard for propriety, seemed willing to overlook his dance partner's lack of same. This oversight we can only attribute to Lady Beatrix's extraordinary beauty (and perhaps to the scandalously deep décolleté of her ball gown). The gown, designed by her close friend, the fashionable dressmaker Vivienne, had not so much as a ribbon of black upon it to mark her father's passing.

Fast motorcars, flouting of mourning customs, indecent exposure of her ankles to public view upon the Cornish beaches? What is the world coming to when a flower of feminine devotion and virtue like Lady Beatrix arrives at such a pass? We can only wait and see what happens next, my dears!

Chapter One

He'd forgotten how beautiful a fine summer day in England could be.

William Mallory, Duke of Sunderland, removed his hat and tilted his head back for an appreciative glance at the dazzling blue sky overhead before turning his attention to the cart piled with his luggage. He studied it for a moment, then turned to the dark-skinned manservant who had just placed yet another valise in the vehicle. "You must learn to pack more lightly, Aman," he said, tossing his hat to land atop the pile. "I don't believe there's room for me."

"Sir?" His valet glanced at the empty place beside the driver and frowned in puzzlement, but he did not contradict his master's words. "As Your Grace pleases," he murmured, which was his usual response to Will's teasing.

The driver of the cart, a gnarled old man who'd

been transporting travelers from Stafford St. Mary's tiny train station to various homes, inns, and Dartmouth beauty spots since well before Will's birth, gave a chuckle. "A fine day for riding," he commented, giving Will a shrewd, knowing look. "And for a race across the moor, perhaps?"

Will laughed. "You know me far too well, Mr. Robinson. Remarkable, given how much time has passed."

"Some things don't change with time, Your Grace," the old man said. "I've a strong young gelding you might like. Not fully trained, mind, but full of spit and fast as the wind."

That was more than enough persuasion for Will. He turned to his valet. "No need for you to ride on the dummy board, Aman. Step up on the box with Mr. Robinson here, and I shall ride to Sunderland Park. In fact," he added, returning his attention to the old man, "I'll hire that gelding of yours for a full week, if I may."

"And have him fully trained by the time you return him, I'll wager," Mr. Robinson answered, and started to climb down as if to fetch the horse in question.

Will forestalled him. "No, no, don't trouble yourself. I'll have young Jim saddle the gelding for me. That is, if he's still with you and hasn't gone off to make his fortune?"

The old man shook his head at that reference to his only son and once again settled himself on the box as Aman climbed up to sit beside him. "Jim's still here, Your Grace, though not for much longer,

I expect. Filled with grand ideas, he is, about going to work in the factories up north, or in the shipyards in Plymouth. He even talks of going off to India. Or Africa, as you did, sir."

"It's not a bad life," Will assured him, but Mr. Robinson seemed unconvinced.

"Begging your pardon, Your Grace, but there's no place on God's earth better than Britain. Besides," he added before Will could debate that point, "he'd break his mother's heart if he goes." Shaking his head at the silly dreams of the younger generation, Mr. Robinson snapped the reins, sending the cart into motion.

Will crossed the road to the stables, and fifteen minutes later, he was taking Galahad, Robinson's fast young gelding, out of the village and along the road to Sunderland Park.

For the moment, he kept the horse to a slow, easy canter, glad to have arrived home on such a gorgeous day. It was warm for England, but even here, near Devonshire's Torbay Coast, even on a summer afternoon, it didn't seem particularly warm to Will. Not like Egypt, where temperatures could be beastly at this time of year. It was good, he thought in surprise, to be home. He hadn't expected that.

Nonetheless, the surrounding landscape of rolling hills and hedgerows gave him a strange sense of unreality. He'd grown up here; he knew every bend in this road, recognized each pasture of Devonshire ponies and Jersey cows he passed. He could identify all the scents in the air—apple orchards and pasture-land and the nearby tang of the sea all mingled in the unmistakable fragrance of home. Everything was just as he remembered it, just as it always had been. Yet it seemed almost alien to him, making him appreciate that Egypt, not England, was his home now.

He turned off the main road, memory guiding him as he crossed the stone bridge that spanned the River Stafford and turned onto the road that led toward Sunderland Park, Danbury Downs, and the wild moors beyond those neighboring estates.

The house at Sunderland was leased these days, of course, but the wealthy American family using the place was touring the Lake District up north, enabling him to have use of it for the rest of the summer. Not that he'd need the place that long. He hoped to have his business concluded and be gone again within a week or two.

Because he wanted to be here as short a time as possible, it occurred to Will that he ought to give the grounds at least a cursory survey instead of spending his afternoon gallivanting across the moor. He was the duke now, after all, and though he cared little for his title, it was his obligation to care for the acres he'd inherited. In the interests of time, estate business ought to come first.

The gelding beneath him, however, seemed to have other ideas. Galahad tossed his head with a contemptuous-sounding snort as if disagreeing with such tiresome priorities, and Will laughed. "No boring tours around the park for you, I take it?" he asked, leaning forward to pat the animal's neck. "We'd both prefer a hard ride on the moor, I daresay."

As he spoke, he realized how much he wanted

that. He wanted to race across the moor at break-neck speed just as he and Paul Danbury used to do when they were boys home for summer holidays. Few people knew he was here, and he supposed even fewer would care. His parents were both dead, and with the exception of a married sister in India and a few scattered cousins, he had no family left. There was no one waiting at Sunderland Park to welcome him home. Even Beatrix wasn't waiting anymore.

Not so fast, Will. Wait for me.

Her voice echoed to him, bringing a memory from nearly two decades ago of a seven-year-old girl in a lacy pink pinafore, a girl with honey-blond curls and big brown eyes, who was running down to the stables on chubby legs, trying to follow him. *Wait for me, Will. I want to go, too. . .*

He didn't remember his reply from that particular day so long ago, but thinking back on it now, he was sure it had been as scoffing and derisive as possible. After all, what eleven-year-old boy wanted his friend's little cousin tagging along?

Odd how things could change. Thirteen years later, he'd been the one pleading, trying for all he was worth to convince that golden-haired girl to accompany him on the adventure of a lifetime. He should have saved his breath.

Anger flared up from deep within him, sudden and hot, but as he'd done so many times before, Will tamped it down and buried it. He and Beatrix had made their choices six years ago, and they both had to live with the consequences.

A sound intruded on Will's thoughts, a rumbling roar discernible even over the rhythmic drumming of Galahad's hooves, a sound that seemed out of place in the bucolic Devonshire landscape.

He pulled on the reins to slow the gelding to a walk, and he listened, striving to identify the strange noise. It was rather like the drone of a bumblebee, only more abrasive and much, much louder. And it seemed to be growing louder with each passing moment.

Perceiving that the sound was coming from behind him, he turned in the saddle, glancing over his shoulder just as an automobile of white-painted steel, red leather upholstery, and polished brass fittings came into view, raising a cloud of dust as it came around the bend in the road.

The driver of the open-air vehicle was clearly female. Though the driver was swathed in a chin-high motoring coat, scarf, and goggles, her sex was evidenced by the coat's enormous leg-o'-mutton sleeves and the scarf of sheer chiffon wrapped around her narrow-brimmed boater hat. Though she wasn't motoring particularly fast, she seemed an impatient sort of female, for as she came closer, she sounded the brass horn attached to the vehicle's seat in a loud, decisive toot-toot.

Galahad gave a violent start at the sound and tried to bolt, but Will pulled hard on the reins and managed to keep control of his mount, at least until the motorcar moved up on his right to pass him.

This loud, rattling horseless carriage coming

alongside proved too much for the skittish young horse. With a whinny of pure terror, Galahad reared up violently, then came down on his forelegs and bucked.

Will went flying through the air and landed hard on the packed dirt of the road. Galahad bolted, giving him an accidental kick in the knee with one hoof as he ran for the woods.

It had been a long time since he'd fallen from a horse, he realized, so long, in fact, he'd forgotten how it felt. He grimaced as he rolled onto his back. He'd forgotten it was this painful.

The motorcar skidded to a halt in front of him, and the driver of the vehicle turned off the engine. "Are you all right?" a feminine voice called to him, a voice that seemed familiar. Too familiar, in fact.

Frowning, he lifted his head and watched as the woman stepped down from the vehicle. When he caught sight of a slim, booted ankle and the ballooning hem of a pair of Turkish trousers, he felt a glimmer of relief. Beatrix wasn't at all the sort of girl to wear trousers, Turkish or not. Nor was she the sort to go bouncing along country lanes in a motorcar. He had to be mistaken.

The woman came hurrying toward him, her long motoring coat flapping behind her as she ran. But her steps faltered as she saw his face, and her lips parted in utter astonishment. "Will?" she murmured as she sank to her knees beside him. "Good God."

She pulled down those goggles, revealing a pair of brown eyes he recognized at once, eyes that had invaded his dreams countless times during his years away. No mistake, he thought with chagrin. Only Beatrix had eyes like that; big, soft, dark eyes, like those of an English doe. Tightness squeezed his chest, and he forced his gaze down a notch.

Her face was just as he remembered it, with the same cupid's bow mouth, the same absurdly tiny nose, and the same soft, round cheeks he'd always known. Faintly, he caught the scent of gardenia in the air between them. Six years, but the fragrance still seemed to be her favorite.

Yet, despite how similar she seemed to the Beatrix of his memory, there had been some changes in her while he'd been away. He glanced down her body, and then looked past her to the nearby vehicle. When had she taken to wearing trousers and driving a motorcar? It seemed strangely out of character, for there'd never been anything of the tomboy about Beatrix. If there had been, he might not have had to go to Egypt alone.

Will met her gaze again, and something fractured inside him, a crack in the layers of indifference he'd spent six years accumulating.

He'd worked so damned hard to forget her, but when this trip home was something he couldn't put off any longer, thinking of Beatrix had become an irresistible temptation. Countless times during the past few months, he'd wondered how it would feel when he saw her again. Now he knew.

It hurt like hell.

Will jerked to a sitting position, sealing the dangerous fracture inside himself before it could open further. He hadn't expected his first encounter with her to be easy, but no matter what happened, no matter what it cost him, he intended to act like he just didn't give a damn.

"Hullo, Trix," he said, proud of the carefree note he was able to put into his voice. "I say, you're looking well."

She glanced over his supine body, then back to his face. "I'm afraid I can't say the same. You look awful. Life in Egypt is obviously just as arduous as I thought it would be."

"Life in Devonshire seems equally fraught with difficulties these days, at least for people on horseback. I approve the motorcar, but who taught you to drive it? The devil?"

"No, Julia."

He thought of her mad cousin and gave a nod. "That's rather the same thing, I suppose."

Beatrix folded her arms. "What are you doing here? Last I heard, you were still in Egypt, looking for King Tutankhamen's tomb. Have you found it yet, or are you still digging up nothing but clay pots and cylinder seals?"

The derision in her voice was unmistakable as she mentioned the life he had now, the life he'd only dreamed of when he was a boy, the life he'd thought she would want to share with him if it ever came to pass; and the anger he'd worked so hard to vanquish flared up again before he could stop it. "The prodigal always returns," he shot back, giving her a pointed glance. "If only to remind himself why he left."

Those big dark eyes narrowed. "You've been gone six years. What's brought you back after being so long away?"

He smiled wide enough to make his jaw ache. "You, sweet pea. What else?"

She made a sound of obvious skepticism. "I should have known not to expect a serious answer from you."

"None of your business. Is that answer serious enough for you?" He tried to stand up, but pain shot through his knee, making him grimace. "Damn," he muttered as he sank back down to the ground. "I really took a tumble this time."

She seemed indifferent to his pain. "I'd have thought six years away would have given you some measure of maturity, but I was obviously mistaken."

Will bit back the angry words that hovered on the tip of his tongue, and strove to maintain his careless air. "Six years?" he drawled after a moment. "My, how time does fly."

"Doesn't it? I'm surprised you would even bother to come back after all this time."

"I don't know why you should be surprised, old thing," he answered, and gave her a wink. "You didn't really think I'd miss your wedding, did you?"

Beatrix stared at the man she'd never expected to see again, unable to think of a thing to say, wondering if she was having a dream—or more accurately, a nightmare.

Still, dream or reality, this was definitely Will. She'd recognized him at once. Some people wouldn't have, she supposed as she studied him, for life in an uncivilized country had clearly left its mark. His hair was still the same dark coffee-brown color it had been when he went away, but the Egyptian sun had tanned his skin to a golden bronze, making his light green eyes seem like glittering peridot jewels. His face was leaner, harder than that of the man she remembered, but the rugged harshness that marked his countenance only seemed to make him even handsomer than he'd been six years ago. With these observations going through her mind, it took her a moment to appreciate the ramifications of what he'd just said.

"My wedding?" she echoed with a dawning horror. She lowered her arms and straightened on her knees. "You've come home for my wedding?"

"Wouldn't miss it for the world," he said, and smiled at her.

Beatrix felt the impact of that smile like a blow to the chest. Will might have changed in many ways, but if she had failed to recognize him, that devilish smile would have set her straight, for with it came a rush of excitement and pleasure so intense that she felt momentarily giddy, as if caught in the violent throes of first love all over again.

Yes, this was Will, who'd led her in her first waltz at her first ball and given her her first kiss. Will, who'd always been able to provoke her temper, stir her passions, and derail her common sense like no other person in the world. Will, the man she'd loved and adored as far back as she could remember, the man who'd jilted her, broken her heart, and shattered her dreams.

"I told you I'd come home one day," he said, his lighthearted voice cutting through her shock. "Hurts to know you didn't believe me."

She looked up into the brilliant green eyes she'd once loved so much, and the silly rush of pleasure and excitement she'd felt at the sight of him vanished as if it had never been, replaced by something darker, deeper, and far more shattering. Rage.

Over five years she'd needed to get over him, and now he decided to come back? Five years of trying to accept that he was gone for good, five years of trying not to hope he'd change his mind and come back to her. And now, when six years had passed, when she was finally over him and she was about to marry someone else, he was here to undo the contentment she'd worked so hard to achieve? If Beatrix had any lingering doubts as to whether her love for him was truly gone, the burning rage within her was enough to banish them.

"Go to hell," she said, and stood up. "Or better yet, go back to Egypt. That godforsaken place is probably hotter and more miserable than hell anyway."

She caught a flash of her own anger mirrored in his eyes, but when he spoke, he was smiling. "Go back to Egypt?" he said, sounding as if he thought her off her onion for even suggesting such a thing. "And forgo the wedding of the season? I couldn't possibly. The scandalmongers are counting on me to make an appearance and upset the applecart. They'd be so disappointed if I failed to show."

"You have not been invited!" she cried. "Neither

Aidan nor I would ever dream of allowing you to attend our wedding."

With that, she turned her back on the man sitting in the road and started toward her motorcar.

"Aidan?" he echoed as she walked away. "Ah, yes, Aidan Carr, the Duke of Trathen. Trading up, aren't you? Trathen's what—tenth in line to the throne, or something like that?"

"Trading up? I'm not doing any such thing. I'm—" She broke off, realizing that she was starting to explain when she didn't owe him any explanations.

Clamping her lips together, she turned away without another word and resumed walking to the front of the vehicle. Still ignoring him, she leaned down, grasped the brass handle, and with the expertise of long practice, gave a hard twist to crank the engine just as Julia had taught her, keeping her thumb back to avoid breaking it on the kickback.

"Wait!" Will shouted over the rumble of the motorcar's engine as she walked around to the driver's side. "You have to take me with you."

"No, I don't," she shot back and climbed into the vehicle. Hitching up her ankle-length motoring coat, she settled herself on the red leather seat. "You can lie in the road until you rot as far as I'm concerned. If you want to go to Sunderland Park, you'll have to walk."

"Walk? But I'm injured, and it's five miles to the house from here."

"Five and a half," she corrected, pulling her driving goggles up to protect her eyes. She turned in her seat to look at him over one shoulder, watching as he struggled to his feet, and she forced herself to ignore the pain that crossed his face, reminding herself of all the pain he'd given her. "Don't worry, Will. I'm sure some farmer will come along and give you a ride. Eventually."

"Beatrix!" he shouted, limping forward toward the vehicle. "You can't just leave me here!"

"Why not?" she countered smoothly. "You had no compunction about leaving me six years ago."

With that parting shot, she turned her back, curled her gloved fingers around the polished wood steering wheel, and pushed the petrol pedal. As the motorcar rolled down the road, it took all the willpower she possessed not to turn her head and look back at the man she'd left behind.

There was no looking back, she reminded herself, keeping her gaze fixed on the road ahead. Not now, not ever.

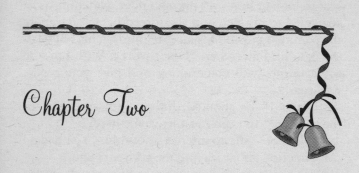

Chapter Two

It wasn't until she turned the Daimler onto the long, shaded lane leading to Danbury Downs that Beatrix allowed herself a glance behind her. By then, of course, the trees and shrubbery that lined the winding road obscured any view of the tall, dark-haired nemesis from her past. Too bad Beatrix's mind wasn't so obliging.

Come with me.

She fixed her attention on the road ahead as Will's voice came back to her, echoing from six years ago, urging her to a course she could not accept.

As if to torment her, her horrified reply also came to her out of the past.

Go to Egypt? Abandon my father, my home, and all our friends? Sleep in a tent, drink water from a canteen, and bathe out of a tin basin? Are you mad?

In her mind's eye, she could still see him holding up that telegram from Sir Edmund, his buoyant ex-

pression at the news it contained hardening into resolve.

*This is what I've always dreamed of. The chance
of a lifetime. I can't let it pass me by, not even for
you, Trix.*

Remembering his face, she felt a shiver of the same
cold dread that had gripped her that awful day, as
she'd sensed everything she'd ever wanted slipping
away from her and into the desolate Egyptian desert.

For three days, they had argued hammer and
tongs. Her father had tried to reason with him,
his father had threatened to disown him. She had
argued, pleaded, even—God help her—begged for
him to stay. None of it had mattered.

Not even for you, Trix.

He'd gone off to find the tomb of King Tutankhamen with his revered mentor from Cambridge days
while she'd written letters of regret to four hundred
and eighty-six wedding guests, with nothing but her
love, an ivory silk wedding dress, and a lifetime of
shattered dreams to console her.

Beatrix realized she was clenching the steering
wheel so tightly that her fingers ached, and she forced
herself to relax her grip, reminding herself that Will
was in the past. She had new dreams now, dreams
that involved a different man, an honorable man
who loved her, who would never abandon her. As
she drove, Beatrix tried to focus her mind's eye on
Aidan's face, but his grave good looks seemed elusive
just now, pushed aside by the brilliant green eyes and
heart-bruising smile of her first love.

It was after her father's death that she'd truly faced

reality; the only man she'd ever wanted wasn't coming back, and the life she'd always envisioned with him was never going to happen. Beatrix squeezed her eyes shut. Because Will had refused to surrender his childhood dream, she had lost hers.

The Daimler lurched, and she opened her eyes to find the stout trunk of an elm looming before her. With a cry of alarm, she gave the wheel a violent twist, bringing the vehicle out of the ditch and back onto the road just in time to avoid a smash-up.

Breathing a sigh of relief, Beatrix shoved memories of the past out of her mind and brought her attention back to the road in front of her. Her cousin had given her the Daimler as a birthday present, and if she was hurt because of it, Julia would never forgive herself. Beatrix concentrated on getting herself and the Daimler safely home.

Passing the lane to Sunderland Park, she took the Daimler a mile farther on, through the open wrought-iron gates that led to Danbury House. She turned onto the sweeping gravel drive, but she didn't stop there. Instead, she circled the motorcar around the south wing to the stables. There was no space in the carriage house for the Daimler, but two stalls of the stables had been thrown into one and a pair of wide doors added to make a place for storing the vehicle. Mr. Warren had left the doors flung back in anticipation of her return from town, and she pulled the automobile carefully into place.

But even after she'd applied the braking lever and extinguished the engine, Beatrix remained in the vehicle. She couldn't have said why she was choosing to linger here, for it was in the stables where her memories of Will had always been strongest. He loved horses, loved everything about them, particularly riding them as fast as possible, a fact that had always left her in perpetual fear he'd break his neck.

She turned in the leather seat of the motorcar, studying her surroundings. To her right, horses' heads were visible over the tops of their stalls—chestnut, bay, black, and piebald. To her left, saddles, reins, and grooming equipment lined the wooden wall. How many times had she and Will ridden together when he'd been home from school? Not many, she supposed. He'd usually preferred to ride with her cousin Paul, who had always stayed at Danbury Downs in the summer holiday. She was hampered by a sidesaddle, and far less able to keep up with Will's reckless speed.

Whenever she and Will had ridden together, he'd been forever urging her to ride astride, go faster, take higher jumps, push herself beyond the rigid limits to which ladies were expected to adhere.

He'd pushed her in other ways, too, she remembered, spiriting her away from prying eyes, stealing kisses from her behind the hedgerows, always wanting more from her, no matter how much she gave, until finally, he'd demanded the impossible.

Come with me.

Will had always been the one to take chances and tempt the devil, not she. Only after he'd been gone five years had she finally realized what he had always known: one couldn't spend one's entire life waiting for life to start. That was why she'd gone to Cornwall with Julia. That was why she'd left her love for Will behind at last. That was why she'd accepted Aidan's proposal after three months of acquaintance. Because time was going by, because she wanted marriage and children, because she'd come to care deeply for Aidan, and because life was short and sweet and meant to be lived, not wasted waiting for someone who was never coming back, someone who hadn't loved her enough to stay.

Egypt's always been your dream, Will. Not mine.

How strange life was. She'd finally left behind the man she'd thought would give her everything she'd ever wanted, and then, as if by magic, a different man had dropped everything she'd ever wanted right into her lap.

Beatrix pressed her gloved hand to her mouth, catching back a sob.

"My lady? Are you all right?"

She jumped, jerking her hand down, and glanced toward Mr. Warren, who was standing beside the Daimler. She wondered how long she'd been sitting here, woolgathering. A while, she concluded, if the chauffeur's frown of concern was anything to go by.

"I'm perfectly well, Mr. Warren," she answered, forcing aside her momentary despondency. When the chauffeur opened the door, she gave him her hand and allowed him to help her step down, but she didn't return to the house straightaway. Instead, she spent a good ten minutes fussing over the Daimler, giving

Warren explicit instructions on just how to refuel, wash, and wax the vehicle. The chauffeur, despite having heard all this from her a dozen times before and having some experience with automobiles, listened with patient forbearance. Finally satisfied, Beatrix left the stables and walked back to the house.

A maid must have spied her approach through a window, for the servant opened the side door for her the moment she reached it. "Thank you, Avery," she said as she handed over her goggles and gloves, and began to unbutton her motoring coat. "Where is Aunt Eugenia?"

"She is in the library having tea."

"Tea? So soon?"

"It's just five o'clock, miss," the maid informed her as she took Beatrix's motoring coat.

Heavens, she must have been sitting in the Daimler at least twenty minutes. With a sound of vexation, Beatrix hurried down the corridor toward the library.

As she approached the door, she wondered if she should inform her aunt of Will's return, but before she could make up her mind, the decision was taken out of her hands.

"Sunderland has come back from Egypt," Eugenia announced the moment her niece came into the room.

Beatrix halted just inside the doorway, unable to fathom how this news had reached her aunt so quickly. She opened her mouth to say she already knew, but then she reconsidered and closed it again.

If she told Eugenia she'd already seen Will, there would be questions, and she'd have to explain, and when Auntie discovered that she'd left the Duke of Sunderland sitting ignominiously in the middle of the road, there would be no end of a fuss. Best all around, she decided, if she feigned ignorance of the matter.

"Sunderland?" She gave a little laugh as she pulled out her hat pin and removed her hat. "Don't be silly, Auntie," she chided gently, hoping her voice carried just the right hint of uncaring amusement. "I think we are both painfully aware that nothing on earth could force Will to come home," she added, weaving her hat pin through the brim of her straw boater before tossing both onto a nearby chair. "I doubt even dynamite would do the trick."

"Nonetheless, he has returned."

Beatrix worked to paste a deprecating little smile on her face. "How did you come by this piece of news?"

"Groves told me, of course."

"Groves?" This time Beatrix didn't have to feign surprise. "Why should Groves know anything about it?"

"My dear niece, butlers always know everything. That is part of their duties."

"Nonsense. Groves should be ashamed of himself, spreading rumors."

"It's not a rumor." An amused voice had Beatrix turning around to find her cousin Geoffrey behind her, shoulder against the doorjamb, hands in the pockets of his striped trousers. "It's a fact. I saw him myself," he added, straightening in the doorway, shaking back the straight blond locks of hair that had fallen over his forehead. "Passed him on my bicycle not ten minutes ago."

"I don't believe it," Beatrix countered. "You were only ten when Will left for Egypt. You couldn't possibly have recognized him after all this time."

"He was limping along the Stafford Road," Geoff went on blithely as if she hadn't spoken, stepping past her to survey the cakes on the tea tray. "He was muttering your name and cursing like a sailor. Given those two facts, who else could it be?"

"Limping?" Eugenia cut in before she could reply. "Oh dear. Did he sustain an injury in Egypt, I wonder?"

"Will wasn't hurt in Egypt," Geoff informed his mother with obvious relish as he took a seedcake from the tray. "He was injured right here in Stafford St. Mary, not more than half an hour ago, thanks to our own dear, sweet Beatrix."

"What?" Eugenia cried in lively astonishment and turned to her. "Beatrix, what is this all about?"

"Nothing," she denied, even as she thought of Will's knee and felt the faint whisper of a slightly guilty conscience. "He's not injured," she added, as much for her own reassurance as for her relations. "It's all a hum."

"It isn't," Geoff contradicted, his mouth full of cake. He turned toward his mother, adding, "Beatrix struck him down with the Daimler."

"I did no such thing!" Beatrix cried, stung by the

accusation. "And I don't see how you know anything about it anyway," she added, going on the offensive. "You weren't there."

"When I saw him limping, I stopped the bicycle and spoke to him. He told me all about it, including that his injuries were caused by that motorcar our cousin Julia gave you. Though how Groves heard about it, I can't even guess, unless he overheard me when I was telling Paul the news."

"You told Paul?"

"Of course. He and Will were deuced good friends, after all, and I thought he'd want to know." Geoff flashed a sly grin at her. "Trathen will probably be interested in this news, too, but I shan't tell him. I'll leave that to you, Trix. You have to tell him, you know," he added as if assuming she wouldn't. "He's bound to find out, and then he'll wonder why you didn't mention it. Besides, he hates that Daimler, and he deserves to know his future bride is running down her former suitors with it."

"Well, this is a fine kettle of fish," Eugenia murmured. "Oh, Beatrix, when you insisted on bringing that dreadful motorcar back from Cornwall, I knew it would mean trouble. It came from Julia, after all. That girl has always been a trial."

"I didn't hit Will with the Daimler," she reiterated through clenched teeth.

Eugenia did not seem reassured. "I've told you again and again, you drive too fast. Your father would never have approved, I'm sure."

Beatrix was sure of it, too, but she wisely refrained from validating that particular point.

"I remember when I visited you both in Cornwall last summer," Eugenia went on. "Why, Julia boasted that she had driven that Daimler along the coast road from Gwithian to St. Ives at thirty-seven miles an hour. Thirty-seven! On those bumpy, twisting roads? Heavens, it's a wonder she didn't kill herself. I told her so, I remember. I was most concerned for her safety."

Which was precisely why Beatrix had seen fit not to tell Auntie she'd been along the day Julia had taken the Daimler to St. Ives.

"I never drive at such speeds," Beatrix pointed out. "I am always a most careful motorist."

"I'm sure you are, dear, but as your dear papa asked me on his deathbed to take care of you, I have the right to be concerned for your safety. And I am not the only one who worries about you with that Daimler. Dear Trathen doesn't like it, either."

"There's a good reason for that, Mama," Geoff put in. "Trathen doesn't like the Daimler because he secretly wishes we were living about a hundred years ago." He gave a derisive snort. "He's so old-fashioned and dull."

"He is not!" Beatrix said, compelled to defend her future husband. "Aidan prefers a carriage to a motorcar, because motorcars are noisy and . . . and . . ." Her voice trailed off as she desperately sought a reason that didn't sound dull as ashes.

"See?" Geoff countered, looking triumphant and causing Beatrix to groan in aggravation.

"Stop quarrelling, you two," Eugenia said. "The fact remains that Trathen agrees with me about that motorcar."

That much was true. Aidan had expressed doubts as to the Daimler's safety and questioned whether driving such a vehicle was a suitable pastime for a young lady. But though she deeply valued Aidan's opinion and was usually happy to accede to his wishes, on this one thing, Beatrix had refused to waver.

Giving up the Daimler would have been like cutting out a piece of her soul. Beatrix closed her eyes, remembering the terror she'd felt as she'd sat beside Julia on the road to St. Ives. How she'd gripped the front dashboard, fully aware that there was no door separating her from the edge of the cliff just a few feet away, sure she'd be thrown out of the vehicle any moment and dashed against the rocks far below.

Yet, along with the terror, there had been exhilaration in it, such glorious freedom. Julia had made her take her hat off, and thinking back on it now, she could almost feel the wind blowing back her hair. She could almost taste the tang in the sea air. She remembered most vividly the moment Julia had suggested she take the wheel, the way her throat had gone dry and her heart had begun to thump frantically in her chest. To this day she didn't know why she had agreed to her cousin's wild suggestion, for she didn't consider herself an adventurous sort of person, but for some reason she had agreed and had slid behind the wheel. And there, in that one, shining moment a year ago, she'd been transformed, and there was no going back.

What a glorious holiday that had been, reminiscent of the carefree days when Will, Paul, Geoff, and

Julia had come home to Devonshire for the summer holidays, when they'd gone to Viscount Marlowe's villa on Pixy Cove for August and they'd snuck out with Marlowe's sisters to bathe in the sea at midnight and tell ghost stories in the caves. But though her time in Cornwall with Julia had been a bit like those blissful childhood days, she'd been surprised to discover that she hadn't missed Will with the same heartrending pain of previous summers. Life, she'd realized, went relentlessly forward, and Cornwall was where she'd gotten over Will. Cornwall was where she'd met Aidan.

"Beatrix?"

"Hmm? What?" She opened her eyes and forced her mind back to the present and what Eugenia was saying.

"Since you struck poor Sunderland, his injuries are rather our responsibility. Perhaps we should send Dr. Corrigan after him?"

Beatrix made a sound of impatience. "Auntie, I did not hit Sunderland with the car. His horse shied when the Daimler came round the curve, and he wasn't able to subdue the animal. It threw him—"

"And when he landed, the horse kicked him, making it difficult for him to walk," Geoff finished for her. "He'll have a deuced fine bruise from it, I'm sure."

"Exactly!" Beatrix said, making a face at her cousin. "His horse caused his injuries, not me."

"No, all you did was leave him there." Geoff shook his head in mock sorrow at her lack of compassion. "Wounded and in pain."

"Oh, Beatrix." Eugenia sighed, staring at her in disappointment. "You knew he was injured, and you abandoned him? You didn't return him to town or summon help?"

Jilting her six years ago on the eve of their wedding, she supposed, wasn't sufficient provocation for leaving him in the road.

"Oh, for heaven's sake!" she cried in exasperation. "He wasn't really hurt. He took a tumble off his horse, that's all, the sort of thing that might happen to anyone. It's happened to him more times than I can remember. He's only trying to flick me on the raw by pretending to Geoff that I injured him. And if he were in need of a doctor," she added, turning to her cousin, "what are you doing here? Why didn't you race into the village on that bicycle of yours and fetch Dr. Corrigan?"

"Because Mr. Robinson came by just then," Geoff answered at once. "The old boy had all the duke's things from the train station piled up in that cart of his, and some Indian-looking fellow in a turban was sitting beside him. He gave up his seat on the box to Will—the Indian fellow did, not Mr. Robinson. The Indian stepped onto the dummy board, and Mr. Robinson drove them both to Sunderland Park."

"There," Beatrix countered with satisfaction. "You've just proven my point. If Will were injured, he wouldn't have been able to climb up on the box of Mr. Robinson's cart." She returned her attention to Eugenia. "You see, Auntie? There's no need to fuss over Sunderland. He's perfectly well. What should be of concern is his reason for coming home. My wedding is only two months away, you know."

Eugenia's frown deepened in puzzlement. "What are you implying, Beatrix?"

"I don't know," she confessed. "But I am curious. Why is he here? He didn't come home when his father died, nor when my father died—" Her voice choked up, and it took her a moment to regain her voice.

"Six years away," she continued, "yet now, on the eve of my wedding to someone else, he comes home. Why?"

"Maybe he wants you back," Geoff suggested, helping himself to another seedcake. "Maybe he's come to stop the wedding."

Beatrix stared at her cousin in horror. "He couldn't," she murmured, even as Will's words from a short time ago about upsetting the applecart came back to her. She swallowed hard. "He wouldn't."

"Ohhh," Eugenia moaned, pressing a hand to her forehead. "This is a fine kettle of fish."

Geoff began to laugh. "I can see it now—all the wedding guests assembled, the journalists with pencils poised, the vicar asking if anyone knows any just cause why these two should not be joined in holy matrimony, and Will stands up—"

"What did he tell you?" Beatrix demanded, striding over to her cousin. When he didn't answer, she reached out and grabbed him by the ear. "Did he say that's why he's home? To stop my wedding? Did he?"

"Ouch!" Geoff cried in painful protest. He gripped

her wrist and pulled, trying to free himself from her tight grip. "Let go of me!"

"Beatrix, stop that at once!" Eugenia ordered. "Twisting your cousin's ears is most unladylike!"

She responded by twisting harder. "Geoff, if you don't tell me what he told you, I swear I shall—"

"Ow, ow!" he wailed, tugging at her wrist. "He didn't tell me anything! I'm just having you on!"

Beatrix let go of him with a huff of exasperation and relief. "I should have known you'd rattle on without knowing any facts. Still," she added, frowning as she returned her attention to her aunt, "in this case, Geoff might actually be right."

"Surely you don't think Sunderland's come home to make trouble?" Eugenia looked dubious. "No, I can't believe he'd do such a thing."

"I can," she responded darkly. "He implied as much to me earlier today. And it would be just like him to stand up in church and disrupt the ceremony. He'd think it quite a lark, I daresay."

"I still don't believe it. Sunderland is a gentleman."

"Gentleman?" She stared at her aunt in disbelief. "Does a gentleman abandon his bride-to-be a fortnight before their wedding? Does he refuse to come home even after inheriting his title? Does he ignore his ducal responsibilities and duties? No, Aunt Eugenia, Sunderland is many things, but he is no gentleman!"

"Moderate your tone, Beatrix," her aunt said with a hint of reproof. "I am scarce half a dozen feet from you and can hear your words quite clearly. A lady of breeding does not shout, remember."

She had been shouting, she realized, and she took a deep, steadying breath, trying to employ reason. Surely Will hadn't come to try to win her back. She wasn't conceited enough to believe it, and besides, six years had gone by. And she'd been engaged to Aidan for nearly nine months. If Will wanted to win her back, he'd had plenty of time to make the attempt before now.

Still, whatever the reason for his return, the fact remained that he was here, and she did not put it past him to cause some sort of trouble for her and Aidan while he was home. Whatever his intentions, she intended to discover them.

"I won't be having any tea, Auntie," she said, and marched over to the chair where she had tossed her hat a short while earlier. "I'm going out again."

"Best to leave the Daimler here," Geoff advised, glaring at her as he rubbed his sore ear. "It might be safer for Sunderland that way."

Beatrix assumed a dignified air in response. "I shall have Groves send for the carriage," she answered, and donned her hat.

"But you just came back from the village," Eugenia cried. "Where are you going now?"

"I may have inadvertently injured an old friend of our family," she answered as she secured her straw boater in place with her hat pin and pulled a few tendrils of her hair from beneath the brim to frame her face. "I must go at once to express my deep distress and concern."

She ignored Geoff's skeptical snort as she started for the door.

* * *

Will made a rueful grimace as his valet rubbed a camphor-scented liniment over his swollen knee. "In situations like this, Aman, I believe I would prefer a stiff whisky and soda to one of your concoctions."

The Egyptian servant, who'd treated him for everything from scorpion stings to blackwater fever during the past half-dozen years, corked the bottle of liniment and returned it to the big leather suitcase from which he had extracted it a few minutes earlier. "Indeed, sir?" he murmured in an unflappable fashion worthy of any British valet. "It is a good thing, then, that I asked your housekeeper, Mrs. Gudgeon, to fetch a bottle of whisky and a siphon."

Will smiled. "I'm deuced glad I saved your life that night in Cairo."

"I am of a similar opinion, Your Grace." Aman fetched an ottoman from one corner of the study and lifted Will's outstretched leg onto its padded surface. He then eased the hem of Will's trouser back down over his swollen knee to his ankle, and gave the hem a tug to smooth out any wrinkles in the fabric, and straightened with a satisfied nod. "It would be best, sir, if you did not put any weight on it for a day or two."

Will moved his leg a bit on the footstool, already restless. "I feel like an old man with the gout," he muttered.

Aman retrieved Will's dispatch case from the open suitcase on the floor and held it up in an inquiring fashion. "Perhaps you would wish to write letters while you are indisposed, sir?"

"I'm not indisposed, and you know how I hate writing letters."

Aman had all the placid, fatalistic calm offered by his heritage. He shrugged. "If you prefer to read, sir, I would be happy to bring a book from your library."

Will eyed the Moroccan leather case in his valet's hands and sighed. He did have writing to do, he supposed.

Not for the purpose he'd come home, of course. When a man wanted to ask a member of his former fiancée's family for a loan, a letter just wouldn't do. But he did have other things to write. A summary of the artifacts they'd discovered during the past season, a speech to the Archaeological Society presenting the latest findings, that article he'd promised the *Times*, a letter to Sir Edmund in Scotland—he reached for the dispatch case and gave in to the inevitable.

"I'll need a quill and ink, and something to write on," he told Aman, and gestured to an elaborate Chinese cabinet in one corner of the study. "If memory serves, my father kept a lap desk in there."

Aman retrieved it and the necessary stationery supplies, placing them on the table beside Will's chair. "If there is nothing else you require, sir, I will begin unpacking your things. Shall you dress for dinner?" He didn't blink at Will's sound of derision. "Is that not the custom in Britain, Your Grace?"

"It is, and a damned silly one, too, especially since I'm dining alone." He imagined himself in dinner jacket and tie at one end of Sunderland House's formal dining table, surrounded by gilt-framed paintings and heavy damask draperies, flanked by two long rows of empty chairs, eating from Limoges plates and drinking wine from a crystal goblet, just as he had been forced to do whenever his parents had been in residence. Will could vividly remember the old man sitting at one end of the table in all his ducal glory, and his mother at the other end, staring icily back at her husband. The silence between them pronounced their mutual contempt more loudly than any angry words could have. He felt suddenly smothered. "God," he muttered, running a finger inside his collar, "it's so damned hard to breathe in this country."

"Sir?"

"Never mind." He eased back in his chair with a sigh. "Trousers and a smoking jacket are good enough for dining alone, Aman. And I'll eat in the breakfast room, not the formal dining room."

"Very good, sir." The valet bowed and departed, and Will stared at his outstretched leg with aggravation. Ages since he'd fallen from a horse. Due to Aman's vile camphor liniment, the pain was beginning to ease, but if all went well with Paul, he probably wouldn't have time to take Mr. Robinson's wind-fast gelding racing across the moor. He felt a tinge of disappointment at that. He'd always loved the moor—loved the wild beauty, the rugged tors and mossy dells. The moorland from horseback was one of the things in Devonshire he'd really missed during his years away.

But not the only thing, a devilish voice inside him whispered.

Unbidden, an image of brown eyes and blond hair came into his mind, and before he realized what he was doing, he reached into the breast pocket of his jacket. He pulled out the folded scrap of newspaper, an announcement torn from the society page of the *Times* last January.

> *The Earl of Danbury is pleased to announce the engagement of his cousin, Lady Beatrix, to His Grace, the Duke of Trathen . . .*

Will's hand tightened to a fist, crumpling the yellowed scrap of paper, remembering the day he'd seen it. Rooted to his chair at the club in Thebes, he'd stared down at the news that by then had been a month old, reading the announcement of her engagement over and over again, trying to accept it. He'd torn the announcement out of the paper and stuck it in the breast pocket of his jacket, too shocked to even realize what he was doing.

His surprise didn't stem from conceit, for he'd known she would eventually marry. She was too desirable a woman, she wanted marriage and children too much, not to do so. No, his surprise had stemmed not from the announcement, but from his own reaction to it. He'd felt as if he'd been hit square in the chest, a painful blow, leaving an ache that had taken ages to subside.

But it had subsided. He'd recovered since that day nine months ago. He'd reminded himself it was all for the best. He'd prayed for her happiness, and he'd tried to mean it. Yet he still hadn't been able to toss this stupid little scrap of paper. He always kept it in his breast pocket, always within easy reach.

Go to Egypt? Abandon my father, my home, and all our friends? Sleep in a tent, drink water from a canteen, and bathe out of a tin basin? Are you mad?

The moment she'd said those words, in that appalled voice, her eyes wide with horror at the prospect, he'd known the inevitable end of the story. Three days of arguing, each of them trying with all they had to persuade the other to an impossible choice, each of them hoping the other would be the one to give in, to change, to embrace a life that only the other one wanted.

Go to Egypt? Are you mad?

The truth was, any hope that they could have a life together had ended the moment she'd spoken those words. Or perhaps it had really ended before that, when he'd received Sir Edmund's telegram, and he'd seen a way to escape the pointless life that had been laid out for him since the day he was born.

Perhaps that was why he kept this scrap of paper— to remind himself of how narrowly he'd escaped a suffocating life of pointless duties and silly social rituals, a life he would have hated. Or perhaps, he thought with a wry smile, his reason was simpler. Perhaps he kept it just to prove to himself he was over her.

He realized he'd wadded the announcement into a ball within his fist, and he forced himself to relax his grip. Despite his words to Beatrix earlier today, he hadn't come all this way to watch her marry some other man. God, he couldn't think of a more dreadful prospect. No, he wasn't here because of her at all, and unless she was standing right in front of him, he had no cause to think of her. What he ought to be thinking about was Paul and how to persuade his oldest friend to loan him twenty thousand pounds.

He had to find a way. Even after the British Museum paid for the antiquities he'd brought with him, it wouldn't be enough to fund the excavation for the next twelve months. His own inheritance was nearly gone, and he hoped Paul would either loan him the funds or sponsor the excavation for the coming year. That would be enough time for him to finally uncover what he'd been digging in the Valley of the Kings for almost six years to find: the tomb of Tutankhamen, a tomb only he, Sir Edmund, and Howard Carter even believed existed.

He recalled the disdain in Beatrix's voice when she'd mentioned his work, and it galled him that she knew he'd spent his entire inheritance without finding much more than pottery shards. Oh, they'd discovered plenty of artifacts—tablets of hieroglyphs, cylinder seals, a few bits of lapis and gold, plenty of sarcophagi containing mummified remains. All these were valuable finds, of course, important to science and to him as an archaeologist, but they weren't the reason he'd gone to Egypt. They weren't Tutankhamen.

Tut was there, though. Sir Edmund had unearthed the first evidence of that seven years ago—only a vague mention on a clay tablet, but Tut was down there somewhere, and he intended to find that Boy King before another year went by.

He knew his choice to follow his dream defied all Beatrix's notions of duty, tradition, and even common sense. At this moment, she was probably congratulating herself on her escape, applauding herself for abandoning him in favor of a more successful, more important man. She had always humored his fascination with Egypt and archaeology, but she'd never really shared it.

He closed his eyes and tried to conjure the delicate sweetness of gardenias, working at it until that fragrance seemed as real now as it had a short time ago on the Stafford Road, as real as the heady fragrance that drifted through his bedroom window from the courtyard at home every night in February.

The sound of footsteps along the corridor broke into Will's speculations, and he hastily shoved the crumpled bit of newspaper back into his pocket. He glanced up as the rosy-faced, round little Mrs. Gudgeon appeared in the doorway with a silver tray containing a bottle of amber liquid, a glass, and a siphon—all the necessary accoutrements of Will's preferred medical prescription.

"Ah," he said, gratified by such a welcome sight. "At last."

"Sorry, sir. Someone has come to call, and with the Americans in the north and with most of the staff on board wages, I had to answer the door myself when the bell went."

"Callers already?" That surprised him. English country life was less formal than in town, but if he remembered the proper etiquette at all, it was his responsibility to call on others first, since he was the one arriving after a long absence. He became even more surprised when informed of the identity of his visitor.

"It's Lady Beatrix, sir. I've put her in the drawing room."

"Beatrix?" Will groaned. Devil take it, did she intend to turn up every time his thoughts wandered in her direction? "What on earth does she want?"

"She's come to inquire about the state of your injuries."

Gudgeon might believe that, but he had no illusions that Beatrix gave two straws about his injuries. Besides, if she had, she'd simply have asked Gudgeon, left a card, and been on her way. "She came alone?" he asked, wondering if he'd imagined the housekeeper's use of the singular pronoun. "Her aunt isn't with her? Or some other woman?"

"No, sir. Shall I tell her you are indisposed?"

Will opened his mouth to heartily endorse that suggestion, but then he changed his mind. For Beatrix to come unchaperoned, she must want to see him pretty badly, and that made him curious.

"No, Gudgeon," he answered. "Show her in by all means, but bring me that whisky first."

The housekeeper obeyed, crossing the room to place the tray on the table beside his chair. She poured two fingers of whisky into the glass, added a much less generous measure of soda water, gave the contents a quick stir, and stepped back.

"Thank you, Gudgeon," he said, and picked up the glass. "If my earlier encounter with Lady Beatrix is any indication," he added with a wry grin as he gestured to his knee, "I'll need all the fortification I can get."

Gudgeon did not smile back or betray any other emotion, for it was not her place. She merely bobbed a curtsy and started for the door. But she'd barely taken two steps before she stopped. "Your Grace?"

"Hmm?"

When the housekeeper turned to look at him, Will caught an unmistakable flush of warmth in her cheeks. She glanced at her surroundings, then shifted her weight from one foot to the other and looked at him again. "It's good to have you home again, young master. This house was a sadder place after you'd gone."

That took him back, rather. Gudgeon had been the housekeeper at Sunderland in his father's time, and the old tyrant had never tolerated any personal expression or opinion from herself or any of the other servants. Before he could recover enough to answer, the housekeeper gave him another curtsy and vanished out the door.

So the house had been a sadder place without him? Given his father's sour temperament, that didn't come as much of a surprise. He glanced around the study— his father's favorite room, a room of dark blue paint and walnut paneling that he'd always found particularly depressing. Perhaps that was because here he'd always been called on the carpet for not living up to the Sunderland family image and his father's expectations, something that had occurred with tiresome regularity, especially the fortnight before he'd gone to Egypt. His father had practically shouted the house down after learning his intent to accompany Sir Edmund, and the news of his broken engagement had nearly given the old man apoplexy.

"I wish I could say it was good to be home, Gudgeon," he murmured, and took a hefty swallow of whisky. "But the sooner I'm gone from this place, the happier I'll be."

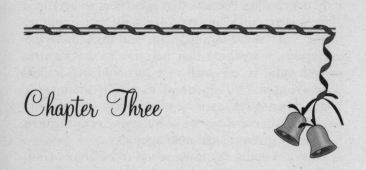

Chapter Three

By the time Mrs. Gudgeon announced her name, Will was prepared for Beatrix's arrival. He'd shifted the footstool a bit so that she could clearly see his outstretched leg from the doorway. If she hadn't left him in the road, he wouldn't have had to walk on his injured knee, and the swelling would have been minimal. Because of her and that automobile of hers, he was laid low in this manner, and she deserved to have a clear view of her handiwork.

"Forgive me for not standing up," he told her with mock cheer. "But that's rather difficult to manage at present, thanks to you."

If he'd hoped for a display of conscience on her part, he was disappointed. "I don't see a splint, so your leg isn't broken." She gave his knee a skeptical glance. "That is, if it's injured at all."

She no longer wore her motoring coat and goggles, he noted as she came further into the study, though she still had on those Turkish trousers, making him remember the time he'd told her she should wear trousers and ride her horse astride so she could go faster, and she'd looked at him as if he'd suggested she go naked. Did she even ride horses anymore? he wondered. If she did, no doubt it was with Trathen. That thought impelled him to take another swallow from his glass of whisky.

"I like the trousers," he told her. "Rather daring of you to wear them, I must say. But really, Trix, since it's of daring that we're talking, isn't coming here without a chaperone carrying things a bit too far? I know I've been away from England a long while, but I'm sure calling upon an unmarried gentleman is still against the rules in civilized society." His hand tightened around his glass. "You're not married yet, you know."

She made a sound of impatience. "Don't be ridiculous, Will. We've known each other for donkey's years. A chaperone is hardly necessary."

"Hmm, I wonder if that's how Trathen would see it. Does he know you're here?"

"Leave Aidan out of this."

"That would be the gentlemanly thing to do," he said amiably. "Lucky for me, I've been living amongst uncivilized heathens so long, I've forgotten how to be a gentleman."

"You never knew how."

He ignored that. "What would Trathen think if he

heard you'd come to see me? What if he knew that scarcely two hours after I arrived, you came running over, alone, to welcome me home?"

"Welcoming you is the last thing on my mind. And as galling as it is to be reminded of how I used to moon over you and follow you everywhere—"

"Not everywhere," he cut in incisively. "Please, Beatrix, do be accurate about these things."

"Those days are long past. I haven't the least interest in running after you now."

"Ah." He settled himself more comfortably in his chair and pasted an expectant look on his face. "You're not concerned about me, and you're not here to welcome me, so you must have come to apologize."

"Apologize?" she cried. "What reason have I to apologize?"

"I'll accept it, of course," he added. "And I'll be jolly civil about it, too, just to demonstrate that a lifetime of the breeding you so highly value didn't go to waste—"

"If anyone should apologize, it's you. I'm here," she added before he could attempt to debate the issue, "because I want to know the real reason you've come home. Is it because of my wedding?"

"I thought you said I wasn't invited."

"You're not. But if you were determined to make a scene in front of over five hundred people, I hardly think lack of an invitation would stop you."

He grinned at that and raised his glass. "True enough," he said, and took another drink. "But now that I'm home, excluding me from the guest list will raise more eyebrows than inviting me would, don't you think? The Dukes of Sunderland are invited to every social event in Devonshire. Deuced impolite of you not to invite me to your wedding. Besides, wouldn't having me there be the best way of proving to everyone that you don't care tuppence for me anymore?"

"I don't need to prove that. Everyone already knows—"

"That you're still holding a torch for me?"

She smiled sweetly. "Only if I can use it to burn you alive."

He glanced down, memory enabling him to see beneath those full, brown velveteen trousers to the generous curves beneath. "As I recall," he murmured, lifting his gaze to her face, "you and I never needed any torches to burn for each other."

He had the satisfaction of watching her smile fade, but other than that, she gave him no reaction but a disdainful stare. "Your memory is flawed."

"Is it?" He stood up, sucking in a deep breath at the pain in his knee, and began walking toward her. "I don't think so."

As he closed the short distance between them, he caught the fragrance of her, and a memory flashed across his mind—their engagement cotillion, a dark corner of the garden, and kissing gardenia-scented skin. Amazing how the scent and sight of her could bring it all flooding back as if six damned years had never gone by. Arousal stirred within his body, and pain, too, and both made him angry, with her and with himself.

"My memory is functioning perfectly," he murmured, leaning closer, close enough that when he spoke again, his breath stirred the delicate wisp of hair that peeked from beneath her hat and curled against her cheek. "Would you like proof?"

She set her jaw. "No."

He ignored that answer, compelled to provoke her on purpose, push her, gain a reaction. "I remember you always favored pink undergarments," he said in a low voice. "Pale pink with tiny satin ribbons and lots of lace."

She stirred, shifting her weight from one foot to the other. Her cheeks flushed pink and she looked away. A reaction at last.

"I remember how the pulse in your throat used to start hammering whenever I kissed you there," he went on, relentless and not even knowing why. "I remember the little mole just above your left—"

"Stop it." She backed up a step, and when he started to follow her move, she lifted her hand, flattening it against his chest. "I said stop. If you don't, I shall be forced to tell Aidan you made advances toward me, and he'll kill you."

"He'll try, perhaps. But first you'll have to tell him you came running over to see me." He paused, smiling faintly. "Alone. Only two hours after I arrived—"

"Oh, for heaven's sake, stop saying that!" She jerked her hand down and retreated several more steps.

This time, he didn't follow. All he'd wanted was a reaction. Besides, his leg was beginning to hurt like hell. Shifting his weight more to the left, he remained where he was, but he couldn't resist needling her.

A petty form of revenge, he knew, but all he had. "Trathen will wonder why you came here, you know. Speaking as a man, I can assure you of that."

"Do you intend to answer my question? Did you come home to make trouble for me? To . . . to 'upset the applecart,' as you put it, and make some sort of scene at my wedding?"

She really thought he'd do that? Will studied her for a moment, noting the anxious way she was biting her lip, the way her hands were clenching and unclenching. Evidently she thought him capable of that very thing. "Terrible for you if I burst into St. Paul's and strode up the aisle, shouting breach of promise, or something," he murmured, not feeling inclined to reassure her. "The society pages would be full of it for days."

She stiffened, and her hands unclenched to rest on her hips. "If embarrassing me is your intent, I can safely say you won't succeed. Having been jilted practically on the church doorstep, pitied as the deserted fiancée, and laughed at for making such a fool of myself over you when you were only stringing me along, I can safely say that nothing you do will ever embarrass me again."

"I strung you along?" He gave a laugh, a laugh that sounded bitter, even to his own ears. "That's the pot talking to the kettle. What about you?"

"Me?" She blinked, clearly taken aback. "I don't know what you mean."

"Don't you? What of all the times you pretended to care about my interests? All my books about Egyptology you borrowed, all the sketches of artifacts you drew for me, the rapt way you listened whenever I talked about excavating a site of my own one day? Pretending, always pretending, to be as fascinated by it all as I was. But that was a lie."

"I wasn't pretending, and I did not lie! I wanted to understand your interests, try to appreciate and share them."

"Yet when the opportunity came to share them in truth, you showed your interest in Egypt to be nothing but a farce."

"I never dreamed you'd actually go! I thought—" She stopped, as if suddenly realizing she was heading into deep waters. Pressing her lips together, she looked away.

"You thought it was a fantasy and nothing more," he finished for her. "Wonderful and exciting to dream about digging up tombs or playing at it like we did when we were children, wasn't it? But only if it never became a reality. All right for you to humor dear Will as long as we were still sitting by the fire here in merry old England, eating plum pudding at Sunderland for Christmas, going to London for the season, Epsom, Ascot, and Henley, coming back to Torquay for August, country house parties in September—"

"Yes!" she cried, interrupting his derisive catalog of a typical peer's life. She met his gaze again, hers defiant. "What's wrong with that?"

"It wasn't the life I wanted! And you knew it. You always knew."

"But it's the life you were born to." She shook her

head, her defiance seeming to fade into bafflement. "You're a duke."

Even now, even after all this time, she still couldn't see beyond their lineage. He doubted she ever would. "Yes, I'm a duke," he conceded, making no attempt to conceal his contempt for that meaningless happenstance of birth, "and you want to be a duchess. First me, now Trathen." He took another drink. "Well, for what you want in life, one duke's as good as another, I suppose."

"His rank isn't the reason I'm marrying him! Do you really think I'm that shallow?"

"I don't know. You seemed to love my position more than you ever loved me, for you abandoned me quickly enough when I didn't want to fulfill it."

"You think I abandoned you?" She stared at him in disbelief. "I'm not the one who broke an understanding that went back to our childhood. I'm not the one who decided to go off to another continent just before our wedding. All our lives—" Her voice choked up, telling him he wasn't the only one who'd felt the pain of their separation. A reaction was what he'd wanted, but somehow it gave him no satisfaction. It just hurt him more. "All our lives, Will, you knew what was expected of us. You knew the duties and responsibilities you were to assume. You abandoned them, and me."

"Yes, there it was, my whole life laid out for me before I was even out of short pants. Can you blame me when a life I'd only ever dreamed of opened up? A life, I might add, you led me to believe you'd be willing to share. Remember that barrow of Roman ruins

I dug up one summer? You sketched all the artifacts, you helped me research and catalog what we found. You visited the British Museum with me every time we were in London for the season. When Sir Edmund offered to take me to Egypt and look for Tut, it never occurred to me you'd balk, though in hindsight, I suppose I should have known you couldn't leave your dear papa."

Too late he remembered her father was dead. He saw her chin quiver at the reminder, and he suddenly felt like a bastard. "Hell," he muttered, and looked away.

"You wanted me to abandon him!" she cried. "How could I? After Mama ran off to Paris all those years ago, abandoning her family and her duties as a countess? And for what? To paint and live like a bohemian?"

"It changed your father when your mother left. He drove any sense of adventure out of you. I didn't really realize just how tightly he had you chained until you wouldn't go to Egypt with me."

"That's not fair! How could I leave Papa and go to Egypt?"

"You were going to be my wife! Damn me for a fool to believe you wanted to be my partner in life, no matter where it led us. But it wasn't me you wanted."

"That's not true."

"You wanted the trappings. You wanted to live in this house, three miles from your father, where everything was safe and familiar and approved by all. Coming with me would have meant defying all that and jumping into a whole new world, and you couldn't do it. It wasn't just about leaving your father. When it came down to brass tacks, you were too afraid to go."

"Afraid?" She blinked, staring at him as if he'd actually said something absurd. "Are you saying I'm a coward?"

"I don't know. Are you? Remember when we were children and Paul, Julie, and I used to dive off Angel's Head into the sea at Pixy Cove? You wanted to do it, too, but you couldn't work up the nerve."

"I don't know what you're talking about!" She tried to turn as if to leave, but he wouldn't let her. Not until he'd made his point.

"You know exactly what I'm talking about," he said, grabbing her by the arms. "We'd all dived off, and we were down in the water below, waiting for you. You wanted to. You wanted to dive off so bad you could taste it, and you stood up there for the longest time, but in the end, you couldn't do it. You sat down and said you'd rather look at the view."

"I was only ten years old! All of you were older."

"What about when I wanted to teach you to ride without a sidesaddle? You wouldn't do it. You wanted to, but you were too afraid someone would see you, namely your father. You were terrified of what he would think."

"That's hardly the same as packing up one's whole life and moving to another country!" she cried, jerking free of his hold. "I wanted marriage and a home of my own. That precious excavation site of yours didn't even include a house. I wanted children, Will. Just where was I supposed to have them? In a tent?"

"I told you I would build a house for you!" he shouted.

"No, Will," she countered in a hard voice. "Not for me. It would have been an expedition house with bedrooms for your staff. I was engaged to a duke, not an archaeologist! And I had every right to continue to expect the security for me and my children that your position afforded us. As for not loving you—" She broke off and took a deep breath. "It took me five years to stop loving you. Five years. I just couldn't believe you were gone forever. I just couldn't accept it. I knew it was over, and yet I kept waiting for you. Waiting for you to realize you loved me, too. Waiting for you to accept your responsibilities at home. Waiting, waiting. I got over you when I finally admitted the truth."

"Truth? What truth?"

"That you weren't worth waiting for."

The impact of her words hit him like a slap across the face, but there was no way he would let her see it. He remained perfectly still, his gaze locked with hers, and it was she who looked away first. "If I see you anywhere near the church door on my wedding day, Aidan won't have to kill you, because I will."

With that, she turned on her heel and stalked out of his study without a backward glance.

The sound of her footsteps echoing along the corridor had not even faded away before he was reaching into his pocket to pull out her engagement announcement. He stared at the crumpled bit of newspaper for a moment, then with an oath, he ripped it savagely into pieces.

He'd see Paul as soon as possible, he decided as he tossed the fragments into the rubbish basket. He'd get that funding, resolve any other unfinished business matters he had in this repressed, class-conscious country in which he'd had the misfortune to be born, and return to Egypt where he belonged, where there was important work to do and discoveries to be made. And when he left this time, he thought, staring resentfully down at the torn bits of newsprint, it would damned well be for good.

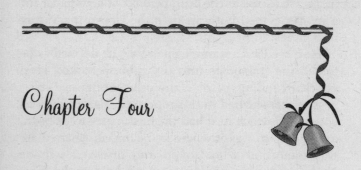

Chapter Four

He was stubborn as ever, Beatrix thought as she strode out the front door of Sunderland House. Stubborn, unchanging, and immovable—rather like the Egyptian sphinxes he adored so much. Still unable to see any point of view but his own. She wished she had opened the door herself rather than allowing Mrs. Gudgeon to do it for her. That way, she could have slammed the massive oak door behind her with a cathartic, satisfying bang. Not a very ladylike impulse, she supposed as she walked to her waiting carriage, but quite an understandable one under the circumstances.

"Drive on, Mr. Warren," she told the chauffeur, stepping into the open landau. She thumped down onto the leather seat and the carriage jerked into motion, but even over the rattle of the wheels and the clip-clop of the horses' hooves, she could still hear Will's condemnations ringing in her ears.

She had misled him? She had abandoned him? He was saying those things to fix the blame on her and ease his own guilty conscience. And only a cad would call her a coward because she wouldn't dive off a thirty-foot cliff into the ocean when she was ten years old.

She remembered that day. And the day he'd tried to persuade her to ride astride. And all the other times he'd pushed her into doing things she knew she shouldn't. Sometimes, like the diving and the saddle and Egypt, he'd failed to persuade her. But there had been other times when he'd succeeded.

I remember how the pulse in your throat used to start hammering whenever I kissed you.

Beatrix remembered that, too. She'd denied it, of course, but did he really believe she'd forgotten? She squeezed her eyes shut. How could he think she'd forgotten all the times when she'd gone out alone to meet him in one of their secret places? All the times she'd let him kiss her when she shouldn't have. And he dared to accuse her of cowardice? She'd put her reputation and virtue at risk dozens of times just for the delicious thrill of his lips on hers. . .

She could feel her face growing hot at the memory, and she opened her eyes with a sound of impatience. She was not a coward. And she wasn't a liar, either, whatever he might think.

She had sketched those artifacts for him because she liked sketching, not simply to please him. And she'd listened to him for hours as he'd told her all about the Romans and the Assyrians and the Egyptians because she had been truly interested. But she'd never thought any of it was real. She'd never thought digging up relics of those past civilizations would be their *life*.

Beatrix stared at the green pastures and hedgerows that stretched for miles all around her, lands that had belonged to the Danbury and Sunderland families for hundreds of years, and her anger dissipated into an old, familiar feeling of bewilderment. He'd said this wasn't the life he wanted, but what did that matter? This was the life they had.

Born into English aristocratic families, she and Will had both been destined for this life from the moment of their birth. It was a life of privilege, yes, and there were elements of triviality within it, she supposed, but it was also a life of duty and responsibility, of caring for the less fortunate and securing the future of one's children and grandchildren through land and title. To ignore it was impossible, and to shun it was unfathomable. One might just as well be a revolutionary, she thought with a shudder. Or an American.

When the carriage arrived at Danbury House, she went back to the drawing room, in desperate need of distraction. Geoff was gone, but her aunt was still there, seated on one of the crimson velvet sofas with a large leather volume on her lap.

"What are you reading, Auntie?" she asked as she came in.

Eugenia looked up. "Ah, Beatrix, there you are. Sunderland all right, I hope, and not too badly maimed?"

"A bruised knee, I'm told. He'll be right as rain in a day or two."

"Excellent. I'm glad Mrs. Gudgeon was able to reassure you about the matter."

The housekeeper had done so, true enough, but Beatrix decided it would be best not to mention that she'd actually spoken with Will. As he had pointed out, calling upon one's former fiancé without a chaperone wasn't at all proper, and here in the country, where there wasn't much to do but gossip, any little thing, however trivial, could be noticed and commented upon. A women's reputation was a fragile thing, and easily damaged. Aunt Eugenia would no doubt point all that out, and Beatrix didn't feel much like enduring a lecture on propriety today. The less said, the better. "Just so," she murmured, and left it at that.

Eugenia smiled and patted the sofa. "Come and sit with me."

Beatrix complied, and as she settled herself beside her aunt, she realized Eugenia was looking at an album of photographs. "Why, that's Papa," she exclaimed, leaning forward to study the sepia-toned image of a man with her own dark eyes and a resolute face. Looking at the image, Beatrix felt a stab of pain, for though he'd been dead over a year now, she still missed her father terribly. He'd always been strict, but she'd always been the center of his life. Looking at the photograph, she forced herself to laugh a little. "Poor Papa. He looks as if he has indigestion."

Eugenia laughed as well. "My brother-in-law

hated photographs. He thought them so uncivilized. But your mother was dabbling in photography at the time—" She stopped and bit her lip.

Beatrix's mother was a subject that had not been mentioned in this house since she was nine years old. She'd never actually been told that her mother had run off to France to paint, accompanied by her lover, a man ten years her junior, or that she'd died in Paris, ill, ruined, and alone. Beatrix had found out those details on her own. Her girlhood friends had thought it all so romantic and tragic, but Beatrix had never been able to see the romantic aspect. All she'd seen was her father's anguish.

Will had expected her to abandon Papa and go running to the other side of the world for what might have been years? If she'd done that, her father would have died alone and abandoned, just as her mother had.

The old resentments, ones she thought she'd conquered, began simmering up, and she shoved them back down. "Show me more of these photographs, Auntie."

Eugenia turned a page. "Ah, my wedding," she said, clearly relieved that there seemed to be no more pictures taken by Beatrix's mother.

Beatrix leaned closer and laughed again. "Oh, Auntie, look at your dress!"

"It does seem quite old-fashioned, doesn't it? That enormous bustle and train. And all those roses. Still, it was a Worth gown." She patted her niece's knee. "Not having a daughter of my own, I'd hoped you would have it made over to wear at your wedding."

"Auntie . . ." she began, then let her voice trail off, for they had discussed all this before.

"I know, dear. You want your own gown. Perfectly understandable. And you want to support your friend in her dressmaking efforts."

She felt a hint of impatience. "It's not an effort, Auntie. It's a business."

Eugenia gave a sniff. "Of a kind. How her brother ever allowed her to engage in it in the first place, I can't think. But then Marlowe is rather permissive in many respects. His publishing company, his divorce from his first wife—oh, I know what you're going to say, dear," she added as Beatrix started to speak. "And I do appreciate that Marlowe's second wife is a most respectable woman in every way. I adore Emma, you know I do. Nonetheless, I do feel there is a certain disregard for convention in Marlowe's household, including the fact that he allows his sister to engage in trade."

"Being unconventional is not necessarily a bad thing." Beatrix ran her finger idly along one edge of the album in her aunt's lap. "Besides, Vivian enjoys her dressmaking business."

"Nonsense. Fussing with account books and bartering with tradesmen and negotiating contracts? How can that be enjoyable? And think of the burden of responsibility! Using one's talents for purposes of commerce?"

Something in Eugenia's words sent a strange spark of excitement through Beatrix's veins. "Oh, I don't know, Auntie. It might be satisfying."

"I don't see how. Oh, inventing pretty gowns for

one's friends is an agreeable pastime, I daresay. And sewing and sketching are both perfectly suitable pursuits for a lady. But to employ those talents for money? To sell the clothes one designs to one's friends? Why, they might not pay, and then one would have to send demands. How disagreeable."

Beatrix forced herself not to roll her eyes. Sometimes, she thought with aggravation, Auntie could be so old-fashioned.

"Still," Eugenia added hastily, sensing she might have gone too far, "dear Vivian's clothes are said to be exquisite. I must confess, I find them a bit too modern for my tastes."

Bizarre was the actual word her aunt had used upon first seeing the sketch of her niece's wedding dress, with its stark, modern lines, but Beatrix was not so tactless as to remind Auntie of that description. She'd wanted something completely different from what she'd intended to wear six years ago, and Vivian, whose dressmaking business called *Vivienne* was known for its avant-garde style, had happily complied.

"You don't like my gown, Auntie?"

"It's a lovely gown." Eugenia turned her head, smiling, but the smile seemed forced. "And it doesn't matter if I like it. Besides, you'll wear the topazes with it, so I'm quite content."

Beatrix thought without much enthusiasm of the opulent topaz and diamond necklace, brooch, and tiara that had been in her family for seven generations. She found yellow jewels of any type unattractive, but the topazes were de rigueur for Danbury brides, and she'd always known she'd be expected to wear them. "Yes," she agreed, "it's all right then. And I shall have your prayer book, of course."

Eugenia's smile widened into a genuine one. "It belonged to my mother, an engagement present from her grandfather. The Duke of Tremore, you know," she added with pride.

One duke's as good as another, I suppose.

Will's contemptuous words echoed through her mind, but she shoved them aside. He might not care about his birthright, his duty, or the security of his heirs, but she cared about hers. And it wasn't as if she had chosen to marry Aidan because of his rank. There were other, far more important considerations. Mutual respect, affection, a shared vision of the future.

By accusing her of mercenary motives, Will was just trying to goad her. In fact, everything he'd said earlier had been offered with just that purpose in mind.

She thought of the infuriating way he had spoken of her father, who had always had her best interests at heart. Why, the last words Papa had said to her before his death had been for her happiness.

We've only one life, Trixie, my girl. Will's gone, and it's time to give up on him, and the past. Promise me you'll make a new future.

And that's just what she'd done. So unfair of Will to say she'd lost her sense of adventure. She'd gone to Cornwall with Julia, and she'd thrown off black crepe mourning clothes. She'd learned to drive an automobile and she'd smoked cigarettes—not that her father would have approved of that!—and though she still couldn't work up the courage to dive off Cornwall's rocky cliffs into the sea, she had walked barefoot in the sand and swum in the sea at midnight with no clothes on. And during that holiday with Julia, she'd learned at last that she could be happy without Will.

Then she'd met Aidan, and that had rather settled everything. When he'd proposed marriage to her, she had taken three days to think it over before accepting. Yes, his ducal rank had played a part, for the security of her children would be her most important duty. And no, she didn't love him—not if love was a wild, passionate, intense insanity. Aidan didn't love her that way, either. They were adults, mature and responsible, and they shared a bond that meant more to marital happiness than romantic love ever could. Aidan had the same vision of the future she did, a continuation of what their parents and grandparents had done before them.

After her mother's abandonment of her family for passionate love, and Will's utter disregard for duty and responsibility, Beatrix was quite happy with a man who valued the same things she did, the things that mattered, the things that endured. With Aidan, she had mutual affection, contentment, and friendship, and she was quite happy to leave passionate, desperate, agonizing love behind.

As I recall, you and I never needed torches to burn for each other.

She stirred restlessly on the sofa, feeling her cheeks heating as those words rekindled memories of midnight assignations in the garden, stolen kisses, and other things she hadn't thought about in ages.

"What's wrong, dearest?" Eugenia asked, her attention diverted from the photographs in her lap.

Well aware of her flushed face, Beatrix shoved thoughts of her first love out of her mind. That was in the past. She was moving toward the future, the future she'd always known she would have, the one her father had wanted for her, one that would carry on the traditions of her ancestors for another generation.

"Nothing, Auntie." She put an arm around Eugenia's shoulders and reached over to turn the page. "Show me more of these pictures."

Will had vowed to see Paul as quickly as possible, but he was forced to wait. The morning after his encounter with Beatrix, Geoff came by Sunderland Park, and during that visit, he mentioned that his older brother had gone to Exeter on a matter of business and would not return for three days.

Though impatient for the meeting, Will benefited from the delay. He was able to conduct other business, surveying Sunderland Park with his land agent and ordering necessary repairs. Aman's liniment did its work, and though he had a fist-size bruise just above his knee, the pain eased. Most beneficial of all, he'd once again managed to push Beatrix into the past where she belonged. By the time he called at

Danbury Downs, he felt fully prepared to discuss the situation with Paul without allowing either physical pain or resentment toward Paul's cousin to affect his demeanor.

He judged four o'clock to be the best time to see the other man, for that was an hour when the ladies were likely to be out paying calls on their friends, but Paul was likely to be at home. He chose not to make his call a formal one; instead, he went on horseback, cutting across the park and approaching the house from the back.

Though it was a cloudy afternoon, it wasn't raining, and the French doors into the study had been flung back. As he came closer, Will recognized his friend framed in the open doorway, confirming that he had timed his visit correctly. Paul was seated at a desk, writing letters, but at the sound of Galahad's hooves on the turf, he stopped writing and looked up.

"By Jove, it is you!" he cried, tossing down his quill and rising from the desk as Will dismounted and tied Galahad's reins to the stone rail surrounding the terrace.

"I heard you were back," Paul went on, coming through the French doors as Will ascended the steps toward him, "but until I saw you with my own eyes, I didn't quite believe it."

The two men met halfway, and Will held out his hand. "It's good to see you, old friend."

"And you," Paul replied as they shook hands. "Care for a drink?" he asked, leading Will into the study. Given an affirmative answer, Paul poured whisky for both of them, then resumed his seat at his desk, gesturing Will to take the opposite chair. The initial greetings over, there was a rather awkward pause.

"Egypt seems to agree with you," Paul finally said.

"Does it?" He gave the other man a rather rueful smile. "Trix said the opposite."

"Did she?" There was another pause, then Paul gave a cough and spoke again. "Well, that's to be expected, isn't it? So, what's brought you home after all this time?"

"Estate business, for one. Wrapping up Father's affairs, that sort of thing. I've put it off far too long."

"Ah." His friend's relief was immediately visible, leading him to conclude that Beatrix had been talking. Offering dire predictions about what sort of scene he intended to make at her wedding, no doubt.

He kept to the business at hand. "I do confess, however, that my primary reason for this journey isn't estate business. I've come home to see you."

"Me?" Paul's brown eyes widened in surprise. He paused, eyeing Will a bit warily. "I'm flattered."

"I've come to ask a favor, and it's a big one." He took a deep breath. "I need a loan."

"A loan?"

"Damned cheek of me, I know, especially in these circumstances. Your cousin and I . . . and all that. But you're the only person I feel I can turn to. We're like brothers." He stopped and gave a sigh, rubbing a hand over his face. "At least, I like to think so, despite . . . despite everything."

Paul tugged at his ear, looking confounded and—strangely enough—a bit relieved. "That wasn't what I was expecting you to say."

Will kept his voice carefully neutral. "No, I should imagine not."

"I feared you might have come home to ask me to intercede with Beatrix on your behalf."

"No."

"Or that you might have come to discern your chance of winning her back."

Will set his jaw. "No."

"A loan," Paul repeated thoughtfully. "For your estates here? Or for the excavations in Egypt?"

"It's for Egypt."

"Of course it is," Paul murmured. "Isn't it always?"

"Paul—" he began, but the other man cut him off.

"How much do you need?"

"Twenty thousand pounds. That would see us through another year."

"Twenty thousand pounds? Will, that's a great deal of money. I take it you've gone through your inheritance?"

"From my mother? Yes. Father, as you might guess, didn't leave me a farthing. Quite the opposite, in fact. I've used the money from Mama to sponsor the excavations since Sir Edmund returned home."

Paul swirled the contents of his glass and took a swallow. "And now you've no money of your own."

"Making inquiries about my finances, Paul?"

His oldest friend shrugged. "It's pretty common knowledge."

"Then you probably also know Sunderland Park is

barely making enough to sustain itself, and that all my other estates in England had to be mortgaged to pay Father's debts and death duties."

Paul confirmed all that with a nod. "And are you sure it's wise to borrow twenty thousand more?"

"It sounds like a great deal of money, I know, but I'll easily be able to pay you back when we find Tut-ankhamen."

"If you find him." Paul set aside his glass and leaned forward. "Let's speak plainly. Almost six years of digging, over a hundred thousand pounds gone, and you haven't found Tut."

"Not yet. But we will. I believe we're close. Carter agrees with me."

Paul didn't seem reassured. "I respect your opin-ion. And certainly Howard Carter's opinion is a worthy one as well. He's quite an important bloke down there, from what I gather."

"He is the chief inspector of Egyptian Antiquities, and he's certain Tutankhamen's tomb is right where we're digging. So am I, Paul. I can sense it. Hell, I can smell it."

Paul didn't seem reassured by either his instincts or his sense of smell. "If I loan you this money, another year might go by without success. Then what? How do you intend to pay me back if that's the case?"

"If we find enough valuable artifacts, you'll be paid anyway."

"And if you don't, the money's gone, and you'll be asking me for another loan twelve months from now."

He didn't deny that possibility. "I'm going to find Tut, no matter how long it takes. Will you help me?"

Paul gave a deep sigh that did not bode well, and Will felt a sinking feeling in his gut. "I can't."

He shouldn't have expected any different. He really couldn't blame Paul for refusing. "I see."

"It isn't because of Trix, Will. When I said I can't, I meant it. I'm not exactly flush myself at this moment."

"Why?" Will straightened in his chair, alarmed. "What's happened? Are you in trouble?"

"Trouble?" Paul repeated, giving the word an odd inflection. "I suppose you could call it that. Like yours, my estates are barely holding their own these days. This beastly agricultural depression continues to affect us all. And my main source of income has rather dried up."

Will frowned, uncomprehending. "I don't understand. I thought you had an income through Susanna."

"I did, but not anymore." His expression hardened. "Susanna and I have separated."

"What?"

"She went to Newport in May. She said it was to visit her parents."

Will appreciated the choice of words, and when he looked into his friend's suddenly wooden countenance, he felt a glimmer of Paul's pain. "But it wasn't?"

Paul looked away. "Her father died while she was there and she decided to remain in the States indefinitely," he said, and began to tidy his desk as if that task was suddenly of vital importance. "She informed me of this in her last letter, which I received two months ago." He returned a quill to the inkstand and straightened a stack of books. "Last month I heard from her attorneys in New York. My income through our marriage has been discontinued. It violates the marriage settlement, but—" He shrugged. "If I sue to have it reinstated, the family will be dragged through the scandal sheets. Susanna knows I would loathe a scandal of any kind. She knows I won't fight her."

"Hell." Will raked a hand through his hair. "Why didn't you tell me about this in your last letter?"

"My marital difficulties are not something I find easy to share. And until the question of divorce is settled—"

"Divorce? Surely it hasn't come to that?"

"She has no grounds to divorce me, but she might try. The only reason for me to pursue such a course would be remarriage, and I can assure you marriage is not something I am looking at in a favorable light nowadays."

Will didn't know what to say. What could a man say? "Hard lines, my friend," he said at last. "I'm sorry."

"Yes, well . . ." Paul stilled, his fingers curled around the edges of the blotter before him. He looked up, but he didn't quite meet Will's gaze. "That's the nature of love. It isn't meant to be everlasting."

The bitterness in his friend's voice rather echoed his own opinion on the subject. "No," he agreed. "I suppose not."

Paul folded his hands atop the blotter. "Let's return

to your situation. Can't you raise funds elsewhere? Find someone else to sponsor the excavation?"

"No. I tried. We've found some amazing items, some of them with immense historic significance. There's a frieze from the Second Dynasty that shows—" He broke off, knowing Paul probably didn't want a lesson in Egyptian history. "The problem is that we've found precious little in the way of gold and jewels. It's difficult to find a sponsor when all you're digging up is pieces of pottery and clay tablets," he said wryly. "Gold and jewels are much more exciting. I didn't want to come to you, given the situation with Trix, but I didn't know where else to go for funds. I've been away from England so long."

"What about bringing in a partner?"

He shook his head, everything in him rebelling at that notion. "I don't mind a sponsor, but I don't want a partner. Tut's mine. No one finds him but me."

Paul shrugged. "Then you have only one option. Marry an heiress. Unfortunately the season is over. Parliament's in recess, and everyone's gone to the country. Not the best time to go heiress hunting."

"Marry an heiress." Will repeated the idea with distaste. "Whore myself in the fine British tradition of our forefathers? No, thank you."

"I married an heiress," Paul reminded him, sounding understandably testy.

Will expelled a harsh breath. "Sorry," he apologized. "I didn't mean that the way it sounded. It's just that—" He broke off, searching for a way to explain why he couldn't consider the course his friend was suggesting.

He thought of his parents' empty marriage, a bargain trading his mother's wealth for his father's title. It had never been about love. He thought of his mother's shallowness and obsession with title and position, he thought of his father's innate laziness and greed, and the words to explain why he couldn't do the same stuck in his throat. "I didn't mean you," he said at last. "I know you loved Susanna. I know you didn't marry her for her money."

Paul held his hand up, palms out in a gesture of truce. "I accept your apology. But to return to the point, I think you're being far too fastidious about this. You're a duke, and though you might not think your title's worth much, there are plenty of women with rich fathers who would disagree, especially among the Americans. The shine's rather gone off the transatlantic marriage nowadays, but there are still quite a few girls coming across the pond hoping to become duchesses. It wouldn't be a quick solution, but it's a feasible one."

Will thought of his father, of the fawning deference accorded the old man because he'd been a duke, of the servants who had stopped their work and turned their faces to the wall whenever he'd walked by and who'd served him on a tray so he wouldn't run the risk of touching them. He thought of his mother, a wealthy American's daughter who'd bought herself a duke, of how ruthlessly she'd slashed the least influential people from her invitation lists, fighting for a position of social respect until the day she died. He thought of himself, a lonely little boy who'd spent most of his time isolated in the nursery until he could be shipped off to school at the age of nine—out of sight, out of mind, and out of the way. "No. I won't do it."

He got up and walked to the French window. Leaning one shoulder against the doorjamb, he looked out at the expanse of lawn, not so well-manicured now as it used to be when they played football on it as boys. Like everything else in their class of life, it had rather gone to seed.

"How many of our lot have married these wealthy American girls for their money?" he asked, staring past the lawn to tufted, orderly squares of growing crops, marked by the darker green of hedgerows. "A dozen? Two? My father, both our grandfathers— hell, if I tried, I could probably name a hundred peers who've done it. It didn't do any of them a bit of good."

Paul groaned at this renewal of a conversation they'd had many times during their days at Cambridge, but Will persevered. "All those American dollars pouring in to prop up our dying aristocracy, and for what? It's still dying. No, I want a life that means something, something more than the next ball, the next race meeting, the next season." He turned to face his friend. "That's why I went to Egypt in the first place."

"Fine." Paul leaned back, spreading his arms in a gesture of capitulation. "Stick to your principles and sneer at those of us who made a different choice. Principles won't help you find Tut."

"If I wait, I won't find him at all. Someone else will. I won't let that happen."

"You could spend your entire life looking for that blasted tomb and never find it."

"Possibly."

"Damn it, Will, isn't it time to stop tilting at windmills? You're nearly broke, you haven't found Tut, and my cousin's marrying someone else. Look what this obsession has cost you. When are you going to give up?"

"Never, but thank you for reminding me of all my failures thus far."

Paul sighed. "I don't mean to kick you when you're already down."

"On the contrary. You give me hope."

"Hope?"

He grinned. "Hope my luck is about to change."

His oldest friend made a sound of exasperation. "Do you ever stop being such a cockeyed optimist?"

"No." Will's grin faded. He was a cockeyed optimist, he supposed, because he had no intention of giving up. "Do you know of anyone who might be willing to sponsor the excavation?"

Paul studied him for a moment, then sighed, giving in to the inevitable fact that Will would never change. "I'll make some inquiries."

Relief flooded through him. "Thank you, Paul."

"This will take some time. We're leaving next week, and—"

"Leaving?"

"Of course." Paul seemed surprised by Will's bewilderment. "For Torquay. We're going to Pixy Cove. We always go to Pixy Cove in August. Surely you haven't forgotten?"

Forgotten those childhood days at Viscount Marlowe's villa on Babbacombe Bay? Never. They'd been some of the happiest of his life. Like going away to school, like overnight stays at Danbury Downs, Pixy Cove in August with Trix, Paul, and Julia had been a refuge, an escape from the hell of his parents' mutual hatred. Pixy Cove was paradise—sea bathing and diving for shells and exploring the caves. He'd never forget those days. Hell, he and Trix had argued about Pixy Cove just the other afternoon.

"Remember how we used to dive off the rocks?" Paul said, as if reading his mind. "You tried to show Trix how to do it once, but she balked at the edge like a skittish horse and wouldn't go, remember?"

As if it were only yesterday, he could see Trix up on Angel's Head, the cliff that hung over Angel Cove, staring down at the others treading water below. She'd wanted to dive off, do what all the other children were doing, but when she'd looked down the thirty-foot drop she'd have had to make to follow, she'd lost her nerve.

A metaphor of their lives, Will thought, and felt a sharp pang of regret. Egypt, like Angel's Head, had been a leap too far for Trix to make.

"I'll be happy to write some letters on your behalf while we're at Marlowe's villa," Paul said, bringing him out of the past, "but I won't be able to do much more than that until I return in September."

Those words brought an idea to Will's mind, a new possibility. "Marlowe," he murmured. "Of course. That's the ticket."

"I beg your pardon?"

"Marlowe's a publishing magnate. He's got scads of money. He might be willing to sponsor the excavation."

Paul acknowledged that with a nod. "Possibly. He's up at Babbacombe Bay already, so you'll have to write to him there."

"Write? Ask a man to give me twenty thousand pounds by letter? That won't do. I shall ask him in person. I'm going to Pixy Cove."

Paul's face clouded with obvious dismay. "But you can't. You haven't been invited."

"True, but I'm sure once you tell Marlowe I'm home from Egypt, he'll invite me. He has to. After all, we're practically family."

Paul groaned. "You do realize Trix will be there?"

"So?"

"With Trathen."

"I'm sure we can all behave in a civil manner."

"You and Trix have never behaved in a civil manner. At least not with each other. You two have been quarreling since she learned how to talk. Marlowe will never believe otherwise. And Trix would never forgive me if—"

"You worry too much, Paul," he cut in with a deliberately breezy disregard for the difficulties. "That's your trouble. Once you reassure Marlowe that there won't be any friction, everything will be smooth sailing."

"Smooth sailing? No friction? Good God." Paul laughed, but he didn't sound amused. "She's going to shoot me when she finds out about this," he muttered, rubbing a hand over his forehead. "And you as well."

That was a possibility, but Will knew he didn't have many options at this point. Going to Pixy Cove would delay his return to Egypt, but that couldn't be helped. He had to secure funds before the excavations resumed in October. "Cheer up, Paul. We're going to Pixy Cove, the most wonderful place on earth." With that, he turned and started out the door. "What could go wrong?"

"Everything." Paul's dour reply followed him out the door, but he wisely chose to ignore it.

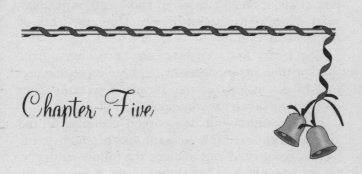

Chapter Five

At first, Will's pretense of optimism seemed destined to become reality.

He spent the day after his conversation with Paul engaged in estate matters with his land agent, and the morning after that, he received a cable from Viscount Marlowe, expressing delight that he was home, assuring him he was indeed welcome at Pixy Cove for the house party as always, and assuring him he wanted to hear all about the search for Tutankhamen.

That afternoon, Will decided to take a walk through Stafford St. Mary. It had been a long time since he'd gone into English society, and just in case funding from Marlowe was not forthcoming, he would need other options. An afternoon stroll in the High Street was an excellent first step toward reestablishing his social connections. A few greetings to old acquaintances, a pint of ale at the White Swan, and a call on the new vicar all helped to integrate him back into the fabric of English social life.

The vicar, Mr. Venables, was a younger, freer thinker than his predecessor, and far more inclined toward discussions of the ancient Egyptians than modern missionary work, much to Will's relief.

His encounter with Sir George Debenham on the village green was both pleasant and productive, for Sir George invited him to come the following day to see the new filly he'd had shipped from Kentucky. He also mentioned Marlowe's house party, and after receiving affirmation that Will would indeed be there, invited him to make the trip up the coast to Pixy Cove aboard his new yacht. Will, who loved sailing almost as much as he loved horses, was happy to accept both invitations.

By mid-afternoon, he felt his innate optimism growing stronger, and by the time he reached Halstead's Bookshop and viewed the extensive number of new books that Halstead had for sale, he began to think the time he spent in England would prove not only profitable, but pleasurable as well.

It was Beatrix, of course, who deprived him of that particular illusion.

He was in the loft above the main floor, surveying the volumes on archaeology in the bookshop's substantial collection, when the bell over the door jangled, followed by the sound of a woman's voice.

"Good afternoon, Mr. Halstead."

Will stifled a groan. For a few short hours, he'd

actually managed to put Beatrix out of his mind. He tried to tell himself it was probably some other woman's voice he'd heard, he tried to return his attention to the row of books before him, but as her footsteps tapped against the floorboards below, bringing her farther into the shop, curiosity impelled him to walk to the wrought-iron rail, just to have a look. When he did so, the faint hope that his imagination had been playing tricks on him vanished.

The woman's back was to him as she approached the counter, but it didn't matter. There was no mistaking Beatrix's luscious hourglass curves, especially without a shapeless motoring coat to conceal them. Perched atop her head was an enormous hat of pale straw, white ostrich feathers, and pink ribbons, but beneath it, her honey-blond hair was plainly visible. And if those two facts weren't evidence enough of her identity, there was her dress. It was pink, Trix's favorite color. He fully expected the scent of gardenia to come floating up to his nostrils any moment now.

She paused in front of the counter. "I've come hoping to see the new Baedeker guides you ordered, Mr. Halstead. Have they arrived from London yet?"

Baedekers? Will's lips curved in a smile. And Trix thought she'd changed?

The proprietor of the bookshop started to respond to her question, but the doorbell jangled again, interrupting any reply he might have made.

Will watched Beatrix glance over her shoulder at the sound of the bell, and it occurred to him that if she were to look up, she'd catch him standing by the rail watching her. He started to step back so that she wouldn't see him, but then she smiled at the man who was approaching her, and suddenly he was unable to move.

Memories came back to him, flashing across his mind as if he were flipping the pages of a picture book. The wide, tooth-gapped grin of a chubby-cheeked little girl proudly holding up her missing tooth for his impressed inspection. The pressed-together curve of cupid's bow lips whenever she was trying not to laugh at something outrageous he'd said. The radiant smile the day he'd asked her to marry him that told him he'd just handed her heaven on a plate.

As he watched her now with those images from the past going through his mind, his throat went dry and he wanted to move out of sight, but he seemed to have no power over his limbs. He could only stand there as if paralyzed, caught by her smile like a fly in treacle.

He'd forgotten, he realized in astonishment. He'd been gone so long, he'd forgotten just how beautiful her smiles were. How could he have let that happen?

Slowly, however, another feeling came to the fore, an uneasy sense that something was wrong. Her smile at this moment was odd in a way he couldn't define, different from all the other Beatrix smiles he remembered, but he could not say precisely what the difference was.

She was smiling at whoever had just entered the shop. "Aidan," she said as a man approached the counter where she stood, and Will realized what was wrong. Her smile seemed different to him because it was not for him. It was for another man.

Tightness squeezed his chest. *It doesn't matter*, he reminded himself. *It doesn't matter anymore*.

He turned abruptly away and returned to the books on archaeology. He grabbed the one on Petrie's excavations in Palestine, opened it, and attempted to read, but he could not shut out the voices below.

"Do you intend to linger here for long, Beatrix?" the Duke of Trathen asked.

"My answer to that question depends upon Mr. Halstead."

"I'm sorry, my lady," the proprietor answered, "but those new Baedeker guides haven't arrived yet."

"Baedeker?" There was a hint of surprise in Trathen's voice. "You ordered a Baedeker? Whatever for?"

Will gave a low chuckle. "Don't know much about your fiancée's reading tastes, do you, old chap?" he murmured under his breath, feeling a hint of satisfaction at his superior knowledge of Trix on this particular topic. The only thing she liked better than poring over travel guides at Halstead's was mucking about with her sketchbook and her paints. Give her either of those pastimes, and she was happy. Add a box of chocolates, and she was in heaven.

"I didn't order a Baedeker, darling," Beatrix clarified with a little laugh. "But Mr. Halstead is having an entirely new collection of them brought in, and I thought if they had arrived, I would have a look at them. I wish to . . ." She paused just an infinitesimal moment. "Improve my knowledge of geography."

"It makes me happy to hear you say that," Trathen said. "Improving one's mind through serious study of a subject is the most valuable of pursuits."

Will rolled his eyes. In his opinion, she ought to tell Trathen her mind was quite improved enough, thank you very much, but she didn't.

"Intellectual pursuits are very important to me," she said, sounding as convincing as a denying child caught red-handed with the strawberry tart.

"Excellent," Trathen answered. "If I am not mistaken, Mr. Halstead has some excellent texts on geography. If you wish to make a study of the subject, those would be of far more use to you than any Baedeker, my dear."

Beatrix said something Will didn't quite catch, but he did hear the other man's reply.

"If you had not intended to stop here too long, perhaps we could call upon Colonel Westholm before meeting your aunt for tea?"

Beatrix laughed. "What you really mean, darling, is that you've decided on your next move in that eternal chess game you and the Colonel are engaged in," she replied, an intimacy and understanding in her words that made Will heartily wish he was somewhere else. If he had to hear her call the other man "darling" one more time, he'd smash his head into a wall.

"Would you mind if I remain here while you visit the Colonel?" she asked, interrupting Will's contemplation of self-inflicted injury.

"Not at all. I shall call back for you in . . ." Trathen paused, obviously consulting his watch. "Half an hour?"

She must have given a nod of agreement to that, for the man's boot heels tapped against the wooden floor of the shop, indicating he was headed for the door. "Intellectual pursuits, Beatrix, remember," he called back, but he was laughing as he opened the door.

"Of course," she called back, laughing with him until the door closed. Then her laughter stopped, and Will thought he heard her sigh, though from this far away, he could not be sure.

"I fear I shall have to go in search of your excellent geographical texts, Mr. Halstead," she said to the proprietor, making Will grin. She sounded as delighted as a child forced to do catechism.

"All the geographical texts are upstairs," Mr. Halstead told her. "Not far from the travel books, my lady."

With those words, Will's grin vanished. He shoved Petrie's book back into place and glanced toward the back of the loft, where—if memory served—there was another set of stairs leading to the ground floor. He ought to escape now, while he had the chance. The loft, despite its rows of tall bookshelves, wasn't large enough for him to avoid her, and any encounter between them was bound to be deuced awkward at best, damned infuriating at worst, and pointless all around. Yet, as he heard her footsteps on the front stairs, his inclination to duck out the back was overcome by what he could only define as a perverse sense of obstinacy.

He couldn't avoid her for long. After all, they'd be at Pixy Cove next week, staying in the same house.

And besides, he'd arrived at Halstead's first, and if she didn't like it, she could be the one to leave. She probably would anyway the moment she saw him. He did not return to the archaeology texts he'd been perusing, however. The same contrariness that impelled him to remain up here also led him to the back corner of the shop, where all the travel guides were kept. If he knew Trix at all, this was where her steps would lead her, and any study of academic geographical texts would go to the wall. He snagged a book on tours of the Nile, settled himself against the back wall, and waited. Sure enough, within moments she came around a tall bookshelf, headed straight for him.

She came to an abrupt halt. "You!"

He looked up, doing his best to act surprised. "Hullo, Trix." Marking his place with one finger, he closed the book and bowed. "This is a delightful surprise."

Beatrix stared at him, appalled. "Can't I even journey to town without running into you?"

He smiled. "Apparently not."

She lifted her eyes heavenward, made a sound of exasperation, and turned to leave.

"Running away?" he called after her.

She halted, and her gloved hands curled into fists. She knew what he was doing. He was implying now the same thing he had the other day—that she was a coward. Beatrix drew a deep breath and counted to ten. When she felt she could respond in a lady-like manner, she turned her head to give him a cool, pointed glance over her shoulder. "I'm not the one who ran away, Will."

He ignored this reference to himself, of course. "Surely you don't intend to go scurrying off whenever you see me?" he asked, and gestured to the shelves. "Halstead's is big enough for both of us, I daresay. Besides, it's rather silly of us to spend the entire time I'm in Devonshire avoiding each other, isn't it?"

Beatrix didn't think it was silly at all. Avoiding him seemed like an excellent idea. But she hated giving any validity to his implied accusation of cowardice, and when he opened the book in his hands as if to carry on with his own reading, she decided that as long as she could ignore his presence, it was best to tolerate him and be civil. She turned back around and walked past him to the shelves of Baedekers, Cook's guides, and other travel books, where she began to peruse the titles. After a few minutes, one caught her fancy and she pulled it from the shelf. She felt a hint of excitement as she opened it to a random page.

There is a charming little pensione located there, not the most luxurious accommodations one could obtain in Florence, but with such splendid views of the Ponte Vecchio that—

"Going on a trip?"

She gave a start, realizing he'd moved to stand right behind her. She didn't look at him, but reminded herself that ignoring him was the best thing to do. If she ignored him, he might go away. She continued to read.

—such splendid views of the Ponte Vecchio that any minor inconveniences are easily tolerated. After all—

" 'After all,' " Will's voice murmured by her ear, reading along, " 'if one wished for nothing more than the convenience of modern baths and the thickest possible feather beds, one might remain in England and stay at a London hotel. Where would be the charm in that?' "

Beatrix sighed and turned her head to look at him. "Do you mind?"

"Sorry," he apologized, but he didn't move.

She raised an eyebrow and waited. After a moment he stepped back, and she returned her attention to her book, but she had barely found her place in the text before his voice once again intruded.

"A quaint little pensione with no bath and no feather bed doesn't seem quite your cup of tea, Trix. Not that it really matters, I suppose."

She should have known ignoring him would be impossible. Ignoring Will was rather like ignoring a case of the measles.

"Do you have a point?" she asked without turning around.

"*Plus ça change, plus c'est la même chose,*" he murmured.

She snapped her book shut and turned to face him. "Just what is that supposed to mean?"

He had reopened his book, and he shrugged without looking up. "The more things change—"

"I know the translation, thank you," she interrupted. "I do speak French."

He turned a page. "Yet you never go to France."

"Do you have a point?"

"You love reading about foreign places, yet you never go anywhere." He shut his book and turned to shove it into the shelf beside him, then once again stepped forward. "All our lives I've watched you do it. Dreaming, dreaming, but never doing what you dream about."

"That's ridiculous."

"Is it?" He leaned forward and took the book out of her hand before she could stop him. "*A Tour of Florence*," he read aloud and looked at her. "You talked about going to Florence years ago. You were fifteen, and you wanted to go with your governess for the autumn to study art, but your father said no. You were crushed. Do you remember?"

Beatrix looked away, unable to bear letting him see that she still remembered, and that it still hurt. Her father had been terrified that she'd do what her mother had done. "So?"

"Your father said no, and that was the end of it as far as you were concerned. You never talked about going to Florence again. And a few years later when your aunt and uncle took Paul and me on a tour of the Continent, you wanted to go, too, but again, your father said no. Seasons in London were all a girl needed, he said. You pretended it didn't hurt, but I know it did." He held the book out to her. "It still does."

Stung, put on the defensive and feeling prickly as a chestnut about it, she felt compelled to retaliate. "I happen to be going on a trip, soon, I'll have you know. It's called a honeymoon. You know what a honeymoon is, don't you, Will?" she added, snatching back her book. "Or perhaps you don't, since matrimony is something you seem allergic to. For our honeymoon, we were supposed to journey to Paris, and then take the Orient Express all the way to Constantinople. But we didn't because you decided two weeks before the wedding to go to Egypt instead. Are you going to blame that on my father, too?"

He didn't rise to the bait. "No, Trix. But you dream of places instead of seeing them. You yearn for excitement, yet you always end up playing safe. It's understandable, given the obsessive way your father always kept you under his thumb."

"Are you saying my father was a tyrant? He loved me."

"In a smothering sort of way, yes. He was a great deal like my father. Both of them were autocratic and arrogant and felt their position entitled them to have control over every single thing in their petty little kingdoms, including their children. I broke away. You didn't."

"It's so easy for you to talk about breaking away and being daring, Will. You're a man. You could defy your father and go off to Egypt. You could do whatever you liked and damn the consequences, especially when you came into your own money. As a woman, I've never been allowed that luxury."

"That sounds like an excuse to me."

"It's not an excuse! It's the way things are. I'd give my eyeteeth to have the kind of freedom your sex takes for granted."

"Would you? I doubt it. It's a bit like the cliff, you see," he added in a gentle voice. "You long to jump off, but you just can't work up the nerve, so you tell yourself you're content to look at the view. Let's not go to Florence or Egypt. Oh no. Let's just read about it, safe and snug by the fire here at home."

Her eyes stung, and she hated him suddenly, hated him with almost as much passion as she had once loved him. "Damn you, Will, if you say one more word, I vow I'll—"

The shop bell jangled below, interrupting her threat to do him bodily harm before she could utter it, and when a male voice called her name, she cast a frantic glance over her shoulder.

"Aidan, already?" She groaned, knowing he couldn't find her up here alone with Will. "Oh Lord."

"What's wrong, Trix?" he asked in a low, hard voice. "Not brimming over with delight to see your fiancé? Does that signify trouble in paradise?"

"If there's any trouble here, it's you." She shoved the guide to Florence back in its place and started toward the stairs, but she hadn't taken more than half a dozen steps before she realized he was following her, and she was forced to stop. "What are you doing?" she whispered.

"What do you think I'm doing?" he whispered back. "I'm returning downstairs."

She stared at him, appalled. "You can't walk down there with me!"

"But I want to leave. I've finished improving my mind through intellectual pursuits."

"Eavesdropping, Will?"

"Hardly." He gave her a look of mock apology. "After all, I was here first. I'd been here for well over half an hour, as a matter of fact, minding my own business, reading my book and pursuing my studies like a virtuous schoolboy when you came in."

She gave a disbelieving sniff and resumed walking. "You weren't virtuous even when you were a schoolboy," she hissed over her shoulder, and when she saw he was still right behind her, she halted again, so abruptly that he almost cannoned into her. "Stop following me!" she hissed.

"But I told you I want to go downstairs."

She cast a frantic glance around, then gestured to the back of the loft. "Take the other stairs. There's a door at the bottom that leads out the back."

"What's wrong, Beatrix?" he murmured. "Afraid of what Trathen will think if he finds us alone together?"

It was absurd, she knew, but yes, that was exactly what she was afraid of. She met his gaze head on and lied through her teeth. "Of course not."

Of course he wasn't fooled. "I think you are. I think you're afraid he'll think we're engaging in something illicit, a clandestine rendezvous in a shadowy back corner, just the way we used to do." He lowered his gaze to her mouth. "Remember?"

She felt her cheeks heating. "Stop it."

"Stop what? We aren't doing anything wrong."

She took a deep breath. She seemed to be taking lots of deep breaths nowadays. "I'm not, at least. But detaining a woman when she is unaccompanied is reprehensible. Knowing you, however, it's not surprising."

"Detaining you? Not at all." He straightened and gestured behind her. "You're free to go anywhere you like. As am I."

"Meaning you intend to follow me despite my request to the contrary, demonstrating to Aidan that we've been alone up here, and encouraging him to think the worst."

"Somehow, I just can't work up any pangs of conscience about what Trathen thinks. Besides, if he thinks less of you for merely being in the same public place as me, then you have quite a lack of trust between you, don't you?"

With those words, her worst fears were confirmed. "So you really do intend to cause trouble. I knew it. What's next, Will? Shall you inform Aidan I went to see you the day you came home, or tell him a lie about how we arranged this little secret meeting?"

"I'm not the one who lies," he reminded her in a savage whisper, but before he could say more, footsteps sounded on the stairs.

"Beatrix?" Aidan's voice called to her. "Are you up here?"

She cast another glance over her shoulder, feeling a hint of panic, then returned her attention to the man before her. "Will, for God's sake—"

He muttered an oath. "Go," he ordered, much to

her relief. "I'll go down the back way. I promise," he added when she didn't move.

Beatrix didn't need any further urging. When she emerged from behind the bookshelves, she found Aidan just reaching the top of the stairs. "Hullo, darling," she greeted, rushing forward to meet him, a little out of breath. "How's the Colonel?"

Aidan laughed. "Confounded, I fear. I checked him with a move he never expected." He turned, offering her his arm. "Are you ready to leave?"

"Absolutely." As she slid her arm through his, she cast a surreptitious glance behind her. Thankfully, Will had gone, but Beatrix had the uneasy feeling he had no intention of staying that way.

Afternoon tea at the vicarage proved to be a welcome distraction for Beatrix. She managed to put Will and his ridiculous comments out of her mind, but afterward, as Aidan drove her back to Danbury in his carriage, Will's words insisted on going through her mind.

Dreaming, dreaming, but never doing what you dream about.

"Is something wrong, my dear?"

Aidan's voice intruded on her thoughts, and when she glanced at him, she found his hazel eyes on her, his expression troubled.

"Nothing's wrong," she assured. Aside from being all mixed up and turned upside down from Will's blasted return, she was just shipshape and Bristol fashion. She forced herself to smile. "Why do you ask?"

"You scarcely said a word at the vicarage this afternoon. In fact," he added, "you've seemed in a pensive mood for several days."

Ever since Sunderland arrived home.

Aidan didn't say those words, of course. He knew Will was here, he must have heard, yet he was too much of a gentleman, far too correct and proper, to make mention of her former fiancé. But what was he thinking? Was he the least bit jealous? If he was, he'd never show it. She had feared what conclusions he might draw if he'd seen her in the loft with Will, but whatever those conclusions might have been, he would never have revealed them. He was a very private man.

"Aidan?" She turned impulsively toward him. "I was wondering . . . do you think we might reexamine our plans for our honeymoon?"

"Reexamine our plans? In what sense?"

"I know we had decided to take a tour of your estates. But I was wondering if we might take a holiday somewhere instead?"

"A holiday?"

"Yes. Somewhere cozy and intimate." She moved a bit closer and looked up at him. "It will be just the two of us, you know."

"Ah, I am beginning to understand the interest in Baedeker." He smiled a little. "Do you have a particular place in mind?"

Images ran through her head at once, images of red tile rooftops and cobblestone streets, of a quaint pensione with a view of the Arno. She could see herself and Aidan sipping espresso in the Piazza del

Campo, or walking through the churches and museums, or picnicking in the Tuscan countryside where he would read and she would paint. So captivating were these images, she could almost hear the sonorous notes of a Puccini aria playing in her head as if on a gramophone.

"Yes," she breathed with a hint of reverence. "I want to go to Florence."

"Florence?" He gave a slight laugh, clearly surprised. "When you said a holiday, I was thinking the Isle of Wight, or possibly Calais. We only have two weeks set aside, remember, and Florence is so far away. It just isn't possible."

Those words were like the sound of the gramophone needle slicing across the disk of her imagination, and the lilting music of Puccini ended in a screeching dose of reality.

She fought it. "I know it's a long way. But we could extend our honeymoon a bit longer, couldn't we? It would be wonderful to see the Duomo and the Ponte Vecchio and Michelangelo's *David*, wouldn't it?"

"Delightful, I agree. But as for extending our honeymoon, we simply can't, my dear. What of Parliament? Our wedding is October 2. The House of Lords sits on October 16, and it's a special session that day, very important. I must be there for the vote."

With those words, Beatrix felt images of Florence fading away into oblivion. "I'd forgotten about Parliament," she admitted, trying to hide her disappointment.

"For us to tour Florence for our honeymoon, I

would have to abandon my Parliamentary obligations."

"I know."

"We discussed a honeymoon abroad, if you remember, and we decided time prohibited it. We arranged to tour my estates instead so that you would have the opportunity to see them all, something we have not yet done."

She kept her gaze fixed on the road ahead, for she did not want him to see the disappointment in her face if he happened to glance at her. "I remember."

"And the tenants would be so let down if they did not have the opportunity to meet you straightaway. Why, I believe the children at Trathen Leagh are even planning some sort of welcoming song to greet their new duchess. We have a duty to our people, my dear. We cannot let them down."

"I know."

"If it means anything to you, I wish I could take you to Florence." He put his gloved hand over hers, and it was such an uncharacteristically open display of affection, it caught her by surprise. Aidan was not that sort. He had kissed her only once, quite properly, upon her acceptance of his proposal, and he was certainly not one for holding hands. "Your happiness is important to me, my dear, and you have been unhappy in the past, I know."

He wasn't looking at her, but as she studied his grave, boyishly handsome profile, she felt a powerful rush of fondness and affection.

Aidan might not be the most demonstrative of

men, or the most expressive, and he was, as her cousins were wont to say, a bit of a dry stick. But he had a loyal, faithful heart. She would always be able to depend upon him. He wouldn't break promises. She could trust him to take care of her and their children no matter what might happen. He would never demand that she do crazy things like follow him into the desert on a bloody treasure hunt. He wouldn't expect her to make impossible, irresponsible choices. Most important, he would never tear her heart into pieces.

She and Aidan were not passionately in love, but they suited. They fit. They both appreciated the responsibilities of their position and accepted its obligations. They both knew this was the life they'd been born to live, a life built around their estates, their families, and the carrying on of traditions that were important and necessary.

"Your happiness is important to me, too," she answered. "And I know it would grieve you to forsake your responsibilities in Parliament for a holiday. I would not ask you to do that."

"Those words means a great deal to me." He smiled. It was an Aidan smile, no more than a subtle curve of the lips, and it didn't twist her heart all around or make her stomach dip or make her giddy with excitement, but that was quite all right with her. She'd had enough of that sort of thing to last a lifetime, and she was perfectly content with what she had now.

You long to jump off, but you just can't work up

the nerve, so you tell yourself you're content to look at the view.

It was ridiculous, she told herself, ridiculous of Will to bring up that stupid story. She didn't want to jump off cliffs. Or ride a horse fast enough to break her neck. And if she was content to be an armchair traveler, what business was it of his anyway?

"Beatrix?"

"Hmm?" She blinked, and Aidan's face came back into focus. "I beg your pardon?"

"You are frowning all of a sudden. Did I say something to vex you?"

"No." She shook her head. "Of course not, I was woolgathering, darling. Forgive me."

He returned his attention to the road, and she worked to force Will's absurd observations out of her mind. Three days back after six years away, and he thought she was the same Beatrix he'd left behind. Well, she wasn't.

She was no longer the scared little girl who couldn't dive off Angel's Head. And she wasn't a lovesick fool, either, mooning over him and waiting for him.

It was just Will, stirring up old memories. Will, who couldn't keep commitments, who refused to honor his responsibilities at home, who went off halfway around the world two weeks before his wedding day without a second thought. Well, she wasn't made that way.

Her life might not be very exciting. It wasn't like jumping off cliffs, or racing along the road to St. Ives in an automobile, or treasure-hunting for Tut's tomb, but it was the life she'd always known she would be expected to lead. And it was the life she wanted.

She glanced behind her at Paul's carriage, which was following Aidan's back to Danbury, and watched Aunt Eugenia smile and wave at her. She smiled back, then she looked again at the man beside her, turning her hand in his to entwine their gloved fingers. Yes, she repeated firmly, this was the life she wanted.

With that, she resolved to put Will out of her mind, and during the days that followed, she was careful to avoid any possible accidental encounters with him— she stayed away from the village, avoided the lane to Sunderland Park, and even pleaded a headache to avoid seeing him at church.

Instead, she occupied her time working with Auntie to make preparations for her wedding, and for the trip to Pixy Cove. She also took long walks with Aidan in the groves and woods surrounding Danbury, and as she listened to him describe his own estates and talk about their future together, she was able to put her priorities back in order.

After a week had passed, Will's return began to seem like little more than a bad dream, and by the time of Marlowe's house party, Beatrix felt she had fully regained her equilibrium. Having managed to avoid him for a full week, and relieved that it would be at least another four before she ran the risk of encountering him again, by which time he might have returned to Egypt anyway, she happily boarded Sir George's yacht, but she had barely stepped off the gangplank and onto the ship before her hard-won equilibrium went sliding away.

Standing on the deck of the *Maria Lisa*, talking to Sir George and looking rakishly handsome in dark blue flannel trousers and buff-colored waistcoat, with the cuffs of his white shirt rolled back and his navy reefer jacket hooked by his fingertips over one shoulder, was Will. He must be accompanying them to Pixy Cove.

With a sinking feeling in the pit of her stomach, Beatrix glanced behind her, but the hands were pulling up the gangplank, and unless she wanted to jump over the side, there was no escape. For the coming four weeks, she would be trapped in the same house with him, and with that realization, the serenity Beatrix had worked so hard to regain during the past week vanished as if it had never been.

Chapter Six

$\mathscr{S}$ ir George and Lady Debenham were passionate about only one thing, and that was sailing. As far back as Will could remember, their favorite entertainment during the hot days of August was to give water parties aboard their yacht, offering a select group of their acquaintances the opportunity for a tour along the Torbay coast.

As the boat skimmed along Devonshire's stunning coastline, most guests at these affairs were content to stand at the rail and admire the view, but not Will. It had been a long time since he'd been sailing, and when Sir George offered him the helm, he was happy to take it.

Occupied with guiding the three-masted yacht across Torbay Harbor and north around the point whimsically called Hope's Nose, Will didn't know Trix was aboard. Being occupied with estate business during the past week, he hadn't talked to Paul. If he'd thought about the Danbury transportation arrangements, he'd have guessed they would have come by rail, as they had usually done in past years. But after he'd handed control of the *Maria Lisa* back to Sir George, he discovered that guess would have been wrong. As he started along the starboard side of the ship toward the observation saloon where refreshments were being served, he spied Beatrix standing by the rail.

She was near the door to the saloon, leaning on the rail and staring out at the sea. The stiff breeze whipped the skirt of her white yachting suit in his direction and stirred the fat blue ribbon bow on the side of her white straw boater. One of her hands gripped the rail to keep her balance on deck. Her other hand was at her neck, and he came to an abrupt halt, transfixed by the aimless, innocuous movement of her fingertips back and forth beneath her jaw. How many times had he kissed her there? he wondered, remembering nights in the moonlight, with the scent of gardenias in the air, and her skin soft and warm against his mouth.

As he stared at her with these images of the past going through his mind, Will felt the slow burn of arousal spreading through his body. Watching her, thinking of those days, he suddenly felt like a randy, desperate youth all over again, and when she lowered her hand, exposing that tempting little bit of bare skin above her collar, his mind began conjuring up images far more explicit than anything he'd actually seen during their many midnight rendezvous so long ago.

Desperate to regain his composure, he lifted his gaze a notch to her profile. Her expression was pensive, almost dreamy, with an upward curve at the corner of her mouth that made him wonder what she was thinking about right now.

Probably her wedding to Trathen, he thought, hoping that splash of cold reality would dampen the desire for her that was now coursing through his body, but instead it only piled resentment he had no right to feel onto the fire of lust blazing inside him.

With a smothered sound, he moved, thinking to go back the way he'd come, but she caught the movement out the corner of her eye, and turned her head with a smile of greeting as if she'd been expecting someone. Not him, he knew, and stopped, speared through the chest by that smile, awash in hot desire and inexplicable frustration, and sure that what he felt was as obvious to her as an elephant in the drawing room.

Her smile faded, reminding him more forcefully than any words that he was not the man she'd been expecting to see and that smile was not for him.

Stupid to stand here, he thought. Stupid to have come back. Stupid to think it wouldn't matter and he was over her and he could pretend to be an indifferent acquaintance for the next four weeks. Stupid, stupid, stupid.

She squeezed her eyes shut, as if to blot him out, and he told himself he didn't care, but he knew that no matter how many times he told himself that, it was a lie. He cared damnably. He always had, he always would, and there wasn't a thing he could do about it, because they moved in different worlds and she belonged to someone else who could give her the life she wanted better than he ever could.

She opened her eyes—those big, soft, dark eyes—and looked into his face. He stood there, helpless, as the past six years fell away and the layers of indifference he'd built to protect himself crumbled to dust.

Walk away, he told himself. *For the love of God, walk away.* But he couldn't. It was too late. She'd seen him. There might be other people who'd seen as well, for the windows of the saloon were directly to his left. He thrust his hands into the pockets of his jacket, wrapping the generous folds of the double-breasted reefer forward to conceal from any curious gazes the most obvious sign of his present feelings.

Still, he couldn't just stand here looking like an idiot. He couldn't pretend he hadn't seen her when it was so clear that he had. And he couldn't turn his back and walk away. If he did that, he'd be giving her the cut direct, the greatest social snub one person could give another, and he couldn't do that, either. Not to her.

He resumed walking toward her, pasting on another artificial, devil-may-care smile. She did the same, turning toward him, her lips tipping up just enough to show anyone who might be watching that they were on friendly, yet wholly indifferent terms. If people believed that, it might avert gossip, but Will didn't think anyone they knew was that big a fool. He paused before her and shifted his weight from one foot to the other, painfully aware that his desire was hidden only by the generous cut of a double-breasted jacket.

He opened his mouth to offer her a good-day greeting so that he could step around her and move on, but the door to the observation saloon swung open and an elegantly dressed man came out with a plate of food in one hand and a glass of lemonade in the other. "My dear, I've brought you—"

The man stopped just long enough to glance at him, a quick, assessing glance, before he came forward to join them where they stood by the rail. "I've brought you some refreshments, Beatrix."

She took the offered plate and glass. "Thank you, darling," she said, causing Will to frown, not because he'd already heard that endearment to Trathen often enough in the bookshop to last a lifetime, but because he was staring in disbelief at what the other man had brought her. Lemonade? For Trix? When there was sure to be champagne on board? And what was that topping the slices of toast Melba on her plate? Caviar? Trix *hated* caviar, and always had.

He began to appreciate the oppressive silence, and he forced himself to look up. He cocked an eyebrow at her, daring her to snub him by failing to perform introductions.

Her cheeks flushed a delicate pink at this social faux pas, and she remedied it at once. "Aidan, would you allow me to introduce the Duke of Sunderland to you? Sunderland, this is the Duke of Trathen."

"Trathen."

"Sunderland."

They shook hands, they both smiled politely, but Will was looking into the other man's eyes and knew he wasn't the only one playing the gentlemanly role expected of him.

There was another awkward pause, and it was clearly up to him to step into the breach by offering his congratulations. His innate hatred for hypocrisy urged him to rebel, but Trathen was about to be a guest in Marlowe's home, and since Will was going to spend the coming weeks beggaring funds from Marlowe, he couldn't afford to antagonize anyone. No, he had to put on the show of British good-sportsmanship, no hard feelings, best man won, stiff upper lip, and all that, when what he wanted to do was crush something, preferably his own skull. He should have walked away from her, social civility be damned in favor of self-preservation.

"I understand," he said, trying not to choke on the words, "that congratulations are in order, that you two are to be married?"

"We are," Trathen said, but though Will could feel the other man's eyes taking his measure, he didn't look at him. He kept his gaze on Beatrix. He watched her take a bite of caviar, and his mood lightened a bit at the grimace of distaste she couldn't quite hide.

"What's wrong, Trix?" he asked with a grin. "Caviar not to your liking?"

She swallowed, and he didn't miss the tiny shiver she gave. "On the contrary," she said, her gaze meeting his head-on. "It's lovely stuff."

"Beatrix adores caviar as much as I do," Trathen said, obviously feeling the need to prove he had some knowledge of her that Will lacked.

"Does she?" he drawled. "Since when?"

The pink in her cheeks deepened, but her gaze didn't waver. "I've developed a taste for it over the years," she said.

"So, Sunderland," Trathen put in, forcing him to give his attention to the other man, "you are attending Marlowe's house party, I take it?"

"I have a standing invitation to Pixy Cove every August. The Marlowes are like family to me."

"Quite. And are you staying in England long?"

Worried, old chap? The words hovered on the tip of his tongue, but he didn't say them. He wanted to, wanted to say them with an arrogant smirk and a triumphant wink and a bravado that he didn't feel in the least. But saying something like that would be ungentlemanly, and despite Trix's words to the contrary, he did know how to be a gentleman.

"Alas, no. I'm only home a month or so, and then I return to Egypt."

Trathen's stance relaxed, but only a bit. "What a pity."

"Yes, a great pity," he lied. "I'd prefer to linger a bit longer, see some old friends in the north, do a bit of fishing . . ." He let his voice trail off, and he gave a shrug.

"But Tutankhamen awaits discovery?" Trathen finished for him with a laugh, and Will wondered if he'd only imagined a hint of ridicule beneath the words. But he laughed, too, being that he was so civilized and all. "Exactly so."

"I wish you good luck with it." Trathen turned to Beatrix. "My dear, I observed your aunt and cousins sitting with Lady Debenham. Shall we join them? That is," he added with a dismissive glance at Will, "if you've finished here?"

"Yes, of course."

When Trathen took her plate, she slipped her free arm through his, they both bid Will a polite farewell, and turned to go.

Will let out a long, slow breath as he watched them walk away arm in arm, and felt his earlier optimism dissolving. "Welcome to hell, Will," he murmured under his breath. "Welcome to hell."

He rejoined Sir George, and fortunately he was allowed to guide the *Maria Lisa* the remainder of the way to Marlowe's slip in Pixy Cove without having to beg for the opportunity. Not that he'd have been above begging at this point. Sailing the yacht was a distraction, and he felt in desperate need of distractions just now.

When they docked, he lingered behind, happy to assist Sir George in supervising the hands with the cleaning of the ship, thereby saving himself the awkwardness of walking to the house with Beatrix and her fiancé. But even a meticulous captain like Sir George was eventually satisfied with the condition of his ship, and when Lady Debenham called down to them from the gazebo above that Lady Marlowe had tea waiting, Will had no choice but to follow Sir George.

Pixy Cove, Viscount Marlowe's seaside villa, was a low, prim, sprawling cottage of yellow stucco, white bargeboards, and red brick. It was perched on a wooded headland overlooking the sea, and a sturdy set of steps led down to the boat dock and the bathing beach, where two clapboard bathing huts provided dressing arrangements for the ladies and the nearby caves sufficed for the men. The house had sixteen bedrooms, four baths with hot and cold laid on, a lawn for tennis and another for croquet, and a beautiful gazebo on the north side where the Marlowe family and their guests could take tea in the afternoon and enjoy the magnificent view.

The tea things had been set out, and a maid in striped gray dress and white apron and cap stood by ready to assist should they need anything for tea. Their hosts, however, were nowhere in sight, and Beatrix's Aunt Eugenia sat with the teapot in hand. "Aunt Gennie," he greeted her with the same impudent familiarity he always had, but she cast him a wary glance from beneath her bonnet as she reached for a teacup, making him want to give her a wolfish smile and assure her he wasn't going to bite her.

Instead, he prayed for a diversion.

Even a sinner's prayers could sometimes be answered, it seemed, for he had barely expressed his silent wish for divine assistance when it came, and from a most unexpected quarter.

The loud drone of a motorcar was heard in the distance, a sound that Will recognized quite well from his painful encounter with Beatrix and her white Daimler ten days ago. It was not the Daimler that appeared moments later, however, but a different model of vehicle, similar in style but painted a deep ruby red and boasting a black interior.

"Oh, look!" Beatrix cried as the motorcar roared into the drive, spitting gravel and dust due to the alarming speed of the driver. "Julie's come after all. She'd written to me that she wouldn't be coming this year. She must have changed her mind at the last minute. Oh, how lovely!"

"Yes, lovely," Trathen echoed in a dry murmur that was polite, but unenthusiastic.

Will couldn't help a grin. No surprise, really, that someone like Julia would rub someone like Trathen the wrong way.

The motorcar came to an abrupt stop about forty feet from the gazebo where they sat, the brake lever was pulled, the engine was silenced, and a slim woman dressed in motoring attire similar to the kit Beatrix had been wearing the day he arrived home gave them a wave as she stepped down from the driver's seat. With her was a brown-and-white bulldog that jumped down from the passenger seat and followed her as she circled to the back of the vehicle. "Hullo, everyone!" she called as she began unbuttoning her motoring coat.

"I see she's brought Spike with her," Paul said with a groan. "Couldn't she have left him somewhere else?"

"Spike?" Will glanced at Paul, surprised by his friend's lack of enthusiasm. "I take it Spike is the bulldog?"

Paul nodded. "And a mean one he is, too."

"He's not," Beatrix contradicted. "He's a bit skittish around men, that's all."

Trathen spoke up. "But, my dear Beatrix, a skittish dog must have training and discipline, or it can become a danger. Unfortunately, given Lady Yardley's rather . . ." There was a momentary pause. " . . . free-spirited character, she will probably do little to check the animal. One day it will bite someone, mark my words."

"Not here," Paul put in. "Marlowe will put his foot down the first time that animal growls at him. She'll have to keep it outside and tied up most of the time."

Her ill-mannered dog aside, Will decided he needed to thank Julia for her timely arrival and for being just the distraction he'd been praying for. "I think I'll give Julie a bit of help with her kit," he said, rose to his feet, and started down the steps of the gazebo.

"Careful," Geoff called him. "Get too close to Julie and you'll find Spike's teeth in your arm."

Will, who wasn't afraid of dogs, walked toward the automobile in the drive. Spike heralded his approach with a series of barks that caused him to stop about a dozen feet away as Julia looked up.

At the sight of him, her piquant pixy face took on a look of utter stupefaction. "Will?" she cried. "Heavens above! Will?"

He started toward her again, earning a warning growl from the animal.

"Wait," Julia ordered, tossing her motoring coat and goggles into the boot and pulling out a leather leash. "Stay right there while I tie up this beast of mine."

She looped the leash around one of the motorcar's wheel spokes, hooked the other end to the bulldog's collar, grabbed her straw boater hat, and came running. "By God, it is you!" she cried, laughing. "I thought I was seeing ghosts of Augusts past."

"Hullo, Julie," he said, smiling.

"I had no idea you were in England!" She dropped the hat, grasped him by the shoulders, and pulled him close, and as he leaned down, she rose on her toes to plant a kiss soundly on each of his cheeks with all the *joie de vivre* he remembered. Then she leaned back to give him a more thorough study.

He did the same. He'd always had a special fondness for Beatrix's cousin, whose adventurous streak matched his own. But as his gaze scanned her face, his pleasure was tinged with a hint of concern, for there were dark circles under her violet-blue eyes. "Are you all right?" he found himself asking.

"Right as rain," she answered at once, her voice airy and light, but somehow Will wasn't convinced. Even in Egypt he'd heard gossip, but he didn't pursue the matter. Julia, he knew, was a law unto herself.

"You seem well enough," she said, and reached up, ruffling his hair with her fingers. "Handsome as ever, you pirate. Tanned skin suits you." She clasped his hands in hers. "Oh, Will, I am so glad to see you! Why, it's just like old days, isn't it? All of us coming to Pixy Cove for August."

She glanced past him, taking note of the people gathered in the gazebo. "Well, almost like old days," she added wryly under her breath as she bent to reach for the straw boater she'd dropped. "Bit awkward, what?"

"Not at all," he murmured, keeping his smile firmly in place, but he suspected he wasn't fooling Julia for a second.

"Don't worry," she said with a wink as she donned her hat. "I make a wonderful buffer. Darling!" she added, smiling past Will.

He glanced over his shoulder to find Beatrix approaching. He stepped back to allow the two women to exchange greetings, then he followed as they walked toward the others.

"Hullo, Aunt Gennie," Julia greeted, bending to press an affectionate kiss on Eugenia's forehead. "Sir George, Lady Debenham, so good to see you. Geoff, Paul . . ." She paused, and her face lit with a sudden, devilish grin. "Ah, and Aidan, too, of course. How delightful."

If her impudent use of his Christian name offended Trathen, he didn't show it. "Baroness," he murmured with a stiff, formal bow.

"I say, Julie, is that a new motorcar?" Geoff asked, eyeing the vehicle in the drive.

"It is. The Mercedes, they call it. I ordered it last year after I gave the Daimler to Trix."

"How fast does it run? Did you calculate the speed?"

"No need to," she answered. "It has a gauge on it that does that for you—a speedometer, they call it. It measured forty-two miles an hour on the straight-away at Nice during Race Week."

"Forty-two!" Geoff whistled, impressed. "Ripping!"

"I don't see the point of traveling at such an unsafe rate of speed," Trathen commented.

"That's because you've never done it, old chap," Paul told him, laughing. "It's deuced good fun. Care for a spot of tea, Julie?"

"No, no," she said, waving a demurring hand as Eugenia reached for the teapot. "I must greet our hosts. Are they anywhere about?"

"Both of them are in the house seeing to some of the other guests," Eugenia offered, waving a hand vaguely behind her. "Marlowe's mother and sisters arrived just after we did. Lord and Lady Weston came with us on Sir George's yacht. We shall be quite a merry party this week," she added, then gave Will a dubious glance, as if he threatened to be a possible fly in the ointment there.

"Excellent." Julia turned to Will. "Walk me there, old thing?"

"With pleasure," he said, offering her his arm, grateful for the escape. "I like the motorcar, but I'm not so sure about the dog, Julie. When did you obtain him?"

"Spike? Oh, I got him two years ago. He's my

constant companion these days. He's a bit hostile to men, but that's all right." She grinned. "Keeps Yardley away. He's terrified of that dog. I had no idea you were home," she added, changing the subject as they walked toward the house. "Are you back for good?"

"No. I'm only here a month or so. I'm trying to raise funds for the excavation."

"Ah. When I first saw you, I thought—"

She broke off, glancing over her shoulder, and he finished for her in a low voice. "You thought I'd come back to stop Beatrix from marrying another man?"

"Something like that. You're not, I take it?"

"No. Should I?"

"I don't know. Should you?"

"Definitely not." He kept his gaze on the house straight ahead, but he could feel her shrewd, thoughtful gaze on him, and he felt impelled to add, "It wasn't meant to be, Julie. Seems she's made a much more sensible choice this time around."

"Oh yes, very sensible." There was an odd inflection in her voice that might have been sarcasm, but before he could take up the point, she steered him away from the side door and around to the back of the house.

"Let's sit back here for a bit," she said, gesturing to a wrought-iron bench overlooking the sea. "I'm dying for a cigarette, but Emma hates the smell, and I always try to avoid offending my hostess until I've stayed at least one night."

They sat down, and Julia pulled a box of matches and a silver cigarette case from the pocket of her skirt. "Want one?" she asked, flipping the case open to display half a dozen neatly rolled cigarettes.

He shook his head, and she extracted one for herself.

"So," he said as she put away the case and opened the box of matches, "were you being sarcastic just now when you said Trix was being sensible?"

"No, no, you misunderstand me." Julia lifted her cigarette to her lips, pulled a match from the box, and used the heel of her boot to strike a flame. She lit the cigarette, then waved the match out and blew smoke in a sideways stream. "I do think it was sensible of her to accept Trathen. I was agreeing with you."

He grimaced, and she saw it.

"Well, what do you want me to say?" she asked, pulling a bit of tobacco from her tongue with the tips of her fingers as she spoke. "I mean, Trathen's a bit stiff, a fact you've no doubt observed for yourself, and he's terribly proper—insists on the old school tie, you know," she added, taking on an arch, painfully aristocratic accent, "and everything according to cricket. Pays attention to who's the right sort and the wrong sort, and disapproves a bit when people shake hands at breakfast."

His opposite, in other words.

"Still," she went on, "he might be wound a bit tight, but he's a good man. He'll make Trix a fine husband."

"Fine husband?" Will made a sound of disbelief.

"Yes. Trathen is the epitome of the perfect British gentleman—honest, honorable, loyal, and true."

"He's a prig."

"Compared to you, perhaps," she conceded, not sounding particularly impressed.

"Damn it, Julie, the man makes her eat caviar!"

"He does?" She sat up a little straighter. "What a cad!"

"Do be serious, will you? I saw them together, and I couldn't believe it. He's so damned superior and highbrow."

"There are worse sins. He's a powerful man with a wide sphere of influence. Not only is he a duke like you, but he's also got oodles of money, and property all over the kingdom. And he truly cares for Trix."

Will began to feel quite depressed.

"And he's terribly good-looking, too." Julia took a puff on her cigarette, pausing a few seconds before she added, "Too bad he's as dull as Fordyce's sermons."

He gave a shout of laughter, cheered a little bit.

Julia grinned back at him, wrinkling her pert nose in rueful fashion. "I say that purely out of spite, but I can't help it. The man dislikes me."

"Dislikes our Julie? Not so!"

"It's true, Will. I fear I'm everything he most disapproves of. I drink and I smoke—horrors!—and I drive motorcars very fast. Worse, I taught Trix to drive and gave her a motorcar of her own. He's forever after her to give it up. That didn't endear me to him. Then, of course, there's all the scandals I've caused."

"Like dancing the fandango on the tables at Maxim's?"

"Heard about that, did you?" She sighed. "My reputation has spread all the way to Egypt, I see. Mind, I've no intention to become a demimondaine. Things aren't that bad, at least not yet. But you're right—that's the sin that probably did it for me as far as Trathen's concerned."

"Because it made the papers?"

"No, because he hates dancing." When Will laughed again, she said, "He does! I don't know why."

"It might make him perspire?" Will guessed.

"Dearest Will! No, it can't be that, for Trathen's quite an athlete. Made the quarterfinals at Wimbledon just last year. No, I think it's because underneath all the ducal hauteur, he's afraid of looking a fool."

Will grinned at her. "So that means we roll back the drawing room rug tonight?"

She laughed. "I fear we shall be a bad influence upon each other this week and rag him mercilessly." She chuckled and took a pull on her cigarette. "Poor fellow."

"Beatrix will come to his defense, I'm sure."

He hoped he said it lightly enough, but he could feel Julia's shrewd gaze on him, and he didn't look at her. He didn't want her to see his face just now.

"I daresay she would, although . . ." Julia paused, and there was something thoughtful in her voice that made him slide a sideways glance at her profile. "I'm not sure he'd need defending," she said. "Trathen may be a stuffed shirt, hopelessly old-fashioned and honorable, but he's not a pushover. He's not *easy*."

Will tensed. "You mean he's a tyrant?"

"No, no, that's not what I mean at all. How can I explain?" She paused, smoking quietly as if considering the question, then she said, "Trathen may never be the life of the party or the soul of wit. But he's also the sort who, to borrow from Tennyson, would ride into the jaws of death with the six hundred. The sort who'd stand like Henley's 'Invictus,' head bloodied and unbowed, no matter what was flung at him."

"It sounds like you actually admire him."

Julia made a wry face. "Nauseating, isn't it, given that he dislikes me so much, but there it is. Trathen's a true *pukka sahib*, and that's a rare breed nowadays."

Will thought of Beatrix on the *Maria Lisa*, eating caviar and drinking lemonade, and he spoke before he could stop himself, asking the question that he'd been shoving out of his mind ever since January. "Is she in love with him?"

"What a tactless question!"

"Is she?" he persisted, not even sure why he wanted to know, not sure he wanted to hear the answer.

"Heavens, I don't know." She took another puff of her cigarette, studying him through the haze of smoke. "Does it matter?"

"Does it matter?" he echoed, rather taken aback. "She's going to marry the fellow. You're part of her family, you love her like a sister. Don't you think it matters?"

"Not really, no. Love can be . . . rather awful. I tried it once, and I can't say it has much to recommend it."

She tossed the cigarette end to the ground and extinguished it beneath her shoe, then tucked her arm through his and stood up, taking him to his feet as well. "Play Trathen a spot of tennis, do. He trounces Paul and Geoff all the time from what I hear, and Marlowe doesn't play, so you're the only one with a prayer of taking him on. I'll even help you," she added. "I'll distract him by lifting my skirt and waving a shapely ankle in his direction at opportune moments."

Will laughed, his good humor slightly restored. "And shall we dance tonight?"

"No, I've got a better idea. We'll play that new music from America—what's it called? ragtime?—on the piano. And we'll sing naughty comic songs. That will shock him right out of his puritanical British sensibilities."

"You're a woman in a thousand, Julie. And you have heaps of money. Would you marry me and fund my excavation so I can avoid this ghastly business and go back to Egypt?"

"Darling, you know I'm already married! As to the rest, I'm mired in debt now that Yardley's cut off my allowance. But," she added as Will opened the door for her, "if you're willing to be seen by some hapless chambermaid at a third-rate hotel, coming out of my room at three o'clock in the morning, Yardley might be moved to divorce me at last, naming you corespondent. Then I'd be free to marry someone else who's disgustingly rich, and I could give you all the money you need."

"You're a brick, Julie. I'll keep your offer in mind."

* * *

Will's room at Pixy Cove had been redone since his last visit six years earlier. The cherrywood furnishings were the same, but the dark velvet and heavy brocade were gone, replaced by a lighter theme of white walls, marine-blue fabrics and a few touches of red and yellow. He suspected that Emma, Lady Marlowe, was the one responsible, and he applauded the change, for now there was nothing but a thin stream of yellow chiffon on either side of the windows to blunt the stunning view of the Babbacombe coastline.

One of his black evening suits had already been pressed and laid out on the bed, and his trunk was in a corner, showing that Aman had already unpacked his things.

He walked to the open window and stuck his head out. Sure enough, the oak tree was still there, halfway between his window and Paul's, with heavy branches that hung over both. He smiled, remembering all the nights they'd climbed down this tree for a midnight swim. Sometimes Trix, Julia, and Marlowe's two youngest sisters had joined them, but it had been much harder for the girls to sneak out, since they didn't have an oak tree ready to hand. Trix, always the most practical of the group, had eventually gotten hold of a rope ladder, enabling the girls to enjoy midnight swims, too, until she'd been caught with it by Marlowe's grandmother. She'd been severely punished for it, too, and Antonia had threatened not to let her come to Pixy Cove the following year. But that hadn't stopped her from sneaking out to meet him in later years for things much less innocent than a swim in the sea.

Memories of their secret meetings at Danbury, Sunderland, and here at Pixy Cove when they were teens flashed across his mind—the garden, the maze, the wine cellar—anywhere they could escape chaperones and be alone for a kiss, a touch. As far back as he could remember, Beatrix had been the only thing he'd been willing to come home for, the bright spot of his life every summer. Now, it was the opposite, because he still wanted her, he couldn't have her, and life was just hell.

He closed his eyes, memories triggering the same desire for her he'd felt as a randy youth, the same desire he'd felt on the boat a short while ago. It had been hard enough to forget those midnight trysts while he'd been hundreds of miles away, but now, when she was so near, when he could look into her dark eyes and smell the scent of her skin, when she was about to marry someone else, it was agony.

He opened his eyes, staring out at the rugged coastline of inlets and caves and tide pools they'd explored together all the summers of their childhood. How, he wondered, feeling suddenly desperate, how was he going to get through the next twenty-eight days?

He couldn't leave. He couldn't avoid her while he was here, and even if he could, he doubted it would matter. Pixy Cove wasn't like Egypt. Here, memories of her were all around him. And if all that wasn't enough to tie him to her for the coming weeks, there was pride. Damned if he'd go running off like a tongue-tied boy in short pants whenever he saw her. Damned if he'd let people see that it hurt. No, no matter what it cost him, he had to stay, he had to smile and pretend to be glad for the happy couple and play the role expected of him—the role of a good sport.

A flash of white caught his eye, and when he looked down, he saw her walking across the lawn in her tailored yachting suit. She wasn't alone, of course. Trathen was right beside her like a shadow.

Will flattened his palm against the glass, reminding himself that Trix was better off with the other man. Trathen would take care of her, and he'd never sneak her away for a quick kissing session in the wine cellar or a midnight tryst in a Babbacombe cave. But as Will watched the pair stroll across the lawn arm in arm, the satisfaction of knowing he'd always be the only man who'd ever been able to coax Trix into disobeying the rules wasn't much of a consolation.

Chapter Seven

Beatrix could not sleep. She changed positions, she counted sheep, she tried to think of other things, all to no avail. The image of Will standing by the rail of the *Maria Lisa* watching her was burned on her brain, and no matter how she tried, she could not rid herself of that image and go to sleep.

She'd been able to read his expression as plainly as she could read a book, for she'd seen that look many times—across the table at a dinner party, during a waltz, in the moonlit gardens at Danbury House.

Desire.

So long since she'd seen him look at her that way, and yet she'd recognized it at once, felt its impact as she always had before. Aidan had never looked at her quite like that, in a way that burned through her clothing, through her skin, into her very heart and soul. Even now, lying in bed and trying to sleep, she felt the euphoric thrill of that look, the same thrill she'd felt so long ago. Sleep was impossible.

She finally gave up trying. She flung back the sheet, got out of bed, and walked to the window. Dawn was breaking, and the seemingly endless stretch of ocean and sky shimmered before her, a dozen shades of gray. Soon, however, it would be gold and pink and vermilion, all the shades of sunrise would reflect off the water and light the scattered clouds. It was going to be breathtaking.

Beatrix ran to her armoire. She slipped into under-garments, donned a simple shirtwaist, skirt and pro-tective smock, then pinned up her hair and laced on a pair of boots. She paused by the various boxes of art supplies her maid had placed beside the writing desk in her room, then she glanced at the window. She wouldn't have much time, she knew, and after con-sidering her options a few more seconds, she grabbed one of her wooden paint boxes, scribbled a note for her maid, and left her room.

Ten minutes later, art box slung over her shoul-der, she was descending the iron ladder to Phoebe's Cove. Her favorite of the many isolated coves along Babbacombe Bay, Phoebe's Cove was also one of the prettiest. Marlowe had named this particular spot for his youngest sister when he'd bought the place two decades earlier, and it had always been a favorite bathing spot, for it was a deep inlet sur-rounded on three sides by caves perfect for exploring, a little stretch of sandy beach for building sandcastles, and a calm, deep, turquoise pool of water for swimming. Massive rocks jutted out of the sea beyond the cove, adding to the spectacular beauty of the scene. Beatrix selected her spot, sat down on the sand, and opened her art box on her lap. She removed her set of pastels and a sheet of drawing paper, then closed the box and placed her art materials on its closed lid.

She glanced at the horizon, chose a color, and began. She sketched quickly, striving to capture the scene before the sun rose too high, and as she worked, she managed to forget about Will. Intent on her task, she was able to blot out the image of his face and the desire she'd seen there. She was able to rid herself of the vestiges of girlish euphoria he'd once been able to evoke just by looking at her. She forgot the past and how he'd been able to send her pulses racing just by touching her hand, or start her heart hammering with a brush of his lips against her neck, or make her shiver by whispering her name.

As she worked, she was able to regain her former contentment with her decision and her future, a future with Aidan, a future that would have none of the agonizing insecurity and dark passions of her past. With Aidan, she would have something far more durable—friendship and affection. As she drew the scene before her, Beatrix's mind also began to find a proper perspective. She attained a calm and serene state of mind.

Then Will showed up and ruined it.

"Pretty as a picture."

She gave a start at the sound of his voice, and when she glanced over her shoulder, she found the cause of her night's insomnia standing only a few feet away.

"You again!" she cried, tossing down her pastel in utter frustration. "What are you doing here?"

As she spoke, she gave a quick glance over his body and realized in dismay that he was barely even dressed. He was wearing nothing but an old white linen shirt, a pair of dark, disreputable football breeches, and scuffed leather loafers. Slung over one shoulder was a towel that answered her question even before he spoke.

"I'm having a bathe, of course," he answered, giving her a look as if he thought her a hopeless pudding head. "Why else would I be down here at this hour of the morning?"

She scrambled to her feet, watching in dismay as he shrugged the towel off his shoulder, kicked off his loafers, and yanked his shirttails out of his breeches.

He was undressing, she realized in horror as she watched him unbutton his cuffs.

"This has always been my favorite spot for sea bathing," he went on, lifting his hands to undo the three buttons of his shirtfront. "Don't you remember?"

She hadn't remembered, not until this very moment, probably because ever since his return home, her brains had ceased to function properly. But as he crossed his arms and grasped the hem of his shirt, she somehow managed to find the wits to speak.

"Stop!" she gasped, appalled. "You can't bathe here. Not right now. I'm painting the sunrise."

"So?" He pulled the shirt up over his head and tossed it aside. "I won't stop you."

Beatrix wanted to reply, but anything she might have said was lost at the sight of his bare chest. She knew she should not stare, but she simply did not have the ability to tear her gaze away. As a young girl, she'd caught glimpses of him without his shirt, of course. When he and Paul were boys, they'd often gone sea bathing without their shirts, but they'd been forced to abandon the practice of swimming bare-chested even before she and the other girls had exchanged their pinafores for long skirts. It had been somewhere between fifteen and twenty years since she'd last seen Will without his shirt. She swallowed hard. His body was very different now.

His shoulders and chest were wide, tanned by the hot Egyptian sun and shaped by years of hard excavation work into a bronze wall of muscle and sinew. His chest tapered downward to an absolutely flat stomach, and his trousers were slung low on his lean hips, revealing the deep indent of his navel and the shadowy hint of dark hair below it. Her gaze dropped another notch, she gave a choked sound and hastily forced her gaze back up, but she only managed to get as far as the flat brown disks of his nipples. She could feel her face growing hot.

"You can't—" She stopped, her protest caught in her dry throat, her gaze riveted to his chest, the heat in her face spreading through her entire body. "We're alone."

"Alone? Trix, how can you say that? What about the pixies?" He bent to retrieve his shirt, flipped back the cuff, and pulled a small metal object from a fold in the fabric. "I even remembered to bring a pin."

He held up the shiny sliver of metal, a gift for the pixies to ensure he wouldn't be pixy-led. The myth of leaving pins or other small gifts for the pixies to prevent being bewitched by them was as much a part of their childhood at the cove as sea bathing and eating ice cream and sneaking out at night, but Beatrix had forgotten to bring a pin this morning, and she wondered if perhaps she was being pixy-led in consequence, for her heart was pounding in her breast with a force that hurt, and her wits were utterly gone.

He moved to weave the pin back into the fabric of his cuff, and as he did, Beatrix took a deep breath, got hold of her common sense, and reminded herself that she didn't believe in childish magic anymore, or the myth of one true love that lasted forever, and her inability to think at this moment had nothing to do with pixies, and everything to do with the scandalous fact that the man in front of her was half naked. "The pixies don't count!"

He gave her a look of mock pity. "Say that at your peril. It would be a shame if they turned that adorable nose of yours into a sausage for saying things like that."

She gave a vexed sigh, unappeased by compliments or nonsense talk. "I mean that the pixies—if they really existed at all, which they *don't*—are not chaperones! You can't bathe here while I'm here."

"No?" A glint of mischief flashed in his brilliant green eyes, and he gave her that pirate smile as he tossed the shirt aside. "Just watch me."

"But it's not proper!" she cried, turning as he walked past her and strode toward the water.

"Sod proper. A dare's a dare." His steps didn't falter for even a second, and she scowled at his magnificent bronzed back as he strode into the water. He walked out until the water hit him mid-chest, then he stretched his arms out, bent his head between them, and dove under, vanishing from view.

She didn't wait for him to reappear before she began packing up her supplies. This was a completely improper situation, and she had no intention of being here when he came back to shore. By the time his head broke the surface of the water, she had placed her pastels back into her art box and closed the lid. As he began swimming away from her toward the sea, she jumped up, slung her art box over her shoulder, and with her partially completed picture in her hand, she started toward the ladder. Her goal was to be gone before he could perceive her departure, but she had barely reached the ladder before his voice called to her.

"You're running away again."

She stopped and glanced over her shoulder to find him standing on one of the big rocks off shore, watching her. His wet breeches clung to his hips and thighs like a second skin, and he stood so still that his hard, chiseled body might have been part of the rock itself, a carving of a sea god by some unknown ancient sculptor. Though she was too far away to look into his eyes or read his expression, she knew he was looking at her the same way he had yesterday on the boat. His desire seemed to pull at her with all the power of an undertow, threatening to take her down to drown.

With a shuddering gasp, she turned her back on him and went up the ladder as fast as she could. He was right, of course. She was running away from him, but this time, she didn't intend to stop. Even after six years, he could still start her heart hammering and send her wits to oblivion at the slightest provocation. Even now, she felt the pull of his desire, but he wasn't the man she was going to marry, and running away from him was the only thing she could do.

It took thirty-eight full laps across Phoebe's Cove for Will to cool the lust raging through his body, the same lust that had started yesterday on the boat, tortured him all through dinner, kept him up all night, and spurred him in desperation to take a morning dip, only to run squarely into the entire reason for his torment. He'd chosen this spot because it was his favorite place at Pixy Cove. Damn him for not remembering it was hers, too.

He'd seen her before descending the ladder, of course, but he'd come down anyway, drawn to her like a moth to a flame, unable to resist the chance to be near her when no one else could see what he felt.

He'd been abominably rude, he knew, dressing down right in front of her and scorning her perfectly valid concerns about chaperones, but damn it all, he'd wanted her to feel something of what he felt. He wanted her to burn as he burned, ache as he ached.

He'd succeeded, too, at least a little, for she'd gone pink as a peony and stared at him as if she'd never seen a man's bare chest in her life before.

Which was probably true, he reflected as he somersaulted in the water, flipped his body over with a hard kick, and started swimming back across the cove. He knew he'd never bared his chest in front of Trix—not since he was a boy, anyway—and he certainly couldn't imagine Trathen doing so. And Trix had been so sheltered all her life—hell, she hadn't even been allowed to go to Italy because of her father's obsessive fear that she'd be so corrupted by the atmosphere of artists and the statues of naked men, she'd never come home again. Fear that she'd turn out to be like her mother.

After two more laps across the cove, Will felt that he was once again in control of his body and his emotions, enough so that at least he could sit down to breakfast at the same table with her and not feel as if he emanated desire like a house on fire. He emerged from the water, toweled off, and slipped on his shirt. Damp towel slung round his shoulders, he started for the ladder.

He was halfway up before he remembered the pin. He paused, considering, then descended the ladder again and crossed the sand to one of the caves that ringed the cove.

Stepping inside, he blinked several times, waiting until his eyes had adjusted to the dimness, then he glanced around, trying to remember just where Marlowe kept the jar for this particular cove. It had to be here—there was at least one jar for the pixies in every cove along Marlowe's property.

He searched for several minutes, and he began to think his memory was at fault and he was in the wrong cave, but then he spied it perched on the rocks piled to one side, above the high water mark. He climbed up on the rocks and pulled the pin from his sleeve, then took the glass jar down from its perch and dropped the pin inside. It was a glint of shiny silver atop a pile of corroded brass buttons, bits of colored glass, and rusty pins—tokens that he and Trix and dozens of other children had left for the pixies over the years to gain their goodwill. Smiling a little, he put the jar back where he'd found it and left the cave.

He didn't believe in pixies anymore, of course, but it was a tradition. Besides, to get through the remainder of the month without going insane, he would need all the help he could get.

During the next few days, Beatrix took great pains to avoid Will, hoping to put that awful sunrise encounter out of her mind, but it wasn't easy. She went for long, quiet walks with Aidan, or rode in the motorcar with Julia to do a bit of shopping in Torquay. Or she spent time with Emma, talking about the other woman's three children—Ethan, Robert, and little Ruthie—and dreaming of the days ahead when she'd have children of her own. All these were successful distractions that enabled her to avoid Will.

In the evenings, however, avoiding him was much

more difficult. Thankfully, her place at dinner was near the other end of the long dining table, but afterward, when the children were in bed and everyone else was gathered together in the drawing room, there was no escape. On the third evening of the house party, when Lord Weston suggested auction bridge, that newfangled version of whist, she was happy to participate. Auction bridge was a complicated enough game to occupy her mind and keep her from thinking about the man across the room and how he looked without his shirt.

Cutting for partners, she found herself paired with Aidan against Lord and Lady Weston. Cards were dealt, and play began, but she managed to hold out for only a few rounds before her gaze inevitably strayed across the room to where Will sat with Julia at the piano. They were playing duets, and Lord Marlowe's sister Phoebe stood by his shoulder, turning the pages for them.

Like all the men in the room, he was wearing a black evening suit, but the image of him a few mornings ago was still vivid in her mind. Nothing untoward had happened, she kept reminding herself, but every time she looked at Will, the image of his smooth, bronzed skin and sculpted muscles came into her mind, and every time it did, she felt a searing flood of heat and a wretched pang of guilt.

It had been wrong of her, very wrong, to stand by as a man undressed in front of her, and every time she thought of it, Beatrix berated herself for having allowed it to happen. The moment she perceived his presence, she should have gathered her things and departed. The fact that she had not done so, that she had not turned her back on him and walked away immediately, was something she could not excuse.

Not that she blamed only herself. Will was even more at fault for subjecting a lady to such an unthinkable display. It had been deliberate, she knew, and provocative, meant to unsettle her in just this way, but knowing that didn't help Beatrix ease her own conscience.

"Beatrix?"

"Hmm?" She returned her attention to the table and realized Aidan had said something to her. "I beg your pardon?"

"It's your bid."

"Right. Sorry." She rubbed her fingers across her forehead with a laugh as she invented an excuse for her absentmindedness. "I'm accustomed to whist. This auction bridge is still a bit new to me. Umm . . . three hearts."

The bidding moved on to Lord Weston on her left, then to Aidan, then to Lucy, Lady Weston, on her right. It went around one more time, trump was decided, and play commenced. Beatrix tried to concentrate on the game, but despite her hopes, her attention began to wander again after only a few minutes of play, and it was all she could do to keep it away from the man across the room.

On a pair of settees nearby, her aunt was seated with Lady Debenham; Marlowe's mother, Louisa; and his grandmother, Antonia. They were gossiping, no doubt. Standing near them was Marlowe's other sister, Vivian, fitting one of her newly designed gowns for *Vivienne* onto a form. Emma, Lady Marlowe, was sitting near her, mending something pink and lacy. Probably one of little Ruthie's dresses.

As if in tandem with Beatrix's own thoughts, Vivian spoke up. "I can't believe how big Ruthie's grown," she said, nodding to the garment in Emma's hands. "And starting to walk now? When Beatrix and I saw her take those steps earlier today, we couldn't believe it. Could we, Trix?" she added, glancing over her shoulder at the card table.

"No," she agreed. "It was beautiful to see, though." She smiled, remembering the scene she and Vivian had witnessed that afternoon—Emma in the grass with her arms outstretched and her hands clasping Ruthie's fingers as the baby had wobbled forward on chubby legs for three full steps before falling down on her bum in the grass. She felt a wave of longing at the memory, longing for the day when she'd be kneeling in the grass, encouraging her own son or daughter to take those first steps. Children were something she'd dreamed of as far back as she could remember, as far back as when she'd still played with dolls in the nursery and believed Will Mallory would marry her someday. Her smile faded. Like pixies, it had never been real.

"Ruthie is looking quite bonny, Emma, by the way," Julia commented from her place at the piano. "She's got that gorgeous chestnut hair of yours, I've noticed. And Harry's blue eyes. She'll be a beauty, mark my words. Her papa had best keep a close watch on her."

Marlowe, who was playing auction bridge with Geoff, Paul, and Sir George at a nearby table, looked up from his cards long enough to comment. "I intend to. She isn't leaving the house once she turns thirteen."

"Harry!" Emma admonished, laughing.

"What do you intend to do, Marlowe?" Julia asked, her fingers tapping piano keys in an aimless tune. "Lock her in the attic to keep her from all the dishonorable young men?"

"Absolutely," Marlowe answered with fervor and returned his attention to his cards.

Beatrix glanced at Will, and as she studied his strong, wide shoulders above the piano, she thought perhaps Marlowe had the right idea. Could she lock herself in an attic until Will went back to Egypt?

He was studying the pages of sheet music with Julia, discussing what they were to play next, but he suddenly looked up and caught her watching him.

He smiled his pirate smile, and it hit her like a shaft through the heart. She inhaled sharply and looked away.

Across the table, Aidan was shuffling in preparation for the next deal, but his attention was not on his task. Instead, his face was turned toward the pair at the piano. In contrast to the busy movement of his hands, his handsome profile was impassive, revealing nothing, but as if he felt her gaze alight on him, he turned his attention to her, and suddenly she felt as if she had a big scarlet A emblazoned on her chest.

When he began to deal the cards, she breathed a sigh of relief, and she willed herself to keep every scrap of concentration on the game. She did not look across the room again during the entire round, but she still found it almost impossible to keep track of the cards being played, a crucial component of bridge, and because of that, Weston and his wife won the round.

"And that's it," Weston said, as his wife pulled in the final trick. "Game and rubber. Excellent play, Lucy," he complimented as Aidan began to tally the scores.

"Oh, let's play this one next," Julia exclaimed, her lively voice ringing through the room. " 'The Maple Leaf Rag.' "

Beatrix watched Aidan lift his gaze heavenward as if praying for patience. It was plain he didn't care for the music Julia was choosing, but he did not say so, of course, or ask her to make a different choice. That would have been rude, and Aidan was never rude.

" . . . and two, and three, and four," Will was counting, and then he and Julia began to play, but they had completed only about four bars before Julia burst out laughing.

"Wait, Will, wait," she cried. "You're going too fast! I can't keep up."

Wait, Will. I want to go, too.

Over the frenetic sound of the piano and the eddying conversations all around her, Beatrix's own voice echoed to her from many years ago, stirring a vague memory of herself as a little girl, sitting on a stone wall and watching the lane at Danbury, waiting for Will to return from a horseback ride with Paul.

Waiting for Will, the story of her life.

Beatrix glanced sideways at the laughing pair across the room, watching them play the already lively tune at an even more frantic pace. They managed several more bars before they muffed it utterly, the song ended in a jangle of discordant notes, and they fell back against the wall behind them at the same time, laughing together.

It hurt, somehow, watching them, but she couldn't look away.

"Oh heavens!" Julia exhaled a heavy sigh, resting her cheek on Will's shoulder. "Next time we play that tune, I'm bringing out the metronome to keep you in line."

"Stuff," Will told her. "Metronomes are for sissies."

Julia lifted her head, shaking back wisps of her black hair. "Still, can we give my fingers a rest and play the next song at a slower pace?"

"Hear, hear," Aidan muttered, and then, as Beatrix looked at him, he once again turned his attention away from the couple at the piano and looked down at the card table, his mouth tightening as if he felt ashamed of himself for making such a comment.

"Why don't you sing something, Julia?" Phoebe suggested from her place near Will's shoulder. "You have a lovely voice."

"Mmm, do," Vivian added around a mouthful of pins. She pulled them out to add, "It's so much fun hearing all the modern songs."

"All right, what about this one?" Without the aid

of sheet music, Julia began to play another ragtime melody. When she began to sing in a deep, bawdy alto about someone named Bill Bailey who wouldn't come home, Aidan stood up and turned to Beatrix, a hint of desperation on his face. "Would you care to take a stroll on the terrace, Beatrix?" he asked her. "It's a lovely night."

She froze, staring up at him, the guilt that had been gnawing at her giving way to dismay. She couldn't do it. She simply couldn't take a stroll along the terrace with Aidan as if nothing was wrong while those damnable images of Will's bare chest went through her mind.

"No," she answered with a glance at the clock on the wall. "I think I shall go to bed. It's quarter past twelve, and besides, I—" She broke off, not wanting to admit she hadn't been able to sleep the past few nights. "I have a bit of a headache," she improvised.

He nodded, but she could feel him studying her face, and such careful scrutiny made her feel even worse. "If you have a headache," he said, "rest is perhaps the best treatment."

"Yes." She forced herself to smile. "I'm sure I shall be right as rain tomorrow."

She rose, bidding a quick good night to everyone, but when she started out of the drawing room, Aidan followed her. "I shall walk with you to the stairs," he said, falling in step beside her along the corridor. "I intend to take a stroll in the front gardens," he added, as if feeling the need to explain.

At the foot of the stairs, they paused. Neither of

them spoke, and the silence between them, instead of being the companionable sort of silence she was used to with Aidan, seemed painfully awkward.

"Beatrix—" he began, but she cut him off, fearful of what he might say, the questions he might ask.

"It is such a lovely, fine night," she said. "I regret that I'm not up to taking that stroll with you. Another night, perhaps—"

"Beatrix." His voice was firm, and as he took her hands in his, her dismay deepened into a sick dread. "We have been engaged for nearly nine months now, but I have only kissed you once."

She blinked in surprise. Of all the things she might have expected him to say, that wasn't one of them. "True," she murmured, wondering why he was choosing this moment to bring up that particular point.

"I have held back from physical displays of affection because that is the gentlemanly thing to do. But perhaps—" He stopped and drew a deep breath, glancing down the corridor toward the drawing room, then back at her. "Perhaps I have made a mistake there."

Oh God, she thought, growing desperate. *Aidan was going to kiss her.* Her guilt deepened into dread.

He released her hands suddenly and cupped her face. "It's a mistake I should like to remedy." Before she could even fashion a reply, he bent his head and pressed his lips to hers.

She waited for something to happen, hoped in desperation for passion to stir, but though the contact of his lips against hers brought warmth, it was the same sort of feeling she might gain from a hot water bottle at her feet or a nice cup of tea in her hands, agreeable and comfortable, but not precisely earth-shattering.

She opened her eyes. Aidan's eyes were closed, and she stared at his brown lashes fanned across his cheekbones with the same objectivity with which she might have studied . . . well . . . blades of grass. They were nice lashes, she thought, straight but thick and dark brown, very attractive.

But surely, she thought in bewilderment, surely the previous time he'd kissed her, the night she'd accepted his proposal of marriage, she hadn't been staring at his *lashes*, had she? That kiss couldn't have been like this one, could it? Warm and pleasant and nothing more? There must have been some spark of feeling in it. There must have been.

When his lips moved to part hers, deepening the kiss, she allowed it. When his arms came up around her to pull her closer, she strove to remember the night nine months ago when she had accepted his proposal and the kiss they had shared.

She got as far as remembering that it had been nothing like Will's kiss before Aidan pulled back, and as she watched his eyes begin to open, she hastily closed hers. She waited until she felt his arms slide away, and then she opened her eyes. His face, so gravely handsome, looked much as always, so steady and sensible, and yet she could sense desire in him. Physical desire.

She'd seen that same look in Will's eyes earlier, but

it wasn't really the same. It didn't make her feel the same way.

Beatrix wanted to sink through the floor. She wanted to grab him and kiss him again and will herself to feel something. She wanted to bolt, call the whole thing off, lock herself in an attic, join a convent.

In the end, she did nothing. When he said, "Good night, Beatrix," she smiled, though it was more as a reflex than an expression of actual feeling, because inside all she felt was sheer, overwhelming panic, and that was nothing to smile about.

It wasn't the kiss that was different. *She* was different. She'd felt something that night he'd proposed, she knew that. But was it the stirrings of passion she'd felt? Or simply hope that she finally had a second chance at love? Whatever it was, that feeling had now faded into the background because of the return of her first love. And her wedding was only two months away.

Beatrix turned before Aidan's perceptive eyes could detect the awful sense of dismay and guilt that must surely be written on her face. She went upstairs, walking slowly until she had turned on the landing and vanished from his view before running full bore to her room.

Safely inside, she closed the door and fell back against it with a gasp of relief. When her maid came out of the dressing room, she saw a frown of concern cross the girl's face, and she could only conclude that Lily could see what Aidan had not.

"Is everything all right, miss?"

She straightened away from the door. "Yes, Lily, thank you. I just have a bit of a headache. I'd like to go to bed."

As her maid brushed out her hair and assisted her out of her evening gown and into her nightclothes, she worked to push aside her panic and think. It was ridiculous, she told herself, that she could have changed during the past nine months. Even more ridiculous to think Will was responsible. How? By taking his shirt off? It was absurd.

Wasn't it?

By the time she had dismissed Lily and slid beneath the sheets of her bed, her panic had thankfully subsided, but in its place was something else, something deeper and much harder to extinguish: uncertainty.

She tried to tell herself this was all Will's fault, that if he hadn't come back, Aidan's kiss would have stirred her deeper feelings tonight. After all, her affection for her fiancé had deepened with the passage of time, and a deeper, more ardent passion would surely follow. But was that true, or was it just wishful thinking?

Beatrix groaned and turned onto her side. Though she closed her eyes, she could not silence the doubts whispering to her, and she hated Will for it, hated him for coming home and stirring up the ashes of a burned-out love. Yet she knew she really had no right to hate him. She was the mistress of her own feelings. She was responsible for them, and for their consequences.

She had loved Will for so long and with such desperation, but nowadays, whenever she thought of those lonely years without him, years of clinging to the futile hope that he would change his mind and come home, she felt only relief that those days were over. She'd given up any stupid, girlish ideas that Will loved her too much to live without her, that he would become a responsible, steady partner in life, someone she could count on. She'd finally accepted reality, and now she felt like kicking herself in the head for allowing one stupid glimpse of him without his shirt to send her somersaulting back to a time when she'd been a complete fool.

It wasn't even as if her engagement had made Will realize he'd made a terrible mistake all those years ago. He hadn't come home to win her back. Nothing of the kind. According to what Paul had told her, Will hadn't come home because of her at all, but for business that involved that damned excavation of his. And even if he had come for her, it wouldn't matter. It was too late, they'd gone their separate ways ages ago, and Will had nothing to offer her. Nothing but the sweet, piercing, momentary joy of a smile and the burning ache of desire. It wasn't enough. It never had been, and it never would be.

Desire did not endure. Fondness, affection, a shared vision of the future, friendship—those were the things that sustained a marriage through decades. Passions were fleeting, and in the end, meaningless.

Beatrix knew that from experience. Her own mother had been carried away by passion, and when the passion died, her lover had abandoned her, and she'd ended up alone, disgraced, and miserable.

She thought of the couples she knew who seemed happy together—Lord and Lady Marlowe, for example, and Lord and Lady Weston—couples who were not only marriage partners, but also contented companions. They might have passion—Beatrix wouldn't know, for no one expressed such sentiments publicly—but she did know they had affection and friendship and a mutually agreeable vision of their lives and their future together.

Beatrix knew all this. She'd been over these things again and again. She'd agonized over them during many other sleepless nights. When Aidan had proposed, she'd spent three days considering the ramifications before she had accepted him. After years of letting her heart lead, she had finally listened to her head. And the kiss they'd shared upon her acceptance of his proposal, a kiss that had been vastly different from the ones shared with Will so long ago, had not changed her mind. She had gone on with her life, made her decision. It was pointless to agonize over it now.

She had no intention of backing out. There was no reason to, and besides, she could never hurt Aidan in such a way. In the twelve months she'd known him, he had become very dear to her, as dear as any member of her family, and she knew, better than most, how heartbreak felt. She'd cut off her right arm before she'd abandon Aidan as Will had abandoned her.

She closed her eyes, but the moment she did, an image of Will came into her mind, an image of smooth, bronzed skin and hard, lean muscles and green eyes filled with hunger. With an aggravated sigh, she opened her eyes again and turned onto her back to scowl at the ceiling.

She refused to let one stupid—not to mention indecent—incident rob her of her common sense. And even if Will removing his shirt had caused her brains to inexplicably take a holiday, once he departed for Egypt, then what? She would be herself again, not this muddled mess of a woman who didn't know her own heart and mind.

Beatrix took a deep breath, striving to be logical about all this. What she was experiencing right now was nothing more than a case of cold feet. She was less than two months from her wedding day. Surely all brides experienced a moment of doubt, a moment when there was a vague sense of dissatisfaction, as if . . . as if she knew somehow that she was settling for less, when something more, something beautiful and wondrous and incredible, might be down the road, and if only she were to wait just a little bit longer. . .

This was ridiculous. Hadn't she waited long enough, in heaven's name? And how could she think for a moment that by marrying Aidan she was settling for less? Aidan was a duke and a man of considerable wealth, power, and consequence. He was good-looking, intelligent, honorable, and considerate. What more could any woman want?

Listing all Aidan's fine qualities had the strange result of making her even more miserable. She huddled into a little ball, plagued by doubts she thought she'd conquered ages ago, and she felt an absurd desire to weep.

Chapter Eight

If Will had hoped for the aid of the pixies—or any other magical forces, for that matter—to get him through the coming weeks, it seemed he was destined to be disappointed. The evening he'd just endured wasn't any easier than the previous ones had been.

Night after night of pretending to be debonair, carefree, and perfectly at ease in the same room with his old love and her new one took quite a toll, but it wouldn't do for him to be dog in the manger about things. Julia had played up beautifully, putting on the same act as he for her own impish reasons, but even with her assistance, the evenings seemed endless.

Tonight had been the worst, the tension nearly unbearable. When the clock struck one and the party broke up, Will was filled with profound relief, but as people began making their way to bed, he found himself reluctant to do the same. Though he'd been up since dawn, he was still too much on edge, too stirred up for sleep.

He caught up with Julia on her way to the stairs, finagled a cigarette and a match, and stepped outside. The lamps in the drawing room and study were still lit, making the limestone floor of the terrace seem to radiate with an incandescent, golden glow.

He walked to the very edge of the terrace, where a rail of carved marble prevented anyone from tumbling to the rocks far below. He lit the cigarette, propped his elbows on the rail, and stared out to the sea. In the moon-lit distance, the water's surface seemed calm as a millpond tonight, but down below, he could hear the waves crashing against the rocks. Behind him, voices bidding each other good night echoed through the open doors and windows.

"Ah, Sunderland, not gone to bed yet, I see."

Will straightened and looked over his shoulder to find Marlowe in the doorway leading from the study. "No, sir," he answered, turning as the other man began crossing the terrace toward him.

"You don't have to call me sir anymore, Will," he reminded with a smile. "You're no longer a boy. Besides, you outrank me."

Will smiled back. "I always did," he reminded, "but old habits die hard. Too many visits to Pixy Cove under your watchful eye, I suppose."

"You mean Antonia's watchful eye." The viscount halted beside him at the stone railing.

"Your grandmother is a formidable woman. I may

be a duke, but whenever she looks at me through her lorgnette, I always feel like a misbehaving lad of ten all over again." He held up his cigarette. "I don't have another," he said, "but I'd be happy to share."

Marlowe shook his head. "Thank you, no. Emma hates the smell of tobacco, so I gave it up long ago."

"That's probably wise. I smoke occasionally, but I strive not to make it a habit. All the workmen on the excavation site smoke like chimneystacks, and I've observed that the ones who smoke the most also cough and wheeze the most. Adversely affects the lungs, I expect."

"Tell me about these excavations of yours. You're searching for some ancient king's tomb, I believe?"

That was the opening Will needed. He talked about Tut, the work they were doing, the discoveries they were making, and the indications that he believed showed they were now digging in the right place.

By the time he'd finished, Marlowe was smiling. "Your enthusiasm is infectious, Will. I find myself wanting to take Emma on a *dahabiyeh* up the Nile. Just to see the Valley of the Kings and let you show me what you're up to." He leaned one hip against the rail and folded his arms. "Danbury tells me you need a sponsor."

"Yes. I have been sponsor for the past few years, but—" He stopped, well aware that confessing that he was broke because of the excavation wasn't an intelligent way to raise funds. Marlowe, however, was astute enough to have figured that out on his own.

"But you've run out of money?" the viscount finished for him.

Will took a pull on his cigarette, and he didn't know which burned more, the smoke in his lungs or Marlowe's words. Still, no hiding it, he supposed. He exhaled and gave a curt nod of affirmation. "We plan to resume excavations in the autumn, as usual, but if I can't find a sponsor, I won't be able to return home. I shall have to remain here until funding is found."

"You regard Egypt, not England, as your home then?"

"Why not?" Will said lightly, but he looked out over the view so the other man wouldn't see his face. "God knows, there's nothing for me here."

"Nothing?"

An image of Beatrix and Trathen strolling arm in arm out of the drawing room went through his mind. "Nothing worth staying for," he said, and took another pull on his cigarette, still staring out at the moonlit ocean. "I don't suppose there ever was."

"I see." Marlowe straightened away from the rail. "I'll be honest with you, Will. Despite your infectious enthusiasm, I'm no Egyptologist myself, and though I might enjoy a cruise up the Nile, I've never been particularly keen on archaeology."

Will's spirits, already low, sank still further, and he began preparing himself for the inevitable refusal.

"However, I am in the business of selling newspapers," the viscount went on, "and my readers are passionately interested in the science of Egyptology. Petrie's writings on the subject have been extremely popular. And if you were to find Tutankhamen's tomb and if it were as spectacular a find as you believe it will be, the news would spread across the globe like wildfire. In light of that possibility, I might be able to sponsor your excavations. Given certain conditions, of course."

Will's spirits began rising once more. "What conditions?"

"I can envision the *Social Gazette* or one of my other newspapers acting as your sponsor, but in exchange, I'd want the exclusive right to publish firsthand accounts of your excavations and photographs of artifacts you find."

"I would have to discuss that with Howard Carter. He's the chief inspector of Egyptian Antiquities now, and it's up to him to grant such requests."

"If you find Tutankhamen, newspapers from all over the world will be clamoring for the story. I would want to be first. I'd want my own reporter and photographer on site with you from the moment you start digging, not locked away in some hotel, waiting for scraps of information. I'd also want exclusive rights to publish any books you might write about your discovery."

Relief flooded through him. "Marlowe, if you sponsor the dig, I'd be happy to write twenty books about Tut for you. When we return to Torquay, I'll cable Carter straightaway, and if he agrees, we have a deal. I can't imagine he would refuse, given that we can't continue without funds. Once he agrees, I'll sit down with you and we'll hammer out the specifics."

"Excellent. I have one other request."

"What's that?"

"It's a tradition for all of us to come to Pixy Cove in August, and since you are in England for the month, I would not have denied you the right to come as always, even if a possible business opportunity weren't in the offing."

"I appreciate that."

"I feel the same way about Beatrix and Julia, too. My sisters are their best friends. I realize Trathen's presence makes things a bit awkward, and I appreciate the fact that you are staying away from him and Beatrix as much as possible, but see if you can persuade Julia to stop antagonizing the man, would you? It's bad enough that that bulldog of hers growls at every man in sight, but she also seems to take great delight in needling Trathen with that audacious manner of hers. Help me keep the peace, will you, old chap, and get her to stop?"

Will, Julia's coconspirator, tried to keep a straight face. "I'll see what I can do."

Beatrix spent another restless night, but she finally fell asleep, and when she woke the following morning, she found her mood had lightened considerably. The light peeking between the draperies at her windows hinted at a perfect summer's day, and when she drew the draperies back, bright sunlight poured into every corner of the room. It seemed a good omen.

She flung up the window sash and leaned out, smiling at the view of Pixy Cove and the ocean beyond. The caps on the water's surface were like glittering diamonds, and there wasn't a cloud in sight. In the far distance she could see the *Maria Lisa* surging out to sea, its white sails rippling in the breeze, and she knew what Sir George and Lady Debenham were up to this morning. She couldn't tell who else was on board, but she suspected Will was with them, and that conclusion added relief to her lightened mood.

As she looked out on the beautiful view, breathed in the luscious ocean air, and savored the warmth of the sun on her face, Beatrix felt certain everything in her world had shifted back into place. She realized now there was no foundation for her bout of guilt, and the dark doubts that had troubled her last night seemed terribly melodramatic.

"Beatrix!"

She looked down to find Julia standing on the terrace below, with a coffee in one hand and a cigarette in the other, Spike at her feet.

"Morning, Julie!" she called back with a wave.

"Barely," her cousin replied, laughing.

"What do you mean?"

"It's not morning for much longer, darling. It's nearly eleven."

"As late as that? Heavens, I quite overslept, didn't I? I'll come down straightaway."

"No need to hurry. Most everyone's gone with Sir George and Lady D. on the boat. They're sailing up to Teignmouth, having luncheon at the Red Bull, and then sailing back down. I thought I'd race up in the

Mercedes, and join them for luncheon. Want to come along?"

She hesitated, not really in a frame of mind to see Will today. "Where's Aidan this morning?"

"Heavens, I don't know. What am I, his nanny?" At Beatrix's reproving look, she sighed and made a face. "He's on the gazebo with Paul. They're playing chess. Can you believe it? Chess, on such a glorious day?"

"That's not really all that surprising, is it? They both have a passion for the game, and they are both very good."

"Too good. They'll be at it all day, I expect. Perhaps even all week, and they'll be forced to declare a draw. Come with me to Teignmouth, do. We'll find some pretty little cove on the way back and have a bathe, all by ourselves. It will be quite like days in Cornwall last summer, remember? Such fun we had." Suddenly her pixy face twisted and she looked away. "God, that seems like a lifetime ago," she murmured as if to herself, and took a pull on her cigarette.

Beatrix frowned, concerned by the sudden hint of melancholy in her cousin's voice. She was a little worried about Julia, who seemed a bit thinner, a bit wilder, and a bit more unhappy each time they met. "D'you know," she said after a moment, "I believe I will come with you to Teignmouth."

"Darling Trix! I'll see to the car. Have a spot of breakfast and join me in the drive. And don't forget your bathing dress," she added as Beatrix pulled back from the window.

"I won't," she called back, and gave a tug to the bellpull, summoning Lily to help her dress. Twenty minutes later, in a blue skirt and striped shirtwaist, with a white straw boater on her head, her putty-colored motoring coat thrown over one arm, and a canvas bathing bag in her other hand, she went downstairs. She handed over her motoring coat to the footman, along with the bag, which contained her goggles and scarf, her sketchbook and pencils, a towel, and her bathing attire. She instructed him to take her things out to the Mercedes, and she went into the morning room.

Breakfast at Pixy Cove was always an informal meal. From eight o'clock until eleven, dishes of eggs, bacon, and kidneys were kept warm on the long mahogany sideboard in the morning room, and replenished as necessary, enabling guests to partake of their morning meal whenever they chose, but because she had slept so late, Beatrix found the kitchen maids clearing away the dishes as she entered the morning room. They offered to bring her a fresh, hot breakfast, but she knew she didn't have time and settled for toast with jam and a quick cup of tea, then she went out to the gazebo to let Aidan know of her plans for the day. To her surprise, she found that although her fiancé was seated at the tea table with the chess game spread out before him, Paul was nowhere in sight. Absorbed in studying the board, Aidan did not notice her approach until she came up the steps.

When he saw her, he smiled. "Good morning.

We began to think you intended to sleep the day away."

For some reason, that smile seemed more open than usual, not in keeping with Aidan's usual reserve. It made her strangely uncomfortable. "Where's Paul?" she asked, feeling in need of something to say.

"Having a stretch and, I expect, thinking out his next move. I rather have him pinned at the moment."

"You do?"

The question caused Aidan to raise an eyebrow. "You needn't sound so surprised, my darling," he said, an almost teasing gleam in his hazel eyes that caught her by surprise. Aidan didn't tease. It wasn't like him. An image of the look in his eyes after their kiss last night came into her mind, and instead of fading away, that little ripple of uneasiness inside her grew stronger. She pushed it aside, reminding herself again that any doubts at this point were just cold feet, trying to hang on to her lightened mood.

"Sorry," she said, "but you and Paul usually need an entire day, at least, for one of your chess games."

"Your cousin is only pinned, not checkmated. He has several means of escape." He took up her hand and pressed a kiss to her gloved fingers. "Why? Did you wish to commandeer me for some other plan today?"

She restrained a silly impulse to pull her hand from his. "Actually, when Julie told me you were playing chess with Paul today, I decided to go to Teignmouth with her in the Mercedes."

He made a face. "Must you?"

"Why do you care?" she asked lightly. "You'll be here all day, hovering over that chessboard."

"I care because I care for you, and Baroness Yardley operates a motorcar with no regard for either decorum or safety."

"That's not true! She's an excellent automobilist."

"Excellent?" He looked skeptical. "She drives as if the devil is after her, and she encourages you to do the same. I realize she is your family, Beatrix, but that woman is a bad influence on you in every way."

Beatrix felt her good mood evaporating. "Bad influence? You talk as if I've no mind of my own."

"Remember Carnarvon's crash two years ago in Germany?" Aidan asked, ignoring her comment, his mind obviously on a different track. "He nearly died because of the reckless speeds at which he drove. Thirty, forty miles an hour. The baroness drives the same way, and on these rutted roads." His voice, much to Beatrix's surprise, was becoming rather testy. "I fear for you every moment you are in an automobile with her. Promise me you will keep her to a more sedate rate of speed?"

She felt a sudden flash of rebellion, and the knowledge that Aidan was only speaking out of concern for her safety did not quite quell it. Still, she did not want to ruin what looked to be a lovely day. "Darling, let's not quarrel."

"Promise me, Beatrix."

She sighed, shifting her weight from one foot to the other. "All right, all right, I promise not to let her drive too fast." Before he could say anything more about Julia or motorcars, or anything else that might mar her good mood, she squeezed his hands and pulled away. "We'll be having a bathe this afternoon at one of the coves along the way back. So expect our return about teatime."

"Don't go too far out when you swim," he cautioned as she turned and went down the steps. "There's some strong undertows past the shallows, you know."

For heaven's sake, you sound like my father. Stop smothering me.

The irritable reply hovered on the tip of her tongue, but she didn't say it. Instead, she merely waved a hand in acknowledgment as she walked away.

The Mercedes was in the drive, its engine on. Julia was at the wheel when she came around the side of the house, and Spike was sitting behind the seats. Beatrix walked to the left side of the vehicle where her goggles and scarf were waiting for her on the passenger seat and her motoring coat was slung over the back. She had to take off her hat to don her goggles, but once those were securely in place and her boater once again secured by her hatpin, she wrapped her chiffon motoring scarf around the hat and tied its ends beneath her chin, then she slipped into the long, lightweight poplin duster and buttoned it.

She stepped up onto the running board, then into the vehicle, giving Spike a pat on the head and settling herself on the seat beside her cousin. "Aidan made me promise I wouldn't let you drive too fast," she told Julia over the noise of the engine.

"Oh, he did, did he?" Julia released the brake lever and started forward. "Forty miles an hour it is."

"Julia!"

"Oh, all right. I shall try to be good today, but only for your sake."

They motored up to Teignmouth at a speed even Aidan might have approved, making it just past one o'clock when they joined the yachting party at the Red Bull Inn for luncheon. Will, however, was not among the party gathered in the main dining room of the inn.

"How now, where's Sunderland?" Julia asked, looking around the dining room. "In the tavern, perhaps?"

"Sunderland didn't come with us, Baroness," Sir George informed her as he pulled out a chair for her at the long dining table.

"He intended to," Marlowe added, doing the same for Beatrix, "for he wanted to send a cable to Thebes. But at the last minute, he decided to stay behind. Writing some paper for the Archaeological Society, he said. He asked me to send his telegram for him."

Beatrix couldn't help being relieved at that news, and she quite enjoyed their ploughman's lunch of pork pie, pickled vegetables, bread, and cheese, though she did have to remonstrate with Julia about drinking ale with the meal since she was driving the motorcar, and ale tended to hamper one's ability in that regard.

"I'm perfectly able to handle one glass of ale," Julia countered, sounding a bit irritated. "Don't fuss, Trix."

Beatrix let the matter drop, and though Julia did drink her glass of ale, she didn't order a second one. Beatrix was glad of it, for she was enjoying her day, and she didn't want to quarrel with Julia any more than she'd wanted to quarrel with Aidan.

They parted company with the yachting party around two o'clock and started back along the road toward Pixy Cove. It was a lovely drive, even though she had to remind Julia several times to slow down on the way back. When they were less than a mile from the house, Julia pulled the motorcar to the grassy spot on the side of the road that overlooked the cliffs, patches of beach, and inlets below. "Where should we swim?"

"Phoebe's Cove?" Beatrix suggested, pointing to a spot just ahead. "It's right down there."

"We always swim at Phoebe's Cove. What about Pelican Point?" Julia suggested, twisting in her seat to point behind her.

"Very well, but if we bathe at Pelican Point, we can't go out very far. The waves are strong there, and I promised Aidan—"

"That tears it!" Julia cried. She yanked back the brake lever and turned in the seat to face Beatrix. "What on earth is wrong with you?"

Beatrix stared at her cousin, stunned by this unexpected attack. "Wrong with me?"

"'Don't drive too fast, Julie,'" she mocked. "'Don't drink too much, Julie.' 'We can't swim out too far. I promised Aidan.'" She paused and pressed her lips together with a sound of derision, then she went on, "Honestly, you're starting to sound just like your father!"

Beatrix shook her head, taken aback, not only by her cousin's tirade, but also by the fact that Julia's words were similar to her own thoughts that morning and compelled her to argue the point. "You ask what's wrong with me, but this . . . this sudden, unprovoked attack upon me and my fiancé and my father, too, compels me to ask what's wrong with you!"

"Unprovoked? I think the past few days have given me plenty of provocation. I hadn't intended to come to Pixy Cove this year. Do you want to know why?" She didn't allow Beatrix time to hazard a guess. "Because Trathen was coming, that's why."

Beatrix was baffled. "But why should Aidan's presence bother you? You know him. You introduced me to him last year. Good grief," she cried, struck by a sudden thought. "You're not . . . jealous, are you?"

"God, no!" Julia stared back at her, appalled, clearly thinking she was off her onion for suggesting such a thing. "I hardly know the man. I've only seen him twice before in my life. And besides, I'm married, remember?"

"That doesn't seem to stop you from having affairs." Beatrix tried to say it without letting her disapproval of Julia's goings-on creep into her voice, but of course she didn't succeed.

"When you've been married a decade, you'll have earned the right to lecture others about their dismal marriages," Julia muttered. "Until then, I'd appreciate it if you'd keep mum on the topic."

"I know you're unhappy with Yardley—"

"Unhappy?" Julia gave a shout of laughter, but it was clear she wasn't amused. "Yes, you could say that."

"I'm sorry, Julia, that you're unhappy, but it's unfair to take out any anger you might feel about it on me. I've done nothing to deserve it."

"No? Then stop lecturing me about how I drive, what I drink, and where I swim! And stop being such a killjoy. Damn it, Trix, I didn't drag you off to Cornwall and teach you to drive a motorcar and do the can-can and blow smoke rings and swim in the nude so that you could become this dull matronly sort who disapproves of everything and everyone!"

"That's unfair!" Beatrix felt her own temper flaring. "The only thing I'm disapproving of is what you've become! Being saucy and provoking and playing music people hate—"

"You mean Aidan hates it!"

"Yes, that's precisely what I mean! You've been rude to him ever since you arrived, abominably rude."

"Why shouldn't I be rude? I feel him judging me every moment I've been here with a disapproving eye, and I don't like it!"

"How can you blame him for disapproving? Or me for worrying? Look at you. Dark circles under your eyes, thin as a rail, smoking too much, drinking too much. And let's not even talk about the shenanigans you've engaged in! Honestly, Julie! Doing the fandango at Maxim's? Auntie Eugenia nearly fainted when she heard about that. What were you thinking of, disgracing the family that way?"

"There you go again. God forbid I should disgrace the family. What's happened to you, Trix? Do I have to drag you off to Cornwall again to put some sense back in your head?"

"I don't know what you're talking about."

"I'm talking about *you*. It all started when Will went away to Egypt, and you didn't go with him. In fact, you never went anywhere. You never did anything. It was as if his leaving had sucked all the joy of life out of you. Your father approved of the change, I daresay, for it kept you right under his thumb where he could cosset you and protect you and keep you from leaving him. And you just let it happen . . . let your soul wither away, while you did good works and needlepoint like a dutiful daughter. You were a tragedy in the making."

Beatrix was unable to believe what she was hearing. "I was a tragedy? That's what you're saying?"

"You were becoming one. When your father died, I thought surely you would come out of the . . . the cocoon he'd spent most of your life wrapping you in, but no. When I arrived in Devonshire, I found you draped in black crepe, and everything worse than ever. You were like some sort of cross between Queen Victoria and a Catholic nun."

"My father had just died!"

"When you said you weren't going to Pixy Cove with the rest of us last year, I knew something had to be done. I kidnapped you, if you remember, in the Daimler and took you to Cornwall. I knew I was no replacement for Will and my little cottage at Gwithian isn't Pixy Cove, but I had to do something.

And we had a jolly time, too, didn't we? It was so merry, just like the old days here, and you started to be happy again. When you and I went to the St. Ives Ball and I introduced you to Trathen, I could see he admired you, and I saw that you liked him, and I thought you'd finally started to get on with life. I thought you'd begun to think of the future, not the past."

"So I was! And I am! I became engaged, didn't I? If that's not thinking of the future, I don't know what would be!"

"I was glad when you became engaged to Trathen. When you wrote to me at Biarritz last Christmas and told me the news, I was happy for you, for both of you. But then, in your next letter, you said you and Trathen were touring your estates for your honeymoon, and I couldn't believe it. You, who pores over Baedekers and longs to see Florence, going on an estate tour? How ghastly!"

Beatrix drew a deep breath and tried to get hold of her temper long enough to explain. "I wanted to go to Florence, but we can't. You see, Aidan is sitting in the House of Lords, and—"

"Not that his inclination to tootle around his own properties and call it a honeymoon surprises me," Julia went on as if Beatrix hadn't spoken. "After being in that man's company for the past three days, I don't believe there's a romantic bone in that man's body."

"You have no right to criticize my fiancé in this manner. You're only doing it because he disapproves of your conduct. And I can't say he's unjustified.

You've become fodder for scandal sheets all over Europe!"

Julia, obviously on a tear, continued to ignore her. "And to think I defended your engagement to Will just the other day, when I'm beginning to think it's the biggest mistake you've ever made—"

"What? You talked about Aidan and me with Will?" Beatrix was becoming more outraged with every moment.

"I did! On the very afternoon I arrived, he tackled me on the subject. He asked me if you were in love with Trathen."

"He did?" She was stunned that Will would even ask such a question, and she badly wanted to know what Julia had replied. She shouldn't ask, she knew. Instead, she should dress Julia down for displaying such a lack of discretion and gossiping with Will about her, but her curiosity proved stronger than her outrage. "What did you tell him? I hope you assured him I was very happy."

"Ah, but that's not what he asked me." Julia shot her a triumphant glance that made her feel suddenly uncomfortable. "He asked me if you were in love with Trathen. I said I didn't know."

"What?" Beatrix groaned.

"Well, it isn't as if you and Aidan go about cooing like doves and sneaking off for passionate kisses in the garden every night!"

"I am making a sensible marriage. I am marrying a good man."

"I'm not disputing that. But you don't really want to marry him." Something sparked in Julia's eyes, something cold and dark that made Beatrix shiver, despite the bright sunshine. "I married Yardley because my parents assured me it was the right thing to do. I knew it wasn't, and I did it anyway. Don't make my mistake. Listen to your heart, Trix, not your head." She stopped and took a deep breath. "When you wrote and told me you were engaged, I thought you'd gotten over Will. But you haven't."

"Yes, I have. I care deeply for Aidan. I do!" she insisted when Julia made a sound of disbelief. "And he cares for me just as much, which is why he disapproves of some of the things you do," she added, going on the offensive. "He's concerned because you're my family and soon you'll be family to him, too."

"Saints preserve us," Julia muttered. "And I don't need his concern or yours," she added, her voice rising again. "And I'll be damned if I'll be lectured to by you on his behalf!"

Beatrix's wonderful day was now utterly ruined. "You need someone's concern, since you're so wholly unconcerned about yourself!"

"You loved Will with a passion," Julia went on, disregarding any attempt to turn the conversation toward herself, "and when you didn't go with him to Egypt, it was as if he took your whole world with him. You didn't know who you were anymore, or what you wanted. You've been trying to get your bearings ever since."

Beatrix's anger faded a bit with those words, and she wriggled in her seat as shades of last night's doubts and uncertainties came back to her. "I don't know what you're talking about."

"I know how much you want to be married, how much you want children, and I know you were becoming scared you'd never be able to have those things. When you became engaged to Trathen, I thought you'd at last found happiness again. But Trix, you're not happy."

Beatrix decided she'd heard enough. "I don't have to listen to this. You say you don't want to be lectured to? Well, neither do I!" With that, she swung her legs to the side of the motorcar, stepped onto the running board, and jumped to the ground.

"Where are you going?" Julia asked, watching her circle to the rear of the Mercedes.

"Off on my own!" she shot back, and grabbed her canvas bag from the open boot. "You know, I was in a jolly good mood when I woke up this morning," she added wrathfully as she turned and began marching away. "Thank you for ruining it!"

"If you're not happy," Julia called after her, "marrying Trathen and having his children won't make you so."

"Perhaps you should spend a bit more time worrying about your own happiness, Julie," she shot back over her shoulder, "and stop worrying about mine."

Julia said something, but she couldn't hear what it was, and she kept walking, blinking back tears of fury as she made her way down the steep hill toward Phoebe's Cove. "Why the devil is everyone so cross today?"

Chapter Nine

*B*eatrix dropped her canvas bag off the cliff edge to land in the sand below, and then descended the ladder to Phoebe's Cove. "I'm unhappy?" she muttered through clenched teeth, picking up her bag again and marching toward the nearest of the caves that ringed the cove. "That's rich, coming from Julie!"

She entered the cave, took off her hat, and tossed it aside, then slipped out of her clothes, Julia's words still ringing in her ears. "I'm a tragedy?"

She pulled on her navy-blue taffeta knickerbockers and reached for the matching tunic. She did up the front, careful to fasten all the buttons, right up to the top of the white sailor collar, for she didn't want sun marks on the neckline of her evening gown that evening. Being that she was alone, she disregarded the customary bathing stockings and lace-up bathing shoes, for the feel of the warm sand between her toes might soothe her frayed nerves and the seething resentment she felt toward Julia at this moment.

After belting the tunic with its bright red sash, she grabbed her ruffled white muslin bathing cap and left the cave. As she headed for the water, however, the usual delight of warm sand on her bare feet went unnoticed.

"I don't know what I want?" Beatrix splashed into the water, but when the water was up to her thighs, she stopped, scowling out at the ocean. "That's not true. I know precisely what I want."

"Do you?"

The deep male voice behind her caused her to jump, dropping her cap in the water. She didn't retrieve it; instead, she turned and found the man she was trying so hard to forget only two dozen feet away. He was sitting on the rocks by the mouth to the pixy's cave, leaning back with his weight on his arms.

"You again?" she cried, vexed that her day was going from bad to worse, though she supposed she ought to be grateful that at least he had his shirt on. "Good God, you are the proverbial bad penny!"

He stood up. "Is Trathen what you want, Trix? Really?"

"I'm going to marry him, aren't I?"

"I can't think why. You don't love him."

Beatrix froze, her stomach clenching into a sick knot at those words. Was it so obvious? She opened her mouth to protest, but he spoke before she did.

"Oh, you want to love him," he said and started

walking toward her. "You want to be the sort of woman he wants, so you try to read the books he approves, you act as if you like caviar, when you really don't, and you pretend it's all right to go on an estate tour when you really want Florence. Yes," he added at her sound of outrage. "I overheard. I couldn't help it. You and Julia were shouting at each other as if you were squabbling little girls all over again."

"Do you follow me around, eavesdropping on me?" she cried, even though she knew there was no possible way he could have done that.

He stopped a few feet from the water's edge, and a smile curved one corner of his mouth. "I hate to say this, but I was here first."

The ramifications of what he must have heard penetrated her consciousness, and she felt sick. "Go away."

"Are you going to answer my question?"

"Was there a question? I thought you were making a speech."

"Why do you pretend an estate tour is an acceptable honeymoon, when it isn't what you want?"

"Ah, I should live by Will's selfish credo, then? Do only what I want and be damned to everyone else?"

"This isn't about being selfish, it's about being honest. I know you, Trix, I know you down to your chubby pink toes."

Her toes curled into the sand beneath the water. "I don't have chubby toes!"

"Yes, you do, and they're adorable toes, but that's not my point. My point is that you don't really want him. Oh, you want what he represents. You want the life he's offering you, the same one you wanted with me, the same one you've idolized since you were a little girl playing with dolls in the nursery—dukes and castles and happy-ever-after, but it's not real. You're trying to trick yourself into thinking it is. You're trying so hard, you're choking down caviar and lemonade, trying to believe you like them."

"I like lemonade! I do," she insisted at his sound of skepticism. "What, when you leave, I'm frozen in place without you, unchanged by the passing years? It so happens there are many things I've learned to like without you."

"Caviar, too?"

She opened her mouth, but she couldn't dispute him on that. She was still trying to figure out why Aidan liked something that tasted like salty, wet sand. She pressed her lips together and looked away.

"See?" he said in the wake of her silence. "He hates that Daimler of yours. How long before he persuades you to give it up and you start trying to tell yourself you never really liked motoring all that much in the first place?"

"Aidan might prefer a carriage to a motorcar, but he would never forbid me to have anything that made me happy."

He didn't seem inclined to debate the point. "Tell me something," he said instead. "Why did you ever fall in love with me?"

She blinked, startled by such an abrupt turn in the conversation. "What do you mean?"

"I mean Trathen is everything I'm not. He cares about his titles, and his estates, and all the same things you seem to care about. He's nothing like me. So if you love him and he's what you really want, what on earth inspired you to ever fall in love with me?"

"Oh, I don't know," she said, desperate to make light of it. "The mad idiocy of youth?"

"That's not it."

"Oh really? What, then? Since you seem to possess more insight into my character, my heart, and my mind than I do, why did I fall in love with you all those years ago?"

"Because secretly, under all the respectable dutiful-daughter rubbish your father tried to stuff you with, you crave excitement and challenge, even danger. You don't always like it, mind you, and you balk sometimes, but inside, you crave it. It's like that cliff when we were children."

"Stop talking about that!"

"You stand up there, and you're staring down and you're dizzy with excitement because you've just seen me jump off, and you want to do it, too. You lick your lips and you want it so bad you can taste it. But then you start to think too much. You remember your father said you couldn't go up on Angel's Head, and what if you fell and got hurt, and before you know it, you're sitting down, saying you're just going to admire the view. But inside you're berating yourself because you lost the nerve to jump."

"I don't know what you're talking about."

"Oh yes, you do. You wanted to go to Egypt until it became a reality, and all the ramifications of defying your father and leaving home hit you in the face."

"This is absurd. I used to defy Papa to come meet you at midnight, didn't I?"

"Only after we were engaged. That way, if we got caught, he couldn't be all that disappointed in you. You let me kiss your neck and unbutton your dress, but only so far. Three buttons was the crossing line, if I remember it right—"

"Stop it!" she cried, slamming her hands over her ears. "You have no right to say these things to me."

"I'll stop when you look me in the eye and tell me you're going to marry that man because you're in love with him. Come on. Say it."

"I—" She stopped. God help her, she couldn't lie to Will. She just couldn't do it. "I don't have to say anything to you," she said instead. She started out of the water, veering to the right so that she could go around him when she reached the shore.

"See? You can't say it because you don't feel it. Trathen's a very sensible choice for any woman who wants to be married. Very safe, very sensible. I know you won't believe this, but if—" He broke off and looked away.

She stopped, unable to resist waiting to hear whatever he was going to say.

"If marrying Trathen would make you happy," he said at last, returning his gaze to her face, "I wouldn't say anything. But Julie's right. You're not happy, and with him, you'll never be."

She shook her head, denying it, hating him for saying it. "That's not true."

"Yes, it is. Because you don't love him, and you're the sort of woman who can't ever be truly happy marrying a man you don't love."

She inhaled a sharp breath, but the words to deny it caught in her throat.

"Some women can," he went on before she could recover enough to speak, "but not you. It just isn't in you."

She forced herself to say something. "Or maybe your male pride just can't accept the idea that I might be able to love someone besides you."

He shook his head. "You don't love him, and I can prove it."

"This should be interesting," she said, and folded her arms, readying herself for whatever outrageous thing he said next. "Go on. I'm waiting with bated breath for this so-called proof."

His gaze locked with hers. "You don't look at him the way you used to look at me."

"That's it?" She bent down and reached for her sodden cap, which was floating in the water nearby. "That's your proof?"

"As far back as I can remember, whenever you used to look at me, your face would light up as if someone had lit a candle inside you. Your face doesn't light up like that when you look at him."

Pain shimmered through her at the reminder of the lovesick girl she used to be. Her cheeks burned with humiliation at the memory, and she struggled to fire off a sufficiently scathing reply. "Of all the conceit!" she scoffed, slapping her cap atop her head. "If that's what you call evidence—"

"Your smile's different, too."

"What?" Water from her soaking wet cap was running down her cheeks, and she rubbed her face, cursing herself for being so at sixes and sevens that she hadn't even wrung the blasted thing out before putting it on her head. "Nonsense!"

He ignored that, of course. "And then there's the way you say his name."

"I don't know what you're talking about. I think you're crazy, I truly do. Too much sun in Egypt, I think."

"I'm not crazy, and I know exactly what I'm talking about. You don't say his name the way you used to say my name." He took a step toward her and then another. "Your voice is different."

Beatrix felt a pang of alarm as she watched him come closer, but she decided not to make any attempt to duck past him and run. She lifted her chin, rubbed water away from her face again, and stood her ground, striving to maintain her dignity, though that was a difficult thing for a woman to do when her sopping wet cap was getting water in her eyes and her bathing dress was glued to her body like a second skin. "That is the silliest thing I've ever heard."

"Silly, is it?" He reached the shore, but to her dismay, he didn't stop. Instead, he came striding into the water, boots and all, and as Beatrix watched him approach, her anger and dismay began dissolving into panic. By the time he reached her, her heart was pounding so hard in her chest, she was sure he could hear it even over the sound of the waves crashing on the rocks at the edge of the cove.

His gaze roamed over her wet, upturned face, and he smiled, clearly finding her appearance amusing, but when he spoke there was no laughter in his tone. "Whenever you said my name, there was always this soft little wobbly catch in your voice, like a hiccup, as if my name were two syllables instead of one." He paused, and a fleeting shadow crossed his face that might have been regret. "It's gone now, of course, but it was there once."

She swallowed hard, hating him for reminding her of the way she'd once felt about him.

His lashes lowered, then lifted. "I don't hear that little wobble when you say his name."

She forced herself to speak. "Wobble, indeed! You have a vivid and convenient imagination. You hear what you want to hear."

"Whenever I heard that, I felt it was as if you were so happy and excited to see me that you wanted to throw your arms around my neck and kiss me senseless—"

"That's ridiculous!"

"—but you knew you couldn't," he continued, ignoring her interruption. "Young ladies don't do that sort of thing. It's not proper. It's not dignified. And your father would have had apoplexy, of course. So you had to suppress what you felt, but you couldn't hide it from me. I always knew." He leaned closer, that faint smile still curving one corner of his mouth. "I could always tell how you felt about me," he said softly, "by the look in your eyes and the smile on your face, and the wobbly little way you always said my name."

She didn't want to hear any more. It was too humiliating, too painful, too damned embarrassing. But pride kept her from showing it. "Awfully meager evidence, in my opinion," she said, and once again started past him, deciding it was time for a strategic retreat.

But he wouldn't let her get away yet. "Wait," he said, and grasped her arms. "I have one other very important piece of evidence, one that would prove beyond a shadow of doubt you don't love Trathen."

"What evidence is that?"

Without warning, he wrapped an arm around her waist and pulled her hard against him. "This," he said, bent his head, and kissed her.

The moment his lips touched hers, she felt a strange, weightless sensation, making her think perhaps he'd just dragged her off that damned cliff at Angel's Head. Down, down, she felt herself falling, heart in her throat, and she couldn't stop it. Down she fell, into the abyss of the past, when she was a girl in love, and William Mallory's kiss was as necessary to her life as the food she ate and the air she breathed.

His free hand cupped her cheek, his fingers touched her face. His mouth opened, his lips parted hers. His arm around her waist tightened, pulling her even closer. Her memory responded at once, sending desire coursing through her veins. Yes, this was Will—his mouth tasting openly of hers, his fingertips caressing her cheek, his body hard and strong against hers.

She strove for sanity. The past was gone, and even as part of her longed to go back and relive those blissful, euphoric days, another part—the sane and rational part, the older and wiser part—reminded her that in less than two months, she was marrying someone else, someone whose kiss felt nothing like this, but who wouldn't leave her for a pile of relics thousands of miles away.

She tore her mouth from his. "Wait," she gasped. "I think—"

"That's always been your trouble, Trix." His arm tightened around her waist, and his free hand cupped the back of her head, his fingers tangling in her damp hair. He tilted her head back, sending her cap falling into the water again. "You think too much."

He recaptured her mouth, and she felt her resistance slipping away as shimmers of pleasure ran through her body. So long since she'd felt this way. So, so long. Will's kiss was a delight she'd almost forgotten, yet it was all so familiar—the taste of his mouth as he parted her lips with his, the hard feel of his body pressed to hers, the rough, sandpapery texture of his cheek against her palm as she touched his face.

"Oh my God!"

Julia's voice, she realized as the startled exclamation penetrated her stunned senses. Julia? She opened her eyes.

Will must have heard the voice as well, for he broke the kiss, relaxed his hold, and turned to look over his shoulder.

When she peeked past him, she saw no one, but when she glanced up, she saw Julia standing at the top of the ladder, an expression of utter astonishment on her face. She was not alone, for Paul stood beside her, frowning like thunder, and behind her, looking over her shoulder, tight-lipped and grim-faced, was Aidan.

Beatrix pressed a hand over her mouth, looking into his face, feeling sick as the ramifications of what had happened, of what he'd seen, hit her with all the force of a punch to the stomach.

Aidan didn't speak. He didn't say a word. He simply turned and walked away.

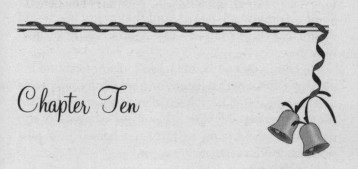

Chapter Ten

In an instant, Will fully appreciated the damage he'd done. It was in Julia's horrified face. It was in Paul's angry scowl. And it was in Trathen's stiff, abrupt departure.

"Oh hell," he muttered, and turned to look at Beatrix, but he didn't have the chance to say a word.

"You bastard." She swung before he could block the move, her palm hitting his cheek with enough force to swing his head sideways, and then she was running past him, sloshing out of the water and across the sand, headed for the ladder. "Aidan, wait!"

Will, his cheek stinging from the slap, his body on fire from the arousal of her kiss, and his mind still dazed from the chaos inside him, didn't try to stop her. He'd done that already—with disastrous results—and pushing his luck was not a good idea.

Besides, if he did go after her, what could he say? She'd called him a bastard, and that pretty much said it all. He certainly felt like one. God knew, he'd acted like one.

He hadn't meant to. He hadn't meant to sound his opinions, force her to listen, or haul her into his arms and kiss her. But he'd been driven to make her see the truth—that she was a beautiful woman far too passionate and loving to imprison herself in a passionless, loveless marriage.

Not that saving her from making a huge mistake had been a pure and noble motive on his part. No, he couldn't salve his conscience with any heroic rot of that sort. He wanted her, pure and simple. Six years of trying to forget her, of trying not to want her, had been an utter waste of time. He watched her as she ascended the ladder, and the sight of her clinging bathing dress and bare legs only sent the desire he felt flaring even higher, desire that, if her outrage was anything to go by, would remain unrequited for the rest of his life.

"Hell," he said again, and wanted to kick himself in the head.

Beatrix had by now vanished from view. Her cousins, however, did not seem inclined to go after her. Julia hovered on the cliff edge, glancing over her shoulder, then back at him as if uncertain quite what to do. Paul, however, had no such ambivalence. He started down the ladder.

Will inhaled a deep breath and let it out slowly, knowing Paul's intent was to give him a sound thrashing, and since he wholly deserved it, the only thing to do was meet it like a man.

He came out of the water and waited on the sand as Paul approached. When the other man halted in front of him, he made no attempt at explanations. Lust, after all, was not an explanation.

"You son of a bitch."

When Paul's fist came flying at him, he didn't even try to duck. He felt a shattering pain in his jaw, saw stars, and then he felt his body falling backward into the sand and everything went black.

Beatrix called Aidan's name several times as she raced after him toward the house, but he did not stop, and by the time she caught up with him, he had crossed the terrace. "Aidan, wait, please. We have to talk about this."

He stopped, his hand on the door handle, but he did not open the door. Nor did he turn around. "You're right, of course."

She halted, too, out of breath and at a loss for words. She'd been so occupied with running to catch up with him that she hadn't had time to think. And now she had no idea how to explain what had happened. How did one explain something like that?

Aidan, however, cut straight to the chase. "This isn't going to work, Beatrix. I think we both know that."

She opened her mouth to disagree, but her lips were still tingling from another man's kiss, and she couldn't seem to find words to deny what was so obviously the truth.

He didn't turn around. He didn't look at her. "I know we both went into this with our eyes wide open," he said. "For my part, I have never expected that romantic love would be part of marriage for me. It seldom is for those of our class. I had always hoped for mutual respect and affection, and when we met, I knew I had found that. I thought it was enough for both of us."

She wrapped her arms around her midsection, miserable and heartsick. "When you proposed to me, it was like the answer to a prayer. Everything you said made perfect sense to me. How romantic love doesn't last, and how we both want marriage and children and we could build a good life together, even without being in love."

"I believed we could do that, Beatrix."

"Despite the evidence to the contrary," she said with a little humorless laugh, "I still believe it."

"Do you?" He squared his shoulders and turned around to face her. "I am not blind, you know. During these past three days, I have seen the way he looks at you, and the way you look at him, and though six years has gone by, I know that whatever was between the two of you still exists. When I saw you with him—"

A sob tore from her throat, interrupting him. "I don't want him, Aidan. I don't."

"What you mean is that you don't want to want him. But you do."

She wanted to deny it, but how could she? The evidence to prove it had been seen by three other people. And even if no one had seen, would it matter? Could she marry Aidan, live with him, knowing Will's ghost could pop up at any time like some damned jack-in-the-box and come between them? Right now she hated Will, but could she ever be sure she would stop wanting him? Could she do that to Aidan? Or to herself?

She looked down at the diamond engagement ring on her finger, winking at her in the sunlight, blurring with the tears in her eyes, and she knew she could not. She wrenched it off. "Oh, Aidan," she cried, looking up at him again as she held out the ring, "I'm sorry. I'm so, so sorry."

"It's not your fault." He nodded to the diamond. "Keep it. I shan't give it to anyone else, you know."

She pressed her lips together, holding back tears, shaking her head in refusal. "Take it, please."

He did, reluctantly, almost as if his only reason was gentlemanly chivalry. "It's not your fault, Beatrix," he said again.

But as she watched him turn away and walk into the house, she found no comfort in those words. Aidan might not blame her, but she did. For the momentary thrill of another man's kiss, she had hurt a man she'd come to regard as a dear friend, tossed aside everything she had ever wanted in life, and come face to face with a brutal, relentless truth: no matter how she tried to think with her head, her heart still didn't want to listen.

The question was what to do about it. As if in answer, Julia's words from earlier in the day came echoing back to her.

When Will went to Egypt, you didn't know who you were anymore or what you wanted, and you've been trying to get your bearings ever since.

It was time, she realized—long past time—to get her bearings. It was time to make her own life, not a life that depended upon a man, or on society's expectations, or on an antiquated girlhood dream. No, it was time to decide what she truly wanted for herself and work to make it happen. That was really her only choice now.

On the other hand, she could just shoot Will with a pistol. That, she thought as she considered it, was quite an appealing idea, too.

Will woke up to pain. He inhaled sharply, feeling something cold being pressed against his eye. He stirred, shaking his head, and when he was able to open his eyes, he found Julia kneeling beside him, using Beatrix's waterlogged bathing cap as a compress.

She pressed it gently against his face again, and he winced, muttering a curse.

"Lie still," she ordered, gently pushing him back down when he tried to sit up. "Paul coldcocked you, and you've been unconscious for several minutes. If you move too fast, you'll probably keel right over again."

"Is he gone?"

"Paul? Yes. After he hit you, he turned straight away. He didn't even wait for you to fall." She turned on her knees and leaned toward the waves lapping against the shore to dunk the bit of muslin back in the water. "He just marched away, climbed back up the ladder, and left."

Will gingerly touched his cheek. "I take it he saw the whole show?"

"If you mean the kiss, yes. We all saw it. Bloody hell, Will," she added, sounding as if she didn't know whether to laugh or cry. "What were you thinking?"

"I wasn't," Will answered wryly. "Rational thought didn't enter into it, I'm afraid."

"So it would seem." Both of them fell silent as she held the compress against his face and Will struggled to clear his head.

He took deep breaths, concentrating on the pain in his cheek and jaw, trying to gather his wits. Beatrix's kiss was still vivid in his mind—the sweet taste of her mouth against his and the luscious shape of her body in his arms.

It was at least ten minutes before he felt sufficiently master of himself again to think clearly. When Julia moved to wring out the compress and reapply it, he stopped her with a shake of his head and sat up.

Julia settled herself beside him on the sand. "So, what happens now?"

"Damned if I know." Six years of trying to hate Beatrix had been for naught, he thought in frustration, propping his elbows on his bent knees and cradling his head in his hands. "I'll leave at once, of course."

"That's probably wise. If you don't, Paul will likely kill you. Or Trathen might."

"Or Trix might beat them to it."

"True," Julia agreed with equanimity. "And I'd say you deserved it."

He lifted his head, staring out at the sea. "And I'd have to agree with you."

A loud whistle had both of them turning their heads to look up at the cliff behind them where Geoff stood by the top of the ladder. "Is it really true?" he asked, his boyish face eager with curiosity.

Will and Julia exchanged glances, and she leaned closer to him. "That didn't take long," she muttered, then returned her attention to the cliff above. "Is what true, darling boy?"

"About Beatrix and Trathen calling it off?"

"They did?" Will and Julia asked the question at the same time.

Geoff made a sound of impatience that he would have to offer explanations instead of obtaining juicy details. "Trathen was at the slip to meet us when we docked," he said, and started down the ladder. "He said something had happened and he had to leave this afternoon, and he gave Marlowe his apologies for not being able to stay. He didn't say why he was leaving. He just said important business has called him away."

"Then how do you know the engagement's off?" Julia asked him.

Forgoing the last few rungs of the ladder, Geoff dropped lightly to the sand. "A few minutes later, after we'd gone into the house, I heard Mum moaning about how awful it was, and how all the gifts would have to be returned again, and Beatrix caught her up sharp and said she didn't want to talk about it anymore."

Will gave Julia an inquiring glance and she shook her head. "None of us would ever tell what we saw," she whispered, and turned again toward Geoff as he came toward them.

He halted by where they sat and frowned at Will. "What's happened to your face?" he asked, momentarily diverted. Then awareness dawned in his expression, and he gave another whistle. "Dash it, did you get in a fight with Trathen over Trix? Is that why he's leaving?"

"Not Trathen," he corrected, knowing what was probably going to be a black eye would have to be explained somehow. "I got in a fight with Paul."

"My brother? Whatever were you fighting with him about?"

"Never mind," Julia interposed. "We can talk about that later. Is that why you came down here? To tell us about the broken engagement? How did you know we were down here?"

"I didn't, not until I saw you. Beatrix sent me to fetch her things. She'd been bathing, she said, but forgot to change when she came out of the water, and she asked me to retrieve her bathing bag and her clothes from the pixy cave. But that's a bit odd," he added, "because girls don't usually forget about things like that. Propriety, you know. She and Aidan must have had a fight. That would explain her forgetting, wouldn't it? And if they had a fight, that explains the broken engagement, too."

Julia cast a sideways glance at Will. "Why don't you go back to the house, Geoff? We'll be up in a minute or two. Don't worry about Beatrix's things. I'll bring them up with me."

"Lots of secrets around here today." Reluctantly Geoff turned away and retraced his steps back to the ladder. "I was hoping you two would know what was going on," he added, sounding aggrieved.

"Well," Julia said when Geoff was out of earshot, "this is a fine mess. What are you going to do?"

Will scarcely heard. He was staring out at the sea, and all he could think of was how he'd destroyed Trix's dreams all over again.

He could remember her standing on the stairs at Danbury House, refusing to even see him off at the train station, her eyes red-rimmed and puffy from crying, her cupid's bow mouth uttering an ultimatum.

If you go, don't expect me to be waiting for you when you come back.

He closed his eyes, his own short, angry reply echoing back.

Fine. Don't.

Those words, along with a hefty dose of pride and youthful stupidity, had ruined any chance of compromise, blown up any bridge between the world he wanted and the one she wanted, destroying her dreams in the process. And now he'd just done it again.

He stood up.

"Careful," Julia admonished at his abrupt move. "You took quite a blow."

"I'm all right." He started toward the ladder.

"What are you going to do?" she called after him.

"Make things right," he said over his shoulder. "If that's possible."

He found Beatrix on Angel's Head. She had changed her clothes, donning a frock of marine blue that seemed brilliantly vibrant in the twilight. Her hat was in her hand, and as she stared out over the sea, the breeze stirred the wisps of gold hair at her temples.

She seemed lost in thought, and she didn't notice his approach. When he was less than a dozen feet away, he stopped and gave a cough to draw her attention. She glanced in his direction, scowled, and immediately looked away again, staring out at the sea. "Leave me alone. If you don't, I will find a pistol and cheerfully shoot you."

Not an auspicious beginning for the purpose he had in mind, and though it was a fate he undoubtedly deserved, he hoped she didn't really mean it. "Paul's already hit me on your behalf. Is that good enough?"

"Hit you, did he? That explains why you look as if you have a toothache, but no, that's not good enough. Go away."

He ignored that. "Paul is quite the pugilist. Knocked me unconscious. I only tell you that to make you happy."

She didn't answer, but in profile, he saw her lips twitch just a little, and that gave him hope.

He came to stand in front of her, blocking her view, forcing himself into her line of vision because for what he wanted to say, he had to be able to look into her face. There was only one way to say something like this. He took a deep breath and said it. "I think we should get married."

"What?" She blinked. She shook her head as if thinking she must have heard him wrong. "I beg your pardon?"

"I think we should get married."

She scorned that suggestion with a snort, turned away, and started back toward the house. His voice called after her.

"I take it you don't agree?"

She didn't even bother to answer, and he started after her. "Look, Trix, I know I behaved abominably, but—"

"You won't hear any argument from me on that score!" she interrupted, still striding toward the house.

"I have absolutely no defense to offer. I know I've wrecked your life again, and I'm more sorry than I can say, and I know an apology can't make up for what I've done. Offering marriage is the only way I can think of to repair the damage I've caused."

"Repair the damage?" She stopped so abruptly, he almost cannoned into her from behind. Without thinking, he brought his hands up, grasping her hips to steady them both, but the moment he did, he felt desire flaring up inside him again. Cursing himself, he jerked his hands down.

"Repair the damage?" she repeated again, her voice rising as she turned around to face him. "I am not a broken fence or a smashed motorcar! The damage you've done can't be repaired."

He could see tears glistening in those big brown eyes, making him feel like even more of a cur. "Christ Almighty, Trix, please don't cry."

"Why shouldn't I? Would that make you feel bad? Would that be another burden on your conscience? Sorry, but your sense of guilt is not my problem." Even as she spoke, she was blinking as if to keep the tears back. "And I won't marry you. I don't love you. Quite the opposite, in fact."

"From your point of view, how valid an argument is that? You didn't love Trathen, yet you were going to marry him."

She made a sound of contempt through her teeth. "So you think you can just step into his shoes? You think I believe one groom is as good as another? I may not love Aidan, but I care for him a great deal. It could have grown into love, if you hadn't come back and ruined everything."

He rubbed his hands over his face, searching for something to say, but he couldn't defend himself or his actions. "We had love once, Trix. We might be able to have it again."

"I don't want it again! Not with you. It took me five years to forget you. And then, just when I finally succeeded, you came back, caused my fiancé to break our engagement, and ruined my life for the second time. And you think stepping up and marrying me now will wipe the slate clean and make everything all right?"

"No, of course not, but marriage is all I have to offer you. And besides . . ." He paused, knowing he was about to skate out on the thin ice. "There's still something between us, Trix. You can't tell me you don't feel it, too."

"Oh, I feel something for you, Will," she said, her voice deceptively sweet. "Indeed, I do. It's called loathing."

He must truly be an optimist, he decided, and an incurable one at that, because her words only served to send his hopes up a notch. "That's a lie," he said softly. "You don't loathe me. You should, no doubt about it. You want to, because I deserve it. But you don't. You're too soft to hate anybody."

Her narrowed eyes told him she didn't think that was a compliment.

He tried another tactic. "When I kissed you, I know you were remembering how it used to be with us."

She opened her mouth as if to deny it, but when she didn't speak and tried to turn away instead, he grasped her arms and pushed his advantage. "See? You can't deny it because that would be a lie, and you can't lie worth toffee. You never could."

She shrugged, trying to get him to let go. "Leave me alone."

"Admit it, Trix. You felt the same desire I did. Even after six years, it's still there."

"Desire is not love!" she cried, wrenching free of his hold. "It's not. You never loved me. If you did, you would never have left me in the first place!"

"And I could say that if you loved me," he shot back, "you would have come with me instead of staying home."

"Thank you for proving my point! We were never in love. "Now will you leave me alone?"

"No. I'm not going anywhere. I'm not leaving you alone ever again. Instead, I'm going to win you back."

"Win me back?" she echoed. "Good Lord, haven't you done enough to torture me?"

"I can see I'm going to need to take a more romantic approach to this whole thing." He drew a deep breath, grasped her hands, and dropped to one knee. "Marry me."

Words failed her. She shook her head, staring down at him, feeling dazed, as if she were lost in some sort of strange dream. Maybe, like Alice, she'd gone down a rabbit hole or through a looking glass, because nothing, absolutely nothing, made sense anymore. Will was once again proposing marriage to her?

It wasn't possible. It was as difficult to imagine as . . . as pigs taking flight. And yet this scenario was not new to her imagination. In fact she had envisioned it many times, secretly, in the back of her mind.

When he'd gone off to Egypt, she had run the gamut of emotions—disbelief, shock, rage, grief, hope, and many others. But there had also been times when she'd dared to think that he might, just might, come back, admit he was wrong, and grovel on his knees. She'd had plenty of daydreams about that, especially the groveling part. And though the details of this fantastic, impossible scenario had been different each time she'd imagined it, one thing had always remained the same—the pleasure and delight she felt whenever she imagined just how she would turn him down.

Never had she thought she would have the opportunity to actually do it.

Remembering all the times she'd dreamed of a moment such as this, Beatrix smiled and looked into the gorgeous green eyes she had once loved so much. "No," she said, and found that word every bit as sweet in reality as it had always been in her imagination. "I will not marry you."

"Beatrix—"

"You had your chance," she cut him off, relishing each word. "And for you to come crawling back now—"

"Crawling?" That actually made him smile, the cad. He tilted his head to one side, slanting her a considering glance. "If I did crawl, would that persuade you to marry me?"

"No."

"Not even if I did it on my belly? In the mud? In my best evening suit?"

She pressed her lips together and looked away, hating the fact that even in these ghastly circumstances, after he'd been a cad beyond belief, even now, he could still—almost—make her want to laugh. But when she spoke, her answer was firm and her will was resolute. "No."

"I could beg, too," he suggested, but when she shook her head, he stood up, relaxing his grip on her hands enough that she was able to pull free.

"I will never marry you," she declared. "Not now, not ever. Not in a thousand years. Not for all the tea in China. Not," she added, loving the act of refusing him too much to stop quite yet, "if you were the last man on earth."

He studied her face for a moment. "You're enjoying this, aren't you?"

"Yes." She widened her smile, savoring it. "I confess, I am."

"You don't encourage me to hope? That way," he added as if being helpful, "you could increase my agony by suspense and enjoy it longer."

"Hmm . . ." She paused, pretending to consider it. "That is a tempting thought," she said after a moment, "but no. I am not encouraging you to hope."

"I see." He nodded, but if he was disappointed, he didn't show it. "Then there's only one thing I can do."

She crossed her fingers. "Go back to Egypt?"

"No." He gave her that wicked pirate smile. "Change your mind."

Lifting her eyes heavenward in exasperation, she gave it up. She stepped around him, and as she continued toward the house, she wondered if Marlowe had a pistol anywhere in the house.

Chapter Eleven

Will studied her as she marched toward the house, her foamy white petticoats flouncing up from beneath the hem of her blue dress like stormy ocean waves, and he appreciated that winning her over was going to be a much harder, much more difficult task than it had been the first time around.

After all, by the time he'd proposed to her the first time, she'd already been in love with him most of her life. In fact, he couldn't remember a time when Trix hadn't been in love with him.

The door slammed behind her.

Until now.

He let out his breath in a sigh, staring at the closed door. He'd taken her love for granted back then, accepted it as an inalterable fact, something that would always be, like laws of physics or the opening of

Parliament. Even after he'd read that she was marrying someone else, he still hadn't quite believed it was possible. That, he realized, was the reason he'd kept her wedding announcement within easy reach for the past eight months. To help himself accept the impossible.

He'd taken her love for granted six years ago, and then he'd thrown it away as part of the rebellion that had caused him to go to Egypt in the first place. Barely twenty-three then, and already his whole life neatly laid out for him—estates, position, beautiful, adoring girl all handed over easy as could be, when he'd done absolutely nothing to earn them.

He thought of Beatrix's angry eyes and wounded heart, and he knew that this time around, at least when it came to winning the beautiful girl, nothing was going to be easy.

Much to her consternation, Beatrix found her enjoyment at Will's expense rather short-lived. She was passing the drawing room on her way to the stairs when Aunt Eugenia's voice called to her. "Beatrix? Darling, come in here."

She stopped with a grimace. After the fuss Eugenia had made a short time ago about the breaking of her engagement to Aidan, the last thing Beatrix wanted was another round of Auntie's tearful theatrics. Still, there was nothing for it. She'd been seen.

Reluctantly she backed up a few steps to the drawing room, where Eugenia was gathered with Marlowe's mother, Louisa; his grandmother, Antonia;

and Lady Debenham. They were already dressed for dinner, sipping glasses of sherry and—undoubtedly— speculating about what could have prompted Beatrix and Aidan to part.

"Yes, Auntie?" she asked, bracing herself for another discussion of how they would have to explain this to all their friends, and how there would be gossip about it that would go on for months, and how Eugenia had never thought she'd live to see the day when a relation of hers would break not one, but two engagements, and how she'd never seen any woman of her acquaintance manage to be both jilted and jilt in a single lifetime.

To her surprise, however, Eugenia seemed to have recovered from her earlier woeful shock. In fact, at the sight of Beatrix in the doorway, she actually smiled.

"My dear, dear niece!" Setting aside her teacup, Eugenia rose to her feet and came bustling forward, hands outstretched, looking inexplicably pleased about something. "Now I understand everything."

Beatrix frowned. "You do?"

"Of course." Eugenia clasped both her hands and leaned forward, kissing her astonished niece's cheek. "Why didn't you simply explain before how it was?"

She glanced past Eugenia, and the other ladies were smiling, too, looking at her indulgently. Even Antonia was beaming at her in uncharacteristically benign fashion. She gave them a polite but puzzled smile in return and murmured, "I'm sure I don't know what you mean, Aunt."

"Not that it's precisely *comme il faut*," Eugenia added with a tinkling little laugh.

"Most certainly not," Antonia said, tapping her folded lorgnette against her knee for added emphasis. "Not at all."

"But is it terribly romantic," sighed Louisa. "Even you must admit that, Mama."

"True," Antonia conceded, expression softening again. "Very true."

"Romantic?" Beatrix echoed, eyeing them all with doubt, feeling utterly at sea. What could be romantic about a second broken engagement? And how on earth had Eugenia's complete turnaround on the subject come about in the space of half an hour? "I wouldn't be inclined to view it as romantic myself," she said. "Chaotic, perhaps. Difficult."

Her adjectives were ignored.

"Romantic, yes," Lady Debenham put in, "but still, the practical aspects must be considered." She set down her cup and looked at Eugenia. "One can't simply substitute one name for another and carry on, my dears. After all, some of their things have been monogrammed."

Beatrix shook her head, certain she must be Alice, for this was beginning to seem eerily similar to the Mad Hatter's tea party.

"I'm sure that Beatrix will manage to be very subtle in her explanations, and our friends will be understanding about it. They know Beatrix, after all."

Beatrix grimaced at that, but Eugenia didn't seem

to notice. She sighed. "Oh, dear niece, to think that he's loved you all this time, suffering from afar, and that only now, after your engagement to Trathen has been broken and Trathen has left, has he felt free to speak—"

"Auntie," she cut in on this lurid, utterly fictional account, "what are all of you talking about?"

Eugenia blinked at the blunt question. "Sunderland, of course. His proposal. We saw it all, my dear," she added, waving toward the open window, "and we couldn't be more thrilled. Though we were a bit surprised—"

"What?" Beatrix looked in the direction her aunt was pointing, and as she stared out the window to the clear, unobstructed view of Angel's Head in the distance, comprehension came in a flash. She pressed her fingers to her forehead with a groan.

"We couldn't hear your conversation from here, of course," Eugenia went on, "but when we saw him fall to his knee, we understood everything. After all, first love is always the strongest."

They all sighed.

Beatrix knew this muddle had to be dealt with at once. She lifted her head. "Aunt Eugenia, ladies . . ." She took a deep breath. "Will and I are not engaged."

There was a stunned little silence in the wake of this announcement, then Eugenia spoke. "But Beatrix, we saw him fall to his knee. We saw him take your hands."

"I know what you saw, and yes, Will did propose. But—" she added, interrupting a chorus of satisfied ahhhs, "all of you seem to have taken my acceptance of his proposal as inevitable."

"Well, of course, darling," Eugenia said, sounding surprised by her statement. "He is a duke." As if that explained everything, she turned to the other ladies. "Could Beatrix and Sunderland keep the same date, do you think? So much simpler for our friends—"

"For the last time, Will and I are not engaged! I have refused him, and I will continue to refuse him until he gives up and goes away. There is no engagement, and there isn't going to be a wedding!"

With that, she turned her back on four disappointed elderly faces and departed from the drawing room. "Heavens," she added under her breath as she ran up the stairs. "I feel as if I've just told a group of two-year-olds there isn't going to be a Christmas!"

"Trix?" Julia's voice came through her closed bedroom door, along with a soft knock. "Trix, dearest, are you in there?"

"Come in, Julie," she called, rising from the bed as her cousin entered the room with her canvas bathing bag.

"Geoff asked me to bring your things up." She paused, then gave Beatrix a rueful grin. "All right, I confess, I volunteered. I wanted to apologize. I was a beast earlier, and I'm sorry." She tossed the canvas bag onto the bed and stuck out her hand. "Pax?"

Beatrix smiled a little at the word, their way of making up ever since their girlhood. She came forward and clasped Julia's hand in hers. "Pax."

They sank down onto the edge of the bed side by side. "Well," Julia said after a moment of silence, "bit of a to-do, what?"

"That's putting it mildly."

"If you're worried that what happened might get about, don't. None of us will say a thing about what we saw. We'll all keep mum."

"I know." She paused, then added, "How did all of you come to be standing up there anyway?"

"When I drove back to the house, I ran into Paul and Aidan, who were just leaving to go for a walk. I gather they'd reached a sort of stalemate in their chess game—staring at the board for hours, you know—and decided a walk would clear their heads. Aidan asked where you were, and I said you were down at Phoebe's Cove, and we decided to walk down and join you. None of us had any idea Will was down there."

"Neither did I," she added with a sigh. "You know Aidan and I have broken our engagement?"

Julia nodded. "After you went after Aidan, Paul marched down to have it out with Will. Hit him with a knockout blow."

Beatrix smiled, thinking of Will's swollen face and taking a great deal of satisfaction in it. "I'll have to thank Paul for that."

"Yes, well, after Paul went stomping off, I stayed behind. Someone had to. Will was unconscious, poor man. Lying in the sand, dead to the world, waves washing up only a foot away. If it had been high tide, he might have drowned."

Beatrix gave a sniff, unimpressed.

"Anyway," Julia went on, "we were still down there when Geoff came for your things and told us about you and Aidan calling things off. I'm sorry, darling." She paused a moment. "Did Will . . . umm . . . say anything to you?"

"Oh yes. He said plenty of things, all of which were absurd." She saw Julia waiting expectantly, and she gave a sigh. "Oh, you'll hear about it soon enough, I suppose. He proposed."

"I knew it!" Julia bounded up from the bed with a delighted squeal. "Why didn't you say so straightaway? When's the wedding?"

"You sound like Eugenia." She rubbed a hand across her forehead irritably. "I refused him."

"You did?"

"Of course I did! Why does that surprise everyone?" She jumped to her feet, feeling prickly as a chestnut. "Do all of you think I'm some sort of desperate, grasping spinster, ready to marry any man who comes along?"

Julia smiled at that, making her feel even more irritable. "Of course not, darling. But we aren't talking about just any man. We're talking about Will."

"Exactly so. Will, the man who jilted me six years ago," she reminded and began to pace, feeling her anger flaring back up. "The man who decided to come back after I was over him, the man who accosted me when I was alone and compromised me in front of my family and my fiancé, the man responsible for both of my broken engagements. Oh yes," she added, halting to glare at Julia, "we are definitely talking about Will, because only Will could cause that much chaos in one woman's life!"

She watched her cousin pressing her lips together as if to hide a smile. "Don't you dare laugh!" she ordered and started pacing again. "This is not amusing. He said he wants to make things right between us. Can you believe it? As if that were possible."

Julia settled back down on the edge of the bed. "You don't believe him?"

"Of course I don't! Why should I? He's doing this to ease his conscience. Now that I've refused him, his conscience is clear and he can leave."

"Ah, but what if he doesn't leave? What if he doesn't give up?"

Beatrix made a sound of derision, turned and started back across the room. "What do you mean? Of course he'll give up. It only took three days of discussion on the issue for him to give up last time!"

"But what if he doesn't? Would you give him a second chance?"

"He doesn't deserve a second chance."

"That's rather ruthless, darling, and I might add, not at all like you."

"Yes, I'm soft as butter, or so I've been told." Beatrix set her jaw, remembering how Will had said she was too soft to hate anybody, but she disagreed. She hated him a great deal, actually. More important, she didn't feel soft at all. Quite the opposite, in fact, for within her was a sense of resolve that was quite new to her—new, frightening, and curiously liberating. "I'm not being soft anymore," she assured Julia. "From now on, I intend to be hard as nails, at least when it comes to that man."

"Hard as nails, hmm?" Julia smiled. "Fair enough. But answer my question. What if Will doesn't give up? What if he decides to stay and work to change your mind? Then what will you do?"

He'd threatened to do that very thing, but she wasn't any more impressed by it now than she'd been before. She stopped pacing. "We are talking about Will," she reminded. "Expecting that man to stick to his promises and act responsibly is more foolish than waiting for pigs to sprout wings." When Julia continued to look at her as if waiting for a serious answer, she shrugged and gave it. "I'll just refuse him again."

"Yes," Julia said, nodding as if that was the answer she'd been waiting for. "That would be the next move in the game, wouldn't it?"

"What are you talking about?"

"How can I explain? You and Will are a bit like . . . like peas and carrots."

She scowled, folding her arms. "More like oil and water."

"Because you're always quarreling? But my darling, you two like quarreling."

"What?"

"You do. You enjoy it. Both of you do. Most men don't. They want domestic peace. But not Will. He loves the challenge and excitement of it, and so do you. You both find it terribly exciting, and that's what I mean by peas and carrots. You two have been quarreling and making up your entire lives, and loving every minute of it. You just might be meant for each other after all."

"Nonsense!" She unfolded her arms and started pacing again, unaccountably nervous at the prospect. "That is the stupidest thing I've ever heard."

"It's not stupid. You loved each other once."

She rallied, shoving fear aside. "No, Julie," she corrected. "I loved him. He did not love me. And it's moot anyway because I don't love him anymore."

Julia gave her an impish grin. "You were giving a fine imitation of it this afternoon."

Beatrix felt her face coloring up, and she stopped pacing by the window, turning toward it so Julia couldn't see her face. "That's not love," she said over her shoulder. "That was a momentary madness. And besides," she rushed on, wretchedly self-conscious about the entire humiliating episode, "It's not as if anything else has changed. Married people have to live in reasonably close proximity."

"I don't see why. Yardley and I don't." She paused and grinned. "At least not if I can help it."

"I'm serious, Julie. To be married—happily, at least—two people have to want the same things, share the same view of their life—" She stopped, appreciating that particular view of marriage hadn't served her any better than passionate, violent infatuation. "The point is," she went on after a moment, "marriage and I are clearly not meant for one another. It seems I'm meant for a different destiny." She sighed. "I just wish I knew what it was."

"So even if Will mends his ways, even if he loves you madly and intends to prove it, you've decided on spinsterhood?"

"I haven't decided anything, but whatever my future holds, Will just isn't part of it."

"You know, darling," Julia said as she stood up, "that might be taken for famous last words."

She ducked when Beatrix threw a pillow at her. Still laughing, Julia darted out the door.

In winning Beatrix over, Will knew he would need all the allies he could muster. In light of that, the first thing he needed to do was make peace with Paul. They'd been best friends all their lives, patching up quarrels with nothing more than a handshake, but this wasn't just another fight. Still, he hoped that once he explained his intentions, Paul would be able to forgive him for what had happened this afternoon.

Paul was in his bedroom, Will was told, dressing for dinner. When he knocked and heard Paul's answering permission to enter, he didn't do so. Instead, he opened the door just enough to look inside. "Mind if we talk?"

His friend looked away. He nodded to his valet, who had paused in the act of doing up his tie. "Go on, Fitch," he ordered.

The servant resumed knotting his black silk napoleon, but Paul did not turn his attention to Will, or even glance in his direction. Instead, he kept his gaze on the mirror past his valet's shoulder and said nothing.

Will looked at the other man's rigid profile, took a deep breath, and said what he came to say. "It's not a dalliance, Paul. It never has been. You know that." When his friend still didn't look at him or reply, he said the most important thing.

"I'm going to win her back."

That did the trick. Paul turned his head, causing the valet to stop again, and he stared at Will as if he were truly insane. "Win her back?" he echoed in disbelief. "Will, she hates you."

He thought of the smile she'd pressed from her lips when he'd offered to crawl on his belly in his best suit, and he shook his head. "No, she doesn't."

"Mum told me that when you found out her engagement to Trathen was off, you asked her to marry you instead, but that she refused you."

"She did refuse, but that's all right. I'm not giving up. I intend to persuade her to change her mind, marry me, and come to Egypt with me."

Paul laughed, shaking his head as if this were the stupidest notion he'd ever heard in his life. "She wouldn't have you back, man, not in a thousand years. And as for persuading her to move to Egypt, I remember how that turned out the first time. Win her back? You haven't a chance in hell."

"The odds of success do look rather slim at present," he conceded. "But I'm doing it anyway. It's the right thing to do. I just want you to know . . ." He paused and ran his finger around the inside of his collar with a little cough. "I want you to know that my intentions are honorable."

Paul raised his brows at that, looking understandably skeptical. "Well, that will make a nice change from what I witnessed earlier today," he murmured dryly.

Will didn't flinch. "You are her closest male relation, so I wanted you to know I'm not dallying with her."

He didn't wait for an answer, but instead he started for the door.

Paul's voice followed him. "You aren't even going to ask my permission to court her?"

"No."

"What makes you think you'll be able to persuade her to go to Egypt with you this time, when she refused to go with you six years ago?"

He paused, hand on the doorknob. "Because this time, I'm not giving up until she says yes."

"Pestering her to accept you. Hmm, that's an interesting strategy."

He grinned at the other man as he opened the door. "I prefer to call it courtship."

Chapter Twelve

Deciding to make one's own destiny was all very well. Figuring out what that destiny actually was, Beatrix knew, was the tricky part.

She didn't go down to dinner that evening. Instead, she had it on a tray in her room, in no mood to be anywhere near Will. Besides, she wanted to think, to decide what to do next.

All her life, she'd been raised with the firm belief that marriage and children were the inevitable course of her life. Now, however, she felt providence was telling her she'd best consider other options. Yet whenever she thought of the future that loomed ahead of her—of spinsterhood, with good works in the parish, helping Eugenia with the garden, sewing and sketching, gossiping and shopping in the village—in short, the life she'd been leading—she felt the same sense of emptiness she'd felt when Will had left for Egypt.

Marrying him would have been the simple thing to do, the obvious thing, the easy thing, the thing everyone else seemed to want her to do now that Aidan was gone. Her family would be relieved to see her settled and secure and suitably married to *someone*, even if the last-minute exchange of one duke for another was a bit unorthodox. After all. . .

One duke's as good as another.

Damn Will anyway. She stopped fiddling with the cold food on her plate, and set down her fork. Shoving the tray aside, she propped her elbows on her writing desk and her chin in her cupped hands, and stared out the open window into the moonlit night.

Will didn't love her, and she didn't love him anymore, and as much as she hated to admit he was right about anything, he'd been brutally accurate in his assessment that she could not be happy in a marriage that wasn't based upon love. That was why she'd had to keep talking herself into marrying Aidan.

But if not marriage, what else was there? A woman of her position did not generally take on a profession. There were exceptions, of course. Lady Weston owned an employment agency, had owned it since before her marriage. Vivian was a very well-known modiste. Emma, Lady Marlowe, had worked as Marlowe's secretary prior to marrying him, and to this day, she was a successful writer in her own right. Beatrix sat up a little straighter in her chair, feeling a spark of interest. What if she followed their example and took up a profession of some sort?

Beatrix considered that for a few minutes longer, then left her room and went downstairs. The children were in bed by now, but everyone else was still gathered in the drawing room. Will was seated at the secretaire with quill and ink. Julia was at the piano, and Vivian was fitting yet another new design onto a mannequin. The older ladies were sipping sherry and talking, and everyone else was engaged in cards, backgammon, or chess.

Conversation paused as she came in, and it was Julia, heaven bless her, who broke the awkward silence. "Trix, just the person I need," she said in a natural, breezy way, as if nothing out of the ordinary had happened today. "Come turn the pages for me. Vivian is terrible at it."

"Well, I do have my hands full," Vivian defended herself around a mouthful of pins.

Beatrix could feel Will's gaze on her as she walked past the secretaire on her way to the piano, but she didn't even glance in his direction. She positioned herself beside Julia's seat to turn the pages, and as her cousin sorted through sheets of music to choose another song, she glanced at the evening gown of sky-blue and ivory silk Vivian was piecing together on the mannequin nearby. "That's a lovely gown, Vivian."

The slender redhead removed the pins from her mouth. "Thank you. It's for the spring collection."

Beatrix nodded, studying it. "Do you have artists sketch your designs for you?"

Vivian looked a bit surprised by the question. "No, actually, I do all the sketches myself. I don't think I could have anyone do the drawings for me. I create the design as I sketch it, you see. Why do you ask?"

She took a deep breath. "I am thinking of ways I

might employ my artistic skill in some sort of commercial enterprise."

"What?"

Eugenia's exclamation of dismay made her wince, and she could hear a few murmurs of surprise from the older ladies, but she was undaunted. "If you draw your designs yourself, I suppose I shall have to think of another way to employ my skills. Lucy?" She turned toward the bridge table. "Does your agency have any posts available for illustrators?"

Lady Weston paused in card play, but before she could respond, Eugenia spoke again.

"Dear Beatrix, why do you ask such questions? You can't possibly become an artist!"

Beatrix set her jaw and looked her aunt in the eye. "Why not?"

Eugenia gave a little laugh. "Because it simply isn't done, dearest! Not by ladies of our class. Your sketching is a lovely pastime, and quite enjoyable for you, I daresay. But you cannot employ that talent for money. It's quite impossible"

"Again, I fail to see why it's impossible."

"Because it is!" Eugenia's voice was rising in agitation. "If what happened to your mother isn't sufficient to explain why—"

"Trix," Paul interrupted, his voice loud enough to override his mother's high-pitched accents. "Perhaps we should discuss this another time? Here and now are hardly the appropriate place and time for a discussion about your future."

Beatrix appreciated the uncomfortable silence. She glanced again at Lucy, realizing that she had just put her friend in an awkward position. "Never mind," she said, withdrawing before there could be any further argument on the topic. "You're right, Paul. This isn't the time. Since it's a lovely night, I believe I shall take a walk on the terrace. Excuse me."

She walked over to the French doors leading onto the terrace and stepped outside. She stalked to the rail, breathing deeply of the ocean air, trying to cool her frustration. Damn it all, why did a woman's life have to be so restricted, so narrow . . . so smothering?

This, she realized with a new sense of appreciation, must be akin to what her mother had felt. Given her family's expressed disapproval, she could not turn to her friends for assistance with any artistic venture. Marriage was no longer a possibility, at least for the foreseeable future, and unless she could persuade her family to see reason, she would have to defy them outright. Defying one's family, her mother had learned, came with a high price, and it was one Beatrix really didn't want to pay. On the other hand, she wanted a new life, a life of her own, and she had no intention of giving up. What she needed to do was find a way to bring her family up to scratch. But how?

Footsteps sounded behind her, and when she glanced over her shoulder, she found Will crossing the terrace to stand beside her.

"Do you really wish to be an illustrator?" he asked as he approached.

"What I really wish is to be alone," she said, and returned her gaze to the ocean view in front of her.

Of course he didn't listen. He moved to stand

beside her at the rail, and when she cast a sideways glance at him, she found him watching her. "Do you want to be an illustrator?"

"I thought I might, but my family isn't taking to the idea, as you have plainly seen."

"Excellent," he cut in as if her family's concerns were of no consequence. "I'll hire you."

"You want me to draw something for you?" She returned her gaze to the water, remembering all the sketches she'd done for him of the Roman antiquities he'd dug out of a barrow at Sunderland years ago. "Artifacts, I suppose?"

"Yes. I brought quite a few pieces back with me. They belong to the Egyptian Antiquities Service, but I am presenting them on loan to the British Museum for an exhibition. The intention is for the exhibit to generate interest in the work we're doing at Thebes and raise funds, perhaps even gain a sponsor. But Lord Marlowe has now agreed to sponsor the dig."

"So for what purpose do you need sketches?"

"Marlowe wishes me to write a series of articles about our excavation work, complete with photographs and detailed illustrations of the various pieces we've found. I'm certain I can convince him to employ you for the illustrations. In addition, the museum will want sketches for the catalog that will be published for the exhibition itself."

"I see." She paused a moment, tempted, even a bit excited by the idea, but she knew it was impossible. "I can't work for you."

He leaned one hip against the rail and folded his

arms across his chest. "I don't see why not. You want to be an illustrator. I'm in need of one. Seems pretty straightforward to me."

"You can't really think employing me would be a good idea."

"On the contrary," he said, smiling. "I think it's one of the best ideas I've ever had."

"But I hate you!"

Much to her irritation, his smile widened. "You don't hate me," he said, sounding so damned confident about it that she wanted to kick him in the shins. "You want to hate me, but you don't. Not really. And besides," he went on before she could argue the point, "if you intend to be an artist with commercial ambitions, you will occasionally have to work with people you don't like. One of the more tiresome aspects of earning one's living, I'm afraid."

She couldn't argue with that, she supposed. "I don't trust you."

"Very wise of you," he said gravely. "I'm quite untrustworthy, as you know from past experience. But I promise to behave myself, unless of course you cast aside your sketchbook, fling yourself into my arms, and beg me to make love to you, in which case I simply can't be responsible for my actions."

She made short shrift of that possibility with a derisive snort.

"It could happen," he insisted. "I live in hope."

"My family doesn't approve of me becoming an artist. They'll never agree to this arrangement."

"Why? Because they're afraid you'll run off to

Paris with some man? That you'll become morally corrupt and wanton?"

"Given what happened this afternoon," she said, giving him a wry look, "Paul, at least, has some justification for that fear."

"Leave Paul to me. I'll convince him to let you do it. He already knows my intentions are honorable."

"You, with honorable intentions?" She was trying to sound scornful, but much to her mortification, the words came out in a breathless rush. She swallowed hard and tried again. "That must be such a novel concept for you."

"I can be honorable, Trix. Do I need to remind you of the three-button rule?"

She shook her head, knowing she was running out of excuses. "I told you, it would never work. All we ever do is argue. And after what happened today, it would be awkward and . . . and embarrassing for us to work together."

"I kissed you. So what? People kiss all the time. You would be shocked if you knew who kisses who at most country house parties. And we have certainly done our share." He shrugged. "I don't feel embarrassed. I don't feel awkward."

But she did. Memories of the kiss they'd shared this afternoon, as well as all the kisses from years ago, flooded her senses, making her feel as if she must be blushing all over.

She drew a long, deep breath and strove to think clearly. "It wouldn't be proper."

"Despite your family's rather antiquated notions about professions for women, many well-bred ladies engage in commercial enterprise nowadays. Several of them are in that room, by the way," he added, with a nod toward the drawing room. "And besides, if I'm the one hiring you, your family won't care. In fact, I suspect they'll be delighted."

"Delighted? You saw their reaction when I brought it up. They hate the idea."

"Ah, but not if you work for me. They won't see your employment as a serious intention on your part to adopt a profession. Instead, they'll regard it as part of our courtship."

She grimaced at that, knowing he was right, remembering how Auntie Eugenia and the other ladies had reacted to the mistaken impression that she'd accepted Will's proposal. "A belief you will no doubt enforce at every possible opportunity."

He didn't deny it.

"I know what you're up to," she said with an accusing look.

He tilted his head, giving her an innocent one in response. "Am I up to something?"

"You are only offering to hire me because you want to soften me. You think if I sketch these artifacts for you, you'll persuade me to change my mind about marrying you."

"You know me far too well, Trix," he said agreeably. "I'm transparent as glass. Remind me never to play poker with you, or I'll lose my shirt. Something which does happen sometimes when I'm near you, by the way. Be warned."

Tongues of fire curled in her belly, and she shoved images of him without his shirt out of her mind. "Why?" she demanded in a fierce whisper. "No one will ever know what happened between us this afternoon. No one who saw us would ever reveal it, which means my reputation is not in jeopardy. So why are you doing this?"

"I told you, I want to do right by you. I cannot forget that I have twice caused your plans for matrimony to go awry, and I am compelled to take some measure of responsibility for my actions. Since you won't allow me to do the honorable thing by marrying you, at least allow me to help secure your future another way. It's a matter of honor."

"Honor?" She gave a laugh. "Honor?"

"All right," he capitulated. "That's all bunkum. Honor has nothing to do with it."

He glanced at the drawing room windows again, then unfolded his arms and leaned closer to her. "I want you. I want you as much as I ever did. I've spent six years lying to myself about it, and I just can't find the will to lie anymore. Now I've got a second chance with you—"

"You do not have a second chance!"

"And I'm taking it," he went on as if she hadn't spoken. "I want to win you back. I want you in my arms, in my bed, in my life."

Heat was flooding her face and spreading through her body as he spoke. Her lips tingled under his heated gaze, and without thinking, she licked them nervously.

His gaze lowered to her mouth, and for a heart-stopping second, she thought he was going to kiss her, right there in full view of whoever might be looking through the doorway, but he didn't, and when he straightened away from her, she didn't know if she was relieved or disappointed.

"Now you know my entire diabolical plan," he said. "Are you going to accept my offer of employment or not?"

"If I don't?"

He gave her an apologetic look. "I really don't want to have to resort to kidnapping."

She made a sound of exasperation and looked away, staring out at the ocean, grateful for the breeze to cool her heated skin. "What would my wages be?" she asked before she could stop herself.

"Three shillings per drawing."

"Five."

He didn't even bother to quibble. "All right. Five."

She bit her lip. She shouldn't even be considering this. On the one hand, he was offering her the perfect opportunity to do what she wanted, namely, take control of her own future. On the other hand, she didn't trust him an inch. Worse, she didn't trust herself.

"What's wrong, Beatrix?" he asked as she remained silent. "Are you afraid I'll wear you down until you just can't resist me anymore?"

Beatrix turned to face him, lifting her chin a notch. "Not at all," she said with dignity.

"Good. Then you'll do it?"

She couldn't really tell in this light, but she just

knew there was a challenging glint in his eyes, daring her. She felt as if she were standing up on Angel's Head again, looking down at a thirty-foot drop—dizzy, excited, and scared. "Yes," she said before she lost her nerve, knowing she was probably out of her mind. "Yes, I will."

Chapter Thirteen

Will stared at her, not quite able to believe what he'd just heard. "You'll do this? Seriously?"

"Yes. If I truly want to control my own destiny, I have to start somewhere. It would be silly to refuse a perfect opportunity." She made a face. "Even if you're the one providing it."

He gave a laugh, confounded. When she'd walked into the drawing room and announced she wanted to become an illustrator, it was a heaven-sent opportunity, but he'd never expected her to agree. After all, he'd told her the absolute, unvarnished truth about his intentions, admitting it was all a ploy to win her over. The fact that she was agreeing to it gave Will a spark of hope he hadn't felt for years.

"All right, then," he said with another laugh, trying to think how to proceed. "We'll . . . umm . . . we'll start straightaway. It's only fifteen miles to Suriderland by road, so tomorrow I'll borrow Marlowe's carriage for the day, my manservant and I will go down there, and I'll select some artifacts to bring back. That way, we can begin working on the catalog together the day after."

"It seems as if you're going to a great deal of trouble, carting artifacts up here. Wouldn't it be simpler to just wait until we return home? It's only three weeks."

"Exactly." He darted a glance at the open door to the drawing room, discerned that no one was watching them, and before she could protest, he planted a quick kiss on her mouth. "I don't want to give you any time to change your mind."

By the time he returned from Sunderland the following evening, it was close to midnight, the house was dark, and everyone was in bed. He slept late the next morning and missed sitting down to breakfast with the others, but when he came downstairs, the warming dishes were still on the sideboard, and he helped himself to scrambled eggs, bacon, and kidneys, and inquired of Marlowe's butler as to Beatrix's whereabouts.

"Lady Beatrix," the butler informed him, "is in the gazebo with Lady Danbury."

"Thank you, Jackson. Would you tell my valet to fetch my dispatch case, quill, ink, and one of the crates we brought from Sunderland Park down to the gazebo? And have Cook make a Turkish coffee for me as usual and bring it to me there, if you please."

"Very good, Your Grace." The butler bowed and

started off to perform these errands, but Will stopped him again.

"And Jackson, also have Lady Beatrix's maid bring her sketchbook and drawing pencils down there as well."

"I believe Lady Beatrix has those items with her already, sir."

"Excellent." Will went outside and took the path partway down the cliff to the gazebo, where Beatrix was seated with her aunt.

She did indeed have her sketchbook, but she wasn't using it. It was on the tea table along with a box of her drawing pencils, and she and Eugenia were at the rail of the gazebo, watching the beach below.

"Good morning, ladies," he said as he mounted the steps. "Gorgeous day, isn't it?"

Both of them turned, but it was Eugenia who spoke first. "Ah, Sunderland. You must have returned last night after all."

"We did, Aunt Gennie. We were delayed several hours by a broken carriage wheel, and by the time we arrived, it was very late."

He turned to Beatrix and gestured to her sketchbook. "I see you're ready to begin work."

"Yes," she said in some surprise. "If you are."

"I am. I'm having Aman bring some of the artifacts here, if you don't mind?" He turned to Eugenia. "Trix has very kindly agreed to do some drawings for me."

She beamed at him. "Yes, of your Egyptian treasures, I understand. Most exciting."

"Sir?"

He turned to see Aman approaching with a crate in his hands, balancing a silver desk set on top and carrying Will's Moroccan leather dispatch case slung over his shoulder. Behind him, a kitchen maid in gray muslin dress, white apron, and cap carried his coffee on a salver.

"Good morning, Aman. Set everything on the table, and then you may go." He turned to the maid as his valet came up the steps, and Beatrix moved her sketchbook and pencils to make way for the crate.

"How you can drink that foul beverage is beyond understanding, dear Sunderland," Eugenia said, breaking into his thoughts. When he turned around, she leaned forward to peer doubtfully into his cup. "It looks like tar, not coffee."

"It's Turkish coffee, Auntie," Beatrix explained. "Since Sunderland and I are spending the day working, perhaps you would prefer to go down to the beach and join the others?"

"Of course, of course," Eugenia said, smiling happily at them both. "You two young things enjoy yourselves. But remember," she added, wagging a finger at them, "I can see you from down below."

Beatrix groaned, but Will couldn't help laughing as Eugenia trundled off.

"See?" he told her when Eugenia was out of earshot. "I told you she wouldn't mind if you did sketching for wages as long as it's for me."

"Only because she's now convinced we're a hairsbreadth from being engaged. Honestly," she added in exasperation, "if I ever do manage to actually marry someone, I think Eugenia will be more radiant than the bride!"

"Not if you marry me. On our wedding day, you'll be so radiantly happy, you'll probably throw your arms around my neck and kiss me senseless the minute the vicar's finished. It will shock everyone in Stafford St. Mary."

"You have such a vivid imagination. Now," she added, gesturing to the crate before he could pursue the topic any further, "why don't you show me what you want me to draw?"

"Very businesslike of you, Trix." He lifted the lid off the wooden crate, carefully rummaged through the straw and pulled out a plain, square wooden box. "I think we should start with something beautiful, don't you?"

"That's your idea of something beautiful?" she asked, eyeing the box with doubt as he placed it on the table.

"It is, actually." When he lifted the lid to display the contents, he heard her sharp intake of breath at the sight of the band of gold, lapis, carnelian, and turquoise.

"What a lovely bracelet!" she exclaimed.

"It's an amulet, actually, worn around the upper arm." He pulled it from its velvet-lined case and held it out to her.

She reached out and took it gingerly, giving him a wry look. "Very wise of you to begin with the jewels," she murmured.

"What better way to captivate a woman's interest?"

As she studied it, he moved to stand behind her and leaned down. "That's history you're holding in your hands, you know." He reached over her shoulder, running his finger over the tiny, inlaid jewels. "This belonged to a woman named Moabset who lived approximately five thousand years ago."

"Do you know anything else about her?"

"Quite a bit, actually." He breathed in the scent of gardenia, and he knew if he turned his head, his lips would brush the soft skin of her cheek, but he appreciated that they were in full view from the beach below, and he knew from memory that despite her dithery manner, Eugenia had eyes like a hawk.

He straightened and forced his mind back to the matter at hand. "Her tomb had been raided, and most of the contents were gone, but somehow the thieves missed this."

"Left it behind by accident, possibly?" she guessed, turning to look up at him with a smile. "After all, if you're carrying out booty by the armful, you could easily drop something like this."

"Possibly. It was the only piece of jewelry in the tomb, but from an archaeologist's point of view, it was a treasure trove. There was a great deal of pottery, some clay tablets, other things like that, which told us quite a bit about her. Pottery shards, wall paintings, and tablets always tell us far more than the gold and jewels ever could. We found her sarcophagus, too, by the way, and her mummified remains. It was very exciting."

"Exciting?" She considered that for a moment, then she nodded. "Perhaps it would be exciting," she conceded, carefully studying the amulet. "But it's also a bit macabre, don't you think? No wonder you liked reading Edgar Allan Poe as a boy."

"Trix, every boy likes Poe."

She wrinkled up her nose with distaste, making a face at him. "I can't think why."

"Trix, 'The Tell-Tale Heart' is a ripping good story, and you know it."

She gave a laugh. "I still remember the night you read that aloud. We'd all snuck out and gone down to Phoebe's Cove. You, me, Paul, Julie, Phoebe, and Vivian. We had a bathe, and ate sandwiches, and made a fire in the pixy cave. And you read 'The Tell-Tale Heart' to us."

"'I heard many things in hell,'" he quoted and gave a diabolical laugh. "'How, then, am I mad?'"

"Oh, stop!" she cried, laughing with him even as she shivered. "I was never so scared in my life! Even Paul jumped out of his skin when you shouted out the part about ripping up the floorboards to find the beating heart at the end. He was more scared than any of us, I think."

Will grinned. "He'll never admit it."

"Probably not." She placed the amulet back in the jewel case and reached for her sketchbook and drawing pencil. "Is that why you find archaeology so fascinating? Because you like digging up tombs?"

"No, it's because I love watching history unfold in front of me. An archaeological site is all the layers of a civilization accumulated one on top of another, and we uncover them from the bottom up. It's important work because it's uncovering people's lives. That's history."

"I remember how you dug up that barrow when we were children. I know how it's done. But—" She broke off and looked away, tapping her drawing pencil against the table for a moment. Then she stopped and looked at him again. "What about what's here in England?" She gestured to their surroundings. "Our lands, our estates, have sustained our families for centuries. That's history, too, isn't it?"

He thought about that for a moment, trying to find a way to explain. "But that's a history we already know because we've lived it ourselves."

"What you're really saying is that England bores you."

He heard the suddenly flat tone of her voice, and he knew he wasn't doing himself any favors by admitting the truth, but if they were ever going to find common ground, they had to start with honesty. "In a way, yes, it does."

"Why?"

"Because there's no adventure in it, no sense of discovery. At an archaeological site, you're unearthing an entire community, layer by layer, generation by generation."

"We have generations, too, Will," she said gently, gesturing behind her to the beach below where the children were playing. "And I think their future is more important than anyone else's past. However fascinating Moabset's life might have been and how exciting it might be to uncover it, I don't think any of that is as exciting or as important as watching one's own children grow up."

"I don't disagree with you about that, Beatrix. I never have."

She frowned a little, looking down at her pencil. "What about giving your children a home? A secure future? Isn't that important?"

"Of course."

"Then why did you spend your entire inheritance on an excavation in Egypt?" She looked up with accusing eyes. "For what purpose?"

He stared at her, the implications sinking in. "You think I've been irresponsible."

"Yes. Yes, I do."

That hurt, like a wound in his chest. "You think if I'd put my inheritance into Sunderland that would have been better?" He didn't wait for an answer, but went on at once, "Landed aristocracy is a dying breed, Trix. They need to earn or marry the money to keep their estates solvent. The examples are all around you. Marlowe, who went into publishing. Your cousin, who married an American heiress—"

"What?" She looked at him in shocked disbelief. "Paul didn't marry Susanna for her money."

"I'm not saying he did, but the fact is, to keep up Danbury he would have needed to obtain money from *somewhere*. These estates don't pay for themselves anymore. If I had sunk my inheritance into Sunderland, it wouldn't have made a bit of difference. The money might have taken a little longer to be gone, but it would still have been wasted."

"I know land rents alone aren't enough to maintain an estate. I understand that. But why couldn't you have used your money to do something here at home?"

"Like what?" He shrugged. "I could have invested my inheritance in something else, stocks or industry, but those aren't sure things, either, you know. I could peg away at an ordinary job in the City, but what's a duke qualified to do?" He leaned forward, knowing he had to make her understand his point of view on this. "I know you feel that by putting my inheritance into archaeology, I made an unwise investment in my future, but I don't agree. That's why finding the tomb of Tutankhamen is so important to me. When I find Tut—"

"If you find him."

"No," he countered stubbornly, "*when* I find Tut, I'll have a secured income for the rest of my life. Books, articles, lectures. And I'd easily be able to find sponsors for future excavations."

"So you intend to be an archaeologist forever, then?"

Something in the question, in the way she asked it, with a tinge of both disappointment and resignation, made him feel defensive. "Why not? If I have to earn a living, why not earn it doing something I love?"

"Because it isn't just about you, Will. If I had married you, it would also have been about me, and our children. You would have been perfectly all right with carting us along to the next excavation. Maybe you'd have had enough money to take care of us, but maybe not. Adventure is all very well when you're a young bachelor on your own, but it isn't any way to raise a family. You accused me of being afraid to go with you, and you were right. I was afraid. Because of the fact that you were willing to upend my life, risk my future and that of our children to do what you wanted in life—without any guarantee of security for our family, and without even consulting me about the decision, I might add. These things told me that you would not be a reliable partner in life, and I realized I couldn't trust you or count on you."

He shook his head, stunned that she would think him so cavalier that he would ever neglect her. "I would always take care of you and any children we'd have, no matter what."

She set aside her pencil, her brown eyes looking at him with steadfast resolve. "That's something you'll have to prove, if you truly want to marry me now. You've lost my trust once, and before I would ever consider accepting you now, you would have to show me beyond a shadow of a doubt that you would be a responsible husband and father."

If Beatrix had hoped throwing down the gauntlet would dampen Will's determination and make him go away, she realized at once that she had severely underestimated his resolve.

His eyes locked with hers, and he nodded. "Fair enough. But," he added at once, "I think this sort of thing works both ways."

She frowned, puzzled. "Both ways?"

"Yes. You say you don't trust me, and . . ." He paused to draw a deep breath. "I admit, you have cause for your distrust. I'll be honest. I never thought about children. I should have, I know, but in my defense, let me say that most men don't. Not until we have them." A hint of wry amusement came into his eyes. "When you and I used to meet in the gardens at Danbury, for instance, children were never what I was thinking about."

Heat flooded her face, and she looked away. If she wanted to be brutally honest, she could have conceded similar feelings, for all those times when they'd met secretly and she'd been in his arms, the only thing she'd been thinking about was how wonderful it felt. But she decided at this point, it served no purpose to be *that* honest.

"Irresponsible of me, I admit," he went on, "but true. And when Sir Edmund asked me to go to Egypt with him, I jumped at the chance. I was twenty-three years old, with my entire future already planned for me, and I realized that I might not ever have another opportunity like that. I knew that if I didn't go, I would regret it for the rest of my life. I cabled him back and accepted without talking it over with you because it honestly never occurred to me that you would refuse to come with me."

"It should have."

"Perhaps, but please let me finish. Most of our lives, you've gone along with me, with what I wanted. A few exceptions here and there, like the cliff at Angel's Head, and not riding horseback as fast as I would like, and putting certain limits on things. Three buttons, and things like that—"

"Do you have a point?" she cut in, feeling the heat come up in her cheeks.

"But for the most part, you've tagged along on

whatever crazy thing I wanted to do, as long as I could persuade you that your father wouldn't find out. And we were about to be married, so I think it's fair to say you never gave me much cause to doubt that you would come with me to Egypt."

"Why?" she shot back. "Because a good wife goes with her husband whether she wants to or not?"

"No, damn it! Because we loved each other. Because I made you happy. Because you wanted to be with me and go on adventures with me. When I dug up that barrow, you enjoyed it, too, and you loved sketching all the artifacts. You loved sneaking out to the pixy cave when we were children, and listening to me read Poe and being scared, and you loved meeting me at midnight, the thrill, the possibility of getting caught. You love adventures, Trix. You do," he insisted when she shook her head, trying to deny it. "When your mother left, you were only nine years old, and from then on, your father tried to wrap you up and lock you in and keep you from doing anything that might take you away from him. He smothered you, and I think one of the main reasons you fell in love with me is because I enabled you to get away, to be free."

She jumped to her feet. "Don't you dare try to blame the fact that you jilted me on my father!" she cried, her temper flaring. "That's all your own doing."

"Not all my doing, Trix. Be fair and admit that you bear some of the blame, but more to the point, so does your father. And you're angry," he added at her sound of outrage, "because deep down you know I'm right."

She shook her head again, still denying it, hating the fact that it was absolutely true.

"You want to know what I think?" He rose and came around to her side of the table.

She folded her arms and took a deep breath, striving for control. "Not particularly."

He paid no attention, of course. "Maybe it was cocky of me to be so sure I could persuade you to go to Egypt, but I think I would have succeeded, and you would have had the time of your life. There was one thing, though, that I didn't take into account. And because of that one thing, I lost you."

"What one thing?"

"Your father. His absolute determination to keep you from ever leaving him. I know damned good and well the only reason he agreed to our marriage was because if you had to marry anyone at all, you would at least be marrying someone who only lived a few miles away. He wanted you to be right by him forever and never leave him. Hell, I think if he hadn't been able to talk you out of coming with me to Egypt, he'd have locked you in your room."

"That not fair! And it's not true!"

"When you issued an ultimatum and told me to choose between Egypt and you, I couldn't believe it. I thought you'd welcome the chance to finally, truly be free. But then I realized what you were really doing was throwing down the gauntlet because you'd already made your choice—dear Papa rather than me.

That's why I went without you. How could I stay, knowing that until the day he died, you'd always choose him over me?"

"So why didn't you come home when he died?" she cried, tears stinging her eyes, furious that she was about to cry when she'd sworn ages ago she'd never shed any more tears because of Will. "Not that it would have done you any good," she added at once. "But didn't you even think that I would be free to choose a different path then? One with you?"

"After five years? I thought it was too late, that it was over between us, and that we couldn't ever reconcile because—" He broke off and looked away for a second, rubbing a hand across his forehead. "I can be afraid of things, too, Trix. Can you understand that? What if I came all the way back here, with nothing to offer you, and you turned me down again? Then what? And then you got engaged to Trathen, and that seemed to be the final nail in the coffin for us. But when I saw you again, that day on the Stafford Road, I knew it wasn't over."

"It is over! How many times do I have to say it?"

He tilted his head as if seriously considering that question. "At least four hundred eighty-six thousand, seven hundred and fifty-two times. Then I might— might—start to accept it. Although, really, knowing how hard I tried to get over you before, I doubt even that would be enough."

"I told you, I can't trust you. I can't rely on you. You're irresponsible, and reckless, and . . ." She paused, running out of adjectives. "And just too cavalier about things. How would I know you would be a good father?"

"Well, I certainly wouldn't be like your father, a fact which tells in my favor, if you ask me. But," he added before she could dispute that point, "you told me a moment ago that I would have to prove myself, so that tells me I have a fighting chance. I propose we make a bargain."

Beatrix frowned, wary, sensing there had to be a trap of some sort involved in any bargain he proposed. "What kind of bargain?"

Instead of answering, he pulled out his chair and sat down, then reached for his dispatch case. Opening it, he extracted a sheet of paper, opened the inkwell, and pulled the quill out of the inkstand. Whistling to himself, he began to write.

"What kind of bargain?" she repeated, watching him.

"Just wait." He resumed whistling and writing what seemed to be a list, while she watched him, growing more apprehensive by the moment.

After a few minutes, he stopped and put the quill back in the inkstand. He picked up the sheet of paper, reviewing whatever he'd written as he blew on it to dry the ink. Giving a nod as if satisfied, he rose and came back to stand in front of her, presenting the sheet to her with a flourish.

" 'Report and catalog for the British Museum,' " she read. " 'Article for the *Times*, Presentation to the Archaeological Society—' " She stopped reading and looked at him. "I don't understand. What is this?"

"The things I need to do while I am here in England. You've told me, and quite rightly, that I have to prove I can be a responsible husband and father. But I also know that the crazy things I've led you into have made you happy. So to prove all these things, and remind you of just how wonderful our life would be together, I propose that I demonstrate my ability to be responsible by accomplishing each of these tasks, and every time I cross one off the list, you have to come on an adventure with me."

Pressing a smile from her lips, she tapped her finger against one item that had a big black line through it. "You already have something crossed off."

He leaned over the sheet, reading upside down. "Ah, yes, finding a sponsor for the excavation. That task is already done. Marlowe has agreed to sponsor it for the year."

"And you wrote it on this list anyway because . . . ?"

He didn't blink an eye. "An hour after everyone's gone to bed," he whispered. "At the dock."

This time she did laugh, but she couldn't help it. He was so outrageous. "Oh no, no. This is crazy."

"True, but it's also an adventure. So you'll come?"

She bit her lip, wavering. She had to admit, having adventures with Will again did sound like fun. On the other hand, life couldn't always be fun and games.

As she struggled to decide, Julia's voice echoed to her from their quarrel the other day.

It all started when Will went away . . . it was as if his leaving had sucked all the joy of life out of you.

It was true, she realized. How nauseating to know she was so susceptible to this man, that even now, he could pull her into things she knew she really shouldn't do.

She gave an aggravated sigh, sensing she was about to make a huge mistake, scared that the only thing she was going to get out of this was more crushed dreams and shattered hopes, and possibly a damaged reputation. And yet, despite all that, she could feel excitement rising inside her, a gigantic bubble of anticipation. She felt as if . . . as if it was June again and Will was coming home from Eton, or Cambridge, or Europe, or wherever he'd been, and she was watching the lane from her window at Danbury, knowing he was home, waiting for his horse to come racing up the lane to her house, dying to know what new adventure he had in store.

"All right, all right," she said, giving in. "It's a bargain. But only if you accomplish your work first."

He grinned and returned to his side of the table. Pulling out his chair, he sat down opposite her. "Well, come on," he urged as she remained standing there staring at him in chagrin. "It's your work, too, remember? So stop lollygagging and get started or we'll never be able to go play."

"I'm going to regret this," she murmured, sinking back down into her chair. "I really don't know how I let you talk me into these crazy things."

He chuckled as he dipped his quill in the inkwell. "You've been saying that ever since you learned to talk."

Chapter Fourteen

*B*y teatime, Beatrix had managed to draw only
three of Will's Egyptian artifacts. It was slow
going, for each piece had to be drawn from
several different angles, but she found herself getting
caught up in the work, just as she had when they were
children and he'd dug up that Roman barrow at Sunderland Park. It was rather exciting to sketch things
so ancient, and fun to speculate about the people to
whom these things had belonged.

Despite that, however, she did find her attention
wandering to the man across the table. She couldn't
resist darting quick glances at him over the top of
her sketchbook as he composed the descriptions and
notes that would accompany each of her drawings.
Not once did she catch him looking back at her. A
fact that she found just a little bit aggravating, espe-

cially since she was the one demanding proof that he could be responsible.

At this moment, he was composing a detailed description of the alabaster kohl jar that sat between them on the table, their last piece of the day. He was in his shirtsleeves, with the cuffs rolled back, and as she watched him write, she could see the flex of sinew and muscles in his forearms, making her remember the strength in his arms as he'd pulled her hard against him the other day. When he stopped to pick up the piece of alabaster for closer study, she studied his long, strong fingers, remembering the caress of his fingertips against her cheek. When she dared a peek at his face, memories of his lips on hers in that lavish, open kiss sent warmth radiating through her body.

He set the piece back down on the table. "Is there a problem?"

"Hmm? What?" She came out of her reverie with a start, lifting her gaze from his mouth to his eyes. "I beg your pardon?"

"I asked if there was a problem. You haven't put pencil to paper for at least five minutes. Instead, you've been staring at me."

"Sorry. I . . ." She paused to compose a reason for staring at him, but she realized there was none, at least none that wouldn't be terribly embarrassing to admit. "I wasn't staring at you," she said, her face coloring up as she uttered the lie, her gaze returning to her sketchbook. "I was . . . I was staring into space and thinking about something, that's all."

"I see," he murmured. "What were you thinking about?"

She resumed sketching, but she could feel his amused gaze on her, and since she couldn't confess that she'd been admiring his body and remembering his kisses, she invented an excuse to be staring at him. "I was wondering about this adventure you're taking me on tonight. What do you have planned?"

"I can't tell you. If I did, it wouldn't be an adventure, would it?"

She gave an aggravated sigh. "You have to at least give me a hint."

Stubbornly he shook his head. "No hints."

"But what do I wear?"

He grinned. "Nothing?" he suggested, sounding hopeful.

She blushed again, threw a drawing pencil at him, and gave up, but all through tea, and dinner, and entertainments in the drawing room afterward, her thoughts kept returning to what lay ahead. With Will, she knew it could be anything, and by the time everyone went to bed around half past eleven, her anticipation, curiosity, and excitement were making her feel as jumpy as a cat on hot bricks.

Dressed in her Turkish trousers and a simple shirtwaist, she sat by the window in her darkened room, staring out into the night, waiting as the clock in her room ticked away the minutes. She couldn't see the dock—it wasn't visible from here. She could only make out the tip of the *Maria Lisa*'s mast in the moonlight, but she knew he was already down there, waiting. She'd seen him in the moonlight a few minutes ago, walking down the path.

She didn't dare follow him until she was sure everyone was asleep, and time seemed to crawl by. With each minute that passed, she felt her anticipation grow, and her doubts with them. What if they were caught? She'd have to marry him then. She wouldn't have a choice.

Perhaps she shouldn't go.

But even as that thought passed through her mind, she dismissed it. Who was she trying to fool? She'd go. She'd known that all along. After all, she reasoned as the clock struck one and she slipped out of her room, a bargain was a bargain.

Would she come?

Will didn't know. She might lose her nerve. Trix did that sometimes, usually just at the moments when he was sure she wouldn't.

But then he heard the delicate crunch of gravel on the path, and a moment later he saw her, hurrying toward the dock in the moonlight, and he let out a slow breath of relief. He walked up the dock to meet her and took her hand. "C'mon."

"What are we doing?" she whispered.

"It's an adventure, remember? You'll just have to wait and see."

With her in tow, he retraced his steps to the end of the dock, where a rowboat was bobbing in the water. "In you go."

She eyed it doubtfully, but allowed him to help

her in. "Where are you taking me?" she asked as she seated herself in the stern.

He didn't answer. He stepped in after her, took the center seat, and pulled the oars from the bottom of the boat. After popping them into the locks, he held the ends with one hand and leaned toward the dock, using his free hand to untie the rope and shove them away from the quay. The boat went gliding silently out into the cove.

"Are we going to Diana's Cove?" she asked, obviously impatient with his refusal to answer any questions.

"Save your breath and stop guessing." He used one oar to turn the bow seaward, and then, with a glance over his shoulder, he began rowing. "I'm not telling."

She made a sound of vexation. "I'd forgotten how stubborn you are about these things," she muttered under her breath, but when he brought the boat out of the cove and began rowing south along the point, she began to laugh. "I know where we're going."

He grinned at her in the moonlight and pulled on the oars. "Do you now?"

"We're going to Smuggler's Island."

His grin faded, and he sighed, shaking his head. "Really, Trix, I wish you wouldn't guess these things so quickly. It's much more fun when I can keep you in suspense."

It took about ten minutes for him to bring the boat around the point, into the bay beyond, and over to the wooded island several hundred yards off shore. He brought the boat in until the sand scraped bottom, then removed the oars from their locks and returned them to their place beneath his seat. He yanked off his boots and socks, rolled up his trousers, and jumped into the water. He held the boat in place as she removed her own shoes and stockings, and though it was just torturing himself to watch her do it, he didn't look away. The view of Trix's pretty feet and shapely calves was just too tempting a sight for him to resist.

She followed him into the knee-deep water and helped him beach the boat well above the water mark. "Now what?" she asked.

"C'mon." Grabbing his boots, he beckoned her to follow him. She started to reach again for her own shoes, but he stopped her. "You won't need them."

She gave him a puzzled look, but he didn't enlighten her. Instead, he led her to the edge of the beach, where the sand ended and the woods began. There he paused long enough to brush the sand off his feet and put his boots back on, and then he turned to her. Wrapping one arm around her waist, he hooked his other arm beneath her knees and lifted her.

She laughed, curling her arms around his neck as he carried her into the woods. "Trying to impress me?" she asked.

"Yes," he confessed, turning down a well-worn path that led through the woods and around a rocky bit of the shoreline. "Is it working?"

"That depends. Where are you taking me? I know,

I know," she said as he still didn't answer. "You're not telling."

"Don't need to," he said, emerging into a clearing. "We're there."

"There?" she echoed, sounding even more puzzled than before as she looked up at him, but when she saw him nod to something behind her, she turned her head, and gave an exclamation of surprise and delight. An ancient elm tree stood on a jutting bit of headland overlooking the sea, and hanging from one of its stout branches was a swing. Its plank seat and twin ropes swayed ever so slightly in the ocean breeze, and behind it, above the endless stretch of ocean, a crescent moon hung in the night sky, surrounded by a million stars.

"It's beautiful!" she said, laughing. "But I don't remember a swing being here when we were children."

"There wasn't one. Marlowe and his boys put it up this summer. I heard them talking about it the other day, and they told me where it was. I remember how your nanny didn't like you to play on the swing Paul and I put up at Danbury."

"I remember, too," she murmured. "But you used to swing me up really high when she wasn't looking. And I'd laugh and give the show away, and Nanny would look up from her knitting and scold you like anything."

He leaned close to her ear. "Care to have another go now that you're all grown up?" he murmured.

She nodded, and he carried her over to it. When he set her down, she settled herself on the seat. He grabbed the ropes and took a few steps backward.

"Hold on," he said, and gave the swing a shove forward to start it going.

"What a lovely view," she said as she came falling back to earth, and he gave her another push.

"Perfect spot for a swing, eh?"

"Mmm," she agreed, and with that, both of them fell silent as he pushed the swing for her. She leaned back in the seat and stretched out her legs in front of her, moving with the motion of the swing in a rhythm every child learned and every adult remembered.

He gave the swing a harder shove, and she sailed up precariously high. "Will!" she cried, laughing protest, but he paid no attention. The next time she came back down, he sent her even higher, laughing with her as she went up, up, up toward the stars. "It's a good thing I didn't wear a dress tonight," she told him as she came back down. "That's why Nanny didn't let you swing me up high, you know. My dress might go flying up."

Her nanny wasn't the author of that silly rule, he knew perfectly well, but he decided there was no point in bringing up the fact that her father was a controlling bastard whose ideas of what was appropriate recreation and behavior for his daughter dated from medieval days.

"Well," he said instead, "if you ever do finally agree to marry me, and if we have daughters, they'll be allowed to go as high up on the swing as they want."

"You say that now," she said over her shoulder as he pushed her toward the stars again, "but what about later?"

The fact that she wasn't protesting the possibility of marrying him gave him another spark of hope. He might, he just might, be able to win her over after all. "Later?" he asked, not pushing the swing as hard this time, but letting momentum alone carry it so that it would slow down. "What do you mean by that?"

"What about when they're older?"

"I still don't know what you mean. They'll be able to go on swings no matter what age they are."

"I'm not talking about swings. What about when they meet young men who want to sneak them out of the house for midnight adventures?"

She swung back down toward him, and he caught her, stopping the swing by wrapping his arms around the ropes and her and digging his feet into the sand beneath them. "I'm not worried about that."

"No?"

"No." He relaxed his hold and leaned down, tilting his head to press a kiss to her temple. "I sleep lightly, and I'm an excellent shot."

That made her laugh, and she didn't pull away when he kissed her cheek. "So shooting your daughters' suitors would be your solution?"

He nodded, inhaling the delicate scent of gardenias as he brushed his lips against her ear. The skin of her earlobe felt like velvet against his mouth. "Yes."

She turned her head, twisting in the swing to look at him. "That's so hypocritical," she accused, but she was smiling when she said it.

He moved around to the front of the swing and sank to his knees. Grasping the ropes to hold the swing still, he leaned closer to her. "Very hypocritical," he agreed, and his lips brushed lightly against hers. The contact sent fissures of pleasure through his body. "What can I say?"

He wanted to kiss her fully, feel her mouth open and willing beneath his, but before he could act on that delicious impulse, her voice—suddenly serious— stopped him.

"But there's really no point in discussing how we would raise our daughters, is there, Will? Because we're never going to have any."

He drew back again. Letting go of the ropes, he cupped her face in his hands. "Don't say never, Trix. I told you before, that's a very long time." He paused, then, forcing offhanded lightness into his voice, he said, "Besides, I'm still hoping to persuade you to come back to Egypt with me."

"If that's the case, you're wasting your time. I don't want to go to Egypt."

"Why not?" He pressed a kiss to her forehead. "There isn't anything stopping you anymore," he pointed out as gently as possible.

"Yes, there is, Will." She gestured to their surroundings. "My life is here. In Devonshire. And I like it that way." She drew a slow, deep breath. "That day in Halstead's Bookshop, when you said I dream of going places but I never go, I can't deny that, for it's true. But I've never really minded being an armchair traveler."

"You only say that because this is what you're used to. You would love to travel, if you stopped wishing about it and actually did it."

"I confess, I would like to go to Florence one day,

and I'm not saying I wouldn't like to see the Pyramids or take a boat up the Nile or unearth some pretty Egyptian jewelry or alabaster jars, but I don't want that to be my life. I do like adventures, but only as long as they aren't too scary and I can come back home when they're over to my soft bed and my afternoon tea and my English rain and my cottage garden. Because deep down, I'm just an ordinary English girl, and I want an ordinary English life."

She paused a moment, then went on, "What you overheard Julia say to me the other day was true, too. It wrecked me when you left, and it took me years to accept that you really were gone for good, that you weren't coming back, and that you didn't want the life I did." He started to speak, but she pressed her fingers to his mouth, stopping him.

"After Papa died," she said, lowering her hand again, "that was when I finally realized how short life was, and how mine was going by. I knew I had to accept that you weren't coming back, that I had to make a life without you. Julie dragged me to Cornwall, and we had a lovely holiday, and then I met Aidan. You're right that we weren't in love, but we were fond of each other, and he wanted all the same things I did, and it seemed that marrying him was the right thing to do. Some might call that settling for less than you really want because Aidan and I weren't deeply in love, but at twenty-five, I was already well and truly on the shelf, and I wanted to be married and have children more than anything, you see."

Will didn't want to hear this, but he knew he had

to. "And now I've ruined all that for you. Again." He gave a sharp sigh and looked away, letting his hands fall to his sides. He felt his desire fading, along with some of his optimism. "I wish I could make it right."

"You can't. Because we don't want the same things, Will, and without wanting the same things, we can't be happy together, no matter how many adventures you take me on. You see, I like my plum pudding at Christmas, and coming to Pixy Cove in August, and watching the races at Ascot. I like the smell of apple blossoms in the spring and roasting chestnuts in the autumn. Those are the things that matter to me. And I've never been able to understand why they don't matter to you."

They'd had this discussion so many times, he thought in frustration, and it never seemed to go anywhere. It never accomplished anything. "It isn't that they don't matter to me. They do."

"But not enough to stay."

"It isn't only that. I want my life to mean something. I want what I accomplish to be more important than the next race meeting or the next London season. And the work I do in Egypt isn't just something I love. It enables me to earn a living. You're telling me I need to be responsible, but I think what I'm doing is responsible. It's important work. Here, I would have nothing to do and no way to support you or any children we might have."

"I have a dowry."

"No." His voice sounded hard, even to his own ears. "I will not live off my wife's money."

She nodded slowly, as if she hadn't expected any other answer. "*Plus ça change, plus c'est la même chose*," she murmured, and a wistful little smile curved her lips. "I've ruined our adventure now, haven't I?"

"No." He cupped her face in his hands again, savoring the soft warmth of her skin against his palms. "You haven't ruined anything," he said, and his words were confirmed by the fact that as he caressed the cupid's bow pout of her lips, his desire for her began flaring up again and spreading through his body.

He reached behind her head and began pulling out her hairpins.

"Will," she whispered, reaching behind her head, pressing her palm to the back of his hand, stopping him, "what if someone sees us?"

"You always say that," he whispered back, smiling. "We're on Smuggler's Island, remember? Around the point and a mile away, and if that's not enough to reassure you, we're on the seaward side and it's the middle of the night. Who's going to see us? Pirates?"

She made a stifled giggle at that and lowered her hand to let him begin pulling out hairpins. When he succeeded in removing all the pins, he tucked them in his trouser pocket and freed her hair from its bun. It came down, and he spread it out around her shoulders, where it gleamed in the moonlight like waves of liquid platinum. In his fingers, it felt like strands of silk.

He raked his hand through it, wrapped a handful of it around his fist, then tilted her head back. Her lips parted and her lashes lowered a fraction, the first sign of yielding in their favorite adventure of all, but just as he had done all those years ago in the gardens at Danbury, he held back, controlling his own desire, reminding himself to wait for hers to catch up. He slid his hands back into her hair and brushed his lips lightly across her cheeks, her forehead, down the bridge of her adorable, doll-like nose, and back to her gorgeous mouth.

The moment his lips touched hers, waves of pleasure fissured through his body, pleasure born of need not yet fulfilled, of desire never sated, of anticipating the next time when, perhaps, satiation would come. It had taken six years for him to forget this, but the memories were rushing back now, renewed and heightened so that his need for her seemed higher than ever. This was Trix, this was her kiss—her soft, full lips pressed against his own, her tongue touching his, her sweet taste. This was her body, all lush curves and soft, velvety skin and the heady scent of gardenias.

He eased his tongue between her teeth, and when her mouth opened, it sent him right over the edge of desire and into full-blown lust. He pulled her off the swing and onto her knees, her arms came up around his neck, and he lowered his hands to cup her buttocks, pulling her fully against him as he began to imagine a fantasy he hadn't allowed himself in years. A fantasy that had given him sleepless nights ever since he was seventeen years old, a fantasy that had never been fulfilled.

He imagined pulling her down into the sand

and taking off her clothes. He imagined her breasts cupped in his palms and her naked hips against his and her hair falling around his face.

He groaned against her mouth, feeling his wits slipping. He broke the kiss and buried his face against her neck, working to regain his control, even as he slid his hand along her neck to where the softness of her skin gave way to the crisp muslin fabric of her shirtwaist.

He unfastened the first three buttons, then pulled the edges of her collar apart and pressed kisses along her collarbone, his excitement rising even higher at the sight he'd exposed, the bare skin from beneath her jaw to the shadowy cleft between her breasts, and he knew he could not take this any further without annihilating what remained of his self-control, knowing she wasn't ready for where all this kissing and petting was bound to lead. Their adventure was over. At least for tonight.

With another groan, he pulled back before he could change his mind, and stood up. "We should go back," he said, and held out his hands to help her up.

When she was on her feet, he knew he ought to step back so that she was out of reach, but he couldn't bear to leave off touching her completely, and he began buttoning her shirtwaist. It wasn't easy, for his hands were shaking with the effort of holding back.

She stared at him as he fumbled with the three buttons, her eyes wide and dark, her hair falling like waves of moonlight on either side of her face. "I'd forgotten how it felt, Will," she whispered. "I'd forgotten."

He left off fastening buttons and caught her by the arms, then pulled her close and kissed her again, a hot, quick, fierce press of lips. "I tried," he told her, his voice a ravaged whisper as he lifted her in his arms again. "God knows," he added with a hoarse chuckle, "I tried my damnedest."

As he carried her back to the beach, he strove to regain his control, but when she stepped into the boat, the sight of her bare calves was almost his undoing, and he very much feared that cooling his lust enough for sleep was going to be impossible. Neither of them spoke as he rowed back to Pixy Cove, but once the boat was docked and they were walking back to the house, he paused on the path. "You go on."

She paused beside him, surprised. "Aren't you coming?"

"No. But I'll see you tomorrow, either at breakfast or at the gazebo afterward. We start work at nine o'clock. Don't be late."

"I won't." She smiled at him in the moonlight, a wide, radiant Trix smile that was for him and would always be only for him. "I'm not the irresponsible one, remember?"

He laughed, hope rising inside him like a wave. He watched her as she walked the steep path up to the house. He waited, watching her window, wondering if she would remember, and when he saw the brief flash of lamplight that always told him she was safely back in her room, he grinned into the dark.

"Good night, Trix," he murmured, and then he turned and started down another path away from the house, heading to Phoebe's Cove. There he did what he'd often done during previous romantic adventures with her. He stripped, marched naked and still fully aroused into the water, and started swimming.

A few more adventures like this, he thought wryly as he took laps back and forth across the cove, would result in either matrimony or insanity. Just now, he wasn't sure which. God, he hoped it was the former.

Chapter Fifteen

When Beatrix came down the following morning, Julia and Eugenia were in the dining room with Lady Marlowe and little Ruthie, having breakfast. Will, she learned, was already down at the gazebo working on the artifacts, and everyone else had gone with Sir George and Lady Debenham to Smuggler's Island for a day of picnicking.

At the mention of Smuggler's Island, Beatrix's thoughts immediately went to the night before, and a swing in the moonlight under the stars. Trust Will to come up with something like that, she thought, smiling as she poured herself a cup of tea. Pushing her up high on the swing when no one could see because she hadn't been allowed that joy as a girl.

She stared at the oil painting of Pixy Cove that hung behind the sideboard, and as she remembered other childhood adventures, she felt a bubble of pleasure rising inside her, pushing up against her chest. Will had always come up with special things to do, which was why life had seemed so colorless after he went away and why she'd needed so long to accept that he was gone.

She'd become sure over the years that he'd forgotten her, forgotten everything—days at Pixy Cove exploring the caves at midnight and reading Poe, and how much she'd loved going high on the swing at Danbury when Nanny wasn't looking, and how she'd wanted to go to Florence when she was fifteen. She'd convinced herself Will had forgotten all that; eventually, she'd even half forgotten it all herself.

I tried. God knows I tried my damnedest.

The pleasure inside her deepened and spread, becoming so keen, so poignant, that it almost hurt. She tried to suppress it, tamp it down, remind herself that what he'd said last night didn't really change anything, but her efforts didn't stop the feeling inside her, and she recognized it for exactly what it was. She was happy.

Her happiness didn't stem merely from reliving their childhood experiences of midnight adventures. She'd also enjoyed the work they'd done together yesterday. She'd enjoyed sketching those artifacts. In fact, she mused as she stirred sugar into her tea, she'd enjoyed the sketching she'd done for him yesterday more than she had when they were children and he'd excavated that Roman barrow. Perhaps that was because this time, she was choosing to do it not for the boy she'd loved, but for herself.

The big grandfather clock in the foyer began to chime the hour, and she came out of her reverie with a start. Nine o'clock? And she'd told Will she wouldn't be late. Quickly she gulped down her tea and raced for the door. "I'm joining Will in the gazebo," she called back over her shoulder. "We'll be working all day."

"Beatrix," her aunt called back to her, "wait for me, if you please."

"Can't, Auntie. I'm already late."

"Beatrix!" Eugenia's voice rose, shrill and firm. "You cannot be alone with him. Wait for me while I fetch my needlework, and I shall come with you."

She stopped in the doorway with a sigh of impatience. "For heaven's sake, Auntie, we shall be outside in broad daylight. What on earth could we do that would be improper? We are working, not courting!"

"Yes, I know, dear. Of course you are. But I am your chaperone."

"I could come with you," Emma offered. "I've nearly finished breakfast. Although my bringing Ruthie with me might be a distraction if you wish to accomplish any work. She's been such a fussbudget of late."

"I'll be your chaperone today, darling," Julia offered, standing up. "I'm finished with breakfast." Picking up her teacup in its saucer, she started for the door, adding carelessly over her shoulder, "Don't worry, Auntie. I'll see that Will doesn't ravish her over the artifacts."

Julia followed Beatrix out of the dining room,

adding in a murmur that only she could hear, "At least not until after lunch."

Both of them burst into giggles as they crossed the corridor and entered the drawing room.

"You really are a most inappropriate chaperone," Beatrix told her as they paused by a bookshelf near the French doors. "You're the one who taught me to smoke cigarettes and drive a motorcar and dance the can-can. Poor Auntie. If only she knew just how wayward I became in Cornwall."

"It would give her heart failure, I'm sure," Julia agreed cheerfully. She pulled out a book from the shelf, and the two of them left the house. "Is that true, by the way?" Julia asked as they walked down to the gazebo. "What you said in the dining room?"

"What I said?"

"That you and Will are not courting?"

Beatrix felt defensive all of a sudden. "I told you already that he proposed and I refused him. I agreed to do these drawings for him, but it's all . . ." She paused as memories of the previous night flashed through her mind. When she spoke again, she strove to sound convincing. "It's all perfectly innocent."

"Is it?" Julia stopped walking. When Beatrix stopped also, her cousin gave her a fleeting smile that had a hint of concern in it. "Be careful, darling," she said gently. "You might fall in love with him all over again. And this time," she added, overriding Beatrix's protest, "I fear even Cornwall and the Daimler won't save you."

Julia walked on, but Beatrix didn't move. Instead,

she stared after the other woman in dismay, rooted to the spot, her momentary happiness eclipsed by panic. Julia was right. She could fall back in love with Will again, easy as winking, and if that happened, even six years, another man, and a Daimler motorcar might not be enough to help her recover.

When she and Julia arrived at the gazebo, Will was already there, immersed in work. His valet had replaced the artifacts they'd finished working on yesterday with a fresh lot, and he was studying a turquoise ring beneath a magnifying glass as she and Julia approached.

He set it aside and rose to his feet as they came up the steps. "Good morning, Julie." He turned to Beatrix, and there was a smile in his eyes that told her he was thinking of last night. "Trix."

She gave a quick nod and looked away, her panic deepening into outright fear—fear of being hurt again, being jilted, living without him—and the simple pleasure and happiness of yesterday began sliding away.

"Now remember, you two," Julia said in a droll mimicry of Eugenia, "I'm watching you from down below." With that, she continued on down the path to the beach, leaving them to work.

Beatrix took a deep breath, let it out slowly, and leaned over the table, pretending to study the various pieces of jewelry in the velvet-lined boxes before her as she worked to tamp down her fears. She was working for him and nothing more, he was leaving in a few short weeks for Egypt, and she was making a new life for herself as an illustrator. Even as she reminded herself of these facts, she had the sinking feeling her efforts would prove as futile as her efforts to forget him had been.

She could feel his gaze watching her across the table, and she forced herself to say something. "Did you want all these pieces sketched today?"

"Only if it's possible."

"I don't know if it is." She bent closer to study a splendid scarab of lapis and gold. "Some of them are very intricate."

"I understand. The gentlemen at the British Museum are excited about our findings, and want to see the artifacts as soon as possible. And I am scheduled to give a speech to the Archaeological Society on September tenth. But there isn't a set date by which I have to show them the sketches."

She touched her fingertip delicately to the beaded chain of an elaborate jeweled collar. "I thought you wanted to be on your way back to Thebes straightaway after your speech."

"That was my intention originally. The journey to Thebes takes about two weeks, and the excavation season officially begins at the start of October. During that first fortnight things are a bit chaotic with everyone returning to Thebes at various times. Since I have been living in Cairo during the summer months, I'm usually one of the first to arrive at the site, and with Marlowe sending a journalist and photographer, I had thought to make the journey back ahead of them, but I might postpone my departure a little longer." He paused, then added, "If you want me to."

She looked at him and found him watching her with a tenderness in his face that seemed unbearable. "Why should it matter to me?" she asked fiercely, and tore her gaze away. "We're not courting. Go back to Egypt whenever you please."

"I can stretch my journey out a little, stay a couple weeks longer, if that's what it takes."

"If that's what it takes to do what?" she asked, and jerked to her feet, prickly and defensive. She was angry at him because he wasn't offering to stay, he was only offering to put off his inevitable departure. And she was also angry at herself because she was already missing him and he hadn't even left yet. "Do you think a couple more weeks will change my mind and persuade me to go to Egypt? If so, you're wasting your time."

"It's my time, Trix," he said gently. "And I wouldn't think it a waste."

She opened her mouth to reply, but at that moment, Will glanced past her and stood up. When she looked over her shoulder she saw Emma coming across the lawn toward them with Ruthie in her arms, and Eugenia walking beside her, and she gave a sigh of relief. In their presence, Will couldn't talk to her of the impossible things he wanted from her.

"Ladies," he greeted them and circled the table to walk down the steps. "Hullo, Ruthie."

The baby, who recognized her name, looked toward him as he approached, and her face lit up, bringing back Will's words of a few days ago.

As far back as I can remember, whenever you used to look at me, your face would light up as if someone had lit a candle inside you.

She studied little Ruthie's expression, and somehow, she found it a bit comforting that she wasn't the only one susceptible to Will's charm, even if his other conquest was only one year old.

She watched him kneel on the grass and hold out his hands to the baby, and when Emma set her on the grass, she stretched out her arms toward Will with a joyous gurgle, but when she started toward him, she only managed to take three steps before she went down on her bottom.

She'd landed in the soft grass, but for some unaccountable reason, her face puckered up and she began to cry. Emma started to reach for her, but Will was quicker, scooping her up and settling her into the crook of his arm, her pale blue dress and her chestnut hair a beautiful contrast to his dark green waistcoat and white shirt. When he smiled at her, she stopped crying, and when he began to talk to her, making silly faces, she laughed and patted at his cheeks with her chubby hands.

Watching them, Beatrix felt a strange, awful sensation—as if the world were crumbling and breaking up and re-forming into a place she hadn't dared to dream about for years.

She'd asked Will the other day how she could rely on him to be a good father to his children, and though his reply—a rather disparaging assurance that he wouldn't be like her father—had angered her, when she saw him now, holding little Ruthie and making her laugh, Beatrix knew she had an answer to her question. He would be a good father, if only . . .

She stopped smiling, and the hard reality set in as the qualification passed through her mind.

If only he would change.

He looked up and caught her eye. He pointed straight at her, murmuring something to the baby, and Ruthie looked at her, too, smiling.

Watching the two of them hurt her eyes, as if she was staring into bright sunlight, and she turned away, blinking rapidly as she returned her attention to her work and picked up her drawing pencil.

He wasn't going to change, she reminded herself, trying to harden her heart and shore up her defenses. For him, life was all fun and play and adventures in Egypt. He wasn't ever going to want to live in the world she lived in, and he wasn't ever going to live up to his responsibilities at home. And that was what truly made her afraid and proved her a fool. He wasn't going to change, and no matter how much time passed, no matter the evidence to the contrary, she kept hoping he would.

Will had thought working together might renew the excitement Trix had felt all those years ago when they'd dug up the barrow, spark her interest in Egypt and the work he was doing there, and bring the two of them closer together. But during the two weeks that followed, he appreciated that it wasn't going to be that simple.

She drew sketches of the artifacts, but she did not ask him any questions about them. He tried to engage her in conversation, discussing the various pieces, describing the excavation work, telling her about the ancient Egyptians. But though she listened politely, she expressed no further interest, returning to her work without seeming inclined to explore the topic further. She made any modifications he requested—a different angle of a particular piece, or a closer view—without any discussion. If she had ideas of her own, she did not express them. She was as business-like as any employee could be toward her employer, and nothing more.

In the evenings she stayed close to Eugenia and Emma, giving him no opportunity to draw her out, bring her closer, show her his point of view. And his frustration grew, because he knew he couldn't force her to meet him halfway. She had to come there on her own.

As the days passed, he often took the opportunity to observe her as they worked together, trying to determine what more he could do to win her over. His chance to rectify his past mistakes was slipping away, and time became more and more his enemy with each day that went by.

Instead of coming closer to him, she was pulling away. He could sense it, but he didn't know what to do about it. As he worked to find a way to bring them closer together, one thing she'd said kept echoing through his mind.

You would not be a reliable partner in life. I knew I couldn't trust you or count on you.

Trust was the crux of it all, really. She didn't trust him, and if he were honest with himself, he'd have to concede that he didn't quite trust her, either. He, too, had felt the pain of a broken heart. But he still wanted her, and he was willing to take another chance because he had a gambler's heart. She didn't.

The problem was that trust, especially once it had been broken, took time to develop, and time was not on his side. As August gave way to September and the time to leave Pixy Cove drew closer, he could feel a sense of desperation and despair setting in. Upon their return to Stafford St. Mary, he would have to depart almost immediately for London to give that speech to the Archaeological Society on the tenth. Upon his return to Devonshire, he'd have two weeks, maybe three, before he had to leave, for he had to be in Thebes by the fifteenth of October. He couldn't stretch things out any longer than that. And even then, two weeks in Stafford St. Mary didn't seem nearly enough time to change Trix's mind. In addition, it would be much harder to find time alone with her than it was now, for they wouldn't even be in the same house. It could be done, of course—they'd snuck out plenty of times in the days before he went away. But it was trickier to arrange, there was more risk of being caught, and with the way she was pulling away from him, the chance she'd take those risks seemed less and less likely.

He kept watching her, listening, waiting, hoping like hell for something—an opening, an opportunity, an idea—anything that would show him what to do next, but it wasn't until the afternoon before they were ready to leave Pixy Cove that he found the opportunity he'd been waiting for.

He'd finished his descriptions for the catalog and was putting them in order with the sketches she'd done, waiting for her to complete her last drawing, but when he glanced at her across the table, he saw that she wasn't working. Instead, she was staring out toward the other side of Pixy Cove, lost in thought.

"Penny," he said.

She gave a start at the sound of his voice and looked at him. "I beg your pardon?"

"I said *penny*, as in *penny for your thoughts*."

"Oh, sorry." She shook her head. "I was just thinking of that day on Angel's Head."

That surprised him. "Really?"

She nodded, and turned her head to look back out at the cove. "You were right, you know."

Will was becoming more surprised by the moment. "In what respect?"

"I wanted to take that dive," she confessed.

"I know you did."

She gave him a rueful smile. "But you can't know just how many times I've berated myself since then because I didn't do it. You were right to say I was afraid."

"Everybody's afraid sometimes, Trix. And it's not as if it was anything important. It was just a silly dare."

"I know, but I've always regretted it."

He glanced at the sky, thought about the moon, and calculated the time of the next high tide. "If that's true, why don't you do something about it?" he suggested as he gathered the papers before him into a stack and worked to sound as if their future didn't hinge on what she decided. "Instead of regretting it, why not change it instead?"

"Change it?"

"Yes." He held out the stack of pages to her. "Other than that drawing you're working on, the catalog is finished and I can cross that off my list of duties to fulfill. I've done my part, I've been responsible, and that means that tonight, it's time for another adventure."

The moment he smiled at her, she realized what he had in mind and she began shaking her head. "Oh no," she said, laughing a little. "No, no, no."

"Angel's Head," he told her, opening his dispatch case to put the catalog inside. "One o'clock. Wear your bathing dress."

"You're off your trolley if you think I'm diving off that cliff at Angel's Head with you."

"It'll be your only chance until next year."

"It'll be the middle of the night!"

"There's a full moon tonight. It'll be almost as bright as day. C'mon, Trix," he coaxed as she continued to shake her head. "It'll be fun."

"You always say that."

"And I'm always right. Admit it. Every adventure you and I have ever had has been fun." He closed his dispatch case and stood up, slinging the case over his shoulder. "I'll bring food, and after you take that dive, I'll make a fire in the pixy cave there, and we'll have a picnic. Maybe I'll even read you some Poe." He circled the table, and as he passed her, he added, "Don't forget to bring a pin for the pixy."

She tossed down her pencil and stood up. "Diving off of Angel's Head in the middle of the night is crazy!" she said to his back as he started down the steps of the gazebo.

He paused to look back at her over his shoulder. "You say you've regretted not doing that dive ever since you were ten years old. This is your opportunity for a second chance." He grinned. "I don't know about you, but I've become a firm believer in second chances."

Beatrix knew she must believe in second chances, too. Either that or Will's particular form of madness was contagious. Because at one o'clock in the morning, by the light of a full moon, she was sneaking out of the house to meet Will at Angel's Head so she could dive off a cliff. She'd have told him again how crazy this was, except that right after dinner, he'd unaccountably disappeared, not joining them in the drawing room.

For over two weeks, she'd propped up defenses and kept him at bay. She'd played the part of the businesslike, indifferent employee, but underneath the mask she'd put on, she'd spent the past fortnight feeling miserable and afraid, and the effort to keep those defenses up was exhausting her. She didn't want to be hurt again, and yet sitting with him this afternoon, staring out at Angel's Head, she'd realized that all her efforts to avoid hurt were an utter waste of time because she'd start hurting the moment he left for Egypt, and she was meeting him at Angel's Head for this adventure because she didn't want to waste any more time hurting while he was still here. Because there was no point in anticipating the future by sacrificing the present. And because life was short and sweet and meant to be lived, and that was the lesson she'd been trying to learn for six years.

He was already there, waiting for her by the edge of the cliff, wearing nothing but his old football breeches and loafers, but she was too nervous to appreciate the delicious sight of his bare chest in the moonlight.

As she approached, she heard him give a heavy sigh, and she watched him shake his head. "Why do they make you women wear such silly things to swim in?" he asked, and before she could stop him, he plucked her ruffled muslin bathing cap off her head and dropped it to the ground, ignoring her indignant protest. "Beatrix, be practical. You can't dive with that thing on your head." He grasped her arms and turned her slightly to examine the back of her head. "Good," he said with approval. "You braided your hair nice and tight. You'll have to take off your bathing shoes and stockings, though. They'll only weigh you down."

Seeing the sense of that, and deciding her own fears were already enough to weigh her down, she unlaced her leather bathing slippers and pulled them off, along with her stockings, and she tried not to think about what she was about to do. She wanted to do this, she wanted to prove to herself that she could, but when he asked if she was ready, she was seized by doubts.

"What if the waves bash me on the rocks?" She watched the smile curving his mouth, and she scowled. "Don't you dare laugh! It could happen."

"No, it can't." He took her gently by the arms. "Listen to me. The cliff overhangs the rocks a good ten feet, and the waves aren't strong enough to carry you because we're in a cove. Look," he added, pointing below. "The reflection of the moon barely makes a ripple. It's almost as calm as a millpond down there. You won't be bashed on any rocks."

"What if it's too shallow and I hit bottom?"

"The depth of the water's at about forty feet right now. You won't hit bottom. It's no more dangerous than diving off the dock."

"Yes, it is." She peered over the edge. "The water is a lot further away."

"But it's perfectly safe. Watch." Before she could blink, he was gone, going over the edge with no hesitation, his splendid body in perfect form, head down, legs together, back arched, and arms outstretched in a perfect swan dive. He straightened his arms over his head, and when he hit the water, she barely saw the splash.

When he surfaced, she let out a breath she hadn't even known she'd been holding. He didn't call up to her, for if anyone happened to be awake back at the house, they might hear him. The windows at Pixy

Cove were always open. He merely beckoned her with a wave of his hand, treading water below, waiting just as he'd waited sixteen years ago, for her to follow him.

She stared down at him in the cove below, wondering how she always let him talk her into these things. She wasn't like him. She couldn't just dive off a cliff, or race the moor on horseback, or go off across the world.

She must have stood there a long time, because he waved his arms in a negative crossing motion, indicating she should stay where she was and not take the dive. He didn't have to worry about that, because she was losing her courage more with every passing second. She peered down at him, watching as he started swimming for shore. A few minutes later, he came up the ladder to rejoin her.

He paused beside her, raking a hand through his wet hair. "If you'd rather look at the view," he said, "that's all right, too."

"I want to do this. I do. I've always wanted to do it. But I—" She looked up into his face. "I don't think I can. Damn," she added, feeling her courage slipping irretrievably away.

He put an arm around her shoulders and pressed a kiss to her temple. "It isn't as if you'll never have another chance. Angel's Head isn't going anywhere, you know."

That didn't make her feel any better. She leaned over the edge a little and gulped. "It's such a long way down."

"It's only thirty feet."

"Only thirty?" she echoed faintly. "Is that all?"

"You don't have to dive off, you know. You could just jump instead."

"That might be better." She peered over the edge again. "Diving off the dock at Pixy Cove is one thing. This is—" She broke off and gulped again. "Different."

"How about if we jump off together?"

She turned to look at him and watched him hold out his hand to her. "If you decide to do it this way, though," he added before she could reply, "you can't hesitate. Once we go, we go. No shying at the last second, or we really could get hurt, and I don't know about you, but I don't want a dislocated shoulder. So I'm trusting you. That's what it is, you know. Trust. Do you trust me?"

She looked down at his hand held out to her. She looked into his eyes, his gaze so sure and steady, and she knew, for whatever reason, doing this was important in a way that was far beyond his childhood dare and her childhood regret.

"All right," she said, and clasped his hand before she could change her mind. "We'll go together."

"The cliff overhangs the cove a good bit here, so it's really just a matter of stepping off."

She nodded. "I'm ready."

"We go on three." He swung their clasped hands forward. "One."

She felt old childhood fear tighten in her stomach.

He swung their hands again. "Two."

She told herself nothing would go wrong and took a deep breath.

"Three."

And they went over together, a jump off a cliff and a leap into space. A leap of faith. And for one incredible moment, she knew how it felt to fly like a bird.

Chapter Sixteen

She held his hand all the way down, letting go only when their feet hit the water. A moment later, Will felt the edge of her bathing dress glide up his arm as she rose toward the surface. He gave a hard kick, following her, and when he broke the water, the first thing he heard was the sound of her laughing. He turned his head and found her treading water only a few feet away, a big grin on her face.

"That was smashing!" she cried, rubbing water out of her eyes with one hand. "Absolutely smashing! Far better than any swing could ever be!" She laughed again. "What on earth was I so afraid of all those years ago?"

He reached for her, cupped a hand to the back of her head, and pulled her toward him for a quick kiss. "The unknown."

She glanced up at the cliff in the moonlight, then back at him. "Could we do it again?"

They did, three more times, hand in hand all the way down. Afterward, he went up the ladder alone and retrieved their shoes and her stockings, then he took her to the pixy cave. He'd already brought everything down for their picnic, and when he lit the lantern, she was able to see what he'd done—the big blanket spread out on the sandy ground, and the picnic hamper, and the fire by the entrance already laid with driftwood.

"So this is why you vanished after dinner," she said, and smiled at him, one of the old Trix smiles, a smile that lit up her face and made him feel like a king. "You were setting all this up."

But then she shivered, her smile faded, and she rubbed her hands up and down her arms.

"You must be freezing." He set their shoes on a nearby rock and reached for the big canvas bag he'd brought down earlier. Opening it, he pulled out the robe he'd brought for her, the warmest robe he owned, a thick, soft garment of claret-red merino wool with a flannel lining. "Here," he said, handing it to her and reaching back into the bag for matches. "I didn't know if you'd think to bring a change of clothes."

"I didn't," she confessed, unfolding it, but as she started to put it on, he gave a cough. "You might want to take off your wet bathing dress first," he advised. "You'll be warmer that way," he added, though he wasn't wholly motivated by concern for her. "We can dry your things by the fire while we eat. Don't worry," he added as she hesitated. "I won't peek while you change."

She laughed. "That's what you always used to say. Turn around."

He pretended to be affronted. "I thought you were supposed to be learning to trust me again."

Beatrix shook her head, unmoved. "When it comes to this, I never trusted you. Turn around. And no sneaking a peek when you think I'm not looking."

He sighed and turned his back, kneeling down to light the fire. "I brought you a picnic and everything," he grumbled. "The least you can do is let me have one little peek."

She gave a harrumph, dashing that hope, but there was no stopping his imagination. He listened, striving to hear what she was doing over the crackling sound of the fire, imagining her removing the wet garments. First her tunic, exposing her bare shoulders. Then her knickerbockers, sliding them down her bare legs. And then her combination, working the buttons free and pulling the edges apart to reveal her breasts, full and round with rosy pink nipples. Christ, he thought as his body responded to these erotic images, he had to stop or he'd drive himself insane.

He fiddled unnecessarily with the fire and tried to suppress the arousal flaring up in his body, but when she told him he could turn back around, he realized his efforts were wasted. The garment covered her, swamped her, in fact, and he couldn't even see her hands—and yet he found the sight of her in his robe wildly erotic. Perhaps, he thought, lowering his gaze to the sash tied around her waist, that was because now only the flimsiest barrier separated his hands from her naked body. Or perhaps it was because he could see her pretty toes peeking out from beneath a sea of fabric. Or perhaps it was the sight of her lacy muslin combination spread out on the rock by the fire. He forced his gaze back to her face, but that didn't help, because she was staring at his chest, and all he could think of was how it would feel to have her hands touching his bare skin.

"We should eat," he said, needing to say something. "We don't have more than about two hours before we have to go back."

She nodded and sank down cross-legged onto the blanket, carefully arranging the folds of his robe around her. That was when she noticed the ice bucket and bottle behind the picnic hamper. She gave a throaty chuckle. "Champagne?"

"I thought of bringing lemonade." He pulled the bottle out of the half-melted ice and reached for a glass. "Since you became so fond of it during my absence that you gave up champagne in favor of it."

She sighed. "I only gave up champagne because Aidan can't drink."

"Can't drink?" he echoed as he filled their glasses. "What do you mean?"

"He said more than one glass of wine or spirits makes him quite drunk and when he's drunk he has a tendency to do wild things."

Will tried to imagine Trathen doing anything wild and failed utterly.

"I never could imagine Aidan drunk and wild,"

she went on, almost as if reading his mind, "but he assured me that's what happens when he drinks too much. He always limits himself to one glass of wine, but he loves champagne, and if he starts drinking that stuff, he finds it hard to stop. Because of that, I felt it was unfair to drink champagne in front of him, and we decided that it would be best to stick to lemonade."

Her smile faded, and he was struck by the change. "What's wrong?"

"Nothing. I was just thinking of Aidan." She bit her lip. "He didn't deserve what he saw that day."

"No," Will agreed, handing her a glass of champagne. "But it happens." Deciding it might be best to stop talking about her previous engagement, he added, "I also thought about bringing caviar tonight, since you love the stuff so much. But at the last minute I changed my mind."

"Thank goodness," she murmured, and gave the same sort of shiver he'd seen that day on the *Maria Lisa*. "Horrid stuff. Tastes like wet beach sand."

He gave a shout of laughter. "It does, rather," he agreed as he set the bottle back in the bucket. He took a swallow of champagne, placed his glass on a flat part of the rock beside him, and pulled the picnic hamper closer to open it.

"I brought bread and cheese," he told her as he laid them on the blanket. "And," he added, rummaging in the basket again, "I also brought these."

She gave a delighted exclamation as he brought out a pair of long-handled forks. "So we can toast our bread and cheese over the fire!" she cried, laughing.

"As we always do at Pixy Cove. Well," he amended, handing one of the forks to her and starting to tear the bread into pieces, "at least as we used to do until Antonia found the rope ladder, realized we were all sneaking out at night, and started watching you girls like a circling hawk. I wouldn't have been surprised," he added, "if she'd begun sleeping outside your door."

"She didn't, but her maid did. Don't you remember?" He shook his head and she went on, "You probably never saw her, since your rooms have always been on the other side of the house. She sat in a chair by the servants' stairs at the end of the corridor. Julie tried to sneak out again once or twice, but the maid always woke up and caught her. I didn't even try. I'm just grateful Antonia didn't write Papa and tell him we'd been sneaking out all along, or the fat would have been in the fire and I'd never have been allowed at Pixy Cove again. But I suppose Antonia decided to keep mum and not tell Papa because I was too young for any of it to be a scandal anyway. I was only, what, ten or eleven by then?"

"Ten," he said and began to pare cheese off the block. "It was shortly after the day you wouldn't dive off Angel's Head with me."

"That's right." Beatrix took the bread he handed her, speared it with her fork, and laid the slices of cheese on top, then stretched her arm toward the fire to toast her makeshift sandwich at the edge of the flames.

He did the same. "And after Antonia figured out what we'd been up to," he went on, "you were so scared of getting caught doing anything naughty. You refused to sneak out for midnight adventures with me for another seven years, not until after we were engaged."

"Is that why—" She broke off, and when he looked at her, he found her looking back with an uncertain expression. "Is that why you proposed?" she asked. "So that we could . . . could . . ." She paused again, and he thought she blushed, though in the light and heat of the fire, it was hard to tell. "You know," she said softly.

He was astonished. "Is that what you think? That the only reason I proposed was because I just wanted to make love to you and couldn't manage it any other way?"

"I did wonder." She wriggled on the blanket, ducking her head, looking uncomfortable. "Especially after you went away. I couldn't help thinking you must never really have loved me at all."

He studied her bent head, her golden hair shining in the firelight, and he felt a fierce, hot ache inside his chest. "I always loved you, all my life," he blurted out, and immediately tore his gaze away, staring at their hunks of bread and cheese side by side. A long silence stretched out, the crackle of the fire the only sound before he said softly, "I never stopped."

Those words hung in the air, suspended in fire smoke and sea air and childhood memories, and joy rose up inside her like a bubble. She caught back the happy, silly sob in her throat, holding it back so he wouldn't hear it. She bit her lip, keeping her gaze on her lap, trying to hold on to reason. It was just words. He was leaving. They weren't going to spend their Augusts together at Pixy Cove or sneak off for kisses in the wine cellar or the garden. They wouldn't be putting presents for their children under the Christmas tree, or doing any of the other things she'd wanted. That dream was dead. It had died six years ago.

"Careful," he said, and she looked up through a blur, realizing her bread was burning at the edge. She jerked her arm back, saving her meal just in time.

"I know it doesn't do any good to say things like that," he told her in an unbelievably level, ordinary voice, "because you've already refused to marry me. But I thought you should know. More champagne?"

"Why can't you stay here?" she whispered without looking at him, her heart constricting with pain.

He refilled their glasses without answering and set the bottle back in the bucket, rattling the little bits of ice that remained. "Because they are expecting me at the excavation. I have work to do there and people counting on me. I know you think I'm not a responsible sort of fellow, but I can't let them down. And you won't come with me, so there we are."

She nodded. She really hadn't expected any other answer, and yet a dull ache formed at the center of her heart, and she didn't want to think about how things would be when he left and she was alone again and there were no more adventures.

They ate their bread and cheese in silence, and it wasn't until they were putting the remaining food back in the picnic hamper that he broke that silence. "I think I'm the one who's ruined our adventure."

"No, you haven't. It's been wonderful. Maybe next year, I'll actually dive off Angel's Head." But she knew without him, she wouldn't. "Maybe, if you—" She broke off, afraid to say what she wanted to say. She turned, shifting on the blanket to stretch out her legs beside the fire, giving herself time to find the nerve. "Maybe if you come back next August, you can watch me do it."

He didn't answer, and she shoved down her disappointment. Silly of her to think he'd promise her he'd come back, silly of her to wish for it. But when the silence continued, curiosity impelled her to glance at him, and when she did, she saw that he wasn't looking at her face. He was staring at her legs where they were partly exposed between the edges of the robe, and in his expression was the same hungry desire she'd seen that day on the *Maria Lisa*.

Warmth washed over her, warmth that had nothing to do with the fire, warmth that radiated through her entire body. She thought of that kiss by the swing, the kiss at Phoebe's Cove, and all the other kisses they'd had, and she decided it was time for something more. She downed the last of her champagne in a couple of swallows and took a few deep breaths, working up her courage. He wasn't coming back, she knew that. And she wasn't going. And she knew there was one more adventure they had to have before he left. "It's been a wonderful escapade," she said, and stood up. "The best we've had yet."

He rose to his feet as well. "I'll take you back."

"Why?" she asked, tugging at the ends of the sash around her waist. "What makes you think our adventure is over yet?"

He watched her, desire turning to dismay as she started to pull the robe apart, and to her amazement, he grasped her wrists, stopping her.

"Don't," he said with surprising fierceness. "For God's sake, don't. I'm going back to Egypt, remember?"

"I know."

He cupped her face and looked into her eyes. "In all the midnight adventures we've had, we've somehow always managed to keep our heads about this. But once we pass a certain point, it will be almost impossible to call it off, which is why we always had the three-button rule, remember? And if we go too far, it'll be too late."

"Because I'll lose my innocence, you mean?" She smiled a little and turned her head to press a kiss into his palm. "I told you before, life is short, and I think we've denied ourselves this particular adventure long enough, don't you?"

She stood up on her toes to kiss him, but he evaded her. "Trix, listen to me," he said in desperation, and she sank back down with a sigh. "It's the champagne talking, not you. We can't do this. If we do, we'd have to marry."

"Why? Because there might be a baby?" She watched him shake his head a little, as if he couldn't believe what she was saying, and she couldn't help laughing a little. "What? You think I think babies come from cabbage patches?"

"Well, I don't know," he said, sounding quite testy all of a sudden. "Your mother left when you were nine, and knowing Eugenia, I can't imagine you ever received a true explanation of the facts of life. And it's not as if you and I ever discussed it. At least not a proper discussion. As I recall, our conversations on the topic were limited by our three-button rule and a lack of time and privacy."

"Julie explained all about babies to me ages ago. When you and I became engaged, she told me everything about it. I'd already suspected certain things, of course, because of you." She began blushing, which didn't help her feel like an adventurous seductress, and she felt the moment of opportunity slipping away. "But I'm willing to take a chance, just this once. We might never have another. The time is now, Will," she said. "It's still about two hours until dawn. And we have privacy here."

"What about the three-button rule?" he said, sounding desperate.

She smiled and pulled the robe off. It fell behind her in a heavy swish. "This doesn't have buttons."

Will turned his back on her with an oath. "For the love of God, Trix, stop it. I'm trying to prove to you I can be responsible so you'll marry me. But if you don't put that robe back on, I can't be answerable for my actions. I just can't."

"That's all right." She came up behind him and

slid her hands along his smooth back, savoring the feel of his muscles beneath her palms. "I don't expect anything. I just want this, because it's all we have."

He gave a shudder beneath her touch, but he didn't pull away. "Trix, don't—"

She pressed a kiss to his shoulder, and with a stifled sound, he turned around, catching her up before she could recover from her surprise.

"I warned you," he said, and his mouth came down on hers. The kiss wasn't like any other they'd ever shared. It was hard, bruising, almost violent, and she knew with a surge of excitement that she'd pushed them both beyond any possibility of stopping. His arms came around her, hers slid around his neck. The contact of her bare skin against his was like nothing she'd ever felt in her life. It was delicious. She groaned into his mouth.

He deepened the kiss at once, his tongue caressing hers, sliding deeper, then pulling back in a way that was carnal and demanding. His skin felt scorching hot against hers, making the warmth in her body deepen and spread.

He pulled back, breaking the kiss long enough for both of them to take one gasp for air, then he was kissing her again, slow, soft, drugging kisses that had them both sinking to their knees.

He cupped her face and explored her mouth, probing deep, tasting, then gently suckling her lower lip. The warmth in her grew stronger, hot where her breasts were pressed to his chest, even hotter where his hard arousal was pressed against her belly. She remembered this from years ago, and yet it wasn't the same, for there weren't layers of clothing between them. She stirred, her arms tightening around his neck, her body rubbing against his, seeking more of this exquisite friction, her breath quickening.

She felt herself falling again, only this time it wasn't like jumping off a cliff into the sea. She was sinking to a soft flannel blanket with Will's hard, strong body covering her, drowning her in heat and fire.

When he didn't kiss her again, she opened her eyes, to find him hovering above her, breathing hard. His eyes were unreadable in the firelight, but his face above hers bore a harsh expression, almost as if he were in pain. "I'll try to stop in time," he said, his voice a hoarse whisper. Before she could reply, he was kissing her again, and his hand opened over her breast.

She jerked in shock, for she'd never allowed him to go this far, and she wasn't prepared for her own reaction—the luscious wonder of it that had her arching upward into his hand. He cupped and shaped her in his warm palm as he pressed kisses to her throat, her collarbone, and the curve of her breast, and it all felt so wonderful, she couldn't help moving, wriggling beneath him, wanting more, but she didn't know what more was coming that could possibly feel as delightful as this. She felt warm and tingly all over.

He kissed her breast again, and her hand came up into his hair, raking the damp, silken strands, pulling him even closer, with a moan.

He obeyed that soft command, opening his mouth

over her nipple, then closing gently to suckle her. She cried out at the hot delight of it, delight that spread in ripples of heat until her whole body felt as if it was on fire. She began to move more forcefully under him, yearning to be even closer. He shifted his body on hers, and she felt the hard, aroused part of him intimately pressed to the apex of her thighs. She'd known this part of him existed ever since she was seventeen, and he'd pressed her against a wall in the fruit garden one midnight at Danbury. She slid her hips against that part of him now, heightening her own desire, making her feel terribly wicked and adventurous. Every sensation seemed heightened. She was naked and he was nearly so, and she was moving with an abandonment and desperation she'd never felt before.

He seemed to sense what she felt, and he lifted his head. "Tell me to stop," he ordered, but even as he spoke, his palm cradled her breast, and his fingers gently toyed with her nipple, teasing her. "Just tell me to stop."

She shook her head, desperate, frantic, terribly afraid he would stop and these wondrous feelings would end. "N-no," she managed, arching upward against his hand, hips sliding wantonly against his hardness. "No stopping."

"You're killing me by inches," he muttered against her skin. "If I die before you marry me, it'll be your fault." He rolled off her, shifting his weight onto his side. His palm glided along her waist and spread across her stomach.

He paused, looking at her, and his eyes glittered like jewels in the firelight. "Part your legs," he said, and when she did, he slid his hand between her thighs and his fingers touched her there. And then . . . oh heavens, the sensation was so sharp, so piercingly sweet, she cried out, her whole body jerking, her thighs closing convulsively around his hand.

"You're so soft," he murmured, pressing kisses to her breast, her collarbone, her neck, her face. His hand moved, pushing, and she relented, relaxing her legs a little. The tip of his finger slid up and down in the crease of her most intimate place, and the pleasure became so acute, little sobs tore from her throat. His voice, so low, only heightened her excitement. "So, so soft," he murmured. "So wet. You're nearly ready."

She only knew what he meant in a vague sort of way, and she couldn't have replied even if she wanted to, for the caress of his fingers was making that impossible. She seemed to have no control of her body. She could only strain and jerk helplessly against his hand, striving toward something that hovered just out of reach. She had no control of her voice, for the only sounds she could make were tiny whimpers of need and desperation. She didn't even have control of her thoughts, for the only thing she could think was *More, more, and don't stop.*

"I won't stop," he said, and she realized she'd uttered those thoughts aloud, a moan of complete surrender, but there was no time to be embarrassed.

Suddenly everything within her seemed to explode in a violent paroxysm of ecstasy. He continued to caress her, vowing not to stop, and waves of that first white-hot sensation kept coming over her again and again, finally easing into a blissful, panting oblivion.

She felt him moving beside her, and when she opened her eyes, she saw him on his knees, unbuttoning his breeches. Still dazed, she blinked, lifting her head, trying to see what that hard part of his body looked like. She caught the barest glimpse, and all she had the chance to do was say his name.

"Will?"

He moved at the sound of her voice, as if hearing the panic in her voice. "It's all right," he said hoarsely, pushing his knee between her legs. "Just open for me."

She did, parting her legs as she had before, but instead of lying on top of her, he knelt between her spread legs. Cupping her buttocks in his hands, he pulled her upward toward his groin.

His face was harsh, even in the soft firelight, and his breathing labored as if he'd been running. His shoulders and chest were like a bronzed wall, blocking out everything but him. She gasped as his hardness touched her where he'd caressed her moments before, and she tried to sit up to see what was happening, but he groaned, his hands tightening, squeezing her buttocks. "Don't move, Trix. Christ, don't move."

He was so afraid she'd move, pull back, bring him to his senses before it was too late, that he surged forward, pushing into her, not fully, but enough that he heard her gasp of surprise at his penetration. He could feel her barrier against the tip of his penis, and he pulled back a little, then pushed forward a little, groaning at the exquisite tension, straining not to go too far and ruin her, but God, she was so moist and hot, and when he felt her body tighten around his cock, when he could feel her climaxing again, he could feel his wits slipping away. Her body was moving in spasmodic jerks, her hips pressing upward against him, wanting him fully, an instinctive, unintentional torment that he didn't think he could bear, and he gritted his teeth. Her barrier touched his cock again, a tease and a warning, and he knew it was now or never.

Until you prove you can be responsible . . .

Christ Almighty. With a groan of agony, he tore himself away, pulling out of her just in time. He lowered his body onto hers, his cock pressed against the soft, melting wetness of her, and frustration and pleasure overcame him in equal portion. "Oh God," he groaned, shuddering as he climaxed between her thighs. "Oh my God."

Her breath was hot against his neck, her arms tight around him, his weight pressing her into the blanket. "Why?" she panted. "Why did you stop?"

He shook his head, unable to speak, pleasure still rocking his body. He drew the experience out as long as he could, knowing it might be the only time in his life he would ever lie with her, wishing it could go on forever, knowing it could not.

After a few moments he drew a deep, shaky breath and opened his eyes. He raised himself up and moved to lie beside her on his back. He buttoned his breeches and tried to regain some semblance of sanity before he answered her question.

"I don't want you to have to marry me just because a baby's on the way," he finally said. "And," he added before she could reply, "don't ever tell me again that I'm irresponsible." He rubbed his hands over his face. "Hell, after what I just did, I think I'm downright heroic."

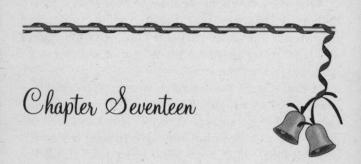

Chapter Seventeen

They left a pair of pins in the pixy's cave before returning to the house. As they'd always done on their midnight adventures in the past, Will stayed outside, watching for that brief flash of light in her window before returning to his own room via the sturdy old oak tree.

This time, there'd been no need for a long, hard swim before going to bed, but Will was far from satisfied. Tearing himself away from her at the last moment had been one of the hardest things he'd ever done, almost as hard as leaving for Egypt.

He lay in bed, staring at the ceiling, listening to the roar of the sea outside his open window, but in his mind, all he could hear were her soft cries of pleasure. All he could see was her face, radiant in the moonlight of Angel Cove and in the firelight of the pixy cave. Her eyes, big and dark and lovely. Her smile, like the sun coming out behind clouds, just to shine on him.

Trix, he thought, closing his eyes. All his life, the only woman he'd ever wanted.

He felt a sudden wave of melancholy and tried to shake it off. He had to journey to London to meet with the fellows of the British Museum, and give that speech to the Archaeological Society, but he'd be gone only a week, at most. And there was a full fortnight after that before he had to leave again.

He couldn't stay longer. Marlowe was funding the excavation, gambling the cost against Will's certainty that where he'd chosen to dig this year was where they would find King Tut, but Marlowe wouldn't continue if Will pulled out. And by October, an entire staff would be readying themselves for the new season, counting on him to be there with the funding to carry on.

He knew he wouldn't make the same mistake he'd made six years ago. He might have to go, but he would come back in the spring. And he would try again to win her. He'd keep trying until she married someone else or hell froze over, but if she wouldn't come with him now, he would have to leave her behind.

At that thought, pain shimmered through him like a cold wind through an empty house.

Trix, he thought in despair and rolled onto his belly, burying his face in his crossed arms. *I don't want to say good-bye.*

* * *

The call of her name and an insistent knock on her door awakened Beatrix, pulling her out of a heavy, languorous slumber.

She'd been dreaming, she realized, dreaming of Will's mouth on hers and his hands touching her. And his body, pushing against hers, into hers, in that luscious, exquisite way.

"Beatrix?" Aunt Eugenia's voice came through the closed door, a shrill sound that made her wince and pulled her out of romantic dreams of Will as effectively as a pail of ice water. An emphatic knock followed. "Beatrix, dear, are you in there?"

She shook her head, trying to clear her sleep-dazed senses. "Of course I am here, Auntie," she called, sitting up. "Come in."

Eugenia opened the door, took two steps inside, and stopped, giving a vexed exclamation. "Oh heavens, you're not even dressed yet!"

She blinked, rubbing her eyes. "That's because you just woke me up," she said around a huge yawn.

"And it's a good thing I did. You'll have to dress yourself, for Lily will need to fully occupy herself with packing your things."

"Packing?" She cast a startled glance at the window. "My goodness, what time is it?"

"It's nearly ten o'clock, and—"

"Ten?" She slid another glance, a guilty one, at the window. "I can't imagine what made me sleep so late," she mumbled, feeling as if the reason was written on her face.

If it was, Eugenia didn't appear to notice. "Well, don't just sit there lolling about," she said with an impatient wave of her hand. "You've no time for it this morning. You only have half an hour to dress, pack, and have your things downstairs. Sir George wants to be under way by half past ten. Although," she added as she turned toward the door and Beatrix jumped out of bed, "it's taking him longer to prepare the *Maria Lisa* than he thought it would, so you might have a bit of extra time. With Sunderland already gone—"

"Will's gone?" Beatrix stopped halfway to her armoire and stared at her aunt. "What do you mean, he's gone?"

Eugenia paused, turning in the doorway. "He left early this morning, dear. Well before breakfast, I understand. He decided to go straight to London from here, evidently, rather than sail back with us. Something involving the British Museum—a speech, perhaps?"

"But that's not until the tenth," she murmured, her joy at the prospect of seeing him ebbing away into disappointment. "Nearly a week away. Why did he leave already?"

"Heavens, dear, I don't know, but Marlowe was leaving this morning for London, and Sunderland decided to go with him. They wanted to catch the ten o'clock train from Teignmouth, so his valet packed up all those artifacts of his, and Paul and Geoff took them to Torquay in the carriages, and—why, whatever's the matter, dear?"

She roused herself from her disappointment, and found her aunt smiling at her.

"He'll only be gone a short while, a little over a

week, he said," Eugenia went on, still smiling. "No need to look so forlorn, dearest."

"I'm not forlorn," she denied as her aunt walked out of her room. Just because Will was gone for a week was no reason to be forlorn. He'd been gone for six years prior to that. "I'm not forlorn!" she insisted just before Auntie closed the door.

It was a lie, of course, but at some point, a girl just had to learn not to wear her heart on her sleeve.

Will threw himself fully into work. London in September was, for most people, as entertaining as watching grass grow. But archaeologists and scientists were not the sort to care about the current plays or the latest gossip or the social whirl, and many of them chose to come to London at this time of year for meetings and the sharing of new discoveries. No worry about finding accommodations, everything was less expensive, hansom cabs were plentiful and traffic was tolerable.

He called on old professors from Cambridge who were in town; he had dinner with some of the other archaeologists he'd met over the years. His speech to the Archaeological Society was well received, and his excavation work at Thebes applauded.

He and Marlowe met at the viscount's publishing offices and made arrangements for funding of the excavations. A photographer was chosen from those on Marlowe's staff, but Will reserved the right to choose his own illustrator, still holding out hope. Marlowe's only response was a slight raising of eyebrows, a murmured, "So that's the way the wind's blowing, eh?" and an agreement to concede the hiring of any illustrator to Will.

Will met with the curators of the British Museum, handing over to them the artifacts on loan for their exhibition and the catalog he and Trix had compiled. Her drawings were praised more than once, and he was very pleased that her talents were appreciated, but he was glad when that meeting was over, for he was trying not to think about her too much.

He tried to build his protective walls back up a little, hoping to toughen his heart for the very real possibility that he would be returning to Thebes alone and spending the next eight months without her, for he doubted one erotic—and incomplete—night together would be enough to change her mind. But though he'd spent six years building those protective walls, now that they were down, it just wasn't possible for him to prop them back up. He ached with wanting her, day and night, more than ever.

He stared out the window of his room at the Savoy, one shoulder against the jamb, staring out at the London traffic that clogged Savoy Street and the Strand beyond. The noise of the city was loud, but he barely heard it. All he could hear was Trix—her soft, panting cries of need.

More, more, and don't stop.

And he'd stopped.

He must have been out of his mind.

He'd had her naked, her willing body underneath his. Never before had it gone that far; even in the most impassioned moments of their youth, they'd never gone past three buttons. This time, he'd been inside her, for Christ's sake, on the verge of taking her virginity. He needn't have stopped. And he could have used the fear of pregnancy afterward as a way to force the issue and bring her to heel. The perfect chance combined with the perfect excuse, and he hadn't done it. Years of unrequited desire, and he'd finally reached the threshold of paradise. With one thrust, he could have claimed it, but he'd pulled back.

Yes, he was definitely out of his mind.

He wasn't completely out of time yet, he reminded himself, still clinging to hope. And if he failed this year, there was always next year. Just now, however, next year seemed a damned long way off, and though he suspected she'd rather sworn off marriage to anyone, not just him, he couldn't be completely sure of that.

Despair echoed through him again. Damn it all, if only she wasn't so stubborn. She clung to English country life and its ideals like a limpet clung to a rock.

Two weeks, he thought, rubbing a hand across his forehead. He had two weeks.

What would it take? He'd told her he still loved her, and that declaration had gone over about as well as a lead balloon.

I always loved you. All my life. I never stopped.

His words had hung in the air as he'd waited for her to say she loved him, too. But then had come one of those long, hellish, awkward silences, an indication their feelings were not mutual.

She didn't love him anymore.

He shook his head again, rejecting that notion entirely. He'd lost faith in their love six years ago, and it had been the biggest mistake of his life. He refused to lose faith again.

Think, Will, he told himself. *Think*. What would woo her and persuade her to marry him and come with him? More adventures, more picnics and champagne might help, he supposed, but those things seemed so inadequate—

There was a knock on the door, and he glanced over his shoulder, but when Aman emerged from the bedroom, he returned his attention to the window.

Picnics, champagne and adventures did him no good if all that resulted was what had happened the other night at the pixy cave. That night had been agony enough; another two weeks of it could well nigh kill him. He'd never pull it off anyway. He just didn't have the fortitude to hover at the very edge of sexual gratification like that over and over and deny himself.

"Sir?"

Will turned to find Aman closing the door to a youth in livery. "Hmm? What?"

"A telegram for you, sir."

His valet brought the communiqué to him. He opened it and a glance at the bottom told him it was from Howard Carter.

ELECTRICITY NOW AT VALLEY OF KINGS STOP
COULDN'T WAIT FOR YOU STOP WORKMEN

STARTED NIGHT DIGGING STOP YOU CORRECT RE
NEW AREA STOP FOUND STEPS TO NEW TOMB STOP
MAYBE TUT EXCLAMATION COME AT ONCE STOP IF
YOU NOT HERE OI OCT COMMA WILL OPEN TOMB
WITHOUT YOU AND SELL STORY TO PRESS MYSELF
EXCLAMATION CARTER STOP STOP

A new tomb? Will read the missive again, and as he did, he felt a sweet wave of triumph. He'd been right, they'd been digging in the wrong place. And now, because Carter had listened to him and moved the excavations, a new tomb had been unearthed, a tomb that could be Tutankhamen. Excitement shot up inside Will like a bottle rocket, and he gave a shout of laughter. He'd been right, deuce take it. He'd been right.

"Good news, sir?"

He looked up, grinning, feeling like a schoolboy with honors. "Good news? Good news?" He clasped Aman by the shoulders and gave him a little shake. "Man, it's the most splendid news that could possibly be!"

Aman remained his usual impassive self. "Indeed, sir? I am happy and relieved for you. Telegrams usually convey bad news."

Will took a deep breath, trying to curb his excitement and jubilation enough to think things out. There was no delaying his departure now. It was already the eleventh of September. If he was to be back to Thebes by the first of October, he needed to leave immediately.

But what about Trix?

He wouldn't have that extra fortnight in Devonshire he'd been counting on. He thought of cabling her, but though she might—*might*—come to London to say good-bye to him, he doubted it. She hated good-byes, and always had. And even if she were to journey down from Devonshire, she wouldn't be persuaded to come to Egypt. Especially since they weren't even married.

Think, Will. He shoved the telegram into his pocket and raked a hand through his hair. "A Bradshaw," he muttered. "I need a Bradshaw."

"Bradshaw?" echoed Aman. "Do you mean the railway guide, sir? Are we departing London?"

"Yes, Aman. We have to return to Thebes." He yanked out his watch. It was half past three. "Isn't there a night train out of Victoria to Exeter at ten?"

"Yes, sir. That is the train we took when we first journeyed to Devonshire. But I thought you said we are going to Thebes?"

"Right." He shoved his watch back in his pocket. "We are. By way of Devonshire." He didn't stop to explain. There was too much to do and he didn't have time. "Forget the Bradshaw. Get hold of Cook's," he said, striding toward the bedroom, Aman trailing after him. "I need to make travel arrangements. London to Devonshire, and one night in Stafford St. Mary. Two nights, if we can," he amended, wanting as much time with Trix as possible. He glanced around. "Where's my jacket?"

The valet retrieved the gray afternoon frock coat he'd been wearing earlier and held it open for him.

"Then back to London," Will went on as he slid

his arms into the sleeves. "Or we could take a ship out of Plymouth to Calais, if that would be quicker. I don't know. Whatever is the most efficient way to reach Paris in time to catch the Orient Express to Constantinople."

"The Orient Express departs from Paris on Wednesdays and Sundays, sir. I believe there is also a connecting train from Calais to Paris."

"The things you know amaze me, Aman. Now," he added, starting out of the bedroom. "We'll take the Orient Express to Constantinople, a ship to Cairo, and a *dahabiyeh* up the Nile to Thebes." He opened his dispatch case, looking for ready money. "The trick is that we have to arrive before October 1. Have you got all that?"

"Yes, sir."

"Good." He counted out pound notes, pulled his money case out of his pocket and shoved notes into its leather interior, and replaced the case in the breast pocket of his jacket. "I think I'll still have time to dine with Sir Edmund this evening, but be ready to depart from here by nine, so we can catch the ten o'clock express out of Victoria. Best to hurry over to Cook's, and then start packing."

Aman nodded and opened the door. Will walked through it, then stopped. "And tell them we'll need to book passage for three people."

"Three, sir?"

"Three," he said firmly, refusing to believe otherwise. With that, Will went down to the Savoy's opulent lobby to request a taxi, and when it arrived, he ordered it to take him to the Faculty Office, where he allowed his hopes free rein and applied for a special license to wed. From there, he went to Lloyd's, then Fortnum and Mason, and then Bond Street. He then returned to the Savoy, changed for dinner, and met Sir Edmund in the hotel's main dining room. Though it was enjoyable to see his mentor again, and exhilarating to share the news from Thebes, Will was happy when the meal ended, for he was eager to be on his way back to Trix. But after bidding farewell to Sir Edmund, Will did not take the lift back up to his rooms to fetch Aman. Instead, he left the Savoy. He still had one thing to do before he returned to Devonshire to win the woman he loved. He needed to find a courtesan.

During the week that followed Will's departure for London and her own return to Stafford St. Mary, *forlorn* proved to be a fairly accurate description of Beatrix's mood.

She tried to tell herself it was because of the tedious details of canceling her wedding. It was customary for invitations to be sent and gifts to be received only within the fortnight preceding the wedding day, so thankfully Beatrix was spared the obligation of sending letters of regret and returning presents after this broken engagement. However, consideration for her friends demanded a brief confirmation of the news by letter.

Society papers were already discussing the fact that Lady Beatrix Danbury's engagement was off. Because she'd been at Pixy Cove, she'd been shielded from the gossip during the first few weeks following her broken engagement, but now that she was back in Stafford St. Mary, the humiliating news seemed to be everywhere. She saw heads together when she came into church on Sunday, she heard conversations cease when she walked into a card party on Tuesday, she felt speculative gazes on her as she visited shops in the High Street on Thursday. The fact that she had failed to secure not one but two handsome and eligible dukes in her lifetime, and that the return of duke number one had surely been the cause of duke number two's departure, was information discussed ad nauseam in all the society pages. The news, Beatrix had no doubt, had been greeted with jubilation and relief by marriage-minded debutantes throughout England and America.

Though she tried not to care, Beatrix found being fodder for the scandal sheets infuriating and humiliating, especially when she read the comments of Mrs. Delilah Dawlish, gossip columnist for the society newspaper *Talk of the Town*. Every time she read the woman's oft-repeated refrain: "Broken engagements seems to be the pattern of her life, my dears!" she wanted to shred the paper and Mrs. Dawlish into little pieces. The speculations about whether she'd been the one to jilt or be jilted were tiresome, Eugenia's wailing about their family being the subject of all this gossip was aggravating, and with Julia's departure for the Continent, Beatrix was left with no one in Stafford St. Mary whose sense of humor could help her shrug it all off.

She packed up the beautiful wedding dress Vivian

had designed for her, only one or two of her tears staining its lovely white silk. She gave it to the vicar's wife to be donated to the next village girl whose banns were posted, a girl who would no doubt be thrilled to wear it.

As etiquette demanded, she arranged for the gifts Aidan had given her during their engagement to be returned to him—a book on the workings of Parliament, an intricately carved ivory fan she'd once admired in a shop window, and a silver locket with her father's picture inside, though she did take her father's picture out before packing up the locket. She sent these gifts to Trathen Leagh, Aidan's estate in Cornwall, along with his letters. Her letters to him had been returned to her already, and she took those to the storage rooms in the attic. She took the time to read them before she put them away, and as she did, she realized why it had been so easy for her heart to return to Will when her head had tried to push her to Aidan.

Her letters and his had been full of news, replies to questions about their mutual health, their families and friends, talk of what they would do with the gardens at the various estates or amusements they would enjoy during their seasons in town, but neither his letters nor hers contained anything remotely passionate. Reading it all now, she felt a hint of the same warm affection and fondness she'd always felt, and she knew that was all she would ever have felt for him. Unlike Julia, she had never found any aspect of Aidan's character jarring or irritating, and if Will had never come back, she and Aidan would have shared a pleasant, nice, and deadly dull life together.

Mere compatibility and fondness, she now realized, were not enough for her. She'd tried to believe otherwise, and had she married Aidan, she would have made the best of things, and she might never have remembered the difference, if Will had not come back.

But he had come back, and now the difference between what she'd had with him and what Aidan had offered her stood in such stark contrast, they were like black and white. Yet she knew she was somewhere between those two extremes, and with Will, there never seemed to be any half shades or half measures. There never seemed to be middle ground or compromise. Once you jumped off the cliff, you jumped, and there was no turning back.

But what if he proved himself? a little voice whispered. She tried to shut it out, but it persisted, whispering teasing possibilities. *What if he stayed and made a life here? What if he showed her that he could stick with things at home? What if he began to take his ducal responsibilities seriously?*

Maybe then, she thought, maybe then she'd take the risk. But it was silly to wish for that, she knew. Will had never been like that, and never would be.

She stared out the attic window at the lane leading to the Stafford Road. How many times had she looked out her bedroom window just like this, waiting for Will? Waiting for him to come home from Eton. Then from Cambridge. Then from the Continent. Waiting for him to declare his love. Waiting for him to propose. Waiting for him to marry her. Waiting for him to come home from Egypt. And now, waiting for him to come back from London.

All the years of her life, she'd felt as if she'd been chasing heaven, thinking she'd found it, only to watch it slip away again. She was not going to wait for Will, because it wasn't enough for heaven to come waltzing by with a few words of love and a few weeks of courtship in between seasons on another continent. Heaven also had to stick around for more than a month or two at a time, and Will had never been the sticking-around sort.

She had her own life to think of, a life that seemed rather in limbo. Her first post as an illustrator was over, it seemed, but she would find another. She didn't know how she would deal with the objections of her family, but she'd find a way. Paul, she supposed, could be persuaded to her point of view, given the other ladies of their acquaintance who had engaged in various professions. Eugenia would probably never accept it, but that was just too bad. Beatrix liked her newfound profession, and she had no intention of giving it up. She wasn't like her mother—she wasn't going to go running off with some man and disgrace the family, but neither was she going to sit around waiting for a husband to provide her with an enjoyable, worthwhile life.

She turned away from the window thinking to go downstairs, but her eye caught on a pair of steamer trunks and a pair of valises, luggage that had been brand-new six years ago, bought to hold her trousseau during her honeymoon with Will. Above it, another set of luggage, for another honeymoon and another man. The first set, she thought wistfully, had been packed with more innocence and joy than the second set.

She'd loved Will for most of her life, but she had no intention of falling back in love with him. If she did, she'd be hurt again as she'd been hurt before. Last time, it had almost destroyed her. This time, she just wasn't willing to take the risk.

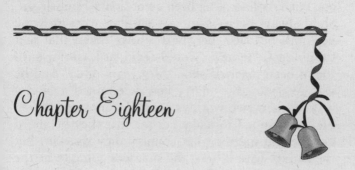

Chapter Eighteen

Beatrix was in the garden, cutting late roses, when Will arrived at Danbury the following afternoon. Eugenia led him to the library window and pointed out where she stood by the arbor, then she sat down in the chair nearest that particular view.

Keeping an eye on them, he thought with amused exasperation. That was all right, as long as she didn't intend to be like Antonia's maid and plant herself outside Trix's door tonight.

He walked outside and made his way through the potager to the rose garden. There he paused at the edge, smiling at the sight of her amid the roses. In her simple shirtwaist and skirt with an apron over them, a big straw hat on her head, and a basket of long-stemmed roses over her arm, she looked just like what she was: an English country girl doing the flowers. But Trix had never been an ordinary English girl. She'd always been *his* girl. When they were growing up, until he'd lost her, he'd always taken that fact for granted. He never would again, at least not until they'd been married about fifty years or so. And he was determined to marry her, determined to find a way for their two worlds to combine into one shared life, determined to make her see that they belonged together no matter what country they were in. But she had to want it, too, and that was going to be the tricky part. Especially since Cook's had been unable arrange an itinerary with any extra time in Devonshire. He had only tonight to win her over.

As he came closer, she looked up, and when she saw him, she nearly dropped her garden shears. "Wi-ill!"

He stopped on the path, as surprised as she sounded, for he'd just heard that wobbly little hiccup in her voice, and hope rose within him in a powerful wave. He had a chance. He knew he had a chance.

She didn't smile at him as he came to stand beside her. When he reached her side, she tugged nervously at the wisp of hair at her neck with one garden-gloved hand and returned her attention to the rosebush.

"So, you're back," she said the obvious in an off-hand sort of way, as if trying to show him she didn't care tuppence about the fact, but it was too late. He'd heard that little hiccup in her voice, and she couldn't take it back. Trix still loved him in spite of everything. He began to laugh. Damned if that wasn't some kind of miracle.

She looked at him, a puzzled little frown etching between her brows. "Why are you laughing?"

He smiled. "I'm just . . . glad to see you. Aren't you glad to see me?"

"Of course," she said primly, snipping roses.

"I missed you." He leaned closer to her. "I think you missed me, too."

"If I missed you every time you went away, I'd spend my whole life miserable. I've learned my lesson about that."

He knew he had to tell her of his imminent departure and his intentions before he attempted to put his plans for tonight into action, but as excited as he was to relay the news that was sending him back to Egypt, the words seemed to choke him as he tried to force them out. "I have something to show you," he said, and pulled the telegram out of his pocket.

She pulled off her garden gloves and set them on the grass with her shears and her basket before she took the sheet of paper from him and unfolded it.

"You found Tut?" she cried excitedly, her gaze scanning the lines of the telegram.

"Possibly. We don't know yet if it's Tutankhamen."

"Still, there's something there, isn't there? Something big, something important. Right?" She looked up, and when he nodded, she began to laugh. "Heavens, you were right after all. You were right. This means—" She stopped, suddenly appreciating what it did mean. Lowering her gaze, she read the telegram again, and he watched her face as her excitement for him faded away. She swallowed hard.

"You're leaving, of course," she said without looking at him.

"Yes, Trix," he said gently. "Tomorrow."

"Tomorrow? So soon?"

He heard her surprise and pain. His hopes rose another notch, even as her pain hurt him, too. "I have to, if I'm to arrive in Thebes by the first of October. My train from Stafford St. Mary departs at noon, and if I don't make that train, I miss the connecting train from Exeter to Dover. If that happens, I miss the day's ship to Calais, which delays my arrival in Paris, and I miss the Orient Express to Constantinople—"

"The Orient Express?" she cried, her face twisting at the mention of the train they were supposed to take together for their honeymoon six years ago. "You're taking the Orient Express?"

"It's the fastest way to Constantinople." He paused, leaning closer to her. "Want to come?"

Her face froze. Her pleasure at his triumph was gone, her pain at his impending departure was gone. Her face was a mask. "No," she answered, and thrust the telegram at him.

He shrugged, pretending a nonchalance he didn't feel in the least. "It's just as well. Since we're not married, it would make quite a scandal if we ran off together. Unless you've changed your mind about marrying me?"

"If I did, would you stay?"

He took a deep breath. "No."

She bent down to pick up her shears. "Then I haven't changed my mind." She resumed snipping roses, but it seemed haphazard, with no regard for the quality of the blossoms.

"If you keep that up," he said, watching her, "that bush will be naked."

She stopped. "Since you're leaving tomorrow, I assume you came here to say good-bye?"

"Actually, no. I was hoping to do that later. I came to see if you might be willing to go on one more midnight adventure with me."

"Indeed?" She didn't ask what he had in mind. Instead, she knelt on the grass, dropped her shears into her basket, and began gathering the roses she'd cut.

"This adventure is a little bit different from the ones we've had in the past," he explained. "For this one, you have to come to my house."

"Your house?" She paused and looked up at him. He waited, watching as the implications sank in and a pink flush came into her cheeks. "I see," she said, and resumed her task. "A repeat of the other night?"

"A bit like that, with one exception." He knelt on the grass and grasped her hands in his, and when she looked into his face, he said, "This time I want to finish what we started."

"Do you?" Her voice was cool, but that was a pose. He knew it when her tongue darted out to nervously lick her lips and she turned her face away.

"I think you know what I mean." He wanted to take her in his arms right here and now, pull her down into the grass with him and persuade her with kisses, but he couldn't. He darted a look over his shoulder, but he couldn't tell if Eugenia was still sitting by the window because of the glare off the glass. Still, it didn't matter whether he could actually see her. He and Trix had years of experience with this sort of thing, and he'd rather developed a sixth sense about it. He could feel Eugenia's watchful gaze boring into his back even from here.

"Beatrix." When he said her name, she tried to pull her hands away, but he held them fast, drew a deep breath, and rolled the dice. "I love you. I've always loved you, and I think you know that. I want you, and after that night at Angel Cove, I think it's safe to say you want me just as much."

She lifted her chin a notch, but she still didn't quite look at him. "You're the one who didn't want it," she said, a little quiver in her voice. "I practically threw myself at you the other night, and you . . . you stopped."

"I told you, I was being responsible. But . . ." He paused, trying to find a delicate way to say this. Unfortunately there was none. He leaned closer, keeping his voice low, even though there was no one within earshot. "There are ways to prevent a baby. Ways better than the one I used the other night."

"Oh." The blush in her cheeks deepened to a rosy pink, and as she caught her lower lip between her teeth, he knew she was wavering. He waited, but when several moments went by and she didn't speak, he began to feel hope giving way to desperation. The thought of going to Thebes without her, of the eight lonely months to come, seemed unbearable.

"I'll be gone a long time," he said. "And before I go, I want this adventure with you. I'll be wholly honest here. I intend to ply you with champagne, take shameless advantage of you, and make mad, passionate love to you. I'm hoping to persuade you to marry me and come with me tomorrow."

"You mean elope?"

"Yes. It's only fair to tell you that although I applied for a special license while I was in London, we won't able to pick it up. We have to take the train out of Exeter straight to Dover, which means we'll either have to marry on the ship across the channel, or wait until we reach Egypt. Either way, it will still make a scandal."

"And you think I would agree to disgrace my family by eloping with you?"

"I'm hoping you'll decide it's worth it."

She looked at him, but he couldn't read anything in her dark eyes. "And if I refuse?"

"I'll come back next year and try again."

She sniffed, not seeming particularly impressed by that. "If you come back next year."

"It's all right if you don't come tonight," he went on as if she hadn't spoken. "Because I am not giving up. Not this time. Say no, and I'll be right back here on your doorstep come June." He paused, then added, "But June is an awfully long way off, and if you want to come on this adventure with me before I leave, I'll meet you by the lodge gates at midnight. Will you come?"

She stared down at her lap for what seemed an eternity before she replied. "Yes, Will. I'll come."

"You will?"

"Yes." She pulled her hands from his, picked up her basket of roses, and stood up. "I like champagne."

Despite her promise to meet him, he wasn't sure she would, and when he saw her crossing the stretch of lawn that separated the park of Sunderland from that of Danbury, he dared to let his hopes for a future with her rise higher. He straightened away from the gate, and went to meet her.

She was wearing riding boots and those Turkish trousers, along with a dark, hooded cloak, and the hood of the cloak shadowed her face, preventing him from seeing her expression. "Are you sure you want to do this?" he asked as he halted in front of her and bent down, trying to look her full in the face.

"Yes," she answered, and pushed back the hood of her cloak. "I'm sure."

"You don't want to back out?"

She smiled a little. "Shy at the jump, you mean? Stop at the edge of the cliff?" She shook her head. "No."

"All right, then. C'mon." Needing no further persuasion, he grabbed her hand and led her across the park and through the grounds to the house. He'd left the south door unlatched, and he took her in through that entrance, across the south wing, and up to his bedroom. He'd already prepared everything, but after shutting the door behind them, he lowered the flame of the lamp a little bit, shifted the bottle of champagne to another angle in the ice bucket, and pushed the plate of fruit and cheese a bit farther back on his dressing table, feeling strangely nervous. Perhaps because on all their previous adventures, there had been certain rules, and tonight those rules were gone.

He spied the black velvet envelope he'd bought in London. Stupid, he thought, and picked it up. He should have put this by the bed.

"What is that?" she asked as he walked past her, and he stopped. One really didn't discuss these things with anyone, particularly not women, but she had the right to know. "They are called condoms." He opened the black velvet packet lined with red silk, and pulled out one of the flattened rubber disks inside. "They . . . ahem . . . prevent a woman from becoming pregnant," he said. "I bought them in London."

"Heavens." She took it out of his hand to examine it more closely, understandably curious. "Where does one find these?"

"Brothels. Prostitutes." He took it back from her. "Not that I went to a prostitute. I mean, I did, but not for . . . not for that." He waved the condom. "I went for this. I mean . . . God," he choked, shoving the condom back into its envelope and tossing the envelope onto the bed. "I feel like I'm seventeen again and I've just come home from Eton and made the amazing discovery that you developed breasts while I was away. I can't seem to say a single intelligent word to you right now."

That made her laugh, but he did not feel like laughing at all just now. Doubts assailed him. "No going back," he felt impelled to point out. "Once it's done, Trix, it can't be undone."

"I know." She began unbuttoning her cloak, still smiling, and her composure made him even more ill at ease. He shifted his weight, suddenly at a loss for what to do next, and he realized he'd never actually seduced Trix before, not like this, not with such blatant, lascivious intent. She'd already refused to marry him, seemed not the least bit inclined to change her mind and elope with him tomorrow. And the stakes were so damned high. Maybe this was a mistake. Taking a woman's virtue when you weren't married to her and you were about to leave the country was a mighty irresponsible thing to do.

He closed his eyes for a second, drawing a profound, shaky breath.

"Nervous?"

Her question caused him to open his eyes. "Yes," he admitted. "You?"

"No." Her smile widened, and then for no accountable reason, she started to laugh. "I like that you're nervous."

"You do?"

"Yes." She shrugged, letting the cloak fall away from her shoulders as she turned toward him. "Because I'm the one who's usually in that position on these adventures of ours, and you're the one who's all breezy and confident."

"Yes, well, that's often just an act." He raked a hand through his hair as she halted in front of him. "Pure bravado on my part."

She slid her arms around his neck. "There's nothing to be nervous about, you know," she said, stood up on her toes, and kissed him. "I don't bite."

He cupped her face, and when his lips parted, hers

did, too. He took her mouth in a long, slow kiss, then his hands slid between them. As he unbuttoned her jacket, his knuckles brushed her breasts, and arousal flared instantly, like lighting a match. But he knew he had to keep it in check, for he had a long way to go tonight if he was to win more than her body. Even as he reminded himself of that, he paused to cup her breasts in his hands, and as his palms embraced them, he realized she wasn't wearing a corset.

He knew what her breasts looked like, for the image of her disrobing in front of him a week earlier was still vivid in his mind, and as he imagined it again, shaping her breasts in his palms, his arousal deepened and spread.

After a moment, he reluctantly slid his hands away from her breasts. He yanked the hem of her shirtwaist out of her Turkish trousers, and he broke their kiss so he could see what he was doing as he began unfastening the buttons down the front of her shirtwaist. It was an agonizingly slow process, for the buttons were tiny, and there were dozens of them. It didn't help that his hands were shaking as he strove to keep his desire in check.

"Just so you know," he said, trying to sound terribly man-of-the-world, "next time I tell you I'm going to seduce you, wear something easy to unfasten."

She sniffed. "Well, next time," she said, matching his blasé tone, "I might not let you seduce me at all."

He stopped, chagrined that he already seemed to be taking her for granted again. "No?"

"No. I might seduce you first."

He laughed at that, and the tension inside him suddenly broke apart. "You just might at that," he said, desire replacing nervousness as he unfastened the buttons down the front of her shirtwaist. "It won't take much," he assured her. "Just smile and say hullo the minute you see me."

"That's all?"

"That's all. I'll be putty in your hands after that. Trust me."

"Trust you?" She tilted her head, as if considering it. "I'm not sure when you are unbuttoning my shirtwaist, you can be trusted."

He laughed again, a low, throaty chuckle. "You have a point." He slid her shirtwaist off her shoulders, and as it joined her jacket on the floor, he caught his breath, for he could see the faint circle of her nipples beneath the thin lawn fabric of her chemise, and his arousal ignited into full-blown lust. He had to see her breasts again. Right now. He couldn't wait a moment longer.

"Lift your arms," he ordered, and when she did, he grasped the hem of her chemise and tugged it up over her head, baring her body from the waist up.

His throat went dry at the sight, for she was even lovelier now than the image in his mind from their night at Angel's Head. He cupped her breasts again, savoring the lush, full shape of them in his palms. He toyed with them, caressing the satiny white skin and velvety pink nipples, until he could hear her breath coming in little catching gasps.

"You love me," he said, rolling her nipples in his

fingers. "You do. Admit it. Say you'll marry me and come to Egypt with me."

She shook her head, and he knew she wasn't ready to concede anything yet. Her hands came up, pushing his aside. For a moment he thought she was pushing him away, but instead, she began to unbutton his shirt, and it was her turn to start issuing orders. "Take it off."

"I can't." He lifted his wrists. "You didn't undo my cuffs."

"Oh." She laughed and reached for one, fumbling with his silver cuff links, and as she turned to drop them onto his dressing table, he pulled his shirt over his head and tossed it aside.

She turned back around, and when she did, she immediately reached out to touch him. He inhaled sharply, tilting back his head at the feel of her hands on him, wondering how he was going to bear this long enough to get them both undressed.

But he endured it, for it was sweet, unbearably sweet, to feel her palms glide over his skin as she touched his arms, his shoulders, and his chest, but by the time she reached his abdomen, he couldn't take any more.

Gently but firmly, he took control back from her. "If you keep torturing me this way," he said, grasping her wrists to pull her hands down, "this is going to be a very short seduction."

She slanted him a wicked look. "And that would be bad because . . . ?"

"Because you haven't told me you love me yet."

Before she could reply, he captured her mouth with his, kissing her deep and slow as he unfastened the buttons of her trousers. "I've told you that I love you," he went on as he shoved the trousers down her hips, "and I'm waiting for reciprocity."

He didn't get it. She leaned forward to press a kiss to his chest instead, and lifted her hands to the waistband of his trousers as if to unfasten them as he had unfastened hers. But he knew he couldn't let her. He was rock hard, and if she started touching him there, he'd never be able to hold out long enough to do this properly. They had waited years and years for this, and he had no intention of spoiling their first time by going too fast. Besides, he had another objective in view, one that was just as important to him.

He gently but firmly pushed her hands aside. "I love you," he said, and slid his palms up and down her hips. "Do you love me?" She didn't answer, and he slowly eased one hand between her thighs to cup her mound.

She gasped and her knees dipped a little, but she still didn't say what he wanted to hear. He maneuvered his fingers into the slit of her drawers, ignoring how her legs instinctively clamped together around his hand, but when he touched the silken wetness of her core, he realized he'd moved too fast, for he hadn't even gotten her boots off yet.

Reluctantly he pulled his hand back. "The footboard is behind you," he told her, and maneuvered her backward to sit on its edge.

She did, her fingers curling around the brass railing as he knelt in front of her. He lifted her foot, grasped the heel and instep, and pulled off her riding boot. After he'd repeated the process, he tossed both boots to a corner of the room, and pulled her trousers all the way off. He then pulled off her garters and slid off her stockings, tickling the backs of her knees. She breathed his name on a sigh.

"Like that, do you?" He slid his fingertips in slow, coaxing circles.

She nodded, tipping her head back as he ran his hands up her thighs to the waistband of her drawers. He untied the ribbon and began pulling the garment down. "Lift your hips a little."

When she did, he was able to pull the drawers down, and as they slid to her ankles, he sat back on his knees and took a long look at her.

He'd seen her in so many ways, and in every way she was beautiful, but now, this way, with her head tilted back and lips parted with desire and her body fully bared to him for lovemaking, she had never seemed more beautiful. Her breasts rose and fell with her rapid breathing, round and full, their nipples a rich brownish-pink in the lamplight. The curls at the apex of her thighs were dark gold, and her skin was like warmed alabaster.

Again he touched her breasts, caressing them, shaping them, toying with them. Her breathing quickened further, her arousal heightening, and he took advantage of the moment. "Love me?" he asked, leaning in, one of her breasts cupped in his palm as he opened his mouth over the other.

She moaned, arching toward him, and he suckled her nipple, then pulled back to flick it teasingly with his tongue, striving to keep his desire in check as he worked to stoke hers as high as he could. "Do you?"

She didn't answer, but her hand slid into his hair, cradling his head, trying to draw him closer. He didn't come closer. Instead, he decided it was time for more ruthless tactics. He began kissing his way down her stomach.

Her fingers worked convulsively in his hair. "Will," she wailed softly. "Oh, oh."

He pulled back long enough to draw breath, then he pressed his mouth to the golden curls at the apex of her thighs. She cried out, her hips jerking, but he grasped her hips to hold her still and began to caress her with his tongue, stroking the crease of her sex over and over, lightly, gently, relentlessly.

He eased his hold on her hips, and her body responded at once, moving against his mouth. Her breath began coming in little gasps. He kept lashing her with gentle strokes of his tongue until she was trembling all over and those soft, sweet wails of climax were coming from her throat.

With a final, shuddering gasp, she collapsed, panting, and he stood up, catching her before she fell, lifting her into his arms. He carried her to the side of the bed and laid her down. His gaze locked with hers, he began to strip off his remaining clothes. "Do you love me?" he asked, yanking off his boots.

Wordless, she stared at him. She wanted to answer, say no. But she couldn't. Nor could she say yes. He was demanding something that she couldn't give him. She could give him her body. Indeed, that was why she'd come tonight. But she couldn't give him her heart. Because he was leaving, and if she gave him her heart, she might never get it back.

Her gaze lowered to his hands as he unbuttoned his trousers. As he slid them down his hips along with his linen, she had to look. When she did, she inhaled a sharp, surprised breath at the sight of him so flagrantly aroused. Good Lord, she thought, with sudden understanding of just how he'd done what he'd done the other night. Seeing him like this explained it all.

He waited, letting her have a good, long look, then he bent down to retrieve that black velvet pouch from the floor and removed one of those rubber disks. She stared in amazement as he slid it along the length of his shaft, sheathing himself with a thin veneer of rubber. She made a choked sound, and felt her courage slipping.

He sensed it. He leaned over to kiss her mouth, and eased his body down onto hers before she could change her mind. She opened her arms, a bit reassured, thinking she knew what to expect next. He rested his weight on one arm, suspended above her, and his hand eased that hard, aroused part of his body between her thighs.

"Beatrix, listen to me." His voice sounded hoarse, his breathing labored. "I can't contain this any longer. I love you, and I was going to wait, hold out until you admitted you love me, too, but I can't. I . . . just can't." He smiled, but she could tell it was forced. "You know me. So impatient."

She touched his face, kissed him. She didn't want to hear any more, because she couldn't give him what he wanted and she wouldn't use love as a way to make him stay. "Don't apologize," she whispered, moving her hips, appreciating how tempting it would be. "Just do it, Will. We've waited long enough."

He shook his head. When she moved again, sliding her thighs against his shaft, he gritted his teeth. "Don't, for the love of God. Don't move. Listen."

He took a deep breath, as if striving for control. Sweat glistened on his chest, on his forehead, and his breathing was becoming harsher by the moment. "No adventure we've ever been on has hurt you, but this one will, Trix. It's going to hurt. No getting around that."

As he spoke, his hips began rocking slowly against hers, and she could feel the hard part of him rubbing the place he had kissed her and stroked her before, and that delicious pleasure washed over her again. She arched into him as she had done before, and the pleasure grew stronger, hotter. She moaned.

"Christ," he breathed, and shifted his body to rest his weight on his forearms, burying his face against her neck, and flexed his hips against her. That hard part of him pressed deeper onto her and then, just as before, into her.

She didn't understand. She was caught up in a sensuous, bewildered haze, and as his body entered her, it felt just the same as it had before. It didn't hurt. Perhaps she'd misunderstood.

Suddenly he thrust hard, shoving himself deeper into her, and she heard herself cry out as sudden, burning pain seared her from the inside. She hadn't misunderstood, she realized in hot chagrin. He'd told her the truth.

He covered her mouth with his, catching her sob of shock and pain in his kiss. He held himself rigid above her, kissing her everywhere—her hair, her throat, her cheek, her mouth. "It'll be all right. I promise it will. I love you, Trix. I love you."

As he spoke to her and kissed her, the pain began to recede. "I'm all right, Will," she whispered, wriggling her hips, trying to accustom herself to this coupling business.

He began to move, slowly at first, then more quickly, his thrusts against her becoming stronger and deeper. His eyes were closed, his lips parted, and it was almost as if he'd forgotten about her, but he was stroking her hair and saying her name, and she realized he was simply caught up in the pleasure of her body. She smiled, liking that.

She pushed upward, and he groaned, his arms sliding beneath her as if to pull her closer when he already seemed as close to her as he could possibly be, and she began to think perhaps this part of it might be tolerable after all. She felt sore inside, but that first searing pain had passed. She thrust up again, striving to move with him.

His breathing was ragged against her hair, the thrust of his hips forcing her deeper into the mattress, and Beatrix began to feel again that wonderful thickening pleasure he'd aroused before with his hands and his mouth.

And then, all of a sudden, shudders rocked him,

and he let out a hoarse cry. He thrust against her several more times, and then collapsed, breathing hard, burying his face against her neck.

She raked her fingers through his hair, she stroked the hard, strong muscles of his back and shoulders. When he kissed her hair and murmured her name, happiness rose within her like a fierce, surging tide.

Yes, she thought, this was why she'd come tonight. Because when he was gone, maybe he'd remember this, and he would be happy, too. And maybe when he left this time around, he wouldn't wait six years to come back.

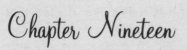

Chapter Nineteen

He was asleep.

Beatrix studied him in the lamplight as she dressed. Oddly enough, in her whole life she'd never seen him asleep. He lay on his stomach, sheets thrown off, exposing his bare, muscled back down to his tailbone.

One of his arms was tucked beneath him, the other was wrapped around her pillow. She smiled at that, liking to believe he thought the pillow was she. Though his countenance still seemed harsher than that of the man who'd gone away six years ago, it was softened now by sleep, reminding her of the boy she'd been in love with ever since she'd been capable of conscious thought.

And she did love him. She'd tried so hard to stop, but that, she supposed, had always been a waste of time and effort. She'd handed her heart over to him before she was three years old, and no matter how she tried, she could never quite manage to get it back. She'd been afraid of that earlier, but now it was done and couldn't be undone.

He'd told her he was coming back, and she believed him. She did. But that didn't alter the fact that he was still leaving. He'd probably go on leaving forever, and every time he did, it would probably hurt just as much as it did right now.

She would go on with her own life here in Devonshire. She liked being an illustrator, and she intended to keep doing it. Perhaps she could do some sketches for Viscount Marlowe's newspapers or illustrate some of the books for his publishing company. Her family might find that acceptable. Maybe next year she'd sketch artifacts for Will again when he came home.

Home. Here in Devonshire would always be her home, but when Will went to Egypt, he'd always take a part of her heart along with him.

She bent down and brushed her lips to Will's cheek, lightly, so she wouldn't wake him. "I love you, Will," she whispered. "I hope it's Tut in that tomb. If it is, maybe you'll come home for good, but if you don't, that's all right, too. I just want you to be happy."

Turning away, she tiptoed out of the room, but she paused by the door for one last look. Their adventure was over, but she wanted to remember this image through what was sure to be a long, lonely winter.

She'd left the north wing door at Danbury unlocked, as she'd always done in the old days when she'd snuck out to meet Will. The north wing was nearly empty, and as always, she was able to tiptoe all the way back to her room in the silence of early morning without being seen by anyone. Exhausted, she undressed, slipped into bed, and the moment her head hit the pillow, she was asleep.

"Ma'am, wake up."

Beatrix stirred, feeling Lily's hand on her shoulder, and she shook off the maid's touch without opening her eyes, fighting to hang on to sleep, for she felt as if she'd barely laid her head down.

"Oh, ma'am, wake up. His Grace, the Duke of Sunderland, has come to call."

"Will?" She opened her eyes. "Will's here?" Still groggy from sleep, she sat up, giving her maid a dubious look, but Lily's next words negated any notion that she'd been dreaming.

"Yes, ma'am. He's in the drawing room, and he wants to see you. Lady Danbury told him you had not come down, but he said it was important that he see you because he's leaving today to go back to Egypt."

She shook her head, trying to clear her sleep-drugged senses. "What time is it?"

"Half past ten, ma'am. Lady Danbury sent me to fetch you and help you dress so that you could come down and say good-bye. You'd best hurry, she said, because His Grace must be at the station to catch the noon train, so you won't have time for a long visit."

She didn't want a long visit. In fact, she didn't

want a visit at all. She'd already said her good-byes, and she didn't think she could bear another one, not in person. "I'm not coming down."

Lily looked at her doubtfully. "Lady Danbury was most insistent."

"I'm not coming down. Lily, go tell His Grace I don't wish to see him. I don't . . ." She paused, swallowing hard. "I can't bear good-byes. He knows that. Tell him I shall see him when he returns in the spring."

Lily nodded and went out. Beatrix didn't go back to sleep. Instead, she got out of bed, slipped a wrapper over her nightdress, and walked to the window. Mr. Robinson's cart was there, along with Will's manservant, and the cart was piled with luggage. Six years, and except for the servant, the view was the same as before.

She knew why he was here, but she couldn't go on this adventure, and that was part of why she'd said her good-byes as he slept. She might have been able to jump off Angel's Head with him, but she still didn't want to live on the other side of the world. And though her father was dead, she couldn't scandalize the rest of her family by an elopement. She didn't want Will to tempt her to try.

She waited by the window, and when Will finally emerged from the house, she watched his back as he walked to the cart.

He started to climb up on the box beside Mr. Robinson, and she breathed a little sigh of relief, but that relief was short-lived. With one booted foot on the box, he paused and turned to look back over his shoulder. He looked straight up at her window.

She wanted to duck out of sight, but she didn't. She could only look back at him, her heart breaking with good-bye.

Go, Will, just go. Don't wait for me. Go find Tut, and when you come home in the spring, then we'll see.

Even though her lamp wasn't lit and he probably couldn't see her behind the reflection of the glass, he beckoned her to come down as if he knew she was there. She didn't move, except to slowly shake her head.

Go, Will, she prayed. *For God's sake.*

At last, after what seemed an eternity, he turned and climbed up on the box. Mr. Robinson snapped the reins, and the dogcart lurched forward in the drive, circling around. As it went back down the long, tree-shaded lane to the Stafford Road, he turned, looking back over his shoulder at Danbury House for what she knew was one last look.

Beatrix watched him go, and even after he was too far away to see, she squinted, trying to keep him in focus as long as she could, until he blurred in a haze of tears and the cart reached the end of the lane. There it turned, disappearing behind the trees that lined the road.

Beatrix stayed by her window, looking down the lane long after he was gone. Lily returned, confirming that Eugenia was in a dither, certain Will had come to propose again and furious that her niece had refused to even see him, but Beatrix didn't care about that. She was trying to protect her heart from further pain.

She stared down the lane, thinking of all the times she'd stood there before, waiting for Will, waiting for her wedding day, waiting for life to start.

Plus ça change, plus c'est la même chose.

Looking down the lane, she suddenly realized what a narrow lane it was. A narrow lane for a narrow life, a life thinned down by her father, by society, by her own fear. Her fear, most of all. She'd always been afraid—of earning disapproval, of stepping outside the bounds, of living a different life than the one she'd always known.

Suddenly resentment rose up inside her, resentment toward herself for living a life bound by rules she never made. Why couldn't girls swing high on the swings until their dresses flew up? Why couldn't they become artists or dig up artifacts or elope with the men they loved? Why was any of that a disgrace?

You long to jump off, but you just can't work up the nerve, so you tell yourself you're content to look at the view.

Naturally. Ladies looked at the view. And that was all they did.

She lurched to her feet so suddenly that her chair tipped backward and hit the floor behind her with a thud. "I don't want to look at the view!" she shouted, slapping her palms against the window. "I want to jump off the damned cliff!"

Lily came running out of the dressing room. "Ma'am?"

She turned to find her maid staring at her in surprise, her hands holding one of Beatrix's gowns. She gave a choked laugh at the maid's alarmed expression. "I envy you, Lily," she confessed. "I truly do."

The girl's blue eyes went even wider. "Me, ma'am? You're a lady. Whyever would you envy me?"

"Because you're free," she said savagely. "No one would care if you decided to swing too high on the swings or take a trip to Florence, or . . . or run off with a man!"

"Run off with a man? Oh, ma'am, my mum would take the skin off my back if I was to do that." Then she realized the implications. "Oh, ma'am," she squeaked in excitement, "are you thinking to elope with His Grace? There'd be a terrible scandal about that, wouldn't there, ma'am?"

She made a face. "Yes, exactly, and a lady never creates a scandal. A lady doesn't draw pictures and sell them for money. A lady doesn't drive motorcars and a lady doesn't walk barefoot on the sand, either! No, ladies have to wear black crepe when someone dies, and have to be accompanied wherever they go. And I'm tired of it."

Lily said nothing, probably because there was nothing to say.

"I feel as if there are chains around me, Lily. Tying me down, keeping me fixed to one place, one life, one ideal, and every time I've tried to break free, I've ended up being more tied down than before. And the odd thing is, it's been my own fault. I decided what life I had to have, what sort of woman I had to be. I helped to create those chains. I helped tie them around myself, and I helped anchor them in place, and I've lived in them for twenty-six years. I chose those things, even though underneath I yearned for something more. Those chains made me feel important. What a humbug I've been.

"Do you know why I learned to drive a motor-car?" When the maid shook her head, Beatrix went on, "Because I wanted to feel free, but I didn't have enough courage to go after real freedom." She gave a short laugh at the other woman's bewildered expression. "And you don't know what in heaven's name I'm talking about, do you?"

The girl shook her head. "No, ma'am."

"It doesn't matter," she said, and started for the door. "It's time to break the chains."

With that, she walked out of the bedroom, leaving her astonished maid staring after her. Ten minutes later, she was back, with two of the valises from the luggage set she'd bought six years ago. Lily once again came out of the dressing room and gave a squeal of surprise.

"Oh, ma'am, you are eloping!"

She laughed, feeling an exhilaration that only Will could inspire. "I am, and there isn't much time." She kicked the door shut behind her and tossed the valises onto the bed, then she unsnapped the brass locks and threw back the lids. "I'll need shirtwaists, skirts—summer things, mostly," she said, nodding toward the armoire. "I'll need a thick, warm shawl, too. And one evening gown, one tea gown, one afternoon frock . . . lingerie, of course. Oh dear, I hope it all fits in two suitcases. I can only take what I can carry."

Lily nodded, pulling pieces of clothing out of the armoire. "How many hatboxes, ma'am?"

"One. Three hats will fit in it—pack a boater, a big, floppy straw, and one little afternoon bonnet."

"What should I bring, miss?" Lily asked as she brought an armful of clothes to the bed.

"You're not coming. Listen to me carefully." She grasped the maid by the shoulders. "If you want to follow me, I'll send for you. If not, I'll write you a brilliant letter of character later, although it might not do you much good, since I shall soon be a scandal and the last person in the world to go to for a character reference. But I'll do whatever I can to look out for you, and I promise you won't get into any trouble because of this, all right? But you can't tell anyone I'm going. Do you understand."

Wide-eyed, Lily nodded.

"Good. Now I have to leave all the packing to you because I need to go down and talk to Lord Danbury before I leave. Lock the door behind me, and take the key out of the lock. If anyone wants in, just keep quiet, and they'll think I've locked it from the outside for some reason. Pack my things as quietly as you can, and only as much as you can fit in these two suitcases and one hatbox. Do you understand?"

"Yes, ma'am."

"And be quick. I have to catch the noon train."

She let go and gave another laugh as she turned away, feeling dizzy. "I can't believe I'm doing this."

She left the bedroom and went down to Paul's study. Thankfully he was at his desk writing letters, and she didn't have to go off searching for him. "Could I speak with you a moment?" Without waiting for an answer, she came in and shut the door behind her. "I'm going away, Paul."

"Away?" Her cousin frowned in puzzlement, standing up as she came toward him across the room. "But we just returned home."

"I know, but . . ." She paused before his desk and took a deep breath. "I'm going to Egypt with Will. We're eloping."

"What?" He started at her in openmouthed astonishment for a moment, then he rallied. "Are you out of your mind or am I?"

"Neither. Will has to leave. Now. Today. And I'm going with him. We're taking the noon train."

He frowned. "I'm your closest male relation, head of the family. Do you seriously expect me to go along with this?"

"I love him, Paul. I always have, I always will, and he loves me, and life is short, and I'm not waiting a moment longer to be with him."

"For heaven's sake, if you and Sunderland want to marry, all well and good, I suppose, but why can't you do it in the proper way?"

"There's no time. He got a cable while he was in London. They may have found Tut's tomb and he has to go back now or they'll open the thing without him."

"Carter found Tut?" Paul asked, momentarily diverted, and when she nodded, he gave a low whistle. "So Will was right."

"Yes. And I'm going with him, and I'm going to do the illustrations for Marlowe's newspaper."

Paul swallowed hard, clearly trying to think out what this would mean. "There'll be a deuce of a scandal. But you know that, of course."

"Yes, I know. I don't care. I'm catching that train at noon. If you choose to stop me, I'll just find another way to leave when nobody's looking and I'll follow Will to Egypt alone."

"Why are you even telling me, then?" he demanded. "Do you realize the position you're putting me in? I, and my mother, too, will be universally condemned for not watching over you better."

"I know, and I'm sorry. We didn't plan this, but if it's any consolation, the condemnation won't last forever. We will marry as soon as we can. Will applied to the archbishop for a special license, but there's no time to go back to London and pick it up. We have to be on the noon train out of Stafford St. Mary to make the connection straight to Dover, so that we can be in Paris by tomorrow night to catch the Orient Express. We'll be married on the ship, or at the British Consulate in Thebes."

She paused only long enough to take a breath. "I'm telling you all this because someone has to send us the special license, in case we decide to marry in Thebes, which would be nice, since that way I can at least have a proper wedding."

"That you can even use the word *proper* in this context amazes me."

"And I'm telling you because I don't want my maid to suffer for what I'm doing, so you'll need to see to it she finds new employment. And someone will have to pick up the Daimler in the village after I'm gone, and you know how to drive. I can't just leave it at the train station until spring."

"Wait. You want me to *help* you elope?"

She bit her lip and nodded, giving him an apologetic look. "Cheeky, I know."

"*Cheeky* doesn't begin to describe it!" he muttered, raking a hand through his hair, glaring at her. "I suppose I should be grateful you're not marrying a clerk or a land agent. And after what I saw at Pixy Cove, I'm not really all that surprised. But if the wedding doesn't come off when you reach Egypt, you'll be ruined utterly. You realize that?"

"I know." She gave her cousin a rueful smile. "And I haven't had much luck actually getting to the altar, have I? But sometimes, to be happy in life, we just have to put love before anything else. I thought perhaps you would understand."

His expression hardened. "I don't know why you should think I would understand that, for love has not made me the least bit happy." He paused, then added in a softer tone, "Still, I'm not like Uncle James, Trix. I'm not going to stop you."

"Thank you."

He stood up. "I'll keep Mum distracted this morning so she won't know about any of this until you're gone and it's too late to kick up a fuss. But you'd better be married within the month, cousin, or there will be hell to pay."

"Thank you, Paul. And you might want to consider taking a holiday yourself." She turned and ran for the door, but with her hand on the knob, she stopped. "I've heard Newport's lovely this time of year."

She didn't wait for an answer, but ducked out the door and closed it behind her.

Will stood at the platform of Stafford St. Mary's train station. The train had arrived from Brixham a few minutes early and was standing idle, its steam engine hissing as it waited for noon to arrive so that it could leave this tiny village and go on to Exeter. Will checked his watch. It was eleven forty-five.

He didn't know why he was bothering to verify the time. He ought to just board the train and take his seat.

Instead, he walked to the end of the platform and stared down the road toward Stafford St. Mary and the land of Danbury Downs that stretched out beyond it, thinking of when he'd first arrived and how alien the rolling hills, hedgerows, and pastures had seemed. It didn't seem alien now; it seemed like home. Trix was here.

He turned away and started back down the platform, for it hurt to look at the pastures and fields of home, it hurt to know he was leaving without her. Most of all, it hurt that she'd left him this morning without even saying good-bye.

Yet how could he be surprised by that? She hated good-byes. And she'd already made it clear she wasn't going to come with him. Hell, he hadn't even succeeded in getting her to admit she still loved him.

He'd pushed her too hard, he supposed, and she'd balked. He didn't blame her. He obviously hadn't earned her trust. And even if she had agreed to marry him, she had every right to demand a lengthy engagement. Asking her to elope because he didn't have time to marry her properly in her own parish was well beyond the pale. He knew all that.

He stopped and pulled out his watch again. Eleven-fifty.

He probably ought to board the train. There was no point in standing down here. Tucking the watch back in his waistcoat pocket, he started back down the line of train carriages to the one that contained his compartment.

He'd write to her every day, he vowed. And he'd tell her what they'd discovered. He'd send photographs, too. Perhaps he could come home at Christmas, but that was unlikely, since two months wouldn't be nearly long enough to excavate the tomb properly. But even if he couldn't get away at Christmas, he could perhaps be here by March. If she'd have him then, he'd take her to Florence for a honeymoon. She'd always wanted to go there. She'd never wanted to go to Egypt.

The first train whistle blew, telling those boarding that they had five minutes.

"All aboard," the conductor shouted. "All aboard for Exeter."

Slowly Will walked to his compartment. Through the window, he could see Aman discussing the placement of their luggage with the porter. He grasped the brass handlebar along the side of the doorway and stepped up, then paused and turned, thinking to take one last look at Stafford St. Mary, but from this angle, the station was between him and any view of the village, and he turned away again and boarded the train.

He'd gambled and lost, and it would be eight months before he could roll the dice again. But he would. After all, he had a gambler's heart.

Paul had dragged Geoff down to the tennis court, insisting that Eugenia come and watch them play, leaving the field clear for Beatrix, and she managed to spirit her two suitcases and hatbox out to the stable without anyone seeing her. She lifted the suitcases into the Daimler's boot, shoved her hatbox between them, and secured everything with a bit of rope. A few minutes later, she was speeding down the lane she'd been viewing through the same bedroom window her whole life, leaving the home she loved, and the family she loved, and the country she loved. But she didn't pause to look back. There was no looking back.

"Wait for me, Will," she whispered, turning the Daimler onto the Stafford Road. "I want to go, too."

But when she saw the puffing smoke of a train's steam engine rising in the distance above the green hills and woods, she gave a cry of alarm and pressed the petrol pedal down harder, praying the train was just coming in or standing at the station, not departing.

She hadn't heard the whistle blow, but that wasn't very comforting, because she wouldn't be able to hear it over the sound of the Daimler anyway. She had no idea of the time, either, for she hadn't wanted to check when she left Danbury. She didn't want to know.

English country roads were not meant for motorcars traveling thirty miles per hour, and each bump and dip and rut lifted her bum off the seat and brought her back down with bone-jarring force. Her heart was pounding in her chest, but it wasn't fear. It was exhilaration and hope and a soaring feeling of freedom.

She was flying in the face of everything she'd ever thought mattered in the world. As Paul had said, if anything about this plan went off the rails, and she and Will didn't marry, she'd be ruined forever. Even if they did marry, the story would still be in every society paper between here and Egypt for months. In this modern age of telegraph cables and telephone wires, the news of their elopement would have spread throughout the British community in Cairo before they even arrived. And afterward, if the tomb Howard Carter had found was that of King Tutankhamen, journalists from all over the world would probably still find the sordid details of the elopement just as fascinating as any of the artifacts Will uncovered.

She didn't care. None of that mattered. She felt as if she had just jumped off Angel's Head again, with her stomach in her throat, and her life flashing before her eyes, and her heart pumping as fast as the pistons of the train's steam engine. This time, she hoped the outcome was just as smashing, rip-roaring fun as that jump off Angel's Head had been. If it wasn't, the crash would be painful.

The shortest way to the train station was straight through the village proper, and she took it, even though she knew anyone in the High Street would drop whatever they were doing and follow her. Lady Beatrix wasn't like that wild Baroness Yardley, after all. She didn't race her motorcar through the street, endangering all and sundry. Oh yes, anyone who'd seen her would follow on foot to discover what had happened to send Lady Beatrix racing along the High Street in that Daimler of hers.

She didn't care.

She turned at the vicarage, careening around the corner on two wheels, spitting gravel and dust and causing Mr. Venables to straighten up from his vegetable garden with an expression of astonishment, and when she glanced back, she found her suspicion confirmed. People were already coming up the road to follow her.

She once again pressed the petrol pedal all the way to the floor, and a few moments later, she was approaching the station. She could see the train, and relief flooded through her. It was still there. She hadn't missed it.

There were several carriages and wagons there, and people milling about, and she brought the vehicle to a jerking halt as close to the station building as she could get, but that was near the very end of the platform. Still, it couldn't be helped.

She pulled the brake lever, jumped out, and ran to the boot, where she began working to untie the ropes that secured her luggage. When she heard the puffing steam engine of the train quickening, she glanced up just in time to see the train lurch forward. It was leaving.

No, no, she screamed in silent agony, wrenching at the knot she was working free. The train began gathering speed, and she thought she'd have to leave her things behind in order to catch it, but then, suddenly, the knot came undone. Flinging the ropes aside, she tucked her hatbox under her arm, grasped the handles of her suitcases, and started for the platform.

And then, just before she reached the steps, for no reason at all, her luck ran out. Her foot came down on some loose gravel and she skidded, losing her balance. She stumbled, dropping her suitcases. She managed to regain her balance, but the hatbox slipped from beneath her arm and rolled away. She left it, and the suitcases, too, scrambling for the steps, but as she reached the platform, the end of the train passed her.

With a cry of dismay, she raced after it along the length of the platform, but the caboose was past the end by the time she reached it, forcing her to stop at the edge. Gulping in air, she watched it go.

Too late, she thought, blinking back tears, feeling a sense of desolation and disappointment that was all out of proportion as she watched the train going farther and farther away. The one time in her life she decided to do something spontaneous, and she'd muffed it. Oh hell.

She swallowed hard, forcing down disappointment, and told herself it would be all right. Missing one train wasn't the end of everything. If she drove the motorcar, she could still make the connecting train at Exeter. If something went wrong, and she missed that train, she'd take another. As she had told Paul, she'd go the whole way to Egypt alone if she had to. She wasn't staying behind. There was a big, wide world out there, and she was going to see it.

"Going on a trip?"

With a gasp, she whirled around and saw Will coming toward her, smiling. "Wi-ill!"

He halted in front of her. "Don't you know when you go on a trip, you need luggage?"

"It's down there," she panted, waving vaguely toward the steps at the other end of the platform. "I thought I'd have to jump for the train, so I had to drop my suitcases. What are you doing here? You missed the train!"

"I couldn't go without you."

"What?"

"I love you, and I'm not leaving." He nodded to a pile of trunks and suitcases by the door into the station. His valet was standing beside them. "Aman and I were just about to fetch Mr. Robinson to take our luggage back to Sunderland."

"But what about the tomb? Carter will open it anyway. He said so."

Will shrugged as if that didn't matter in the least. "I suppose he'll have to do it without me."

"Without you? But it's your life's work. You have to see it come to fruition. You can't just abandon it now!"

He tilted his head to one side, looking at her. "For someone who was so opposed to this idea a few hours ago, you seem awfully in favor of it now. Leaving luggage behind and jumping for trains—"

"Will! Sometimes I wish you'd be serious. You missed the train for me? Are you out of your mind?"

"I have never been more sane in my life. I couldn't go without you, because without you it's all meaningless. We're not eloping."

"But, Will—"

"We'll be married right here in Stafford St. Mary, we'll settle down to village life as the Duke and Duchess of Sunderland. I don't know how I'll support you, but I'll find a way. Sunderland won't ever be profitable, but maybe we can keep it limping along. Tradition's important. And no matter what I have to do, I'll take care of you, Trix. You, and our children, always."

"Like hell you will!"

He raised an eyebrow. "You don't want me to take care of you and our children?"

"Not by living in Stafford St. Mary, I don't! Not now, not when you're about to find Tut. We're going to Egypt, Will. I want to go. I want that trip on the Orient Express, and I want to see Constantinople, and I want to excavate that tomb with you. If Tut's in there, all well and good. And if he's not—"

"And if not?"

She looked into his brilliant green eyes, and though she didn't know how it was possible, she loved him more now than she ever had before. "It's a sealed royal tomb, isn't it? Some Egyptian king's in there, and whoever he is, he's bound to be worth digging up. I'll sketch all the artifacts and you'll write the articles and books about him, and Marlowe will print it all in his newspapers, and you'll be that famous archaeologist who found all these wonderful Egyptian treasures."

"No. I don't want to be famous. I just want you. While I was waiting to board the train, I did a lot of thinking. I knew I'd have to come back next year and try to persuade you again, but then I thought about going back to my life in Egypt without you, and I realized that nothing I do anywhere on this earth matters to me now, not if I can't share it with you." He grabbed her hands. "I've loved you all my life, Beatrix Elizabeth Anne, and I want to marry you. Right here in Stafford St. Mary, with you in a beautiful white dress with a long train, and all our family and friends there, and a big wedding breakfast afterward. It'll be the wedding of the season, just what you always wanted."

"That doesn't matter to me, Will. Not anymore."

"It matters to me. And we're going to have at least two boys and two girls. And our oldest son will just have to accept the fact that he's the duke, and he'll have to live up to his responsibilities at home, and that's all there is to it."

"But what if he wants to go to Egypt instead?"

"He can, but he'd better come home. And our girls will be allowed to swing high on the swings, as high as they want, and go to Florence and paint."

She heard the church clock strike the quarter hour, and she knew they had to be going. "This is all lovely,

Will, and I appreciate it. I do, and maybe we can go to Florence one day, but we can talk about all of that later. We have to be on our way."

"And," he went on as if he hadn't even heard a word she was saying, "maybe one day you'll let me take you to Egypt, and I'll show you what the desert is like at sunset. And we'll stand on the deck of a *dahabiyeh* boat on the Nile—"

"Will," she interrupted impatiently, "I don't want to stand here and *talk* about going to Egypt. I want to do it. We have to get moving or we'll miss the next train."

"Next train? Beatrix, we already missed the train, and there is no next one, not today."

"Oh yes, there is, and we're going to catch it." She let go of one of his hands and tightened her grip on the other, pulling him. "Let's go."

"Go where?" He frowned, unmoving, clearly not sharing her sense of urgency. "Trix, we missed the train," he repeated, as if she hadn't already seen that for herself. "It's gone."

"I know, Will, but we'll catch up with it at Exeter."

"We can't. A carriage isn't fast enough—"

"We don't need a carriage." She pulled again, and this time, he allowed himself to be dragged around the end of the tiny train station so that he could see the Daimler, ignoring the fact that half the village of Stafford St. Mary seemed to be coming down the road toward them. "We have a motorcar."

He looked at the Daimler and back at her. "The Daimler will get us to Exeter in time to make the train to Dover," he said, enlightened at last.

"Exactly! That's what I've been trying to tell you. And also that I love you. And that I truly, honestly don't care where we live, because wherever we can be together is where I want to be." She squeezed his hand and took a deep breath. "From now on, everything we do, we do together. Off the cliff and all the way down. Together."

"All right. Together. Off the cliff and all the way down. But when this Egypt business is finished, we're going to Florence, and then we'll come back here for summer."

"Pixy Cove in August?"

"Pixy Cove in August. And we ought to be able to roast a few chestnuts before going back to Egypt, and once we have children, I think we should spend Christmas here in Stafford St. Mary." He pulled his hands out of hers and cupped her face. "I love you, Trix."

"And I love you, Wi-ill."

She watched him smile that heart-bruising smile, but this time it didn't hurt to see it. Instead, it filled her heart with joy.

"Hell's bells!" he said suddenly. "I've got to get my things and tell Aman our plans. He'll have to follow us to Thebes and bring whatever I can't carry with me."

She glanced uneasily at the curious, approaching villagers. "We have to hurry or we'll have half the village here gaping at us."

"Right." He dashed back toward the platform while she gathered her suitcases and hatbox and returned them to the boot of the Daimler. When Will joined her, he brought one large valise, one smaller one, and his dispatch case. He placed them beside hers and tied down all the luggage as she walked around to the front of the motorcar and cranked the engine. A few minutes later they were racing away, leaving the curious, approaching crowd in a cloud of dust.

"Well, you have to marry me now," he told her, raising his voice to be heard over the noise of the engine as he settled his long legs as comfortably as he could in the limited space. "Your reputation's thoroughly ruined, I fear. Elopement is one adventure we haven't tried yet."

She laughed, tilting her head back, relishing the feel of the wind on her face. "Will, my darling, with you, every day of our lives is an adventure."

What happened after
Aidan left Pixy Cove?
Where did Julia disappear to?
To find out the answers
to these questions and more,
turn the page for a preview of

Scandal of the Year

On sale from

Avon Books

January 25, 2011

idan went for a walk in the gardens of Park Lane, and when he started back toward Kayne House some thirty minutes later, he felt his blood had cooled sufficiently that he could return to the ball.

Aware that being anywhere near Lady Yardley was dangerous to both his peace of mind and his reputation, he intended to keep well away from that woman for the remainder of the evening. But as he started toward the terrace, his intentions were forgotten at the sight of a slim figure sitting on the wide steps. Light from the ballroom spilled over her, thin ribbons of cigarette smoke swirled over her head, and the crimson silk of her gown pooled at her feet.

The moment he saw her, images of that August afternoon went through his mind, making him angry, but he worked not to show it. "Lady Yardley," he said and glanced at the cigarette in her fingers as he approached the steps. "Still smoking, I see."

She smiled a little. "I'm trying to give it up, if that raises me in your estimation." Her nose wrinkled ruefully at his unchanged expression. "Obviously not."

"I bid you good evening," he said, and for the second time tonight, he bowed to her, but as he started to ascend the steps to the ballroom, her voice stopped him.

"I was waiting for you here because I wanted to thank you."

He stopped, curious. "For what do you thank me?" he asked, even as he knew it was probably a mistake to inquire.

With her free hand, she reached for the glass of champagne perched on the step above the one where she sat. Then, turning, she leaned back against the carved stone balustrade of the stair railing and faced him, lifting her glass in salute. "Thank you for not giving me the cut direct earlier. Given the last time we saw each other, I thought you might."

He stiffened. "Contrary to some of my past behavior, I am still a gentleman." But even as he spoke, his gaze was lowering to the shadowy cleft between her breasts, and he feared that when it came to Lady Yardley, he was in fact hopelessly depraved. "At least I strive to be," he muttered and forced his gaze back to her upturned face.

She was looking at him in a thoughtful way he didn't quite understand. "No striving necessary. You couldn't stop being a gentleman if you tried."

He gave a short, unamused laugh. "That's ironic, coming from you. The last time I was in your company, my gentlemanly side took quite a holiday."

She took a pull on her cigarette, and tilted her head farther back to exhale the smoke overhead. "And you've been condemning yourself for it ever since, I daresay."

"Don't worry," he reassured her at once. "I have plenty of condemnation for you as well."

"You should. It takes two to tango, as they say. But I suspect you are reserving most of the blame for yourself."

"Can I be expected to do otherwise, having compromised a lady?"

She smiled, a dazzling flash of white in the moonlight. "Only you would think tumbling a willing and experienced woman was compromising her. That, and the fact that you can still refer to me as a lady prove my point. But you need to stop being so damned chivalrous." She paused, her smile faded, and she added in a softer voice, "It makes you quite vulnerable, you know."

"Vulnerable?" he echoed, surprised by the word.

"To women who are all wrong for you."

He stiffened. "If you mean yourself, Lady Yardley, and that tiresome business last year, I can assure you—"

"I wasn't referring to myself," she interrupted hastily. "I meant Rosalind. And Felicia Vale, too, of course. Yes," she added before he could contradict her about Rosalind, "I saw you looking at her when I arrived, but you're wasting your time considering her. The girl's dim as a firefly."

This confirmation of his own suspicion had the curious effect of making him want to argue the point. "Nonsense. There is nothing wrong with Lady Felicia's intelligence."

"Hmm . . . it's obvious you haven't met her yet.

She talks just like a mouse." As she spoke, her voice rose to an unbearably high, painful pitch. "Just like a teeny-tiny, itty-bitty mouse. Squeak, squeak, squeak." She paused to take a sip of champagne, then added in a normal voice, "She'll drive you mad in half an hour."

Aidan felt compelled to defend the poor girl against this criticism. "Even if what you say is true, a high voice does not imply stupidity."

He might have been talking to the wind. "Lady Felicia would be a terrible duchess. Especially for a brainy chap like you, with your interest in history, science, and politics."

"I haven't an interest in politics," he answered tersely. "Not anymore. It was suggested by certain colleagues that I not attend the House of Lords for the good of the party. Tories and scandals do not mix."

"I'm sorry. I—" She paused and took another sip of champagne. "I didn't know that."

He looked away. "It doesn't matter," he lied.

"Even so," she went on, "with Lady Felicia, you couldn't even discuss politics. I doubt the poor girl knows which party is which."

"That's absurd. Her father's in the House. She must have some appreciation of—" He broke off, realizing too late he was becoming entangled in an argument with a woman whose opinion did not matter to him about a girl he did not know. He drew a deep breath.

"Forgive me," he said, pasting on a mask of cool, puzzled disinterest, "but what is the purpose of your rather ruthless assessment of Lady Felicia's intelligence?"

"Isn't it obvious? You're back on the hunt."

"And if I am, what has it to do with you?"

"Nothing at all. Still," she added irrepressibly, "you might want to reconsider your strategy. Appearing at public balls could prove to be more trouble than it's worth."

"I met your cousin at a public ball."

"In St. Ives. London during the season is a different kettle of fish, as you are well aware. You'll be drowning in invitations by the end of the week, most of them from matchmaking mamas in the lower ranks who want to move up the social ladder."

"Given the curtailing of invitations from my own set because of my association with you, Lady Yardley," he shot back, "I am forced to widen my circle of acquaintance."

She bit her lip. "That won't last forever, not for you. One season. Perhaps two."

"Possibly, but I don't have the luxury of sitting back and waiting for my reputation to be restored. And I don't recall soliciting your views on the subject of my social engagements, or the young ladies with whom I choose to become acquainted, or anything else, for that matter. And I have a title, Baroness," he added, attempting a haughty, dampening tone without the least hope it would have any affect. "Would you mind terribly if I asked you to address me by it?"

She flashed him a grin. "I don't mind at all if you

ask," she responded, as unimpressed by this attempt at ducal hauteur as he'd suspected she would be. "I can't promise to comply, though. Addressing everyone in the proper way is so predictable, and I do hate being predictable."

"I'm delighted to hear it," he countered. "No doubt you will surprise me then, and refrain from offering me any more of your pert opinions."

She held up her hand, waving it in an airy gesture toward the ballroom. "Oh, don't mind me. Go back inside, though I don't know what you expect to gain. Most of the unmarried women here are ladies you've already considered and rejected, the daughters of merchants or bankers you're too fastidious to consider anyway, or debutantes who are too young for you. You are thirty now, you know. Happy birthday, by the way."

She might have a point, but he refused to concede it. A man in search of a wife had to start somewhere. Folding his arms, he said, "Is there a point to any of this?"

"I suppose I'm warning you," she said slowly. "Don't allow yourself to be trapped or entangled with some girl whose character you know nothing about. It could happen if you're not careful."

"You mean because I allowed myself to be manipulated by you, I can be manipulated by any woman, is that it?"

If he hoped his words would sting, he was disappointed. She shrugged, his comment sliding off of her back like water off a duck. "We all have our weaknesses, petal. Yours is your fine, upstanding character."

"How in heaven's name is that a weakness?"

"It makes you particularly susceptible to women who would do anything to secure a man of your position."

"Are you basing this conclusion on your own past ability to manipulate me, or are you just deeply cynical about your own sex?"

"I'm not cynical," she denied. "Just realistic. Most women are prohibited from earning their way in the world, and making a good marriage ensures their future and that of their children. You're a duke. You're also rich and successful, and despite our little tête-a-tête, you still wield a great deal of power. And you're so good-looking, too, without a scrap of conceit about it. What more could a girl ask for?"

He set his jaw. "Yes, that's me," he said, and couldn't help a hint of bitterness. "Every girl's dream."

Her head tilted to one side and she skimmed a considering glance over him that made him wonder if, like him, she tended to dwell on that afternoon in Cornwall. Did she ever remember his naked body the way he remembered hers? The question sent a flash of heat through his body. With an effort, he suppressed it.

"You are, you know," she said, lifting her gaze to his face, bringing his attention back to the current conversation. "You're just the sort of man girls dream about, and their ambitious parents, too. Snaring a duke, even if he is a bit tarnished, would be the *coup de grace* for any family. Hell, thousands of women would marry you for your money alone."

"I would not be inclined to a girl of that sort."

"Rosalind Drummond was just that sort! I daresay

if Creighton hadn't come along so soon, you'd have been able to win her by the end of the season. Felicia Vale is just the same, though she hasn't Rosalind's brains. Neither of them are worthy of you. Honestly," she added with a hint of impatience, "what is it about melting brown eyes that makes your judgment go utterly awry?"

"That's nonsense!"

"Is it? Don't tell me Felicia's eyes weren't tempting you to ask Lady Vale for an introduction."

God, he thought in horror, was he that shallow? The idea didn't bear thinking about. "You don't have brown eyes," he pointed out, "and history proves that when it comes to you, my judgment is not awry, it's nonexistent. And since we are on the subject of my taste in women, Beatrix—if I understand you correctly—is just another mercenary woman who lied to me."

"Trix? No, she's not mercenary in the least, but . . ." Julia paused, considering. "But yes, in a way, she did lie to you."

"She's your own cousin. You are the person who first introduced her to me. Yet you deem her dishonest?"

"There are different kinds of lies. Don't misunderstand me. I love Trix like a sister, and I don't think she's ever uttered a deliberate lie in her life. But when I introduced her to you at the St. Ives Ball, she was still feeling the pangs of heartache over Sunderland going off to Egypt, not to mention the terrible grief and loss she felt over the death of her father. When you met her, she was at the lowest point of her life, and you were just the right balm to soothe her wounded feminine pride and protect her from an uncertain future, the perfect hero charging in to save her. She convinced herself that she could come to love you, but it was a lie. As for you, you took one look into Trix's big, sad eyes, and you told yourself the same lie."

"And how would you know I didn't love her?"

Her answer was simple, direct, and brutal. "Because when Sunderland came back and she broke her engagement to you, you didn't fight to keep her."

"God," he choked, "you do give your opinions honestly, don't you, Baroness?"

"You asked," she said and shrugged, taking a sip of champagne and another pull on her cigarette. "I just wish you'd be equally honest about yourself when it comes to matters of romance. You're a lot like Trix, you know. Honorable and good and trying so hard to always do the right thing. Striving all your life to live up to everyone's expectations and trying to believe virtue is its own reward."

"So it is."

She made a sound of derision, dismissing that contention. "You like to think it is. That's why you accepted my invitation for a picnic that day. You wanted to prove to yourself you could resist me, and you wanted to pat yourself on the back for your virtuous nature afterward."

He inhaled sharply, damning both her perspicacity and his own arrogance. "Well, I was appropriately punished for my conceit in that regard, wasn't I?"

Her mouth took on a sulky curve. "You did what

you secretly wanted to do. You'd be happier if you'd be honest enough with yourself to admit it. Under all the gentlemanly honor you revere, you long for adventure and excitement and a taste now and then of the forbidden fruit."

"Getting drunk and sleeping with a married woman and being publicly humiliated for it is the sort of adventure I could well do without! You talk as if what happened was merely some delicious, harmless little romantic romp in the country, but it wasn't. You used me," he accused in a hard, tight voice. "You wanted a divorce and the only way you could obtain it was by taking a new lover and arranging for Yardley to discover your adultery. And for reasons I cannot fathom, you chose me to be your pawn."

She didn't deny it. She didn't try to defend herself. She said nothing, and her silence only fueled his anger.

"I have to admire your talent for strategy," he went on. "Yardley had overlooked your previous lovers, but how could he overlook it this time when he arrived to find you actually in bed with another man? And then, just to be doubly sure, you gave the whole sordid story to the gutter press, causing a scandal so blatant Yardley had no choice but to set you aside. You played me and you played your husband, moving us around to suit your will as if we were chess pieces on a board. You, madam, are a female Iago!"

Pain shimmered across her face, and his shame deepened. He looked away. "Sorry," he apologized tightly, and worked to force his emotions back into governable order before he looked at her again. "That was uncalled for."

"No, it wasn't." She lifted her cigarette, then changed her mind and crushed it out on the step below the one where she sat. "Why apologize for telling the truth? I did and I am all of which you accused me."

"But why?" he demanded. "I can appreciate that your marriage was unhappy, but to break yours, you caused pain and humiliation to three other people. Doesn't that bother you? Don't you care?"

She jerked, her chin lifting with the same defiance he'd seen her display that day in the Divorce Court. "My husband was a bastard," she said, her pale violet eyes glittering like gray steel in the dim light, her voice so hard and cold that it chilled him. "I loathed him to the very core, and I cannot work up even a tiny pang of conscience over any pain or humiliation he suffered. As for you, you knew what you were doing. I didn't force you to come on a picnic. I didn't rape you. I may have seduced you, but you allowed yourself to be seduced."

His anger died, leaving only a hollow emptiness. What she said was true, and he had no business leveling blame on her for his conduct.

"I'm sorry about Lady Rosalind," she added. "Though I know her well enough to know she's probably not worth my regret, or yours either. And she seems to have recovered nicely from the experience, for she's engaged again, I hear. So, no, to answer your question, I don't care. I would do it all over again."

He stared at her in disbelief, shaking his head. "What did your husband do to make you hate him so?"

"What did he do?" she echoed, and with mercurial suddenness, her face changed. The cold glint in her eyes vanished as if it had never been, and her ruthless expression gave way to amusement. "Fucked the chambermaids, of course," she said lightly, laughing as if it was all a joke. "Don't they all?"

"Many do," he was forced to agree, concluding that Yardley was one of them, but he didn't see what was amusing about it. "But not all do."

"Well, you probably won't," she said and waved her hand toward the ballroom. "Go. Stop wasting your time with me. Go find your duchess."

He hesitated, feeling as if there was more to be said, but he decided they'd both said quite enough already. He turned away.

"But promise me something," she said as he started past her up the steps.

He stopped, but he did not look at her. "What's that?"

"Why anyone would want to marry at all baffles me, I confess, and my advice would be not to bother. But if you must marry—and I can see you are quite determined to do so—promise me you'll marry for love and no other reason, someone worthy of you who would make you happy." She gave him a whimsical smile. "Believe it or not, I want you to be happy, for I do like you, you know. I always have."

He was inclined to doubt that, and her desire for his happiness seemed a bit late in the day to be genuine, but he didn't argue the point. "I am sure that if

I marry a woman whose background and interests match my own, and if we share fondness and affection, genuine love will surely follow."

"Either that," she said dryly, "or you'll bore each other to death. I'd hardly call that love."

"Your view of love and mine are obviously different, Lady Yardley. Good night."

Once again he moved to leave, but to his astonishment, she reached out and actually put a hand on his leg to stop him. He froze and closed his eyes, arousal stirring inside him at her touch. He fought it, hating that she could still evoke with the touch of her hand what had already destroyed his honor and hurt his reputation, hating that she could move him like a chess piece, controlling in him what he could not seem to control in himself.

"An unhappy marriage is hell, Aidan," she said, her fingers curled around his shin. "I should know. Promise me you won't do what I did."

He didn't reply, for there was nothing to say. He was a duke, and he had a duty to marry, with love or without it. Slowly, he pulled away from her touch and went back inside without giving her the promise she'd asked for. He never made promises he wasn't sure he could keep.